Praise for *Dying to Kn*

'This book is a cracker – a genuine page ⟨...⟩
and builds – it kept me guessing all the way. Geneva Leighton is a
brilliant protagonist – tough and resourceful, yet vulnerable and
caring' CHRIS HAMMER, author of *The Tilt*

'Rae Cairns shows us what ordinary people can do in extraordinary
situations. *Dying to Know* is a thrilling and wild ride with love at
its core' HAYLEY SCRIVENOR, author of *Dirt Town*

'Smart and suspenseful, *Dying to Know* is another high-stakes
original thriller from Cairns that does not ease up until the last
page. I dare anyone to read it slowly' SARAH BAILEY, author of
The Housemate

'Wow, what a ride! *Dying to Know* has all the ingredients of
the perfect thriller: a brilliant start, lots of twists and turns, and
characters you really care about. I couldn't put it down' SARA
FOSTER, author of *The Hush*

'This fast-paced thriller hooked me in and kept me guessing. A
gripping read with high stakes and blurred lines between good
and evil' PETRONELLA McGOVERN, author of *The Liars*

'I raced through this addictive, twisty book, desperate to solve the
mystery of Amber's disappearance alongside Geneva. An expertly
plotted and wholly absorbing thriller' NICOLA MORIARTY,
author of *You Need to Know*

'Intriguing, heart-wrenching and compelling, Cairns draws you
in and holds you until the final gasping twist' SULARI GENTILL,
author of *The Woman in the Library*

'Compelling and emotive, *Dying to Know* kept me up late at night
dying to know what happened to Amber and the family she left
behind. Cairns deftly captures the pressures of a modern family
and, in Gen Leighton, has created a character that you'll want
to root for and villains you'll love to hate' RWR McDONALD,
author of *Nancy Business*

'Rae Cairns is the master of gripping thrillers with big hearts. *Dying to Know* is all the more terrifying because of how much you care about the characters ensnared in its dark and twisty tale' ANNA SNOEKSTRA, author of *Out of Breath*

'A rollercoaster ride from the first page to the last, *Dying to Know* confirms Rae Cairns as a genuine mistress of mystery and mayhem! Breathtaking, believable and utterly unputdownable – this is the rollercoaster ride you don't want to miss!' NINA D CAMPBELL, author of *Daughters of Eve*

'What can I say about *Dying to Know* but wow! What a read! One terrifying crime and one extraordinary woman's quest for answers against all odds. Shocking, gut-wrenching and real. It doesn't get any better than that. Brilliant writing and an outrageously tense plot combine in a cleverly crafted, heart-stopping, action-packed thriller that won't let you go. Rae Cairns is my definition of a true grab-you-by-the-throat thriller writer. Be prepared for some sleepless nights as you devour every last word' SARAH BARRIE, author of *Retribution*

'*Dying to Know* is twisty, feisty and full of intrigue. Rae infuses her characters with so much warmth and nuance that you can't help but be drawn into their world and fully invest in it. This kept me up late guessing and moved me to tears. Loved it' VANESSA McCAUSLAND, author of *The Beautiful Words*

'Rae Cairns seems to effortlessly combine a propulsive and gripping plot with a story that will pull at your heartstrings. Complex characters abound and, as Rae teases the reader with the notion that people are not who they seem, twists appear that you won't see coming. I flew through it!' ALI LOWE, author of *The Trivia Night*

'A compelling novel that is both original and frighteningly realistic. I was enthralled and on the edge of my seat as I raced to the last page' BM CARROLL, author of *You Had it Coming*

'Was I dying to know! This is a fast-paced, edge-of-your-seat thriller right from the opening scene ... I could not turn the pages fast enough. What a ride!' ANNA LODER, *ReadA Book*, www.readabook.com.au

Rae Cairns writes crime with heart: thrillers featuring everyday people facing extraordinary circumstances. Her debut novel, *The Good Mother*, was shortlisted for Best Debut Crime Fiction in the 2021 Ned Kelly Awards and longlisted for the 2021 Sisters in Crime Davitt Awards, and draws on her background as a youth worker in Northern Ireland during the final years of The Troubles. Rae has also co-managed a crisis refuge for street children, worked as Program Director for the Sydney Olympic Youth Camp and holds a degree in Performing Arts. She is currently busy writing her third novel.

Rae lives in Sydney with her husband, two children and her dog, Alfie, who snores at her feet while she writes.

www.raecairns.com

Also by Rae Cairns

The Good Mother

DYING TO KNOW

RAE CAIRNS

HarperCollins*Publishers*

HarperCollins*Publishers*
Australia • Brazil • Canada • France • Germany • Holland • India
Italy • Japan • Mexico • New Zealand • Poland • Spain • Sweden
Switzerland • United Kingdom • United States of America

HarperCollins acknowledges the Traditional Custodians
of the land upon which we live and work, and pays respect
to Elders past and present.

First published in Australia in 2023
by HarperCollins*Publishers* Australia Pty Limited
Gadigal Country
Level 13, 201 Elizabeth Street, Sydney NSW 2000
ABN 36 009 913 517
harpercollins.com.au

A catalogue record for this book is available from the National Library of Australia

ISBN 978 1 4607 6195 3 (paperback)
ISBN 978 1 4607 1482 9 (ebook)
ISBN 978 1 4607 4795 7 (audiobook)

Cover design by Andy Warren Design
Cover images: Woman © Nik Keevil / Trevillion Images;
    all other images by istockphoto.com
Author photograph by Emma Stergio
Typeset in Sabon LT Std by Kirby Jones
Printed and bound in Australia by McPherson's Printing Group

MIX
Paper from
responsible sources
FSC
www.fsc.org   FSC® C001695

For my mum, Lynda Parry,
who raised me and my sister on her own,
and who, no matter how tough things got,
always encouraged me to follow my dreams

Prologue

Then

Geneva Leighton pressed send and punched a fist into the air. 'Done!'

'Shhhh!' Amber strode into the kitchen, pressing her finger against closed lips. 'I just got the kids off to sleep.'

Sorry, Gen mouthed. Verifying the facts of her mentor's newspaper article had been like riding a motorbike across an ice-skating rink, blindfolded. But she'd finally navigated to the other side.

Her gaze passed over her sister, who had fed, bathed, and put four-year-old Lily and six-month-old Charlie to bed. Amber's white linen pants remained completely uncreased, not a stain in sight. *Why can't you be more like Amber?* Their mother's honeyed tone parachuted into Gen's head. She ejected it, fast. She had no desire to live like her twenty-five-year-old sister, not now, nor in three years' time when she hit that age. She opened the search engine on her laptop.

Amber approached the dining table. 'So, I take it you've finished?'

1

2 • RAE CAIRNS

'Yep. Now I have to prepare an upcoming witness summary for our reporter on that extortion case.'

'That paper's sure getting their money's worth out of you.' Amber collected the dirty plates, empty mugs and glasses surrounding Gen's laptop and kissed the top of her head as she passed by.

Gen looked up. Her sister balanced the mountain of crockery on the drainboard, then pulled her mobile phone from her back pocket and frowned.

'You all right, Ambs?'

'Hugh said he'd be home by now.'

Of course he had. Their marriage had always seemed solid, but ever since his promotion to the board of his father's real estate company a year ago, Amber's husband was evolving into a carbon copy of his politician father. Selfish, pompous and obsessed with image. Did Amber even see it?

'Where is he?'

'A work function.'

Gen swallowed a scoff. The entire five days she'd been here, Hugh had been out at 'work functions' until after midnight. Not that she minded. Amber was more present without Hugh around, and without her sister, Gen would have had to survive on cornflakes alone to make deadline. The extensive fact-check of the paper's exposé on horseracing was her first real chance to make an impression on her mentor since she'd started her cadetship eight months ago, and Amber had stepped right up to support her. Made her a priority, even though she had two young kids underfoot. She'd always taken care of her. Had been more of a mother to Gen than their biological one had ever been.

Gen studied Amber closely, the pale complexion and the lines of concern etched between her sister's brows. Her gaze skimmed over the Caesarstone benchtop and imported splashback tiles from Italy. The house was lovely, as was living near Balmoral Beach in Mosman, one of Sydney's most well-heeled suburbs, but was the price worth it? All Amber seemed to do lately was fret and fight with Hugh about his new job and the stress and absences it caused. Gen returned her focus to her sister's drawn face.

'Ambs, is everything okay?'

'What?' Amber pasted on a bright smile that didn't reach her eyes. 'Yes. Of course. Everything's fine.' She stacked the dishwasher feverishly then sprayed the stovetop with disinfectant, scrubbing hard and fast. It had always been her way. Gen preferred a good all-out brawl, tackling things head-on, but she'd learnt to leave Amber be when she got into one of her cleaning frenzies. She'd try to coax the problem out of her sister later.

Rubbing the crick in her neck, Gen turned back to her computer and typed in the first name on the witness list. A minute later, the scratching and squeaking sounds of domesticity paused. Gen glanced up. Amber was checking her phone again.

'You know you can talk to —'

Charlie's scream blared through the baby monitor and, like a programmed robot, Amber ran upstairs. Gen zoned out the screams and listed the crucial background details she needed for the summary.

Thirty minutes later, Amber dashed back into the room.

'Any chance you could run to the shops for me? We're out of nappies, and I really need to be here when Hugh gets home.'

Gen screwed up her face in apology. 'This summary is due by midnight, and I've only just started.'

'You really can't spare twenty minutes to help me out?'

'I could go once I've sent it off?'

Amber sighed. 'Can you at least keep an eye on the kids until I get back?'

'Of course.' Gen noted down the next witness's date of birth and marital status then glanced up at Amber. 'Why can't Hugh grab a pack of nappies on the way home?'

'He's not answering his phone.'

'What a surprise.'

'Please don't start. Both kids are asleep, and Charlie's monitor is on the bench. I'll be as quick as I can.'

'Okay.' Gen opened a new tab in the browser.

'Gen, did you hear me?'

'Yes.' She opened Facebook and searched to see if the witness had an account.

'Are you even going to notice if the kids wake up?'

Gen waved a hand towards the front door. 'Will you go already?'

Amber gathered her handbag and keys. 'If Charlie wakes, there's formula in the fridge.'

'We'll be fine, Ambs. It's not like you're going to Antarctica. Go!'

Frowning, Amber checked her phone again and sighed. A moment later the front door clicked shut.

Gen stretched her arms above her head. Playing aunty to Lily and Charlie was amazing, but she was nowhere near ready to be lumbered with the never-ending demands of kids. Maybe one day. Perhaps. In the far, far, far away future. But first she'd nail this cadetship, get offered a permanent position on the paper, then travel the world as a fully fledged investigative reporter.

She clicked on the witness's profile and scrolled through his posts.

＊

An hour and a half later Gen was pacing the pristine beige carpet in the lounge room. Charlie arched in her arms, his screams assaulting her ears. Her head throbbed and pain stabbed behind her right eye. How did Amber do this, day in, day out? Charlie howled again.

'You're okay little man.' She rocked on the spot, patting the padded curve of his bottom. 'Mummy will be back soon.'

She'd better be. Charlie had been bawling for an hour straight. She pulled aside the curtain and checked the front drive. No sign of Amber's car. Where was she? And why wasn't she answering her phone? She dialled again, but it went straight to voicemail. As did Hugh's. Again.

Loud clangs from the hallway's grandfather clock clashed with her headache and spurred a fresh bout of screams from Charlie. She glared at it as she paced. Hugh and his pretentious antique. Anyone would think he was seventy-one, not thirty-one, considering his obsession with collector timepieces. Where the hell was *he*?

A hand tugged at her shirt. She looked down into her niece's chocolate-brown eyes.

'Aunty Gen, I hungry.'

Gen's teeth clenched. Lily wasn't supposed to be out of bed. How long did it take to buy goddam nappies?

The doorbell's shrill tone cut through the baby's cries, and Gen exhaled with relief. Until she remembered that Amber had taken her keys. Barking joined the chorus as the family's yellow Labrador, Bentley, charged for the door. Geneva grabbed his collar, overbalancing in her effort to control him. As she did, a flash of pink pyjamas dashed by, and Lily stood on her tippy toes to unlatch the door.

Geneva lurched forward. 'Lily, no!'

Too late. Humid night air flooded the hall. Two men in dark-blue suits filled the doorway. One was young and tall, his expression earnest and warm. The other was older, stocky, his guarded face lined with the toll of life. Geneva curled her free arm around Lily's shoulders and tucked her in close. She looked back to the younger man. Apprehension clouded his green eyes. Gen's pulse sped up.

'Bentley, sit. Quiet.' Miraculously, both dog and baby silenced.

The older man held out a wallet displaying identification and a badge. 'Detective Sergeant Scott Maitland, ma'am.'

The younger man followed suit. 'Plain Clothes Constable Jesse Johns.'

Gen's gaze bounced between the two officers. She hugged Lily in closer.

'Are you Amber Forsythe?' the sergeant asked.

'No, I'm Gen – Geneva. Amber's my sister.'

He looked over Gen's shoulder into the house. 'Is Mrs Forsythe here?'

'She's gone to get nappies.' Gen checked the grandfather clock again. She lowered her voice. 'She should be back by now.'

'Aunty Gen,' Lily said, and turned her face upwards, her eyes wide, 'are we in trouble?'

Crouching, Gen tucked a stray blonde curl behind Lily's ear. 'No Lilybelle, everything's fine.' Her focus darted briefly to the sergeant then back. 'How about you go to the pantry and grab a biscuit? You can watch *Tangled* while you eat.'

'Mummy said no TV at night.'

She squeezed Lily's hand. 'You can blame me, okay?'

Lily's concern transformed into a grin, and she skipped off to the kitchen with Bentley in tow.

Gen heaved herself and a now-sleepy Charlie back to standing. A heavy quiet filled the entranceway. She almost missed his cries.

Sergeant Maitland stepped further into the house. 'Is there somewhere we can sit?'

'Sorry, come in. Take a seat.' She indicated the expensive cream sofas that no one ever used. 'I'll just put Charlie in his crib.'

Her insides churned as she carried Charlie upstairs. Why did the police want Amber? Was Hugh in trouble? She settled Charlie and retreated from the room, then grabbed her mobile from her back pocket and dialled.

'You've reached Amber Forsythe. I can't get to the phone right now —'

Gen hung up and, biting her cheek, tried Hugh. Voicemail again. She took the stairs slowly, her chest tightening with each step. Whatever was going on here, it wasn't good. Squaring her shoulders, she re-entered the front room, sat on the lounge opposite the officers and forced herself to meet the sergeant's gaze.

'Please, tell me what's going on.'

'Your sister's vehicle was found in the laneway car park behind the independent supermarket in Mosman, driver's-side door wide open, purse left on the seat. We need to confirm her whereabouts.'

'I don't understand.' Gen shook her head and turned to the kinder gaze of the constable. 'She went to get nappies. She wouldn't leave her purse in the car.'

He leant forward. 'How long ago did she depart?'

'Ummm …' She checked the time on her phone still clutched in her hand. 'About an hour and a half, I guess.'

'Have you spoken since then?'

'I've tried ringing a few times, including just now, while I was upstairs, but she hasn't answered. She always answers her phone, keeps it in her back pocket like me. We laughed about it yesterday, how you have to be careful when you go to the loo.' Her face heated. 'Sorry, I —'

The ringtone programmed for Amber's calls, 'Tequila', blared from Geneva's phone.

'Oh thank God!' She leapt to her feet and answered. 'Amber? Where are you? The police —'

'Gen, is that you? I can't see properly, the screen's blurry —'

'Ambs, are you okay?' She covered the phone and whispered to the officers, 'Something's not right. She's slurring her words.'

The sergeant turned away and spoke into his two-way radio, while the constable stepped closer to Gen. 'Put her on speaker.'

Gen's heart hammered as they huddled around her mobile.

'Are you there?' Her sister's voice wobbled with tears. 'Gen?'

'I'm here. Where are you?'

'I'm in a car. The boot.'

What the hell? 'Where?'

'I don't know. We're moving.'

Gen forced herself to swallow. 'Who's we?'

'I don't know. Oh God!' Fast, ragged breaths came down the line.

Gen needed to be the strong one now. 'It's okay, Ambs, take a breath with me.' She inhaled against locked ribs and the constable nodded, pointed to the phone. 'The police are here. They want to talk to you.'

'No, don't go!'

Her throat burned. 'I'm not going anywhere. He's right next to me.'

'Amber, my name is Constable Jesse Johns. We're tracing your phone as we speak. Can you tell me what happened?'

'No.'

Gen's gut wrenched at the hitch in Amber's voice.

'Amber,' the constable said warmly, but firmly, 'I need you to tell me.'

'I don't know. I ... I think he hit me. I can't believe he hit me.'

'Who hit you, Amber?'

'A man. His car ... It was parked next to mine. It had to be him. No one else was around.'

'Did you recognise him?'

'No. Why is he doing this? I don't understand.'

'You're doing really well, Amber. What does the man look like?'

'I don't know. It was too dark.'

'Is he tall or short?'

'He was big, tall, but everyone's tall to me.'

'His hair? Face?'

'He wore a black baseball cap, I think. I didn't look closely, just circled around him to get to my car.'

Sergeant Maitland leant away from his walkie talkie and put a finger up. 'We have a general location, but there's only one tower nearby. We need more information.'

'Oh God, what does he want with me?'

Gen started to shake, and the phone blurred. Constable Johns cupped her hands from beneath, keeping the phone stable.

'Amber, are you restrained?' he asked.

'No.'

'Then I need you to kick out a tail-light.'

'What? I can't.'

Gen leant in. 'You can do it, Ambs. Pretend there's a cockroach on it.'

'Start by prising the cover off.' The constable's tone was both kind and commanding. 'Have you done it?'

'Yes.'

'Now smash the bulb and light casing out with your heel.'

'But he'll hear me.'

'Not over the engine.'

'Come on, Ambs, do it for Lily and Charlie. Kick as hard as you can.' Gen held her breath. One thud. Two thuds.

'I did it!'

'Look out the hole,' Constable Johns directed. 'Is there a car behind you? Headlights? Stick your hand through the hole and wave to get someone's attention.'

Gen held her breath, focused on the shuffling sounds coming from the phone.

A hiccupping sob filled the line. 'There's no one there.'

'Ambs, lock on to my voice.' Gen slowed the pace of her speech. 'You have to stay calm. The police are on their way.'

'Please hurry. Wait. We're turning. Ow!'

'Ambs! What happened? Are you okay?'

'I hit my head. There are rocks pelting the bottom of the car. I think we're on a dirt track.'

'Look out the hole again,' Constable Johns interrupted. 'Can you see anything, any houses, or signs?'

'I thought you knew where I was!'

Gen pushed the back of her hand against her nose, and her chest convulsed with a contained sob.

The sergeant covered the phone's speaker and spoke quietly to the constable. 'The signal's moving on the motorway, near Gibbergunyan Creek, but the squad car hasn't reached Welby yet. Just keep her talking.'

'We're close,' Constable Johns said into the phone. 'You just need —'

'No, no, no! The car's slowing. Please, help me!'

'Stay quiet and still,' Constable Johns ordered. 'Pretend you're unconscious. Hide your phone and keep the call open. I promise we're coming for you.'

The noise of the car engine disappeared, then a door slammed.

Amber whimpered. 'Gen,' she whispered, 'promise you'll take care of my kids.'

'Don't you dare give up.'

'Tell them every day how much I love them.'

'Ambs, keep fighting! We'll find you.'

'Hugh is —'

A click, then the creak of the boot opening.

Silence.

Rustling.

A grunt.

Then a high-pitched scream. 'No. No! Please, no!'

The sound of a scuffle, then a loud thud, a crack.

'Fuck,' came a man's gravelly tone. 'Fuck!' he screamed, his voice filled with pain.

A scratching noise came down the line, as if something was moving against Amber's phone. She must have put it in her pocket.

Gen could make out fast footfalls and crunching leaves.

She glanced up at the constable and saw her flare of hope reflected in his eyes.

Come on, Amber, run!

'Come back here, you bitch!' The kidnapper's voice sounded distant but full of rage.

Constable Johns looked at the sergeant. 'Is the car close?'

'They've turned onto the freeway and are closing in.'

The pounding footsteps continued. Gen could hear Amber's fear, visceral in her ragged gasps.

Then … nothing.

'Amber? Ambs?' Gen yelled into the phone. She whirled on the sergeant. 'What happened?'

'The patrol car's three minutes away.'

'What if Amber doesn't have that long?'

1

Now

'Aunty Gen,' Lily yelled from the hallway. 'I'm off to school.'

Geneva slid aside the shower door and snatched a towel from the rail. 'Are you sure you don't want a lift?'

'I'm old enough to get myself to school.' There was that snippy tone again. In the last two months Gen seemed to test Lily's patience more and more. It was as if Lily's sixteenth birthday had triggered a tsunami of hormones and the once gentle, positive and even-tempered girl had become a hypersensitive, moody enigma. The new snark took Gen by surprise every time. 'Okay, well good luck with the test today!'

Thank God for school. Lily was smart. Really, really smart. In Year 10, but already sitting her final year in accelerated mathematics, she behaved as if maintaining the requirements of her full scholarship at one of Sydney's most exclusive schools was a piece of cake.

Twelve-year-old Charlie, on the other hand, could barely get himself out of the house on weekdays.

Gen dried off and wrapped a towel around her bust. She walked down the hallway and rapped three times on Charlie's door.

'You up yet? I need you to get a wriggle on. I can't hang around this morning.' After an answering groan she returned to the bathroom and retrieved the hairdryer from the cupboard.

She rubbed at the fogged-up mirror with her hand. Her straight hair lay in lacklustre clumps to her shoulder blades. Amber had always called it golden brown, which made it sound more glamorous than it was – nothing like the rich blonde waves Amber had passed down to her daughter. Gen bent over and turned the dryer on her roots.

Amber. Always there like a hovering spirit. Even now, the smallest things reminded her of her sister. It was hard to believe next Friday would be twelve years since she'd been taken. Gen still had to finalise the arrangements for the annual vigil and upload the details to the Find Amber website, but right now, she had to focus. She couldn't afford to be late again. Yesterday the restaurant manager had given her a warning, any more last-minute missed shifts or tardiness and she'd be fired. It might just be another waitressing gig, but it was local and provided much-needed flexibility.

Her cadetship mentor would be horrified by her attitude to work now. But that life had ended the day Amber disappeared. How could she continue in a career that she'd prioritised over everything, especially Amber? Her sister wouldn't have been in that car park if Gen had helped that night.

She brushed her hair into a ponytail, then reached for the moisturiser. She never wore make-up anymore. She'd got that out of her system during her teens.

Gen smiled grimly, recalling Hugh's expression the first time he'd met her. Their mother had practically fallen over him, with his tailored suit and carefully styled hair, but Gen had been less impressed. He'd reminded her of a motorbike she'd once inspected with her dad. It had an immaculate chassis and paint job but leaked white smoke when it started – a clear sign that the engine was shot. The owner had dedicated all his time to perfecting the exterior, but totally neglected the bike's inner workings. All style, no substance. Hugh had seemed the same.

Amber had introduced Gen and Hugh's eyes had widened at her black clothing, Doc Martens, jet-black hair and kohl-rimmed eyes. He'd straightened up as he took in her almost six-foot frame, and she'd offered her hand to him with a smirk.

It hadn't been the most auspicious of beginnings, but they'd managed to negotiate their way around their differences. A level of competition for Amber's attention reared up occasionally, but the truth was every time her sister entered a room, Hugh's face lit up, and Amber had got the family she'd always wanted. Gen had never seen her so happy. Until that final year.

Gen smoothed her unkempt eyebrows into place.

Hugh was due back from Melbourne tonight, thank God. He'd been away for work for the past fortnight, and she needed him to take up some of the slack. The wheels of their unconventional arrangement had been falling off lately, as they often did a little in the lead-up to the anniversary of Amber's disappearance.

A knock at the bathroom door jolted Gen from her reverie.

'Sorry Aunty Gen, I forgot – I need you to sign my excursion slip.' Lily sounded stressed. 'Can I pass it through to you? If I don't leave soon, I'll be late for class.'

'Of course, honey.' Gen cracked open the door and peered around the gap. A slightly bedraggled Lily stood before her, her cheeks bright red, as if she'd been running. 'Dad was supposed to sign it online by yesterday, but he didn't remember and the portal is closed now.' Lily passed through a paper and pen.

Gen leant on the vanity to sign the form. As she stood upright, the alien sound of the home phone ringing echoed through the house. Her stomach dropped. Hugh had wanted to disconnect the landline, but she hadn't let him. Just in case. Footsteps ran to the phone.

'Forsythe residence, Lily speaking.'

Gen poked her head around the corner. 'Lily, who is it?'

'Some guy. He asked to talk to you.'

Rearranging her towel around herself, she walked into the hallway and took the phone from Lily.

'Hello?'

'Ms Leighton?'

'Yes?'

A beat of silence filled the line, then a slow exhale.

'Geneva, it's Jesse.'

His calm, measured tone took her straight back to that night, dissolving every response on her tongue.

He cleared his throat. 'Sergeant Jesse Johns? I was the constable —'

'I remember.' As if she could forget.

'Would it be possible to meet today?'

Lily touched her palm to Gen's forearm. 'Are you okay?' she mouthed.

Gen nodded. 'Sergeant, could you please give me a minute?' She hooked her arm around Lily's head and pressed a kiss to her hair, holding her there a moment longer than she should. Lily took after her mother in stature, so Gen could still rest her chin on her niece's head.

'Everything's fine. Just a hiccup with the permits for the vigil.'

'O-kay,' Lily drawled, scrunching up her nose in disbelief.

'You'd better get a move on or you'll be late. Don't forget to grab the permission slip from the bathroom.'

Lily darted into the bathroom then came out. 'See you at six, after band.'

'Love you. Have a good day.'

'Love you too!' Lily's heavy school shoes clomped down the hall and the front door clicked shut.

Gen raised the phone to her ear. 'Sergeant, what's this about?'

'Are you available this afternoon? I need to meet with you in person.'

'Hugh's working in Melbourne, but he's due back tonight, around dinner time. Is there news?'

'Are *you* free to meet?' he repeated. 'You, alone?'

She wanted to repeat the question he'd avoided but paused. Was she ready for the answer?

'I have work until three.'

'I'll come to your house at four o'clock.'

A bleary-eyed Charlie stumbled towards the bathroom. She lowered her voice; she couldn't risk him overhearing anything. 'Charlie will be home, but he can go out the back, I guess. Is it ...?'

'See you at four.'

He hung up and Gen slumped against the wall. The likelihood of Amber being alive was minuscule, but until this second Gen hadn't realised how hard she'd been holding on to hope.

She strode to her bedroom. Why did it have to be Jesse? So much had been left unsaid between them. She yanked black work pants over her hips and slipped a shirt over her head. It must be about Amber; he wouldn't have called otherwise.

But if it was good news, surely he'd have told her on the phone. A wave of foreboding rippled through her, and she slumped onto the edge of her bed. Her eyes welled and she scrubbed her hand across her face. She had to pull herself together.

'Are you okay?'

She looked up. Charlie's freckle-dusted face stared back at her, his big blue eyes tinged with concern.

'Everything's fine, Charlie.' She ruffled his spiky red hair. 'Just got moisturiser in my eye, stings like a bitch.'

'Hah! You owe a dollar to the swear jar.' Charlie's full lips spread into a huge grin. 'Remember what happens when it gets to the top. You have to take us out for dinner, our choice.'

She reached out to tickle him, but he dodged and ran down the hall.

'You're almost there, you know. I reckon ten more swears. We can have pizza tomorrow night!'

Geneva chased him but she had no hope of catching him. He slid down the banister, laughing hard. She stood at the top of the stairs, wagging her finger at him.

'Just you wait, Charlie Forsythe. When you least expect it, I'll —'

'Careful, or we'll be going out for breakfast instead!'

The day dragged as she tried not to torture herself with thoughts of what the afternoon would bring. It felt like all she'd done for the last twelve years was wait; held on pause, frozen like some cryogenic life form. After the early rush at the restaurant, she threw herself into re-organising the cool room, blasting hard rock music through her headphones, determined to drown out the questions and fears and keep her hope alive.

Now Jesse would be here any minute and all she wanted was to delay his arrival indefinitely.

She carved off two slices of watermelon, its sweet scent sending a wave of nausea through her. Had they found new evidence? But why would they send Jesse? He hadn't been on Amber's case since that first month.

She checked her watch and her jaw tensed. Hugh should be here, but he wasn't answering her calls or messages. Too bad if something had happened to one of the kids. She sighed, the weight of responsibility settling heavily on her shoulders.

'Honey,' she said, and tapped Charlie's shoulder, 'off the computer and take this outside.' She handed him the plate. 'I've got someone coming for a meeting.'

'Thanks Mum.' He grabbed the fruit and charged for the side stairs leading to the driveway.

'Charlie, hang on a sec.' She knelt in front of him. 'I love you more than anything, but we've talked about this.'

'But —'

She rubbed his arm. 'You already have a mum.'

There was no way she could fill Amber's shoes. And she had no right.

He blinked a few times, then shrugged. 'Is it okay if I practise shooting during your meeting?'

'Of course.'

On the rare occasions Hugh was home, he'd complain about the banging on the backboard and the thump of Charlie dribbling the ball up and down the driveway. But Gen found the sounds calming, almost reassuring. They meant Charlie was okay.

She moved to the front room to wait and stared at the framed photo on the mantel. It showed Amber at the beach, baby Charlie held to her chest and little Lily beaming as she rested her chin on her mum's shoulder. It had been taken just two weeks before everything changed. Amber looked so vibrant.

Strong.

Alive.

A weight shifted in Gen's stomach. She had to keep believing. She'd lived through this before with many of the tip-offs that came through the Find Amber website. Gen had set it up three months after her sister's disappearance, when Amber was recategorised as long-term missing and the high-profile investigation was downsized. The site had gotten Gen through the awful coroner's inquest five years ago, when Hugh had successfully pushed for Amber to be declared legally dead. Despite the coroner's conclusions, Gen had forged on with her quest for answers.

Not long after the inquest Gen had thought she'd seen her sister herself. She'd been walking down George Street in the city, heading to a temp receptionist position, and up ahead, a swish of thick blonde hair, the exact same length and colour of Amber's, had disappeared around the corner. Gen had raced after her, but when she'd rounded the corner the blonde had looked back, her oval face nothing like Amber's heart-shaped one. Gen never made it to the job that day. Instead, she'd gone home and posted across every social media platform. Fat lot of good it had done. A few crank leads. A dozen sympathy responses.

Warmth pressed against her leg as Bentley leant into her, as if he understood she needed support. She knelt and scratched his ears.

'Thanks, bud.' She led him out to the deck, gave him another pat as he gingerly lowered his arthritic body into his bed, then she traipsed down the side stairs, just off the kitchen, to collect Charlie's plate.

An engine rumbled and a white vehicle pulled in at the end of the long driveway. She squinted, hoping it was one of the airport transfer limousines Hugh used. Her shoulders fell. It was a ute.

Charlie remained oblivious. He was in the zone, executing a figure of eight leading into a lay-up. He caught the rebound and wove in the other direction, getting that shot in as well. His teachers might complain about his attention span, but when it came to basketball, he had no such problem. He knew the stats of every Aussie and US basketball team, researched everything LeBron James had done to reach the top. Obsessed didn't come close to describing his passion.

The car door opened and a man, easily over six foot, unfolded from the vehicle. Jesse. Dressed casually in blue jeans, he filled out his black tee and leather jacket more than the last time Gen had seen him. He had to be in his late thirties now; his dark-brown hair had turned salt and pepper early. He watched Charlie shoot two more baskets then strode up the concrete drive, his solid body moving with calm assurance.

He skirted the three-point chalk line Charlie had drawn and Gen wrapped her arms around herself. There was a heaviness surrounding him that hadn't been there twelve years ago. Frown lines had crept in around his mouth and across his forehead, the elevens etched between his brows giving him a look of serious concentration. His green eyes met hers, and his lips lifted in a tight smile.

'Thanks for making the time to see me.'

Gen's gaze flicked to Charlie, who was in the middle of another lay-up. 'Let's grab a cuppa inside.'

'Great.'

God, it was so damn awkward between them.

'Charlie, you okay out here for a bit?'

'Mm-hmm.'

'Charlie!'

'Sorry, yes, have to get a hundred more in the basket.'

She led Jesse into the kitchen.

'The kid's good.'

'Yeah.'

'Where's he play?'

'School. He loves it.'

'He should come to the Y sometime.'

'The Y?'

'The PCYC – Police Citizens Youth Club. It's where I'm stationed now.'

'That's quite a change from Tactical Operations.'

'Not as much as you'd think.' He chuckled. 'We could do with another fast player for our under-fourteens rep team – especially one who can shoot like him.'

'Not sure Hugh would go for it.' She lifted a mug in Jesse's direction. 'Tea? Coffee?'

'Coffee, thanks. Black.' At least that hadn't changed.

The buzz of the coffee machine provided a brief reprieve from the small talk. She made herself a peppermint tea, handed Jesse his coffee and led him into the front room, away from curious ears. She took a deep breath. Whatever he was about to tell her had already happened. It couldn't be changed.

'I think you'd better tell me why you're here.'

'Can we sit?' Jesse indicated the lounge.

She stared at him, assailed by echoes of the past. His kindness that day, sitting on this very couch. The terror in her sister's voice. The suffocating fear and guilt.

The loud thump of the basketball rebounding off the backboard returned her to the present. Hugh should be here for this. She reached for the phone in her back pocket.

'Geneva?'

She blinked a few times then sat on the edge of the lounge opposite Jesse. She discarded her mug and clasped her hands together. 'Go ahead.'

'Two weeks ago, a woman's remains were found on a property in Windsor. Early this morning the coroner confirmed a match to your sister's records. I'm so sorry.'

Saliva pooled in her mouth.

'Gen?'

She forced a swallow and met his concerned stare.

'Are they sure? It's been twelve years.'

'Dental records are accurate.'

'Where was she found?' Was. She was already talking about her sister in past tense.

'Windsor.'

'You said that. I mean where exactly?'

'Amber's remains were buried under the concrete floor of a storage shed. The property is being demolished and her remains were uncovered when the slab was removed.'

'Has the owner been questioned? Arrested?'

'He died two years ago.'

Gen bent forward, face in her hands. So they might never find out what happened, never get justice for Amber. Oh God. Amber was never coming back. Pain tore through her chest and her eyes flooded.

The couch sank next to her and Jesse rested a hand on her shoulder. She looked up and the compassion in his eyes almost undid her. She blinked away the tears.

'What was the owner's name?'

'That detail hasn't been released yet.'

'Why? He's dead.' A sour taste flooded her mouth. 'Was he some kind of serial killer?'

'No other remains were found on the property.'

Gen took a breath, forcing herself to ask the next question. 'How did she die?'

'The provisional cause of death is blunt force trauma.' He paused. 'You sure you want to hear this?'

She stared back.

'The coroner compared the blood-coated rock found at the scene of her attempted escape to the injury present on her skull and believes it's likely she died as a result of being struck that night.'

Gen's eyes squeezed shut. Had her sister been dying while Gen had listened on the phone? Her chest spasmed as she fought back sobs. She didn't deserve to cry. It was her fault Amber was dead. She shrugged off Jesse's arm and shifted away, putting some space between them.

'What happens now?'

'The department carried out the next of kin notification to Hugh, then scheduled a press conference for six o'clock tonight. I wanted to make sure you'd been kept in the loop.'

He looked away.

There was something else. 'And?'

Jesse sighed. 'Someone leaked the news to the press thirty minutes ago. It's already trending on social media.'

'Oh God, the kids can't find out like that.' She swivelled to face him. 'Wait! Hugh knows?'

'The family liaison notified him this morning, right before I rang you. Apparently he's stuck in Melbourne for meetings and can't get back until tomorrow.'

'The fucking coward! He's leaving it up to me to tell the kids their mother is dead.'

'No!' A pained whisper came from the hallway. Gen looked over her shoulder and caught sight of the tip of a blonde ponytail fleeing. *Shit. What's Lily doing home this early?*

The front door slammed shut.

Gen leapt to her feet and ran after her niece but froze as she reached for the door handle. She couldn't leave Charlie here alone, not with the media about to descend.

'I've got him. Go.' Jesse waved her off. 'I'll stay until you get back.'

2

Gen charged down the steep, shady walking track of Lawry Plunkett Reserve. The bushland flew past in her peripheral vision. Halfway down, near the remnants of the Balmoral tramway system, she weaved through a bunch of women kitted up in Lululemon, unable to offer an *excuse me* between her audible gulps of air. A minute later she stumbled onto The Esplanade, crossed to the promenade and bent in two, hands on her knees. The second her breath settled she was off again, zeroing in on Rocky Point Island, Amber's favourite part of Balmoral Beach.

Jogging across the small arched pedestrian bridge, she skirted a young couple strolling hand in hand, and paused at the top of the rise. Lily sat on a rock shelf at the island's edge, hugging her legs to her chest. She stared into the distance, looking weighed down by more than any teenager should have to withstand.

Gen climbed down next to her. 'This seat taken?'

No answer.

She sat anyway, relieved to see another slab of rock only a metre below stretching out towards the water. She followed Lily's lead and stared across the Harbour. Heat shimmered around the buildings on the far bank of North Head. She counted in her mind, forcing herself to give Lily space. But when she reached one hundred she couldn't stand it any longer. She turned to face her niece.

Tears tracked down Lily's face.

'Oh Lil.'

'I can't remember what her voice sounds like,' Lily whispered. 'I can't picture her clearly anymore.' Her chin dropped. 'I didn't work hard enough to keep her.'

Gen's chest knotted tighter. 'Oh honey, I had twenty-two years with your mum, and she still feels out of reach to me sometimes.' She cleared her throat. 'I'm sorry you heard about her like that.'

'So it's true, then. What happened to her?'

She tugged Lily closer in. 'She was found on a property near Windsor.'

'Do they know why ... how she died?'

Oh God. She hadn't had time to think this through. But she couldn't lie. 'They think it was an injury to her head.'

'Did someone hit her?'

'Most likely. The important thing is the coroner thinks it happened the same night she was taken.'

'So she didn't suffer?'

Honesty was one thing, but painful conjecture was another. Gen dodged the question. 'Her last words to me were about you and Charlie. She loved you both so much.'

Lily's legs unfolded, and her calves hung over the edge. 'I hoped she still might turn up one Christmas, or at my graduation or something.' She shrugged. 'I know it sounds stupid.'

'I had the exact same thoughts, sweetheart.'

Lily's chin dropped. 'Sometimes it feels like everyone's going to leave.'

'What do you mean?'

'Dad's barely at home.'

Gen's jaw tightened. 'Your dad would be here if he could.'

'That's not what you said.'

'I was dealing with my own crap. Your dad loves you.'

Lily pulled her knees back in. 'Tracey Halnom from school reckons he has another family.'

'Lilybelle —'

'It's what happened to Zara's family. Her dad spent less and less time at home, and then bam, he moved out with his new wife and their new baby. Zara doesn't see him anymore.'

'That's not what's happening here.'

But even as Gen said the words, a prickle of doubt crept up her neck. Lily was right about Hugh spending less time at home lately. How that was even possible was anyone's guess.

She met Lily's imploring gaze. She had to help the kids get through this. If that meant she had to drag Hugh back to them, kicking and screaming, she would.

'Sweetheart, your dad runs a big company.' She resisted rolling her eyes as she echoed the words he regularly threw at them. 'If he could be here, he would. He's getting a flight home tomorrow.'

Lily leant her head on Gen's shoulder. Gen curled her arm around her and drew in a slow breath. Gentle waves lapped against the rocks below, then drew out again.

Lily edged away. Sat taller. 'Who took her?'

'The police don't know yet, but they will.'

'How can you believe anything they say?'

'The police did everything they could twelve years ago. They conducted a massive search for your mum and kept the case active for as long as possible. I trust them to —'

'Jesse's a liar.'

'Honey —'

'He said he'd never give up, pinkie promised. He even gave me his card. Then he disappeared too. I tried ringing the number on the card, but they said he didn't work there anymore.'

A wave of hot rage flared up Gen's neck. Her feelings were one thing, but to leave Lily feeling abandoned too? He would be hearing some choice words when she could get him on his own.

'I'm sorry the police let you down. I promise we'll get an answer this time. I won't stop until I find out what happened.'

'Promise?'

'You have my word.'

The wind picked up and Lily shivered. Gen checked her watch. 'You okay to go back to Charlie?'

'Oh shit, I didn't even think.' Lily leapt up and hooked her backpack over one shoulder.

'It's fine, sweetheart, Jesse's with him.'

'Does he know?'

'Not yet.'

'Were you going to wait for Dad?'

'Honestly, I hadn't had time to decide, but I think I would've had to tell you both. Someone's already leaked it to the media.'

Lily's hand fluttered to her throat. 'It won't be like before, will it? All those people screaming questions?'

'I won't let them get to you.'

'Can we go? I don't want Charlie to be alone.'

'You going to be okay?'

'I guess. Just ... don't ever leave us, Aunty Gen.'

'There is nothing and no one who could take me from you.'

*

As they walked back up the hill, Gen silently rehearsed ways to break the news to Charlie. He was only twelve; she wished she could protect him from this. A weight settled over her. Maybe it would have been better if Amber hadn't been found.

Heat burned her cheeks. How could she think that way?

Gen's phone vibrated with a message. She pulled it out to see a text from Toni, a broadcast journalist and her closest friend.

Heads up, we're out front. All major TV stations present. Sorry.

Damn it. The cul-de-sac would be swarming. She caught Lily's arm gently, pulling her to a stop.

'Sweetheart, that was Aunty Toni. There are reporters outside the house already.'

Lily's eyes widened, fear filling her face.

Gen placed her palms on her niece's shoulders. 'It'll be okay. I'll distract them while you get inside.'

'But then you'll be on your own.'

'I'll be fine. I want you to walk parallel to the back fence. Make sure to stay in the bush until you're in line with the gate. If any reporters are standing there, just wait it out. They'll go when they hear me arrive.'

'I'm so sorry. If I hadn't left —'

'This is not your fault, Lily. Text me when you're inside and I'll come straight in.'

'I can't do this again.' Lily's voice wavered. 'All the yelling and cameras.'

Gen bracketed her niece's cheeks with her palms. 'You won't have to. I will handle it, and this time we have Aunty Toni to help too.'

Gen pulled Lily into a brief hug, then stepped back. 'Off you go. It'll be okay.'

'Will you?'

'I'm tough. You know that.' Gen reached for the necklace her sister had given her for her twenty-first birthday, the one she never took off. She slid the gold and diamond pendant between her fingers as she watched Lily cross into the scrub. *Look after her, Ambs.* She gave her niece a minute, then walked up the path that led into the cul-de-sac.

Five white news vans, sides emblazoned with station logos, took up the entire turning circle, showing absolutely no regard for the neighbours. A hum of chatter filled the street as on-air reporters checked their make-up in small hand-held mirrors while cameramen smoked or tapped away on their phones.

Any minute now someone would notice her. Bat-sized butterflies flapped frantically in her stomach, like birds trapped in a room. She was older this time; she knew what to expect as the focus of high-profile news. She brushed down her hair and searched the crowd until she found Toni and met her gaze. The pounding in her chest eased to a gentle knocking. She set her shoulders and lifted her chin. Game time.

'There she is!' a husky female voice shouted. All heads turned her way and the reporters descended, blocking her path, the barbs of their overlapping questions assaulting her.

'Ms Leighton, how do you feel knowing that the sister you've been searching for has been dead all these years, just as the coroner said?'

'Have the police identified a suspect yet?'

'Where are the police in their investigation?'

'How long have you known about the body?'

'Sources report Mr Forsythe is staying at the casino in Melbourne. Why hasn't he come home to be with his kids?'

Because he's a coward, who can barely cope with his own emotions, let alone those of his children. But Gen couldn't show these vultures a hint of weakness or they would eat her alive. She tucked her chin in and barrelled forward.

'How are Amber's children processing the news?'

'What does the Minister for Liquor and Gaming think about his family being thrust back into the public eye?'

Gen rolled her eyes. Hugh's father and his political career was the last thing she cared about.

'What do you say to the rumours that Hugh was having an affair and had his wife killed?'

'Have the police revealed the motive for Amber's murder?'

'Is it true Amber was having an affair?' a blonde woman shouted in an ugly, thin voice.

Gen shoved her hands into her pockets, one hand clutching her phone. She just needed to last until Lily was safe. She didn't recognise most of these reporters. They were younger than last time. More aggressive.

Her breathing shallowed. The sensation of being boxed in was threatening to overwhelm her.

To her right, Toni and her cameraman hugged the edge of the fence, essentially extending it. Gen continued driving her way forward.

'Have you met with the police yet?' Toni pushed her microphone through the pack, manoeuvring other reporters out of the way. As Gen reached her, Toni stepped aside, providing an escape route.

Gen's phone buzzed with a thumbs-up text from Lily.

'What do you say about the rumours you and Hugh were having an affair?'

Gen's head whipped around, laser focused on the petite blonde with overdone make-up and ironed-out hair.

The woman shoved a microphone in her face, whacking it against Gen's chin in her haste. Gen's resolve evaporated.

'Make up your fucking mind! One minute Amber's having an affair then the next minute it's Hugh and I?' Boom mics filled the air around her; handheld mics crowded her face. Every other space was taken up by the cameras, their red recording lights on.

Geneva retreated a step and turned her back on the arseholes.

The blonde ran forward and blocked Gen's path to the stairs. 'Or could Amber's death have something to do with your father's history as a gang member?'

Just because her dad had been a member of a motorcycle club didn't mean he was in a gang. And he never would have put his daughters at risk. Geneva lengthened her spine. 'Where are you from?'

'Melody Jamison on the ground for Newsfirst online.' The arrogance in the young woman's voice only fortified Gen's contempt.

'Well, Melody, if you ever set foot on this property again, I'll have you arrested.' The woman's eyes widened. 'Now get the fuck out of my way.'

The woman scuttled back to the pack and Gen faced them all.

'Our family will put out a statement tomorrow morning. If I find any of you on this property again, I will call the police.'

Gen marched up the stairs, opened the front door and slammed it behind her. Her hands shook and her eyes filled with tears. *Dammit.* Her outburst would be all over the news and social media.

She'd always used the press to keep the search for her sister going, while they'd used her for content. And their family had been lucky, if you could call it that, because Amber was an attractive, rich, young white woman so the coverage and interest had been widespread and longer-lasting. It didn't work like that for many missing Australians, especially the Indigenous, poor or elderly. But now, even with the fascination and appeal of Amber, much of the media just seemed hungry for clickbait to hashtag on socials. Forget the truth.

Gen blinked until the tears subsided. She shook her hands out, then double-locked the front door. Raised voices drew her to the kitchen.

'You can't tell him to leave!' Charlie yelled.

'We don't even know him!'

Gen entered the room and was hit by the scent of fried onion and garlic. Lily stood on one side of the kitchen island, hands on her hips. Charlie, mirroring her stance, stood in front of Jesse, who was stirring something at the stove.

'He's my friend.'

'He's just a cop.' Lily grabbed a backpack off the dining table and shoved it across the island in Jesse's direction.

Charlie pushed it away. 'He came to see Aunty Gen. He works at a police youth ... something club.'

'Citizens.' It was the first interjection from an extremely calm Jesse.

'I don't care! I don't want him here.'

'That's enough.' Gen placed her palm on her niece's shoulder. 'Jesse helped us *both* out this afternoon.'

Lily jerked away and flicked a sharp look at Jesse. 'I'm going to my room.' She stormed off, clomping up the stairs.

Gen turned to Jesse, who continued stirring the pot as if nothing had happened. 'Sorry.'

Jesse shrugged. 'It's been a tough day.'

'I really appreciate your help this afternoon.' Her eyes darted to the ceiling. 'But it might be best if you go now.'

'No!' Charlie shook his head. 'He made dinner. He should get to stay and eat with us.'

'It's okay, bud.' Jesse collected his jacket and slipped it on. 'Sorry if I overstepped. I didn't know how long you'd be, and Charlie said he was starving. We found the defrosted meat and ...' He gestured in the direction of the pan.

'That was really kind, thank you.'

'I'll stay out front for a while, keep an eye on things.'

'You don't need to.'

He shrugged again.

Could he stop being so bloody helpful? He had no place in their lives.

She glanced at Charlie's crestfallen face. Dammit. Why couldn't the police have sent someone else?

She pulled four plates from the cupboard. 'Charlie's right. You can stay for dinner.' At least if any of those reporters crossed the line, Jesse would sort it.

'What's going on out front?' asked Charlie.

Shit. She'd forgotten how well little ears listened when they weren't supposed to. She turned to Jesse. 'I need to ...' She shifted her eyes in Charlie's direction.

Jesse nodded. 'I'll finish dinner. You take all the time you need.' He disappeared into the walk-in pantry.

Geneva put her arm around Charlie and led him to the lounge on the other side of the room.

'I've had the best afternoon. Jesse coaches basketball. He played one on one with me, and he offered to take me to rep trials tomorrow, if you'll let me, and —'

'Woah, slow down there. I'd love to hear more, but first I need to tell you something.' She angled her body to face him.

'Okay.' He nodded, no defence in place. No shutters. She took his hand.

'The police found some remains.'

'Like bones and stuff?' His gaze dropped, and he ran his thumb back and forth across her knuckles.

'I'm so sorry, sweetheart. They're your mum's.'

Charlie stared at their hands.

'Are you okay?' Gen asked.

'I feel weird.'

'What do you mean?'

He shrugged. 'I don't know. Like, I wish she wasn't dead but, I kinda feel nothing.' He looked up through his lashes. 'Is that wrong?'

'There's no right way to feel.'

'Is that why Lily is angry?'

'Everyone deals with things in different ways.'

'What about Dad? Does he know?'

'He'll be back in the morning.'

Charlie's quiet breaths filled the silence between them.

'You can talk to me, Charlie. I'm here for whatever you need.'

He shifted in his seat, then looked up with a sheepish expression. 'Can we eat dinner? I'm so hungry.'

Wow. Her hand rose to the base of her neck. She wanted him resilient, but did Amber's death really have such little impact?

She looked to Jesse in the kitchen. He gave her an understanding smile. 'Dinner's ready whenever you guys are.'

Ninety minutes later, Geneva walked Jesse to the door. Lily had joined them for dinner, albeit in silent protest, but Charlie had filled the void with a word vomit about last Friday's game between the Sydney Kings and Perth Wildcats. The news about Amber didn't seem to have sunk in at all. Was his reaction normal? Gen sighed. Hadn't she told Charlie there was no right response? She cracked open the front door and peeked out.

'They're gone,' Jesse said from behind her. 'I had a patrol car check.'

She turned to meet his gaze, which seemed to laser through her defences.

'I can stay if you want?'

'I'm not the same person I was twelve years ago.'

'I'd like to help.'

She stepped aside. 'You're a bit late.'

'What's that supposed to mean?'

'You pinkie-swore with Lily that you'd find her mum and then you disappeared. She was four and half, Jesse. I won't let you do that to her again.'

'I know I let you all down. I'm sorry – you have to believe me, I had no choice. I want to make it right.' He stepped outside, then looked back at her. 'I'm not here in an official capacity. My brother, Ethan, is in the Homicide Squad. He knew what this case meant to me.'

'Well, I'd like to deal with the actual investigating officers going forward.'

He slipped a business card from his pocket and handed it to her. The words 'PCYC North Sydney' were on the front, and there was a mobile number scribbled on the back.

'I live in Neutral Bay. I'm only a few minutes away if you need anything.'

'Thanks, but we'll be fine. Goodbye Jesse.'

She pulled the door closed, engaged the lock and released a breath. There was no way she would let that man back into their lives, not after last time.

3

Gen's eyes cracked open then slammed shut, rejecting the bright light pouring through her uncovered window. She lay on her stomach and inhaled a long breath. For that one brief second, everyone she loved was safe. It was the moment she lived for every day, the one before the weight of regret, grief and responsibility settled on her chest.

But today was different. Today she knew beyond all doubt there was nothing she could do, no clue she could uncover that might bring her sister back. And that knowledge threatened to crush her completely.

The remnants of last night's sleeping pill coated Gen's mouth like fur. She rolled onto her back and blinked into focus the white and taupe toned bedroom. Even after twelve years, the only signs the room was hers were a wonky vase Lily had made in Year 7, a photo of Amber with the kids, and a stack of files about Amber's case sitting on the dresser. Gen had willingly stepped in as a place keeper for Amber, like one of those chair fillers at the Oscars. But Amber was supposed to return to her seat.

Someone rapped on her door, then Charlie burst in and dive-bombed onto the bed.

'Better get a wriggle on, Aunty Gen!'

'Inside voice, Charlie.' With a groan, she pulled him into a hug. The scratchy fabric of his basketball singlet tickled her cheek. She checked the time. It was 7 am and he was already dressed in his uniform. Gen groaned again. She should have told him last night that he wouldn't be able to play this morning.

'Come on!' He pulled the covers off her. 'You promised we could get a bacon and egg roll before the game.'

'Charlie, I don't think that'll work now.' The discovery of Amber's remains had been the top news item last night. There was no way she was going to let the kids go out in public today. She needed to prepare them for the questions first. The nosy. The compassionate. The cruel.

'But you promised!'

How on earth could she explain this to him? He seemed fine, as if yesterday had been just another day, but she had to make sure Lily was okay, face off with Hugh, schedule a meeting with the police, check in with Toni and, worst of all, track down her mum.

'You're going to need to skip basketball today.'

'No!'

'How about you grab breakfast while I get dressed, then we can talk?'

'But —'

'Please, Charlie.'

He left the room, uncharacteristically slamming the door behind him.

Geneva swung her legs over the side of the bed, sat up and checked her phone. Social media notifications filled the lock screen. Toni had sent a text, but there was still nothing from Gen's mother. Normally, Gen would accept that a honeymoon on a Mediterranean cruise ship qualified for a 'contact cleanse', but surely 'important news' from her daughter rated a response. Gen hadn't wanted her mum to hear the confirmation of Amber's death via social media. But her mum's focus remained squarely fixed on the current man in her life, as always.

Gen yanked on trackies and the same tee she'd had on yesterday. She opened Toni's text.

Media release typed and ready to go. You want to check it
first? Or run it past Hugh?

The man had chosen not to come home. He'd just have to suck it up. She started tapping a reply.

Has it changed from last night's draft?

Not much.

So, 'fuck off and leave us be, you vultures'.

More or less.

Three dots blinked in repetition as another typing bubble appeared from Toni.

There is a lot of interest.

Gen had had enough of typing. She called Toni.

'Can you add that I've signed to do an exclusive interview with *Sunday First*?'

'You sure?'

'Better you than anyone else. And it's the only way to get everyone to leave us alone.'

'I'll add it to the release but take my time organising the contract. That'll buy you time to decide if it's something you really want to do.'

'Your producer must be about to strangle you for not pushing.'

'Our friendship comes first.'

'Aunty Geneva!' Charlie shouted from downstairs. 'I can't find the Nutella. Are you coming?'

'I need to go. I have to explain to Charlie why he can't go to basketball today.'

'Once I add the interview, you want me to send out the release?'

'I still haven't tracked Mum down.'

'If you leave it —'

'I know, I know. Just send it.'

'You going to be okay?'

'Always. Thanks for your help.'

'I'm here if you need me.'

Slipping the phone into her pocket, Gen opened her door, and the scent of freshly brewed coffee drew her to the kitchen. Had Hugh caught an earlier flight? A frisson of hope fluttered then fizzed out. She'd have heard Charlie's greeting from her room.

Rubbing the sleep from the corner of her eye, she stepped into the kitchen. Charlie turned from the coffee maker with a huge grin on his face and placed a fresh brew on the kitchen island.

Gen's lips twisted to the side. 'Are you trying to butter me up, Charlie Forsythe?'

'Mwah?'

'It's a lovely gesture, mate, but it's not going to change the fact that we won't make your game this morning.'

'It's okay. I sorted it.'

'What do you mean?'

The clang of the doorbell sounded, and Charlie grabbed his backpack. 'I organised a lift.' He ran down the corridor.

'Charlie, wait!'

It could be anyone at the door. She charged after him, then pulled up short. Jesse stood in the doorway, head cocked to the side.

'Morning.'

'What are you doing here?'

Jesse's gaze slid to Charlie and her nephew looked to his feet.

'I called him,' he mumbled. 'He's my lift.'

'Charlie!' Her phone buzzed, but she ignored it. 'Jesse has better things to do than run you to activities.' She placed her hands on Charlie's shoulders and looked at Jesse. 'I'm so sorry to have wasted your morning.'

'Actually, I told him yesterday I wanted to attend his game. With permission from you or his dad, of course.' Jesse raised a brow at Charlie.

'I know I told you I asked, but what does it matter? Dad's away and Gen said she can't go. I need to play today. If I miss this game, I can't play in the finals.'

'Charlie, that's not how to go about this.' Gen turned Charlie to face her. 'And your teammates and their parents are bound to ask questions. That could be hard, even if they mean well.'

'None of my friends are going to care. They know my mum's not around. She never has been. Please, Gen. I need to play this game.'

Her phone rang. She glanced at it; the call was from an unknown number. Probably the press. She hit reject and bent to look Charlie in the eyes.

'I'm not going to reward your behaviour. I'm really unhappy.'

Her phone buzzed again, with a text message from Hugh this time.

Make sure kids are home for dinner tonight. No sleepovers.

'For frig's sake.' The man was unbelievable. He'd been incommunicado since being notified yesterday, and this was all he could think to send her?

'Gen, please.' Charlie's puppy dog eyes made her feel about an inch tall. She looked at Jesse. He raised his hands as if to say, *whatever you need*.

Pressure swelled inside her like an inflating balloon. Should Charlie be allowed to carry on as normal? Was it okay to accept Jesse's help again? She closed her eyes, took a breath, and asked herself the question she always used as her barometer: What would Amber do?

She would put Charlie's needs first. If he played the game, it would fill his morning while she dealt with things, and it would help him burn off some energy, which would be beneficial when Hugh got home and expected his son to behave.

'Go and brush your teeth while I chat with Jesse.'

'But —'

'Teeth, now, if you want any chance of a yes.'

Charlie ran off and she faced Jesse. 'I'm so sorry about this,' she said.

'I'm happy to take him.'

'I know, but —'

'No one will approach him with me hovering, and some normalcy might be good for him. The next little while could get a bit overwhelming, especially for a twelve-year-old.'

'Why are you doing this?'

'I want to poach him for our rep squad.'

Gen's eyes narrowed.

'Okay, okay. You're holding everything together, so I thought I could take one thing off your load.' He pushed his hands into his pockets and grinned. 'And ... I want to poach him for our rep squad.'

He was trying to put her at ease, but she couldn't get sucked in by his nice-guy charm again. 'It would help if you'd take him today, thank you. I promise it won't happen again.'

Charlie raced back into the room. 'So?'

Gen folded her arms. 'There will be consequences for lying.'

'I didn't lie. I ... changed the truth.'

Jesse shook his head. 'Mate, thinking before you speak might be the best step forward.'

Charlie nodded to Jesse, then looked back at her. 'Sorry, Gen Gen. I'll clean the rumpus room tomorrow and do my homework without you asking.'

'You should be doing that anyway.'

'I'll do my homework as soon as I come in the door, every night this week.'

'Again, should happen anyway.'

'I'll —'

Gen put her palm up to stop him. 'I'll think of something. You can go – *if* you agree to do everything Jesse tells you to.'

'He will, or I'll bring him straight home,' Jesse assured her.

Her phone rang again, this time with a call from Greece. She glanced back at Jesse. 'You sure?'

He nodded.

'I need to take this, it's my mum.' She kissed Charlie on the head. 'Be good.' She pointed to her ringing phone. 'Call me if you need me.'

Jesse put a hand on Charlie's shoulder. 'I'm a policeman. We'll be fine.'

She pressed answer as they jogged outside to Jesse's ute.

'Finally!' Her mum's breathy, high-pitched voice came down the line. 'I was about to hang up.'

'Hi Mum.'

'I've told you, now we're adults my name is Lucielle.'

Gen's grip tightened on the phone. 'Did you get my message?'

'That's why I called. What's wrong?'

'Everything's fine. It's just ... the police found Amber's remains.'

'Oh my baby girl! Graeme!' The voice moved away from the phone. 'Graeme, they found my baby.' Lucielle's breathy voice returned. 'Where was she?'

'Buried on a property in Windsor.'

'Windsor?' Her tone made it clear she thought Amber should have been discovered somewhere with a better pedigree. 'Do they know what happened?'

'The investigation is ongoing. But in the meantime, we need to plan her funeral.'

'A funeral? Darling, is that really a good idea?'

'Are you kidding?'

'Don't you take that tone with me. No one was more devastated than I was when Amber was taken away, but nothing can bring her back. A funeral will only stir everything up again. We said our goodbyes at the memorial service following that dreadful inquest. Well, most of us did.'

'Yessss ...' Gen drew out the word as she attempted to rein herself in. 'But now we have her remains.' Surely it wasn't unreasonable to want a funeral?

'What does Hugh say?'

'I was trying to find out when you could get back before I spoke with him.'

'We still have ten weeks of our trip left.' And there it was: the underlying truth. Lucielle didn't want to upset the applecart with husband number three. Nothing had changed; her husband always came first.

Lucielle pulled seven-year-old Geneva and ten-year-old Amber to her side at the full-length mirror. 'This is the beginning of our new life, girls. John will take care of us, you'll see. We'll live in his big house by the harbour, and you'll have new clothes and toys and everything you ever wanted.'

Gen didn't want to live with stupid John. She wanted to move back to her dad's house in Guildford. So they could be a family again.

Lucielle twirled, checking her wedding dress from every angle, looking like a princess. Bor-ring.

'Geneva darling, stand up tall. No man wants to marry a girl who slouches.' Lucielle pulled the baby-pink sash of Gen's scratchy flower-girl dress in tighter.

'Daddy will marry me.'

Her mother scoffed. 'Don't be ridiculous.'

'He would too.'

'You need to behave today. John already thinks you're a bit too rambunctious.'

'Rambunc-what?'

'Just like your father.'

Gen puffed out her chest. Her mum meant that in a bad way, but her daddy was the best.

From behind their mother, Amber shook her bottom, making Gen giggle instead of cry.

Their mother headed into the hotel ensuite, and Amber put her arm around Gen. 'You're perfect the way you are, Gen Gen,' she whispered. 'I grabbed a set of cards to play games at the reception, okay, and then we've got two whole weeks with Dad!'

*

Amber always said their mother was from a different era, and if Gen learnt to understand that she could get on better with Lucielle. Gen needed to try a different tack. 'Maybe you could come back briefly?'

'I really don't think we should put Lily and Charlie through any further trauma.'

'Amber was their mother.'

'I know that!'

Gen took a deep breath.

'Darling, you know how impulsive you can be. I think once you've had time to think about it, you'll agree a funeral's a bad idea.'

Gen exhaled slowly.

'And now you can close that awful website too, move on with your own life.'

There was no point talking any further. 'I guess we'll just go ahead without you. Enjoy your trip.' She ended the call and let out a scream of frustration.

After taking Bentley for a short walk, she had a quick shower, threw on a load of washing and tidied up, wanting no distractions when Hugh got home. She *needed* to stay calm, *had* to make him to step up for his kids, and she'd have a better chance of accomplishing that by coming at him sideways rather than head-on.

She made a cup of tea and took it out to the deck. Sitting at the smoked-glass table, she sipped the drink and closed her eyes. The sounds of the neighbourhood surrounded her: a lawnmower starting up, a kookaburra's laugh, the squawk of a cockatoo, a baby's cry.

'Nice for some.'

Gen's eyes snapped open at the speech-coach-moulded voice. She attempted to control her tone. 'It's the first time I've sat down since yesterday.'

'Where are the kids?'

'Lily's in bed. I let her sleep in.'

'She has her scholarship exam and interview this week.'

Gen swallowed the comeback that burned in her mouth and faced Hugh. His usually perfect hair appeared ruffled, as if he had been running his hands through it. That was his tell. Gen recognised it well from the weeks after Amber's kidnapping. She stood.

'Have a seat and I'll get you a coffee. You must be tired after such an early start.' Gen put a pod in the coffee maker. When the coffee had brewed, she placed the long black in front of Hugh, who accepted it without a word of thanks.

'Where's Charlie?' He took a sip. 'I thought you'd be at basketball with him.'

'He's there. Jesse, the … do you remember the original constable from the case?'

Hugh sat taller, his focus narrowing. 'Johns?'

Gen nodded. 'After you told the family liaison officer you were staying in Melbourne yesterday, Jesse wanted to make sure I knew what was happening.'

Hugh's lips thinned. 'Did you stay in contact?'

'I haven't heard from him in years.'

'You sure?'

'Why do you care?'

'He was over-involved back then.'

Gen took a sip of her lukewarm tea. 'He offered to take your son to basketball this morning because he knew I had a lot on my plate.'

'I cover all the bills so you can look after the kids. They are all that should matter.'

'Hugh, my sister's remains were found yesterday. She's dead. I need to process that.' She took her cup to the sink. 'There are things to be done, a funeral to organise.'

'The funeral home has been notified.'

She jammed her hands onto her hips. 'Don't you feel anything? This doesn't seem to have had any bloody impact on you!'

'I came home, didn't I?'

'For fuck's sake.'

'I heard that!' Charlie's excited shout came from the front entrance. 'Another dollar to the swear jar.'

'Make it two,' Hugh snarled as he stood.

'Dad?' Charlie flew into the room, 'Dad!' He ran over and wrapped his arms around Hugh's waist, his face aglow. Hugh hugged him back, leaning into his son's exuberance and affection. He kissed the top of his head, then looked up and stilled. Jesse stood in the doorway to the family room, Charlie's backpack over his shoulder.

Jesse nodded. 'Mr Forsythe, good to see you got back safely.'

Hugh prised Charlie's arms off him and stepped away. 'Say thank you to the constable, I'm sure he needs to be on his way.'

Charlie ran to Jesse and took his backpack. 'Thanks so much. Today was the best! Can you come and coach next week?' He turned to face Hugh. 'Dad, you wouldn't believe —'

'Go and pack away your things, please.' Hugh's flat tone brooked no argument. Charlie's gaze ping-ponged between the three adults, confusion creasing his face. Gen tilted her head gently in the direction of his bedroom.

Charlie's shoulders sank and he headed for the stairs.

Jesse waved. 'Thanks for today, Charlie. It was fun.'

Hugh strode to his office. Gen glared at his retreating back.

'You okay?' Jesse asked from behind her.

She inhaled deeply, then gestured towards the corridor. 'I'll see you out.'

At the front door, Jesse stepped onto the porch. 'He still needs to control things, I see?'

She scoffed. 'He's never controlled me.'

A car Gen didn't recognise pulled up next door. 'Can we go to my workshop?' she asked. 'I don't want to risk prying eyes or ears, and I have a few questions.'

She led him towards the standalone brick garage set to the front of the house.

Surprise flashed across his features. 'You still working on your dad's bike?'

'It keeps me sane.'

They walked through the side door. Her dad's 1980 Triumph Bonneville took pride of place in the centre of the garage.

'Wow. It looks like new. Do you take it out much?'

'Not as often as I'd like.' She gestured to the Ducati Streetfighter parked to the side. 'The sports bike's easier around city streets.'

'We never did get out for that ride.'

'Yeah.' Her non-answer bounced between them. 'Hey, I want to thank you again for this morning, and for coming yesterday. I would have hated to find out from the press.'

'No problem.'

'I didn't get a chance to ask about the investigation.'

'There's not much I can tell you. I'm not on the case.'

'Surely you know what leads they're following?'

Jesse looked to the floor, his hand massaging the back of his neck. 'I did grill my brother.' He took a breath and met her eyes. 'Gen, there are no leads. None whatsoever. I think you should prepare yourself for the fact that you may never find out exactly what happened to Amber.'

'But the case has barely been reopened!'

'They have nothing to go on. The owner of the property passed away two years ago. His son has lived in the UK since before Amber went missing, and the place has been cleared out. The scene is being released back to the builder this week.'

'What?'

'There's nothing there.'

'But Amber deserves justice. And Lily and Charlie deserve to know why they're growing up without their mum.'

'What if there's no one to hold accountable? At least she's not missing anymore.'

'You mean, at least you can put this case behind you for good now.'

'I never put it behind me.'

'Sure seemed that way.'

'Gen, I had no choice. It's against department policy to be involved with victims' families.'

Department policy? One day he was in their lives twenty-four seven, the next he was gone. No explanation, no goodbye. Just gone. She wasn't falling for his shit again.

'Get out.'

'Gen —'

'I'll talk to the detective in charge of the case.'

'He won't have anything more to say.'

'Neither do we.'

'I promised Charlie I'd talk to you about the rep team thing.'

'Yeah, well, you also promised you wouldn't stop until you found Amber, so … Just go, Jesse. You can see yourself out.'

She turned and pressed her shaking palms down on the bench, keeping her back to him. The door creaked open and then closed, and footsteps retreated towards the road.

She'd promised Lily she wouldn't give up until the police found out what happened. Gen had to convince the officer in charge of the case to keep it open. She wouldn't take no for an answer.

Gen stared at the ceiling. Moonlight snuck around the edge of the blinds, casting the room in blue. She checked her phone: 2 am. Thirty minutes since she'd last looked. She'd tried every sleep technique she knew, but none worked to shut down her noisy thoughts.

She allowed her memories to unwind.

Jesse had seemed sincere when Amber had disappeared. He'd sat with Gen on the front lounge all night after that phone call and had pretty much stayed by her side for the next month. He'd been the only person in her corner while she'd tried to deal with everything, especially the steep learning curve of caring for Lily and Charlie.

Her mother barely had the strength to handle her own grief, let alone the demands of two distraught grandchildren. And Hugh had fallen completely apart, numbing his pain daily with alcohol, absent in his anguish.

But Jesse had turned up every morning, updating her on the case, helping her handle the media, even managing to make her smile. No one but Amber had ever stepped up for her like that.

She closed her eyes. Even that last night, she'd called and he'd come running. She'd heard a trespasser rifling through their bin and panicked. He'd chased them off.

All she'd wanted to do was to soak up his strength. A month after Amber had been taken, Gen was a wreck. So when he'd offered to come in for a while, she'd gladly accepted.

'How about a cup of tea?' Jesse went straight to the mug cupboard, comfortable in the kitchen by now.

Gen pulled her knees to her chest. 'I don't think I can do this anymore.' Her voice caught.

Jesse abandoned the kettle and sat beside her.

'You're doing so well, especially with the kids.'

'They need her back.' She sniffed and placed her cheek on her knees to look at him. 'Is there any news?'

'I was going to tell you tomorrow. Hugh has been cleared.'

'Already?'

'He has a rock-solid alibi.'

'But it's always the husband, isn't it? And he's totally fallen apart since that night. Surely that's suspicious.'

'People grieve differently.'

Her eyes filled. 'But if it's not Hugh, that means this is all my fault. If I'd gone for the nappies when she asked ...' She hiccupped. 'Amber would still be here.'

Jesse's arm came around her and he pulled her in close. She burrowed into his hold.

He caressed her hair with long smooth strokes. 'What you need is sleep.'

Sleep. She'd forgotten what that felt like.

'How about I stay?' he asked.

'The night?' Warmth spread through her.

'I can get up to Charlie if he stirs. I'll sleep on the lounge.'

'You sure? He's waking almost hourly.'

'I have three nieces under five, I'll be fine.' He wiped a tear from her cheek. 'You're not in this alone.'

She caught his hand and squeezed. 'Thank you.'

He pulled her to standing. 'Come on, let's get you upstairs.'

Up in her room he folded back the doona and she climbed into bed. He bent to tuck her in. His breath caressed her face. He inched back a touch and their eyes met.

She slid her arms around his neck and tugged his mouth to hers. After a moment his lips parted, and the kiss heated. He took control, threading his fingers through her hair. His touch felt so good.

Then he pulled away, his face a picture of regret.

'That should ... I'm sorry ... I shouldn't have done that.'

'It's okay, I wanted —'

'I'll be downstairs if you need me.'

He left the bedroom before she could say another word.

The next morning she'd found the lounge empty, a note on the dining table. *Gone to work. Charlie fed and back asleep.* She'd never heard from him again.

4

Geneva gave up on sleep when the kookaburras mocked her efforts at 5 am. Carrying an instant coffee in one hand, she sought the sanctuary of her garage.

She switched on the portable speaker, opened the music app on her phone and selected her 'Dad and Bikes' playlist. The opening banjo riff of 'Black Betty' blared. She leapt to turn the music down but couldn't help a chuckle as she pictured Mrs Rosen from next door being woken by Spiderbait's screaming vocals.

She slit open the package that had arrived the other day from Old Bike Specialists and uncoiled the enclosed cable. The clutch on her dad's bike had been slipping a bit lately. She turned to the Bonneville, and a pang of longing filled her as she was assailed with memories of her dad walking her through this process when she was a kid.

'Come here, wild one. Make sure to have a close look where the cable goes. Trail your hand from the clutch on the handle down behind the headlight.' He'd lifted her up so she could see the path the cable followed and talked her step by step through the process. It became their thing, working on his bike together, until he'd died while on a trip to Vietnam, when she was seventeen.

She ran her hand across the black vinyl seat. The bike was everything her dad had been: simple, sturdy, honest. No bells or whistles. She was so grateful she'd inherited it and his tools when he'd died, and that Amber had let Gen store them in her garage.

God, Amber. A vice squeezed Gen's chest. She'd known her sister would never stay away from her kids, but her heart, her traitorous, stupid heart had always hung on to hope. How long had Amber been at that property? Windsor was so far from where her phone had last pinged. Had her abductor moved her to the farm and kept her there alive?

Gen's gaze slid to the ignition. She almost shook with the need to jump on the bike. To speed away from this house. The responsibilities. The sorrow. The guilt. She closed her eyes. This wasn't helping. Hugh had written himself off with glass after glass of scotch last night; she was going nowhere this morning. The kids needed someone to be available for them.

Refocusing, she pulled at the orange straps securing the bike to the hoist, making sure they held. She didn't bother with overalls or gloves, needing a direct connection with the metal and oils – the only things outside of riding that could ground her today.

She grabbed a spanner from her dad's bright-red tool caddy, knelt at the bike and loosened the two lug nuts connecting the cable. She screwed the adjuster wheel back into the Clovis clamp, so no thread showed.

Next, she removed the dress cover and loosened the nut that kept the cable attached. A new song played quietly through the speakers. 'Sweet Child of Mine'. Her eyes filled and she gashed her knuckles on the exposed screw. She sucked on the wound, concentrated on the metallic taste of her blood. Wallowing achieved nothing. Action was what would fill the gaping hole inside.

She wiggled the cable free from the bike and tossed it aside. Snaffling the new cable from the bench, she removed the rubber seal, raised the oil can to the top and squirted, letting the oil sink in one drop at a time. She pumped the cable in and out of the sheath.

'*Don't overfill it, kiddo. You need to go slow.*'

Going slow was not her forte, everyone knew that.

But maybe she needed to try it to get the police to keep Amber's case open. Be methodical, like in journalism. Focus on facts rather than feelings. She should prepare a list of questions for the lead detective, who was coming over tomorrow to update them.

The side door creaked, and Charlie ambled in, hair poking every which way. 'It's bright in here.' He rubbed at his eyes, then wrapped his arms around Gen's waist.

She kissed the top of his head. 'Careful, monster, I've got oil on my fingers.'

'What are you doing?'

'Changing the clutch cable.'

'Can I help?'

'Sure. Suit up. Gloves on.' She nodded to the drawer where she kept his overalls and disposable gloves.

'You're not wearing any.'

'That's because I'm a grease monkey.'

'I can be one too.'

'You've got the monkey bit down already, but your dad won't be happy if you get covered in gunk.'

Charlie yanked on the overalls and Gen helped him snap on the gloves.

'Okay, first, remove the end nuts.' He did, then she handed him the new cable. 'We're going to thread that back through from the handlebars down. Stand on my feet and lean forward.'

He slid it down slowly.

'That's it, just behind the headlight.' When it was in place, she reattached both ends. 'Now set the finger adjuster.' She pointed it out.

'How many times do I twist it?'

'Three.' She watched over his shoulder. 'Is the thread nicely engaged?

'I think so.'

She squeezed the handle. 'Good job, there's loads of room for adjustment there.' She brought the lock wheel in against the clamp.

'Gen, what happens now?'

She paused. 'I gather you're not talking about the bike?'

'Dad was pretty angry last night. I heard him yelling on the phone.'

Half the damn neighbourhood had. 'I think he might have had a little too much to drink.'

'I hate it when he's like that.'

'Me too, Charlie.'

'Why aren't you angry?'

'I'm ...' Gen picked up the dress cover and put it back on. 'I'm frustrated and sad and still trying to figure my way through all this.'

'Lily didn't even come out of her room last night. It feels like we're broken.'

'Oh sweetheart, we're just a little cracked. We'll be okay again, I promise.'

'I just want everything to go back to the way it was. Is that wrong?'

'Like I told you yesterday, there is no wrong.' She moved to the sink and washed her hands.

Charlie pulled off his gloves and dropped them into the bin.

'Gen, can I please try out for the rep team?'

'You're already on a school team.'

'But I'm different from those kids. They have normal families.'

'There's no such thing as normal.' Gen turned off the taps and grabbed a clean hand towel.

'But they have a dad and a mum and —'

'They might look normal from the outside, but I promise you, everyone has things to deal with. They just do it behind closed doors.'

'I want to find friends who get me.'

Gen paused, regarding him. 'And you think you might find them at the PCYC?'

'Jesse said all sorts of kids go there.'

Bloody Jesse! She took a steadying breath and searched her nephew's pleading gaze. He'd had to face so much more than other kids his age. If he needed this, she'd make it happen. She could keep her distance and space from Jesse and still give Charlie what he needed.

'I'll see what I can organise.'

'Really? Thank you!'

The electric guitar riff of Joan Jett's 'Real Wild Child' came through the speaker. Charlie's smile broadened.

'Can I?' He pointed to the volume button.

She grinned and nodded.

He twisted the knob to high and they head-banged for the rest of the song. No doubt the neighbours would complain, but right now she really didn't care.

'Hugh, dinner's ready. Can you please carve the lamb?'

Gen removed the roast and switched the oven off, leaving the kitchen ringing with quiet.

'No need to screech like a fishwife.' Hugh marched out of his office and went straight to the drinks trolley for the third time that night.

'Could you go easy please, for the kids?'

Satisfaction rushed through her when he put his whiskey tumbler in the dishwasher instead of refilling it.

'I don't understand why you insist on having these dinners every week.'

'It mattered to Amber.' Sunday was the one night her sister had insisted Hugh be home. She said it would keep them connected as a family.

'The detectives are coming at nine tomorrow. Can you be here?' Uncharacteristic vulnerability coloured Hugh's tone, and for a brief moment she could see the boy beneath the man, the person Amber must have fallen for.

'Of course.' She passed him the electric carving knife. 'We'll have to organise something to keep the kids busy.'

'They'll be at school.'

'It's too soon.'

'What else are they going to do?'

'Grieve,' she muttered under her breath. She stood on her toes to grab the serving tray from the top shelf.

If Lily or Charlie didn't want to go tomorrow she'd argue the point, but it may actually be better for them to be surrounded by their friends. Especially Lily. She'd stayed in her room all weekend, had even banned Charlie from going in.

Gen set the tray on the bench. 'I suppose if they go to school the media will leave them alone. I had to deal with a whole pack of them out front on Friday.'

'And don't we all wish you hadn't.'

'What's that supposed to mean?'

'I saw the footage, just like the rest of Australia.' Hugh rolled his eyes, and the buzz of the electric carving knife filled the kitchen.

Gen inhaled a slow breath. She didn't enjoy dealing with the media, but someone had to, or they'd harass the kids. If she ever returned to journalism, she'd make sure to always respect the talent's boundaries. God, how she hated that term: *talent*. It made it sound as if losing a loved one required some kind of special skill.

She removed the veggies from the second oven and arranged them on the white serving plate Amber had always used. 'Any chance we could talk after the kids go to bed?'

'I'm heading out with Tobias.'

'We need to sort the funeral arrangements.'

'I told you, I've already spoken with the funeral home. I'm settling the final details on Wednesday, and she's being buried in my family's plot on Friday.'

'Hugh, that's not solely your decision to make.'

'I'm Amber's next of kin.'

'And I'm her sister!' She turned to him. 'She didn't believe in burials, she always said they're bad for the environment. She wanted to be cremated.'

'I am not having her ashes around to taunt the children.'

'We could scatter her ashes at Rocky —'

'The decision is made. I won't discuss it further.'

'You sound just like your father.'

'And maybe you should behave more like your mother.'

She jammed her hands on her hips. 'What's that supposed to mean?'

Hugh discarded the knife, collected a new glass from the cupboard and stalked to the drinks trolley. 'Charlie! Lily!' His voice reverberated through the space. 'You need to set the table.'

Gen threw her hands in the air. Hugh always reverted to avoidance, control and alcohol when emotions were high.

Charlie ran into the room. 'I'm starving!'

Lily shuffled in a moment later, lost in her mobile phone.

'Lily,' said Hugh in a warm tone.

She stuffed her phone in her back pocket and gave her dad a shy hug. He pulled her in closer and she sank into his hold and smiled.

Gen blinked slowly. This was the father the kids needed. The one he used to be.

'How's your preparation for the scholarship assessment going?'

A flash of hurt crossed Lily's face, which she quickly camouflaged with a fake smile.

Gen shook her head at Hugh, and he mouthed '*What?*' back.

Lily disengaged from Hugh's hold and walked to the cutlery drawer. 'I performed my flute solos for the music department last Thursday and they said I'm ready.'

'That's good, Lily, I'm proud of you. But you still need to keep working hard.'

'I know,' she mumbled.

Gen rolled her eyes, and a scowl set on Hugh's face.

Charlie took the placemats from the cupboard and arranged them on the table. When he reached the end, he froze. Stared at the empty chair. His gaze lifted and he locked eyes with Gen. *Dammit.* She set aside the tongs and went to him.

'It's okay.'

'Do I still set it?'

Every Sunday they set a place for Amber at the table. Lily had started it, that first week. Torn, Gen looked to Hugh. He skolled his whiskey, discarded his glass on the bench and stalked from the room. A moment later the front door slammed.

Lily snatched the placemat from Charlie's hand and returned it to the cupboard. She handed him three plates, carried the food over to the table, and then sat.

'Lily, honey ...'

'What's the point? She's never coming home.' Lily raised her chin as she spoke, but tears filled her eyes.

Gen knelt next to her. 'I think we're going to have to take this a bit as it comes.'

Lily reached for the serving tongs. 'Can we just eat and have a normal night?'

Charlie sat opposite his sister, his eyes filled with worry.

Gen stood and stepped towards the hallway. 'I'll try and catch your dad.'

'Can we please just start?' Lily's voice had thinned, like she was barely hanging on.

Nodding, Gen took her place at the table with the two people who meant more to her than anything in the world, hating herself for not being able to make this right, despising Hugh for putting his own crap first yet again, and knowing that if she let herself acknowledge the chair at the end of the table, the one that sat emptier than it ever had before, she just might fall apart.

Gen raced to her bedroom to finish getting ready after dropping both kids at school. She'd spoken to Charlie's teacher and was confident he was in good hands, but she was a little nervous about Lily. The year supervisor had assured Gen they'd keep an eye on her, but the school was so big. What if a journalist got to her?

Gen brushed her hair into a ponytail. It would be okay. Lily knew to go to the office if there was a problem. Hopefully the group of friends she'd had since primary school would rally around her.

The front doorbell rang right on nine. Gen gathered her files, including the list of questions she'd put together, and headed downstairs.

Hugh led two officers into the house. Bentley trailed behind them, his arthritic hips slowing him down.

'Ms Leighton, nice to see you again.' Constable Venuka Gunarathna, a short, slender woman in her mid-twenties, shook Gen's hand, then knelt to scratch Bentley under the chin.

'Hello boy, how are you?' His tail wagged. Since being assigned as their case liaison officer five years ago, Venuka had shown nothing but genuine compassion, always making time to listen to Gen's ideas and answer her questions.

Gen turned her attention to the man with a square-shaped head and buzz cut, standing at Venuka's side.

'Detective Sergeant Isaac Simpson from the Homicide Squad, ma'am.'

She shook his hand. 'Please, call me Gen.'

He had the same look she'd seen in so many of the police officers she'd met over the years. Direct, no nonsense and hardened.

'I'm hoping you have news?' Gen placed her files on the glass coffee table, ignoring Hugh's dirty look.

The detective gestured to the lounge. 'Okay if we sit?'

'Of course.' She perched on the edge of the lounge and shoved her hands between her thighs.

'As I informed you last week, Mr Forsythe,' the detective addressed Hugh, 'the coroner confirmed the remains discovered on Dennis Stubenitsky's property were Amber's.'

Hugh's heel jackhammered against the floor. He wasn't as unaffected as he liked to make out.

'Stubenitsky died two years ago of natural causes, aged eighty-four. The property has sat vacant ever since. We've been in touch with his only child, Erwin Stubenitsky, who resides in London, but he could provide no reason as to why Amber would have been on his father's land.'

'Erwin owns and runs a high-end restaurant in London,' Venuka cut in. 'He's lived in the United Kingdom for the past twenty years.'

The detective leant forward. 'Dennis Stubenitsky had no criminal record. By all accounts he was an upstanding member of the community, a former chef who'd been instrumental in setting up a local soup kitchen. He and his wife also fostered a number of children throughout their lives.'

Gen rubbed at the developing tightness in her chest. 'What are you saying?'

The detective turned to her. 'We have pursued every lead possible since the remains were recovered, including interviewing the surrounding neighbours —'

'And?'

'Will you let him finish?' Hugh's scolding tone drew heat to Gen's face. She had an awful feeling she knew exactly what was coming.

'All lines of enquiry have been exhausted. The details of the case have been digitised and cross-referenced through our database, but there is nothing else for us to pursue.'

'You can't return it to non-active status yet! It's only been two weeks.'

'I'm sorry, but there are no leads left to follow.'

'What about the concrete she was buried under?'

'Mr Stubenitsky built the formwork himself, although he did bring in a concrete truck. The house has been emptied for demolition and all records, including those of the concreting company he used, have been disposed of. Identifying when the slab was poured would have helped establish a more exact date of death but unfortunately we haven't even been able to confirm an exact year.'

'Are you saying it's possible my sister was held captive for a time before she was killed?'

'Unlikely, but possible.'

'Oh God!' Gen clutched her necklace. 'That is not a no. You have to keep investigating. Surely concrete can be dated. We can get an expert in.'

'There's no way to accurately determine the age of concrete. It can only be inferred, and even then, only within the same decade.'

'Decade?' Gen stood and paced to the window. 'I can't believe this.'

Hugh gave her a steely look. 'For goodness sake, calm down, Geneva. This doesn't change anything.'

'Are you kidding me? Amber could have been held on the property against her will for months – for years! – having who knows what done to her, and you don't think it changes anything?'

'It won't bring her back.' Hugh glanced at his mobile.

'We need to find out what happened!'

Hugh stood. 'Detective,' he nodded, then turned to Venuka, 'Constable, thank you for coming to fill us in.' He reached for his suit jacket and threaded his arms through the sleeves. 'It's my understanding that my wife's remains will be delivered to the funeral home this week. We will hold a small graveyard service on Friday, and then I believe it's in the best interests of my children that we all put this behind us.'

'Hugh! What about her belongings? Her rings?'

'I'm not doing this. It ends here.' He shook each officer's hand. 'I have a flight to Melbourne to catch. My taxi's out front. I'll walk you out.' He gestured to the door with an open palm, inviting them to leave.

'Can you please stay and talk with me?' Gen asked.

Detective Simpson sat back down. 'Whatever we can do to help. And once again, Mr Forsythe, I am sorry this isn't the result we were all hoping for.'

Hugh picked up the overnight bag he'd left by the front door. 'Geneva, you'll be home for the children tonight?'

'When am I not?'

'Please don't discuss the details of what we learnt today with them.'

The door clicked shut and she pushed a hand through her hair.

'Sorry. Hugh and I handle things differently.'

'Can I get you some tea?' Venuka asked.

'No, thank you,' Gen sat on the edge of the lounge. 'But I do have a few more questions, if you don't mind?'

'We'll answer whatever we can,' Venuka replied.

5

Two hours later, Gen turned her Ducati onto the Old Pacific Highway and twisted the throttle, finally able to give herself the escape she'd needed since Friday. Alone, with the sun on her back and the rush of wind filling her ears, the bike was the only place she could inhale a full breath these days.

She settled into the rocking motion of the bends and curves alongside the Hawkesbury River and replayed her conversation with the officers. They'd patiently run through every aspect of the case again, from the initial enquiries twelve years ago to the discovery and identification of Amber's remains. No belongings had been found nearby. No clothing or jewellery, not even her wedding ring.

Gen had asked to visit the property but was told it was being handed back to the building company tomorrow, the house having been cleared for demolition. She'd argued that it was too soon, that something might have been overlooked, but Venuka gently pointed out that the house had been emptied months ago, and the shed already bulldozed.

The police had done all they could, conducting a meticulous grid search of the property and also bringing in cadaver dogs.

But what if they'd missed something? It would be destroyed forever.

She sighed. She really was clutching at straws. If the police had just taken her to the farm, let her see things for herself, it would have been easier to accept that there were no investigative options left.

Ideas circled in her head.

The place shouldn't be hard to find. She had the road and the suburb. How many building sites would be along that stretch? She could visit the property late tonight and do a walk around. According to the detective there was nothing of value left, so there was a good chance no one would be there. Legally speaking, she would be trespassing, but it wouldn't hurt anyone, and if there was security present she could just ride off.

She hit the two-lane section of road and overtook a semi-trailer heading for the brickworks. She'd invite Toni to stay the night, so there'd be someone there for the kids. It would be a big night, riding to Windsor and back, but she couldn't risk the building being demolished before she got a look and put her mind to rest.

She also needed to find a way to contact the owner's son. He might share more information with her than he had with the police.

Once she'd completed those two tasks, she would have done everything she could to find answers. Maybe then her brain would quiet, the guilt would subside, and she could finally move forward in her life.

After her ride, Gen showered then called Toni, who gladly accepted the invitation for dinner and a sleepover. She'd be less happy when Gen shared her plans for the evening.

She sat at the dining table and opened her laptop. Amber's blue eyes gazed back from the lock screen, the dusting of freckles she hated so vehemently accentuating her natural beauty. The water of Balmoral Beach glistening behind her. An open-mouthed Charlie, just six months old, lay in her arms. Gen could still hear his laugh, full-bodied and infectious, as his mum blew raspberries on his belly. Out of shot Lily had built a sandcastle, every turret and shell perfectly placed. At the end of the day they'd all jumped on it, Lily's giggles the loudest of all.

Gen swallowed. When was the last time she'd heard Lily laugh like that? She really needed to make some time to check in with her niece.

Hugh hadn't been at the beach that day, he'd had some conference interstate. As soon as he'd received the big promotion at Forsythe Commercial Real Estate, he'd spent less and less time with Amber and the kids. His father and brothers had demanded so much of his attention. Even now, when the rug had been pulled out from under his kids' feet again, they all expected business to take priority.

Something was really off with him at the moment. The drinking was a huge red flag. She should check in with Tobias, Hugh's best friend. They'd become unlikely mates at university, Tobias as a scholarship student and Hugh as a major donor's son. He'd been a godsend after Amber disappeared, and in the years since. When Gen had made the mistake of voicing her concerns about Hugh's drinking to his family, Hugh's father, William, had gone ballistic, more concerned with keeping any problems out of the press than with keeping his son alive. Tobias had played mediator and whisked Hugh off to a private rehab facility in Queensland.

She couldn't let Hugh get that way again. The kids needed him – now more than ever.

Gen inhaled deeply, then let the breath out on a slow count. He wasn't due home until tomorrow. Sorting him out would have to wait.

She took another breath, unlocked the computer and her fingers hovered above the keyboard. She knew it made no sense, but once she typed the words it would be final. When she'd set up the Finding Amber website, part of her had already known. Even with each new lead – the sighting in a Cairns supermarket, the blurry video footage from a women's refuge in Melbourne, the blank 'Happy birthday from Mummy' cards Gen had intercepted the first three years – even then, a space in her heart had remained barren of hope. Nothing could have made Amber stay away from Lily and Charlie. They were her world.

Had been her world.

Gen blinked against the stinging in her eyes and forced herself to type.

To everyone who supported our search for Amber, thank you. Your encouragement, tip-offs and compassion drove me forward for the last twelve years. I so wanted to return my sister to her two children but unfortunately that's not to be. Three days ago, the police informed our family that Amber's remains had been found. At least now we can lay her to rest.

Amber was a vivacious, warm, loving, kind, vibrant person – an incredible mother, a wonderful sister, a devoted wife, and the most incredible human being I've ever had the honour to spend time with.

This will be my last post on this website. We would greatly appreciate if you would respect our privacy at what is another difficult time in our lives.

Gen hit post and then closed the computer. She ran her hands across the smooth silver casing, lost in thought. The search for Amber might have come to an end, but Gen still

owed it to her sister to do everything she could to help discover
who had killed her and why.

Gen handed Toni a hot chocolate and sat at the other end of the
lounge, tucking her feet up under her bottom. She smirked at
the candy-pink elephant pyjamas her friend had changed into.

'What?' Toni swung a red polka-dot slipper from her toes.
'They're comfy.'

Gen chuckled, grateful to have met this quick-witted,
quirky, loyal woman during her first year of Communications
at Charles Sturt University. Within ten minutes of introducing
themselves they'd been giggling uncontrollably. From that
moment on they'd been the best of friends.

Toni retrieved the television remote from the side table
and pointed it at the wide-screen TV. 'Alrighty, what are we
bingeing?'

Gen scrunched up her face. 'About that.'

'I knew it!' Toni pointed the remote at her. 'What are you
up to?'

'The police are closing Amber's case.'

Toni nodded. 'Makes sense. Their only suspect is dead.'

'But why would a guy from the outskirts of Sydney, a pillar
of his community, drive all the way to Mosman to abduct
a random woman, detour south on the M5 all the way past
Welby, turn off onto a bush track, and then return to his *own*
property in Windsor to bury her? Just because Amber was
found on his land doesn't mean it was him.'

'I know you don't want to hear this, but maybe it is as
simple as that.'

'How did a man in his seventies lift my unconscious sister
into a car boot? She was small, but she wasn't that light. And
when she called, she didn't describe him as old.'

'She might not have noticed his age. He had a cap on, remember?' Toni leant forward. 'Have you considered that this is an opportunity to finally let her go?'

'I can't believe you of all people would say that.'

'I'm worried you're avoiding facing facts because you're scared of what might come next.'

Gen straightened in her seat. 'What exactly is that supposed to mean?'

'You've set aside your own life for twelve years. Your career, having a partner, even travel.'

'I can't commit to a career; not with the long hours that would be expected. And what partner would want to be with me? I need to be available for the kids.'

'They don't seem to have held Hugh back.'

'That's why they need me. Someone has to put Charlie and Lily first.'

'Babe, they're his kids.'

Geneva shook her head. Most people couldn't understand why she had dropped everything to help Hugh, but she hadn't done it for him. It was for Lily and Charlie and Amber. Hugh loved his kids, but for the first few months after Amber's disappearance he'd barely been able to tie his own shoelace, and then he'd thrown himself into his work. If Gen hadn't stepped up, the kids would have been raised by a nanny, or worse, Hugh's parents. Amber would have hated that.

'I know it was hard at first.' Toni's voice deepened. 'But surely you can claim some of your own life back now. Hugh has a career. He dates. He's taking advantage of you, hon. It's time it stopped.'

Gen picked at a loose cuticle. She couldn't do any of that, not until she had more answers.

'Think about it, okay? I'll help in any way I can. I can even tell Hugh to stop being such a selfish arsehole.'

Gen ran her hands over her face and she slouched back into the lounge. 'Talking with Hugh won't help. If anything, it could tip him further off kilter.'

'What do you mean?'

'He's been kind of belligerent lately.'

Toni's forehead creased.

'And really unavailable for the kids. I'm not sure what to do.' Gen grabbed her mug and took it back to the kitchen. 'I feel like I don't know what to do about a lot of things at the moment. Every instinct I have is screaming that there's more to find about Amber's death.' She poured her untouched hot chocolate down the sink. 'I'm thinking of contacting the landowner's son to see if he has any ideas, but first I want to look at the place where she was found.'

'Gen.'

'I have to. What if there's something out there that can explain why he took her?'

'I love that you want to investigate something again – anything – but I don't understand going to a demolition site that the police have already cleared. What will it achieve, other than you possibly getting arrested?'

'Her death just seems so senseless. If I can understand why, I think it'll make it easier to accept.'

'Gen, honey, Amber would want you to be living your own life.'

'Don't. Amber would want to be raising her two beautiful children. And if I had gone to the shops that night she would be.'

Gen put her mug in the dishwasher and met Toni's stare. 'Can you please keep an eye on the kids while I ride out to Windsor and have a look around?'

'Was this what you had planned all along?'

'Maybe. Sorry. Please don't be angry.'

'I'm not angry, just worried.' Toni sighed. 'But I'll watch them.'

Gen gave her a quick hug. 'I don't know what I'd do without you. No one else gets my crazy.'

'One kook recognises another.'

Gen grabbed a black jumper. 'It's about an hour's ride out there so I won't be home before three. Don't wait up, okay? I'll come past the spare room to let you know I'm back.' She shoved her arms through the sleeves, slipped the top over her head then headed for the front door.

'Be safe!' Toni called out.

Gen collected a Maglite torch from the garage, stored it in the top box on the back of her bike and rode off.

Gen slowed outside a property with a building works sign, halfway along the road the detectives had mentioned. It had to be Stubenitsky's. She drove up the dirt driveway and manoeuvred the bike into a thicket of trees, making sure it faced forward, in case she needed a fast getaway. She killed the engine.

The only structure within view was a small, old, unlit weatherboard house surrounded by a two-metre-high chain-link fence. A shadowy patchwork of fields stretched out to the rear of the house. The closest neighbouring property, another small cottage, sat about four hundred metres up the road, its windows dark.

Staying in the bike's saddle, Gen scanned for any sign of a security patrol. All remained quiet. She dismounted and checked the ground for anything that could interfere with tyre grip upon acceleration, then glanced back at the house.

If she had to consider escape routes, maybe this wasn't such a brilliant idea. She closed and opened her fists. *No second thoughts.* This was for Amber.

She removed the torch and her phone from the bike's top box, clicked the phone to silent and slipped it into her pocket. Leaving her helmet on the saddle, she set off in a wide arc around the house.

Moonlight caught on crime-scene tape staked around a cleared area in the backyard. A three-metre-square hole had been dug in the ground. That had to be where the storage shed had stood. Where Amber had been found. Gen's palm pressed to her chest. She took a deep breath then kept going. She paced out the perimeter but found nothing of note.

She walked to the security fence surrounding the house and pulled at the gate, but the thick chain and lock held. She passed a beam of torchlight around the yard. No dogs. Nothing. She put the torch between her teeth, slid one foot into the diamond of the fence pattern and, clutching the wire above her head, pulled herself up. The torch beam bounced with each heave. At the top, she examined the ground below for obstacles, swung her leg over and jumped.

Her left ankle twisted on landing. 'Shit!' Her eyes squeezed shut. It had to be okay. She needed that foot to work the bike's gears. She rotated the ankle first in one direction and then the other, then pressed it on the ground. No shooting pains. Unclenching her teeth, she exhaled. It was just a little jarred.

She ran the torchlight along the slatted verandah that wrapped around the dilapidated house. Flakes of green paint covered the posts holding up the rusted corrugated iron roof.

She approached the stairs leading up to the faded green front door and placed her weight gingerly on the first board. It held. She crept up the remaining steps, testing each for strength before placing her full weight on them. The last stair creaked loudly. She leapt onto the porch and pushed at the front door. It was locked. Reaching into the zippered pocket of her leather jacket she pulled out a credit card. A YouTuber she'd found online had made it look easy enough. She slipped the card into the crack between the door and jamb, searching for the tiny latch that would release the lock. Nothing. She tried again. No luck. So much for easy.

Circling the verandah, she pulled at the ply board covering each window. The fourth one, at the back of the house, gave with a loud crack. She held her breath. Waited a count.

Nothing happened.

She set the board aside, hoisted herself onto the window ledge and slid through, onto a laminated floor. Sticky strands of spiderweb caught on her forehead. She swatted them away, slapping at her hair too, in case the spider had tried to hitch a ride. She shuddered, then took in the small laundry she found herself in. To her right, the plumbing pipes had been capped off below the spot where a sink had once been. Next to that was an empty space for a washing machine, and near the doorway sat wonky shelves, also empty. She directed the torch beam through the doorway and her shoulders sank. The adjacent kitchen had been stripped bare too. Even the cornices had been removed.

A hallway ran from the kitchen. Swinging the torch left and right, she worked her way through the rooms along the corridor. There was a bare space that might once have been the lounge room, a stripped bathroom, and a small bedroom. She reached the front door and crossed to the other side of the hall. She searched the master bedroom and its wardrobe, her gut sinking with each barren space. She returned to the back of the house and ran the beam of light over the kitchen walls. As it hit the doorframe leading to the dining room, her pulse quickened. Up the inside was a list of names written in pencil. She moved in closer and found lines next to the names, each marked with a measurement, like the chart she marked on the pantry wall with Charlie and Lily each birthday.

Erwin 14, 163cm. Rebecca 13, 161cm. Jayden, 13, 158cm. Erwin, 13, 158cm. Bryn, 12, 156cm. Other names, ages and heights continued down the doorframe, but Erwin's was the only name you could track year after year. She pulled out her phone, took photos, then did another circuit of the house. All she found were cracks in the plaster, mice droppings and a couple of dead cockroaches.

The sound of Harley-Davidson motorbike engines broke the quiet of the night. They were approaching from the west. The rumbles grew louder, then halted outside the property. The engines cut out.

She twisted her torch off, plunging the house into blackness. Her heart raced.

Two male voices murmured; she couldn't make out what they were saying. The voices moved closer. She had to get out. She felt her way back down the hallway. A bark of laughter sounded, much closer now. She sped up, but then a creak sounded from the front porch. She froze. How had they gotten through the gate so quickly? Were they security guards?

'Do a perimeter check,' said a gruff male voice from outside the front door. 'I'll get the gear.'

Security didn't ride Harleys. Gen lurched towards the laundry.

Footsteps thumped along the verandah towards the back of the house. She'd never make it out the window in time.

A key slid into the front door lock. Gen's feet rooted to the spot. Her breathing stalled. She was trapped between the two men, like a rabbit being rounded up by hunting dogs.

'Hey Trig, come here,' a half-whispered call came from the laundry window. Heavy footsteps tramped along the verandah towards the laundry. This was her chance. She darted towards the front door.

'Fuck, someone's been here since the police boarded it up.' Trig's voice came from the back of the house. 'They better not have found it.'

Gen grabbed the door handle, ready to bolt for the thicket of trees. She pulled but the door didn't budge. The deadlock was still activated.

The floor vibrated as footsteps approached the front entry. She darted into the spare bedroom and slid behind the door, leaving it slightly ajar and flattening herself against the wall.

Why had she come here? What had she been thinking?

The front door banged open, the sound reverberating through Gen's body.

'Hate this place.'

'Scared it's haunted, Sparks?'

'Fuck off. At least the key was where he said it would be this time.'

Through the door crack she saw a beam of light sweep the hallway. Gen didn't dare breathe.

'Doesn't look like anyone's here,' Sparks said.

'Well the gear had better be, or we're screwed.'

Gen's lungs burned, demanding she inhale, but the men were too close.

Their footsteps moved into the master bedroom. Wood banged against wood. They were lifting the floorboards. Something thudded to the floor.

'All there?' Sparks asked.

'Looks like it.'

There was what sounded like something being stuffed in a bag, then a zipper rasped. 'Time to roll,' said Trig.

'We should torch the place,' Sparks snickered. 'It'd light up like New Year's Eve.'

Oh my God! The house was a tinderbox. She'd have no time to escape.

'Why the ever-livin' fuck would we do that?'

'The pigs might search it again, because of that chick. They might find our prints.'

'You stupid cunt. It's getting demolished tomorrow. Burning the place down would attract attention.'

'Fuck you!'

There was an *oof*, then a grunt.

The walls shuddered with the weight of a body hitting the floor.

'Disrespect me again, dickhead, and it'll be more than one fist.'

Sparks groaned.

'Stop fuckin' around and take the bags to the bikes,' Trig ordered.

One man stepped back into the hall. Gen tensed every muscle so she didn't make a sound. He turned right and stomped down the front stairs.

Wood slid against wood again, then the second man exited the house. The front door slammed, a lock clicked, and a minute later the Harleys rumbled to life and roared away.

Gen's pulse hammered in her ears. She didn't move an inch.

6

After the longest ten minutes of her life, Gen eased the door aside. Nothing happened. She moved cautiously into the master bedroom. The room looked unchanged; there was no sign that Trig and Sparks had ever been there.

Gen inched her way to the laundry and paused to listen when she reached the window. Croaking frogs. She ducked her head out, checking left and right, then climbed through the opening and charged for the fence. She scurried up one side and down the other, not risking a twisted ankle with a jump again, then bolted for the thicket of trees. Reaching her bike, she ducked down behind it, her breath heaving. She checked behind her, then peered over the saddle.

There was no one there.

Her body jittered with excess energy. Questions tumbled through her mind. Who were those men? What had they taken from the house? Had they had anything to do with Amber's murder?

She paced on shaky legs and shook out her hands. She had to get it together; it was too dangerous to ride like this. She inhaled a breath to the count of four, held it for four, exhaled for four, held for four. She'd learnt the square technique soon after Amber went missing but hadn't used it for years.

Slowly, gradually, her pulse rate eased. She pulled out her phone and it lit up with a full screen of missed calls and texts from Toni.

Where are you?

Are you okay?

It's 4 am, answer me!

If you don't answer in the next 10 mins I'm calling Jesse

Shit! Gen typed in a quick text response.

Took longer than expected. Sorry.

Should she mention the men? In case they ambushed her when she left? She typed again.

100% FINE but had to wait for 2 men to leave. Will tell all when I get back.

Toni would help her figure out what to do next.

She pulled on her helmet and gloves, mounted the saddle, and checked for threats one last time. Still quiet. She started the engine, engaged the gears, and accelerated away, a spray of rocks spitting out from her tyres. In the distance, silver leeched into the lower edges of the night sky.

Hitting the throttle, she increased the distance between herself and the farm as fast as possible, checking her mirrors constantly.

Finally, she turned onto her street, blinking rapidly against the tiredness that had grown heavier with each kilometre. The sky was tinged with streaks of orange and red. *Red sky in the morning, sailor's warning.* She hoped it wasn't an omen.

Killing the engine, she coasted down the hill, into the

driveway and parked outside the garage. Chin to chest, she trudged to the front stairs, her feet dragging with every step.

'What the hell were you thinking?'

Her head whipped up. Jesse sat on the third step, dressed in tracksuit pants and a navy hoodie, arms folded.

She closed the distance between them. 'I told you I needed to see the place where she was found.'

'And I told you it wasn't safe.'

'I'm back in one piece, aren't I?'

'Just.'

She tried to move around him, but he stood, blocking her way.

'I should be arresting you for trespass.'

Their gazes locked. His lips thinned.

Gen sighed and sank to the bottom step.

'You don't understand. I have to find a way to keep the investigation alive.'

'Getting yourself hurt won't help.' He sat next to her, and his tone softened. 'What about Lily and Charlie?'

'I'm doing this for them.'

'You sure?'

She rubbed the heels of her hands down her thighs. 'They need answers.'

'They do, or you do?'

'Okay, both. I need answers too.'

He clasped his hands in front and stared at them. 'How would things be different if you knew?'

'You of all people should understand. Didn't you swear to solve crime when you joined the police?'

'No, I swore to protect life and property. And it seems that's a full-time job with you.' He looked at her. 'Tell me about the men.'

'There's nothing to tell. They rode up on Harleys. I hid. I didn't see them.'

'How do you know they were on Harleys?'

'Pretty distinctive sound.' She yawned and scrubbed her hands across her face. She wanted to tell Jesse what she'd overheard, but she needed to debrief with someone she trusted first. Toni would help her get her thoughts straight.

'Jesse, I can barely put a coherent sentence together, and I have to get the kids off to school in two hours, then work. Can we talk later?'

'If you promise it'll happen *today*. And I want every detail – not some watered-down version.'

'Okay.'

'I know you want answers to help you move on, but there might not be anything to find.'

'My gut says there's more to all of this.'

'You can't always trust your gut. Believe me, I should know.'

'What?'

'Story for another time.' He stood. 'I'll be waiting for your call.' She watched him walk to the end of the driveway then let herself in to the house, knowing she had another battle ahead with Toni before she could fall into bed.

Gen found Toni sitting on the back deck, two steaming coffees in front of her. Toni pushed a mug across the table but didn't look at her.

Gen wrapped her hands around the mug and sighed. 'This doesn't make up for ratting me out to Officer Do Right.'

'Mmm hmm.'

Heat seeped into Gen's fingers. She sipped gratefully, the drink warming her from the inside out.

Toni nursed her coffee, not saying a word.

Gen traced a deep scratch on the table with her forefinger. 'I'm sorry for scaring you.'

'Mmm hmm.'

Gen shifted to face her. 'I mean it. I am sorry.'

'What happened out there?'

'I will tell you but, first, how did you get Jesse's number?'

Toni pointed at herself. 'Investigative journalist?'

Gen raised her brows and Toni chuckled. 'Charlie leaves his phone on the kitchen charger overnight. His lock code wasn't hard to guess. LeBron James's birthday.' She took a sip of coffee and nailed Gen with a look. 'Now spill.'

Gen told her everything and by the end Toni's forehead had wrinkled into a frown. 'You're not going to go after those men?'

'Of course not.'

Toni's lips pursed. A flock of cockatoos squawked overhead.

'I *would* like to take a look at the supermarket footage from that night to check if there were any motorbikes around.'

'Sounds like a long shot.' Toni placed her palm on Gen's forearm. 'You know you have to tell Jesse what you overheard.'

'He's not on the case.'

'Well, someone on the force needs to know.'

Gen stared into space, then shook her head. 'I can't tell the investigating officers without admitting to trespassing.'

Toni withdrew her hand. 'Perhaps you should have thought that one through.'

Gen shifted in her seat. 'I also want to follow up on the names on the doorjamb. Maybe one of the Stubenitskys' foster kids knows something.'

'Another long shot.'

'I wish I'd seen what they took from the floorboards.'

'It was probably drugs. The house was abandoned.' Toni faced Gen square on. 'Hon, it's unlikely those men had anything to do with Amber.'

'But they said the cops had been around "because of that chick". They had to mean Amber.'

Toni let a beat pass, then sighed. 'I'll help as much as I can, but I won't break the law.'

'I wouldn't ask you to.' Gen yawned.

'Go to bed. I have the day off, I'll get Charlie and Lily to school.'

'Thank you.' Gen hugged her. 'Don't know what I'd do without you.'

'Neither do I, my friend.'

7

Incessant bleeping blared from the bedside table. Gen slapped at the phone with her hand until she hit the stop button. Five hours sleep hadn't been enough. She dragged herself from bed and made it to work in time for her lunch shift.

It was mid-afternoon when she finally felt like all pistons were firing. She tried to order her thoughts as she headed home. She needed a plan of action before she did anything more, especially before she spoke with Jesse.

Back in her room she spread out every file and folder of evidence she'd compiled in Amber's case – the coroner's inquest report, newspaper articles, her notes from police interviews and the yearly check-ins with their family liaison. She read over all the theories that had been posited to explain Amber's disappearance. The only one about motorbikes had been to do with their dad and his friends, but none of them were involved in the underbelly of motorbike culture.

Her eyes landed on the section marked 'Hugh', and she bit her cheek. Most women were killed by someone known to them, often an intimate partner. And Hugh's behaviour the night Amber went missing made him even more suspect.

He'd been incommunicado all afternoon and evening, his phone untraceable. The next morning, police had discovered him naked in a Sydney casino hotel room after a tip-off from reception. He claimed to have no memory of what he'd done between gambling at the roulette wheel in the early evening and being woken by the police the next day.

But within a day, the police had cleared him. Tobias, Hugh's friend and lawyer, gave him an alibi, swore they'd been together the entire evening. He said they'd stayed in the suite because they'd had too much to drink, and that the only reason he wasn't present when the police arrived was because he'd gone to get coffee.

It never felt as if the police had taken into consideration Tobias's unwavering loyalty to Hugh. Following graduation, Hugh walked into a senior executive sales position at his father's corporate real estate company, leapfrogging far more experienced staff. Two years later he got his dad to put Tobias on retainer as one of the company's conveyancing lawyers. Tobias owed Hugh a lot.

A reminder pinged on her phone. *Charlie BB trials*. She still hadn't managed to talk to Hugh about that. She dialled his number, reaching his voicemail for the gazillionth time that day. His voice droned on, and she shifted her jaw from side to side. Finally, the beep came.

'Hugh, Charlie wants to try out for a representative basketball team at North Sydney PCYC. I've tried calling a dozen times to check with you, but seeing as you're ignoring my calls, I'm just going to take him.'

She hung up and her eye caught on Lily's forgotten music folder. Her gut swirled with anger. She called Hugh again.

'And you need to be home tonight. It's time to get your head out of your arse and put your kids first.'

Gen hung up, dropped her face into her hands and groaned. She'd pay for that, but she didn't care. Hugh's kids needed him.

She checked the time and leapt to her feet. She threw on her shoes, then dashed past Charlie's room, stuffed shorts, shirt, socks and his basketball boots into a sports bag and raced out the door, cursing.

Pulling up in the deserted pick-up zone outside Charlie's school, she spotted him straight away, dribbling a basketball up and down the path. She leant over and threw open the door.

'Sorry I'm late, we'll still get there on time.'

He jumped in and she accelerated away from the kerb.

'How was your day?'

'Had zone try-outs for cricket.'

'How'd you go?'

'What do you reckon?' He grinned at her.

'Alrighty, Mr Modest. You nervous about this afternoon?'

He shrugged. 'I'll just play the best I can.'

She pointed at the floor near his feet. 'There's a banana and some crackers in the bag.'

By the time they'd reached the PCYC car park he'd devoured every scrap of food and changed into his gear. She'd barely brought the car to a stop when he leapt out. 'Come on, Gen, it starts in three minutes.'

She followed him into an industrial-looking building. Shouts, whistles and the thud of basketballs hitting backboards echoed through the cavernous space. She wound her way to the reception desk where Charlie stood, practically bouncing on the spot, holding a pen out towards her. The receptionist, a young woman with a harried look on her face, shoved a clipboard in her direction. 'If you could sign the permission form and the indemnity waiver, the coaches are about to start.'

Gen signed the asterisked sections and handed the clipboard back. 'Trials are on court one,' the woman said. Charlie threw Gen a quick wave and ran off.

After her sleep that morning Gen had realised it would be better to have Jesse on side – he was a policeman after all – but she would keep the boundaries clear. She scoured the courts but found no sign of him. Gen asked the receptionist if he was around and she pointed down a corridor. In a separate hall on the other side of the building she found him hauling a metre-thick blue gym mat against a climbing wall. He moved the huge mat around with ease. She exhaled. Better get this over and done with. She entered the space.

'You need a hand?'

Jesse turned, his features flashing with surprise. 'Didn't expect to see you here this afternoon.'

She shrugged. 'I promised to tell you what happened. Every detail.' The comment sounded more sarcastic than she'd intended, but his posture relaxed anyway. 'I thought you'd be helping with the try-outs.'

'I'm needed here.' He balanced a plank between two gymnastic vaults. A set of parallel bars sat to one side.

'I didn't know you taught gymnastics.'

'I don't. I run parkour sessions three afternoons a week.'

'Is that the thing where people climb walls and buildings and stuff?'

'We run a tamer version here, but it's a great way to draw the more challenging kids into the PCYC. Gives us a chance to connect.' He flashed her a grin. 'Want to give it a try?'

She shook her head. 'Flexibility and coordination aren't really my thing.'

Chuckling, he collected a water bottle then sat on the floor near the door. 'Okay if we chat here? I don't want to miss the early arrivals.'

Gen crossed her legs and sank to the floor next to him. She ran him through the events of the night before.

When she'd finished, Jesse's jaw flexed, as if he wanted to say something but was stopping himself.

'Say what you're thinking.'

'Nothing is gonna stop you looking for answers, is it?'

Gen shook her head.

'You shouldn't have gone there on your own.'

'The house was supposed to be empty.'

'Searches are like that. You never know what will happen.'

Gen bit at her bottom lip. 'I need to follow up on a few things from last night. I'm hoping you might have some ideas?'

'I can't help in my capacity as a police officer.'

'I was hoping you'd do it as a friend.'

'We're friends now?'

'What else do you call someone who helps you with a problem?'

'A sucker,' he mumbled under his breath. 'I won't be able to access records that aren't readily available to the public.'

A skinny boy, maybe ten or eleven, sauntered into the room. 'Hope it's not as easy as it was last week.'

Jesse shook the boy's hand. 'I guess we'll see.' Another boy entered, about the same age but stockier.

Gen picked up her backpack. 'I'll leave you to it.'

Jesse lifted his chin. 'Come and see me when trials are done, I should be finished by then. We can plan a time to meet.'

'You'll help?'

'As if that was ever in question.'

Gen found a table in the far corner of the cafeteria and opened her computer. She pulled out her phone and dialled the number Toni had emailed through.

'You've reached Erwin Stubenitsky, you know what to do. Unless you're a journalist – you can piss off.'

Gen hung up. Poor guy. Memories flared, recent and old, of being hounded by the press. The incessant calls, letters, reporters outside the home with cameras and lights, inbox flooded with interview requests, theories by the late-night TV hosts skirting the edge of defamatory and cruel. Last time, she'd had to change all her contact details, get a new mobile number. Hugh had done the same. For a while it had felt like they'd never have any privacy again. Then a new story broke, and the attention fell away, making day-to-day life easier but also diverting public attention from Amber's case. Back then, Toni had also been a cadet so hadn't been able to help, but now she was doing everything she could, including sending Gen Erwin's phone number and a link to the contact page of his upmarket London restaurant.

Gen decided not to leave a voicemail. It was likely he'd ignore it. Instead, she found the restaurant's email address and began to type.

Dear Erwin,

I would like to express my condolences for the loss of your father two years ago.

My name is Geneva Leighton and I'm Amber Forsythe's younger sister. I don't believe your father killed Amber. I'm trying to uncover new leads before the police close the file and I'm really hoping you can help.

I'd like to ask you some questions about your father's life, your home growing up, and the foster children you were raised with. I give my word anything said to me will be held in confidence.

You can contact me via this address or on my phone number at the bottom of this email.

Yours sincerely,

Geneva Leighton

With a whispered prayer, she hit send, then opened up the report from Amber's coronial inquest from five years ago and began to reread.

Two hours later she heard her name being called from the stairs.

'Gen!' A beaming Charlie ran over, sweaty hair plastered to his face.

'How do you think you did?'

He shrugged, but a grin filled his face. Gen gathered her things and threw her arm around her nephew.

'We just need to pop past and say goodbye to Jesse.'

'He's here?'

'Teaching a class down the corridor.'

Charlie took off, leaving Gen in his wake. She entered the hall and almost tripped over his discarded shoes.

'Jesse teaches parkour.' Charlie turned, eyes wide. 'Isn't that the coolest?'

She smiled.

'He said I can have a go if you say yes.'

Gen checked her watch. 'Five minutes.'

'James,' Jesse called out, 'can you guide Charlie here around the course please?'

The two boys charged at the vertical blue mat and scrambled up it, using knotted ropes to pull themselves to the top.

'He's a natural,' Jesse said.

'No matter what sport he tries.' Pride radiated in Gen's voice. She pulled up the calendar on her phone. 'When are you free this week?'

'I'm working afternoon shifts but can meet any weekday morning and any time on Saturday.'

'I'm working mornings, and we have the funeral on Friday. How about ten on Saturday? Hugh should be home but, if not, Lily can keep an eye on Charlie.'

'It's a date.'

'No.' She held his gaze. 'It's a meeting.'

He stared back for a moment, then nodded towards Charlie. 'He really is good at this.'

Charlie leapt from one balance beam to another like a cat. He swung across a set of monkey bars, ran at a mock fence, vaulted it and landed a metre from their feet.

'That was ... That is ... I have to do that again.' Charlie sucked in breaths, an enormous smile lighting up his face.

'I have space on Thursdays.' Jesse turned to Gen. 'If your aunt says yes.'

Gen took in Charlie's absolute delight. It'd be a great distraction, but Hugh would hate it. Then again, he probably wouldn't even be home.

She nodded and Charlie whooped.

Hugh was supposed to be home early but sent a text at 7 pm.

Client dinner. Home 9 pm.

Charlie had spent the hour between nine and ten with his eyes glued to the driveway, determined to wait up. He'd made it onto the rep squad and wanted to share the news with his dad. Only the bribe of a pancake breakfast convinced him to go to sleep.

Gen pulled Charlie's door closed, then turned to Lily's, but the space under it was dark. Damn it. She really needed to find some time with her niece. Lily had stormed off to her room straight after dinner and hadn't emerged since. She'd clearly been struggling since the news about Amber broke, but it felt like more was going on. More than average teen hormones.

Back in the kitchen Gen eyed the half-full bottle of red but channelled her inner Toni and made a peppermint tea instead. While the tea brewed, she re-read Hugh's curt text message. God, she'd had enough of his bullshit.

As she yanked the teabag from her mug, a key slid into the front door. She strode down the hall ready to let fly, when whispered laughter stopped her. The door opened to reveal Tobias. His dark-rimmed glasses had slipped down his nose, and the unremarkable navy-blue suit and white shirt he always wore were rumpled.

He pulled a bedraggled Hugh through the doorway behind him. Hugh's loosened tie sat skewwhiff. He hooked one arm around Tobias's shoulders and slid his palm along the wall as they bumbled down the hall. The reek of alcohol practically bowled her over.

Hugh lurched forward, arms open wide, his coat sliding to the ground.

'Gen Ben!' His voice boomed.

'Shhh.' Gen pointed up the stairs. 'You'll wake the kids.'

'Uh oh, in trouble again.' Hugh cracked up.

Gen rolled her eyes. 'For fuck's sake.'

Sorry, Tobias mouthed.

'You will be.' Her answer was smothered by Hugh, who pulled her into a headlock and scrubbed his knuckles across her scalp.

'Let me go, you idiot!'

'Come on, you love me. I'm your favourite brother-in-law.'

'You're my only brother-in-law and you stink like a brewery.' She pushed him away and stepped back. The smile dropped from his face, morphing into a hangdog expression.

'Awww, don't be like that. I needed to let off steam.'

'You need to grow up.'

Hugh scowled. 'Always a hard-arse.'

'Always a selfish prick.'

His shoulders drooped. 'Can't you ever cut me a break?'

'Come on, man.' Tobias, always the peacemaker, dragged Hugh in the direction of the master bedroom. 'Let's go.'

Gen retrieved her tea and carried it out to the deck. She leant her elbows on the railing and began constructing a plan to make as much noise as possible tomorrow morning.

After a minute, Tobias joined her. 'Sorry, he wouldn't stop ordering shots.'

'What's going on? He's drinking a lot again.'

'Amber being found has triggered something. He keeps talking about it being his fault.'

'Why?'

'Because he wasn't here that night.'

'Well, maybe he should try learning from his mistakes. The kids need him at home.'

Tobias twisted his wedding ring around. 'He said you want the police to keep the case open.'

'What I want is for him to step up and behave like the dad his kids deserve.'

'They're lucky they have you.'

'They'll always have me, but they need him too.'

Tobias faced her, his expression serious. 'So, what's happening with the investigation?'

'The police are ready to close it.' Gen picked at the cuticle on her thumb. 'But I think I might have found something to keep it open.'

'Does Hugh know?'

'When would I have told him? He's barely home.'

'He has fallen off the wagon a bit lately.'

'So why did you go drinking with him?'

'I thought we could talk things over. That I could get him back on track.' He cleared his throat. 'Do you think, for Hugh and the kids' sake, you could let your search for answers settle down? Just for now, while Hugh puts himself back together?'

'I already contacted the farm owner's son. He's in London. I'm hoping he has some answers about his dad.'

'Surely the police spoke to him.'

'Yeah, but I'm hoping he'll open up to me because I'm Amber's sister. The family used to foster kids. I want to know if any of them kept in touch.'

'I'd leave it if I were you.'

'I want to go over that night with you, too: hear your version of went on with Hugh and why he stayed at the casino.'

Tobias checked his watch then grimaced. 'Happy to, but could we do it another time? Heather is really miffed with me for not going straight home. I should get back to her and the kids.' He walked to the front door.

'Tobias?'

He looked over his shoulder.

'Thank you for getting him home in one piece.'

He shrugged. 'No problem.'

She sagged against the doorframe. She needed sleep, then she'd figure out how to handle Hugh.

8

The glow of the sunrise had almost completely faded from the sky by the time Gen paid for her coffee, wandered to the edge of the beach and sank to the step. She wrapped her hands around the takeaway cup, toed off her sandals and dug her feet into the sand.

In the distance, an older woman swam slow laps across the shark-netted baths. The steady pace looked almost meditative. A wave of longing consumed Gen. She desperately wanted to be on the back of her bike, the one place she could keep her mind completely in the present. But instead, she had to make sure Hugh was functioning for their meeting with the funeral director. It was going to take every bit of her willpower not to march into his room and dump a bucket of cold water on his head.

She sipped her coffee. Blowing up at him would be counterproductive, and the truth was, he held all the power. Her waitressing gig earned enough for incidentals, but nowhere near enough to support a family of three, especially not in Sydney's crazy housing market. Worse still, she had no legal right to be in Lily and Charlie's lives. She was at Hugh's mercy.

If Amber were alive, how would she get Hugh to step up?

Gen sifted sand through her toes. Her sister would win him over with kindness. That had always been her way.

Gen finished her coffee and lined up at the kiosk window to order Hugh a bacon and egg roll – an olive branch of sorts. Hopefully the grease would soak up some of last night's alcohol.

'The significant advantage of a graveside service is that the entire event is conducted in one place, making it perfect for privacy.' Nancy, the softly spoken funeral director, took the signed forms Hugh had pushed across the oak desk.

'Is that everything?' Hugh stood.

'Yes.' Nancy nodded. 'Although, if you would —'

Hugh strode from the room before she could finish. The funeral director gave Gen a confused smile.

'Sorry, he's struggling with all this,' Gen said.

'It's okay, I understand. I was just going to say that, if you'd like, you can include some items that were special to Amber in her casket.'

'I'd like that very much. I'll have a look and drop something off to you.' Gen offered her hand. 'Thank you.'

Hugh's black Porsche was running by the time Gen stepped outside. The car was more suited to a racetrack than a city street. He couldn't even fit both children in it. She slid onto the passenger seat, the smell of leather and new car smothering the stench of alcohol seeping from Hugh's pores. Gen tucked a wayward strand of hair behind her ear then snuck a glance in his direction. He floored the accelerator as they drove out of the car park, his forehead wrinkled in deep thought.

'Are you okay?'

'What's that supposed to mean?'

'Nothing, just … That was hard.'

'You got what you wanted with the extra flowers, so I don't know what the problem is.'

'There is no problem. I just wanted to check if you're all right. Especially after last night.'

'You are not my mother or my wife. How I spend my nights is none of your business.'

'It is when it affects the kids.'

'*My* kids! They're my children and they are fine. You said it yourself at breakfast, Charlie is excelling in sport, and Lily will nail her scholarship assessment next week.'

'About Lily —'

'Geneva, stop. Perhaps you should focus on your own lack of direction and back off the three of us.'

God, he was in full-blown arsehole mode.

He pulled to a stop at a red light. 'Can you book the caterers for the wake?'

'Caterers? It's only going to be family; can't everyone bring a plate?'

'I'm not asking my family to bring food. If you can't manage it, I'll get my assistant to —'

'Fine, I'll do it. Can you stop being ...'

'What?'

'Can we just take this down a notch? Please? It's not an easy time for any of us.'

Hugh turned the radio up, loud enough to prevent further conversation until he dropped her home. She'd barely closed the car door when he sped away and headed back to work.

Gen lowered the attic ladder, climbed up and hoisted her body into the cavity. Plastic storage boxes, all neatly stacked and labelled, filled the space. A musty, slightly sweet scent lingered.

She spied boxes of books, a bassinet and a garment box

containing Amber's Grace Kelly–style wedding dress. She'd stunned everyone that day, the fitted lace-covered bodice flaring out into a full train, the delicate veil framing her elegant features. Standing beside her sister, wearing a shell-pink flouncy monstrosity of a bridesmaid dress that Amber's mother-in-law had insisted on, Gen had felt like a bumbling Amazonian. Amber had laughed and apologised about the dress, completely aware of the sacrifice Gen was making to keep the peace. Gen shuddered at the memory. If she never wore pink again it would be too soon.

She pivoted to check the opposite end of the roof space and froze. A toppling pile of cardboard boxes stuffed to the gills stood against the back wall. Anger surged through her. On the first anniversary of Amber's disappearance, Gen had come home from work to find an absolutely sozzled Hugh lying on his bed, all signs of his wife removed from the house. When he'd sobered up, they'd had a hell of a blue and he'd finally agreed to a few photos being returned to their places, but nothing else.

Gen had planned to go through Amber's things properly, but the parenting role she'd found herself thrust into had quickly taken priority. Every spare second was focused on her niece and nephew. Not to mention how her stomach curdled at the mere thought of rifling through her sister's possessions.

Today though, she was on a mission. She was determined to make sure Amber was buried with some of the things she loved most. Her favourite dress, a photo of Lily and Charlie, and the heart pendant their dad had given Amber on her eighteenth birthday.

Gen took a deep breath, lifted the first box down, opened the flaps and groaned. It was stuffed to the brim with a nonsensical mix of items. Hugh must have just thrown things in willy-nilly. She pulled out a mouldy linen blazer, a crumpled blue blouse, some beach shells, and a book. She kept going. Midway down, twisted among the items Hugh must have swept from Amber's dresser, was the heart necklace, the chain knotted and tangled. Heat flared up Gen's neck. Did he have no respect at all?

She sorted through to the bottom of the box, but there was no sign of Amber's diamond earrings or the gaudy sapphire pendant Hugh's parents had insisted she wear on her wedding day.

Gen wiped at the sweat collecting above her lip and cursed the corrugated metal roofing that charged up the temperature in the unventilated space. She moved on to the next box. This one was full of shoes, bags and scarves. At the very bottom, she spotted a pair of ratty pink ballet slippers, and tears filled her eyes. A flash of Amber pirouetting across the stage in a production of *Sleeping Beauty*. Dance had been everything to her until she'd met Hugh. She gave it up soon after. Gen placed the pointe shoes next to the necklace.

It took two more boxes until she found the blue cotton beach dress Amber had practically lived in when Hugh wasn't around. It was the same colour as Amber's eyes and had set off her olive skin and blonde hair beautifully. She clutched the dress to her face and inhaled, but all she could smell was muskiness. She shook it out, held it against her body and smiled. It would be indecently short on her.

Against Gen's hip, a lump protruded from the dress's pocket. She reached in and her fingers closed around a hard plastic cylinder. A film canister. Her eyes stung again. Amber had taken up photography when Lily was born. She'd bought herself a second-hand Leica, and alongside taking photos of the kids, she had developed a talent for capturing flora and fauna – she'd even won first prize in a local photography competition. Gen paused. The camera hadn't been among Amber's possessions. She rummaged through the rest of the boxes but found no sign of the camera. Her jaw tensed. It had probably made it into a 'worth money' pile, alongside the earrings and sapphire.

Gen turned the black canister over in her hand. A roll of film shifted inside. Could film survive twelve years, especially in the roof's heat? Imagine if she could get the photos processed and share them with the kids. It was worth a try. She gathered the other items she'd saved and took them to her bedroom, trying to temper her excitement at the possibility of finding another tendril of connection to Amber.

She opened her laptop and found a photo lab with good reviews for film restoration. Rewind Images Lab. The website mentioned the process could take a few weeks. She paid for expedited processing and popped the canister into an envelope to drop off later. A lightness filled her chest. How amazing would it be to see the world one last time through her sister's eyes?

After work the next day, Gen had just enough time to deliver Amber's things to the funeral director and drop the film into the post before the kids' buses dropped them home from school.

Lily walked through the door and looked around expectantly.

'Is Dad home tonight?'

'I'm ... not sure.'

Lily's expression went dark, and she headed upstairs. A minute later, her bedroom door slammed. Gen headed for the staircase, determined to get to the bottom of what was troubling her niece.

'I'm doing homework,' Lily snapped when Gen knocked on her door.

'Lily, can I come in please?'

The door swung open, and Lily placed her hand on her hip.

'I wanted to check if you're okay?'

'I'm fine, just have a lot of homework.'

'I know it's been a tough week —'

'I said I'm fine. Can I get back to work now?'

'Ummm, okay.' The door clicked shut before Gen finished speaking. She stared at it. Had she done something to upset Lily? She mentally trawled through their interactions over the past few days but couldn't see how. They'd barely spent a minute together.

Maybe things would get easier after tomorrow's funeral.

Gen dropped Charlie at his first parkour class, then returned home and loitered in the stairwell. What if Lily really wasn't okay? Maybe Gen should insist they talk? Bentley whined from his bed, as if sensing her indecision.

'Was that a yes or no, Bent?' Kneeling, she scratched behind his ears and the Lab rolled onto his back for a tummy rub. She indulged him for a few minutes, then stood. Lily was smart and resourceful. If she wanted Gen's help, she would ask for it.

Still, her gaze caught on the stairs. There had never been any awkwardness between her and Lily, but she didn't want to make things worse. She headed for the garage in search of a task to distract her. Jesse had offered to drop Charlie home, so she had a little time before dinner.

She snatched up the wrench and adjusted the clutch cable on her dad's bike, which was still a little sticky at the handle. Once that worked smoothly, she drained the radiator, flushed it out with fresh water and filled it with new coolant.

She was removing a new radiator cap from its packet when the rumble of a ute came up the drive.

A car door slammed and then another. Footsteps ran

towards the garage. Gen snatched up an old towel from the bench and walked out to the front of her workshop.

'You should have seen me, Gen! ' Charlie said. 'Jesse said I was the best he'd ever seen.'

'And the most modest.' Jesse chuckled. His navy-blue polo shirt stretched tight across his chest, and his shorts revealed the muscled legs of a runner. Gen turned away, focused on wiping the grease from her hands.

'Thanks so much for bringing him home.' She threw the rag in the corner, then faced Charlie. 'Inside for a shower, mister. I'll have dinner ready when you're done.'

Charlie shook Jesse's hand. 'Thanks for the ride home. See you next week!'

He ran up the front stairs and Jesse laughed again. 'Does he ever stop?'

'Never.'

Gen walked back to the radiator and screwed on the new cap. Jesse moved in next to her and ran his hand along the bike's saddle.

'What is it that you like about motorbikes?'

'Ever ridden one?'

'Only dirt bikes as a teen.'

'Fun, but not the same.'

'May I?' He pointed to the bike. She nodded and he straddled the seat. He held the handlebars and Gen had to turn away. He looked good astride her dad's bike. Too good. She began tidying up the tools she'd used.

'In answer to your question, I guess riding is like meditation to me. My body reacts as soon as I put on leathers. Everything slows down and I can think clearly. When you're riding you have to concentrate on the present, what's in your immediate vicinity – the wind and surrounds and the motion of the bike.

When I finish a ride I'm physically buzzing. It's like my whole system gets recalibrated.'

'Sounds like when I run.'

She grimaced. 'Running's my nightmare.'

'Do you ever take anyone on the back of your bike?'

'Nah. I won't take the kids until they're eighteen.'

'No one else?'

She put her hands on her hips. 'Why? You game?'

'Absolutely. Whenever you talk about riding your whole face come to life. Where do I sign up?'

Gen wanted to trust the enthusiasm in his eyes, to surrender herself to their connection, but she'd sworn she wouldn't make that mistake again.

'I better get dinner on.' She reached for the light switch, and he took the hint, following her outside.

'Thanks for dropping Charlie home.'

'Anytime.' His hand ran through his hair. 'I'll see you tomorrow, at the cemetery.'

'You don't need to —'

He put his hand up. 'I'll be there.'

'Jesse, if you're coming as a police officer that's fine, but please don't come for me. The kids will need my full focus.'

'I'll be there if you need me.' Jesse headed for his car, then turned. 'If you ever want someone at your back, on the bike or anywhere else, I'm here.'

He jumped into his ute and reversed out the drive.

Gen's breath bottled in her chest. She could barely remember what it felt like to have someone to rely on. She pinched her lips between her teeth then blew out the held air. Jesse said all the right words, but when it mattered, he would bail again, just like he had before.

9

Gen's scratchy black linen dress rode up as she got out of Toni's car. She pulled it down and strode up the path towards a ridiculously expensive oak wood casket her sister would have hated. Gen struggled to comprehend that it held Amber's remains. The past twelve years had been such a tangle of grief and hope and fear, and it had all come to this.

The knot beneath her ribs expanded.

Toni came to her side and hooked her arm through Gen's. 'You all right?'

She nodded. 'I just hope the kids are okay.'

Hugh had insisted Lily and Charlie travel to the service with him and his parents. He probably wanted them as a buffer. Gen wasn't even sure why the Forsythes were coming. They'd always made it clear they thought Hugh had married beneath him, and it was a private funeral, so there was no reason to keep up appearances.

She exhaled. Today was for Amber. The Forsythes didn't matter. She raised her chin, searching for the two people who did.

Charlie broke from the small pack of black-suited people waiting at the graveside.

'Charlie!' Hugh growled, but his son kept running and wrapped his arms around Gen's waist. She squeezed him tight, then knelt, ignoring the damp seeping in through her stockings.

She took his face in her hands. 'You okay?'

He buried himself back in her arms. 'Dad's going to be angry I ran,' he whispered.

'I'll handle him.' She took his hand and closed the distance to the casket. An ornate wreath of white roses, flowers Amber had always hated the smell of, covered it almost entirely. Hugh stood with his older brother, William Junior, otherwise known as Bill; Bill's wife Trudy; and Tobias, flanking Hugh's parents. To their right Jesse chatted with the now-retired Sergeant Maitland, Constable Venuka, and Detective Simpson.

Gen mouthed a *Thank you* to the group of police.

Behind the casket stood Lily, stiff-backed, vulnerable, and so very alone. Gen threw her arms around her niece, but Lily's body stayed rigid.

'Dad said we have to stay strong.'

'It's okay to let your feelings out.'

'But he said Grandpa will get angry if we cry.'

'Oh honey, emotions are normal, especially at a funeral.'

A shadow fell over them.

'I thought I told you the press were not welcome in any circumstance.'

Gen glanced up at Hugh. 'And I agreed.'

His head tilted to the right, indicating a man fifty metres away, watching from behind a eucalyptus tree. He had a long beard, wore an ill-fitting black suit, and looked to be in his late sixties. Gen didn't recognise him. Before she could refute Hugh's accusation, or challenge the interloper, Jesse marched towards the stranger.

'If we could all take our places, it's time to begin,' the Anglican minister Hugh had insisted on called out. Amber hadn't even believed in God.

Gen guided the children to the row of wooden chairs at the graveside and sat them either side of herself. Hugh raised his brows pointedly, then sat beside Lily.

'We are here to honour the life of Amber Louise Forsythe, who was born in Sydney on May 1st, 1985.

'When someone is taken too young, we long to have more time with them. But as it says in Ecclesiastes, *For everything there is a season, and a time for every purpose under heaven.*'

Gen pressed her lips together. How could there be a purpose in a young mother being taken from her children?

'*A time to be born, and a time to die; a time to plant, and a time to reap ...*'

Charlie burrowed in close, and Lily's hand gripped Gen's so tightly that the tips of her fingers turned white. She didn't care. She would give them whatever they needed.

The minister droned on. 'Amber lived a short twenty-five years, but in that time, she thrived in her role as caretaker to Lily, Charlie and her husband, Hugh.'

Caretaker! Pressure built in Gen's head, throbbing at her temples. Amber was so much more than that. She'd been a beautiful ballet dancer, was passionate about the environment and photography, and had a wicked sense of humour.

Although that had diminished in the last year of her marriage to Hugh.

Gen glanced at the man her sister had fallen in love with. Hugh behaved as if Amber was defined by who she was to him, and the minister spoke as if her sister hadn't existed until she'd become a Forsythe.

'She was a fabulous cook and entertainer, and everyone ...'

Why did eulogies always describe the person who'd died as a sum of their accomplishments? Amber wasn't a bunch of skills. She was real and beautiful and kind and loved, and she had the biggest heart of anyone Gen had ever met.

'... and while it is in our nature to want to understand why we lost such a precious life so young, we need to focus on the things we know. Have faith in ...'

Focus on the things we know. What did she know for sure in Amber's case? She needed to go through every fact with fresh eyes.

Charlie's sob broke through her thoughts. She tugged him in closer.

'In closing ...'

Thank goodness.

'... let us recite the Lord's Prayer.'

Everyone bowed their heads and mumbled the words.

As the attendees dispersed, Gen stepped forward with Charlie to place a flower on the casket. She held one palm to the side of the smooth cold wood. Her breath stuttered.

Miss you so much, Ambs. I promise we will find who did this to you.

Lily stepped up beside her and placed her flower on the casket. 'Love you,' she whispered.

Charlie gripped Gen's hand tighter. He put his flower down gently, tears streaming down his cheeks.

The invisible band around Gen's ribcage loosened a smidgen. He was finally allowing himself to feel the loss.

'Hugh!' William Forsythe barked from the other side of the casket. 'Tell your boy to pull himself together.'

Gen pulled Charlie closer. Before she could respond, Hugh stepped in front of her.

She glared at him. 'The kids are coming home with me.'

He checked Charlie's face, then nodded.

'I'll stay with Dad.' Lily slipped her hand in her father's.

'You sure?' Gen asked.

Lily nodded and she walked over to the minister with Hugh, remaining at his side while the two men talked. Gen watched them as they then made their way to his parents' Mercedes. Hugh fell into step with his brother. As he became engrossed in their conversation, he dropped Lily's hand. Gen took a step towards them, but Toni touched her shoulder and shook her head. She was right. Gen needed to respect Lily's choice.

She squeezed Charlie's hand, then swung his arm, back and forth, all the way to the car park.

She climbed into the rear seat of Toni's jeep and cuddled Charlie into her side. As they drove off, she stared out the window.

Amber was truly gone.

The passing cars and scenery blurred over, and she blinked hard to bring them back into focus. She had to stay strong for the wake; the kids still needed her.

Gen set Lily and Charlie up with the latest Marvel movie in the downstairs TV room, then found Toni in the kitchen. Her stomach rumbled at the array of food set out, and she snuck a salmon blini from a tray.

'Can you believe this?' She followed Toni onto the deck. Classical music droned from below, its passionless execution more suited to an elevator playlist.

'It's somewhat over the top for a small family gathering. Then again when image is what matters ...' Toni shrugged and sipped her mineral water. 'You all right?'

'I'm happy Amber's been laid to rest properly.' Gen's eyes welled, and she closed them, stemming the flow. *Not now.*

'Oh hon —' The trill of Toni's phone interrupted. 'Sorry, it's work.'

'It's okay.' Gen waved her friend away, and leant on the glass fence. Voices rose from the deck below.

'Bill, the election is in three months. I need the polling information now. And Hugh, I need you to chase up that campaign donation promised by Walter. We need to get the ads up and running.'

'William dear,' Hugh's mother half-whispered in her nasally tone, 'I'm not sure now is the time —'

'This is important, Helen. Stay out of it.'

Toni moved back to Gen's side. 'Eavesdropping?'

'William is business as usual.'

'At his daughter-in-law's wake?'

'He's an important man with important work to do.' Gen mimicked William's plummy delivery and Toni giggled, her bright tinkling laugh helping to ease the flatness Gen felt.

Toni held up her phone and made a face. 'They need me to cover a breaking story at the ports. You going to be okay?'

'Of course, but call me later. I want to hear about all the stevedores who are bound to fall in love with you.'

Gen walked Toni to the front door, then nipped up to her bedroom to throw off the dress she could no longer bear to feel against her skin. She slipped on jeans, a white button-down shirt and runners. Her cheeks ached from fake-smiling around the Forsythes all day. Thankfully, now, they had pretty much forgotten Gen and the kids were there.

Would they notice if she snuck Lily and Charlie down to the beach for fish and chips? The kids could probably do with the space to decompress.

So could she. It was the finality of it all. Her brain understood Amber was gone, but that closure everyone talked about remained elusive. Maybe it would come when the mystery was solved. Or maybe the whole concept was just bullshit.

She went downstairs to check on the kids, found them engrossed in the screen, and let them be. Outside, near the pool, Tobias stood talking with Hugh and his family. Gen picked up a bottle of champagne and listened in as she undid the foil wrapping.

'Lily has her scholarship exam and interview next Friday.' Hugh was practically puffing out his chest. 'She's going to nail it.'

'I don't know why you insist on her performing like a monkey for a scholarship she doesn't need,' said William.

Bill nodded.

Hugh raised his chin. 'Actually, it's a badge of prestige at her school. And advantageous for university applications.'

William folded his arms. 'And Charles?'

Gen's jaw tightened. Charlie hadn't ever been a Charles, and if she had a say he never would be. She removed the wire cage from the champagne cork, then gently twisted it loose. She didn't want to draw attention with a loud pop. It was kind of fun watching Hugh squirm.

'He made the regional cricket team, is up for sportsman of the year at school and has been selected to play on a representative squad for basketball.'

'For the private school's area team?'

'As part of the North Sydney PCYC team.'

Helen drew her hand to her throat. 'Are you sure you want him mixing with those children?'

Hugh rubbed the back of his neck.

Gen could practically hear Amber screaming at her to rescue him. She snagged a beer for herself and approached the group, offering the champagne.

'Anyone for a top-up?'

Helen offered up her empty flute, never one to turn down a drink. Tobias walked away, heading down the corridor towards the bathroom.

'Geneva.' William honeyed his tone. She gave him a cool smile and lifted the bottle to fill his glass. 'I thought you'd like to know we are featuring Amber's murder in a report to support a policing and crime bill going before parliament next month.'

Gen froze mid-pour. 'You're what?'

'This bill is an essential —'

Gen raised her palm, cutting him off. 'Unbelievable. You're using the murder of your grandchildren's mother to gain sympathy and votes for your election.'

She couldn't do any more time with these people. And that was exactly what it felt like: doing time. She turned away, but a hand closed over her forearm. It was Bill.

'Can you fill Trudy's glass before you go?'

Gen shoved the bottle into his hand. 'Fill it yourself.' She marched back into the house and down the corridor, stopping only when she was sure no one had followed. Her nose stung with tears. How dare they use Amber for their gain? What about how it might affect Lily and Charlie? Even Hugh? Did no one in that family actually care about anyone else? She focused on her breathing, trying to slow her adrenals down. As her rage began to abate, Tobias strode from the direction of the bathroom. She stopped him as he passed.

'You got a sec?'

'What do you need?'

'You promised we could talk about the night Amber went missing.'

He looked about. 'I'm not sure this is the place ...'

'This is Amber's wake, Tobias. I don't think there's a better time to talk about her. Hell, someone should.'

Tobias searched the room behind her then his posture softened. 'What do you want to know?'

'Talk me through what you remember.'

'We were at the Sydney Conference Centre all day. It was a commercial buildings management thing, with stalls on security, cleaning and the like. When it finished, Hugh said he didn't feel like going home.' His gaze slid from hers and the hairs on the back of her neck prickled.

'Why?'

'He thought Amber might have been ... It doesn't matter now.'

'That Amber might have been what?'

Tobias sighed and ran a hand through his hair. 'Money had gone missing from their joint account and Amber had become distant. Hugh was starting to think she might be planning to leave him.'

Was that possible? Gen scoured her memory.

'No way. She loved Hugh.'

'Well, Hugh didn't seem all that confident of that, and money had become a huge issue. They were fighting a lot.'

Gen took a swig of her beer. 'They fought, but it was because once Hugh joined the board he was never home.'

'Are you sure?'

Gen stood taller. There was no way her sister had been planning to leave.

'Did you tell the police?'

'Not a chance! Hugh didn't want the speculation about Amber's disappearance to get worse. People were already saying awful things, remember?'

'Of course I do.'

'We were also worried the police might not pursue her case as thoroughly if they thought there was a possibility she faked her abduction.'

'You can't possibly have believed she'd leave the kids.'

'We didn't, but we were afraid the police would.'

What a load of rubbish. If, by some remote chance, Amber had faked her abduction, she would have taken the kids with her and faked their abductions too.

'Back to that night. Instead of going home, you and Hugh went to the casino?'

'He wanted a night off from confrontation.'

'Well, I suppose he got it.'

Tobias gave her a disapproving look.

Gen wiggled her toes in her shoes. If she didn't release her pent-up energy somehow, she'd combust. 'What exactly happened at the casino?'

'We played roulette, Hugh drank. He got to the point where they asked him to leave. He insisted we check into a room at the hotel, said Amber would kill him if he came home in that state.'

She folded her arms across her chest. 'Maybe he deserved it.'

'When we got to the room he threw up all over himself, so I put him in the shower. I went to check on him and he was on the floor naked, almost asleep, so I got him to climb straight into bed. Trust me, I saw way more of him that night than I ever wanted to. I stayed on the lounge and kept an eye on him in case he vomited again.'

'He was found in the room alone.'

'I'd gone downstairs to get coffee. I told the police all this in my statement.'

'Why didn't Hugh tell me that he was worried Amber was going to leave him?'

Tobias's gaze moved to the space over her shoulder and a horrified expression crossed his face.

'Because you didn't need to know!' Hugh's voice vibrated with anger.

She pivoted on the spot. 'Hugh, I don't think —'

'You never do, do you? I came to tell you the kids are going to stay with my parents for a few nights.'

'No! They need home. Routine.'

'I will decide what they need! I have to go to Melbourne in the morning, and I don't want them here with you while you're stirring up trouble.'

'If you'd talked to me about that night I wouldn't have had to ask Tobias.'

'You didn't have to do anything, Geneva. You're a guest in my home. I suggest you do whatever you need to do to move on, or I'm not sure I'm comfortable leaving the kids in your care anymore.'

'You can't do that!'

'We all need peace and calm.'

'Then stay here with them. They need you.'

'Someone around here has to earn a living.'

'It's not all about money.'

'You sound like your sister.'

Gen's hand tightened around the neck of her beer bottle.

'I get back Monday night. After that, I don't want to hear another word about Amber's case. It's over. Finished. Closed.'

'Other than when your father needs to exploit the situation?'

'That is enough!'

'Don't you want to know what happened to her?'

'I *do* know. Dennis Stubenitsky abducted her. He killed her and then buried her on his property.'

Gen looked to Tobias for support, but he shook his head.

'Sorry Gen, but I agree with Hugh. You do need to move on.' He slipped past her.

She fixed Hugh with a glare. 'How can you be so cold?'

'I loved Amber as much as you, but all this drama isn't helping anyone. Not the kids, or me, or you.'

Gen forced herself to remain silent, determined not to make things worse.

'I can't tolerate you dragging this out any further. If you want to continue living under my roof, then you need to accept that.' He turned on his heel and stalked away.

10

Gen slid on her leather jacket but ignored her riding boots. She had to get out of there or she might give in to the urge to snatch the kids and run. Charlie had been teary, Lily furious, and it was clear that neither of them wanted to go to their grandparents'. It was all Gen could do not to declare all-out war with Hugh. Instead, she'd told the kids she loved them, that she'd see them on Monday, then she'd kissed them and got the hell out of the house.

She roared out of the garage, not even allowing the engine to warm up. At the end of the street, she turned right and flew through the roundabouts until she reached the freeway. Hitting the throttle, she wove through the cars scattered across the road and, finally, the invisible hands around her windpipe began to loosen.

After exiting the freeway she turned left at the lights. Up ahead, a gleaming Indian Chief motorbike exited the cemetery. The rider wore a black open-faced helmet, jeans and a black leather vest that resembled a biker's cut. As he passed, he dipped his chin briefly, his silver beard disappearing into the V of his cut. Something about him seemed familiar. She checked her side mirror. On the back of his vest was a cartoon-like picture of a yellow and orange bird, wings outstretched, wearing a green military helmet. Not a club design she recognised. Nice ride, though.

She pulled in to the car park, locked her helmet away and headed for her sister's grave.

The casket and surrounding chairs had all disappeared. All that remained was a mound of dirt and the flowers. The scent of freshly turned soil grew stronger as she approached the plot. Gen knelt next to where the headstone would go – some ostentatious marble monstrosity Hugh's mother had picked out. Another of the many battles Gen had lost. She sat on the ground and crossed her legs.

Gen eyed the staid white arrangement weighing down Amber's grave, tempted to boot them away. She spied a spray of yellow on the opposite side. She walked around and picked up the simple bouquet of yellow chrysanthemums. Amber would have loved them. Gen turned the posy over in her hands. There was no card, and they'd been nowhere in sight at the funeral.

Her gaze fanned out across the grounds and caught on the eucalyptus up the rise, where the reporter had stood this morning. *Wait.* That was who the guy on the bike had reminded her of. He'd been wearing different clothing, but the beard was identical.

She lifted up the flowers and studied them, as if they held the key to everything, then placed them at the foot of the grave.

Who left the flowers, Amber?

A silent breeze was the only answer. She sat again and stared at a worm burrowing into the fresh dirt. The cycle of life at work.

Your kids are amazing. Lily runs rings around almost anyone she talks to. And she's loyal to a fault. Remind you of anyone you know?

Gen smiled. Amber's loyalty to those she loved had been unwavering. When they were kids, even when Gen had been a revolting little shit, Amber had always had her back.

Charlie keeps me on my toes in a different way. He's a bundle of cheeky energy with a heart as big as yours.

She could almost hear Amber's whispered, 'And Hugh?'

Honestly, Ambs, he's a mess. He's so caught up in being who he thinks he has to be for his father that Charlie and Lily don't get a look in. I'm trying to get him to spend more time with them.

Gen played with the pendant at her neck.

Why didn't you tell me you two were having problems?

She patted down the mound, smoothing the area at her feet.

I swear to God, Amber, we're going to find out who did this to you.

A butterfly flew in, inspecting the flowers. It favoured the yellow ones too.

Toni's promised to help. Jesse too. And before you get your hopes up, nothing's going to happen there. He's been great with Charlie, though. And he's agreed to go over the case with me tomorrow, so if you feel like sending us any hints from beyond the grave ... Gen glanced around, feeling self-conscious.

I know this is a bit weird, but I never had anywhere to be near you before. I promise I haven't lost my marbles – or at least no more than I already had.

A droplet of rain darkened the earth, then another.

I'll come back soon, Ambs. And remember what I said: any divine intervention would be greatly appreciated. Hell, haunt me all you want. It'd be amazing to have you around again. Love you.

*

The sky darkened with each kilometre Geneva got closer to home, a cool stillness filling the air. As she turned onto Military Road, lightning flashed across the sky, thunder rumbling a second behind, and then the heavens opened up. She headed down a side street and pulled into an underground car park. Might as well grab some groceries while waiting it out.

She walked up the covered pedestrian ramp, entered the supermarket and filled a basket with bits and pieces they were running low on – Charlie's favourite muesli bars, apples, milk – then headed for the toiletry aisle to get Lily's shampoo. She plucked the bottle from the shelf and turned to leave. She froze. The display in front of her was filled with nappies. Gen's cheeks burned. *If onlys* glued her feet to the floor.

'Nutter,' a young woman dressed in a silk pantsuit muttered as she dodged around her.

Grateful for the wrench back to the present, Gen shrugged. Who cared what some stuck-up Stepford wife thought? She never fitted in these well-heeled suburbs anyway.

At the checkout, she scanned her items and then loaded them onto her bike. A flash of lightning lit up the ramp. It wasn't safe to get back on the road yet. She wandered into a nearby cafe. A metal cup on the table held coloured pencils and sheets of paper. Her gaze was drawn to the yellow pencil, a similar shade to the flowers on Amber's grave. She pulled out a sheet of paper and sketched the cartoon bird she'd spotted on the back of the biker's vest. She stared at the completed picture. She had never seen this design anywhere in the motorbike scene. Yet the vest had looked so much like a motorcycle-club cut.

The bird had appeared to be some kind of eagle. She brought up the search engine on her phone, typed in 'Eagle Motorcycle Club Australia'. An invitation to join a game called the Iron Eagles was the only result. Next she tried 'Eagle Soldier MC' because of the green helmet. Again, no matches, only a list of known one-percenter biker gangs, including the Rebels, Hells Angels, and the Mongrels – outlaw motorcycle clubs committed to life on the fringes and their own rule of law. The majority of motorbike riders, the other ninety-nine per cent, were law-abiding citizens who rode for recreation. Like Gen.

She stared at the drawing. She must have remembered the design wrong. Or maybe the man was some kind of wannabe.

By the time she'd finished her tea it was late afternoon and the rain had abated. She ordered takeaway from the Indian restaurant next door, tucked her folded sketch into the plastic carry bag and headed home.

Twisting the key in the lock, she paused, listening for signs of life.

'Anyone home?'

Bentley walked down the hall to greet her but no one answered her question. She gave him a pat and her shoulders relaxed. She couldn't deal with Hugh tonight.

She swung her food onto the kitchen bench, then continued down the corridor to check. She nudged open his bedroom door with her foot but didn't cross the threshold. Craning her neck, she checked the spot where his overnight bag usually sat. The space was bare, like the rest of the room, devoid of personality and neat as a soldier's bunk.

Her stomach growled. She returned to the kitchen, fed Bentley, filled a bowl for herself with butter chicken and rice, retrieved a beer and sat at the dining table. She scrolled through social media while she ate. Outside, the sky had cleared into an early evening tinged with pink. She took a photo and sent it to the kids. Her phone buzzed almost immediately with a reply from Charlie.

Night Gen Gen. Love you.

She called his number, but it went straight to voicemail. So did Lily's. She pressed her lips together. Hugh's parents never made it easy.

She opened her computer to check her emails. Anything to distract herself from the worry about the kids. The screen was filled with opened tabs. She closed them one by one, the last one being the email she'd sent Erwin Stubenitsky. Still no reply. She scraped up the last forkful of rice and chewed absently, weighing up her next move. She needed to take action. If she sat here with her tumbling emotions, she'd go nuts.

She grabbed a notebook from the kitchen and, even though it was early morning in London, dialled his restaurant.

'Stuben's Bistro. Erwin speaking.'

She hadn't expected him to answer. 'Uh hi. My name is Geneva Leighton, and I was hoping to ask you a few questions —'

'When will you leave me alone? I have no comment. Lose this number.'

'Wait! Please! I'm Amber Forsythe's sister.'

Quiet breathing filled the line.

'I sent you an email recently saying I think your dad is innocent.'

'What are you playing at?'

'I'm not. The police conclusion makes no sense. Amber was abducted from Mosman, but her last call came from way south, near Welby. We were talking before her phone cut out, and she didn't describe her abductor as old. She described him as big and wearing a baseball cap.'

'Dad hated baseball caps, thought they looked stupid.'

'Did you tell the police that?'

'I don't think they ever asked.'

'And what was his motive? Why would your dad travel over an hour from where he lived to abduct a random woman, then drive her south ninety minutes, only to turn round and drive another ninety minutes to his own property in Windsor to bury her.'

'My dad was a country man through and through. I doubt he ever even visited Mosman. And he wouldn't hurt a woman, no way. I never saw him lose his temper, not with Mum or us kids. He set boundaries, but he was never violent. Never. And he had no mental health issues. I told the police all this.'

'Did he have the strength to lift a woman from the boot of a car on his own?'

'He still worked around the farm, the stubborn bugger, but I doubt he could've managed a dead weight.' He cleared his throat. 'Sorry.'

'It's okay.' She swallowed. 'Was your dad into motorbikes?'

'Not at all, wouldn't even let me ride a trail bike. His passions were cooking and volunteer stuff.'

'Like being a foster parent?'

'He and Mum did that together, but when she passed Dad turned to cooking for the local homeless shelter. Roped me in. It's how I ended up wanting to be a chef.'

Gen chewed the top of the pen, racking her brain for the right questions to ask. This might be the only opportunity she got to talk with him. 'Did you keep in contact with any of your foster siblings?'

'Some. The ones who were around a bit longer.'

'Can you remember their names?'

'There were the twins – Rebecca and Bryn. They ended up in Queensland with their grandparents. And there was a guy who played on my footy team for the season he was with us, Greg or Geoff or something. Sorry, I can't really remember. It was a long time ago.'

'What about the height chart your parents kept in the kitchen? If I read the names out, could you tell me anything about them?'

'Worth a shot.'

She scrolled to the photo on her phone and enlarged the image of the doorjamb. 'Rebecca, Jayden, Bryn, Christian, Roger, Geoff, Bindy —'

'Wait. Roger. Rog the Podge. He was older than me, lived with us about a year and a half. Kids at school gave him a real hard time for being chubby. He had to change schools and foster homes because of it.'

'Anything else?'

'Dad was upset about Roger after he moved, something about him joining a gang I think.'

'Could it have been a motorcycle club?'

'Don't know. He was obsessed with motorbikes though. Talked about them all the time.'

'Any chance you can remember Roger's last name?'

'I'm embarrassed to say Podge is all that comes to mind.'

'Do you have your parents' records?'

'Threw them away, sorry. Too expensive to store or ship.'

Gen checked the photo of the doorjamb again. 'There are two names left: Freya and Will.'

'I don't remember them. To be honest, once I hit high school I wasn't interested in the fosters anymore. I had my own group of friends.'

'Did you go to the same school as Roger?'

'Nah, I went to the local Catholic one.'

'How much older was he?'

'Five years or so. You think he had something to do with this? Could he have set my dad up?' The excitement in Erwin's voice was like a bucket of ice water over Gen. It wasn't fair to give the man hope.

'Look, I doubt it. I'm just following every whiff of a lead, no matter how small. If I think of any other questions, would you mind if I called again?'

'As long as you promise to tell me what you find. I know my dad didn't hurt your sister, and I'd like the opportunity to clear his name.'

'Of course. I really appreciate you talking to me today. Have the press backed off?'

'It's started to wane, but for a time I wondered if I'd have to close the restaurant.'

'Sorry you had to go through that.'

'It's like having to grieve him all over again, you know?'

'I do.'

'Course. Sorry about your sister.'

'Thanks.'

'I hope you find out what really happened.'

Gen hung up and re-read her scribbled notes. This Roger guy was too young to be the man she saw leaving the cemetery, but could he be one of the guys she overheard at the farm?

She rinsed her plate and packed up the leftovers. The phone call with Erwin had left her with even more questions. She grabbed another beer and returned to her computer, searching Windsor High, Facebook reunion groups and any related articles she could find mentioning a boy named Roger.

At 2 am, after zero success in her research and a failed attempt to sleep, Gen concluded that the most useful thing she could do while the kids were away was to identify the guy at the cemetery. Even if he had nothing to do with Amber's murder, she needed to rule him out. Her cadetship mentor had always insisted that the first rule of investigating was not to get too singular in your focus. Follow every lead.

She needed to show her sketch to some bike enthusiasts and see if they recognised the eagle design. People who she would find at Jerry's Cafe at lunchtime on a Saturday. The popular bike rest stop – a combined outdoor cafe and service station – was situated in Kulnura, a rural suburb of the Central Coast, about a ninety minute ride from Balmoral. So, at 6 am, she sent Jesse a text rescheduling until late afternoon. At 10 am, she jumped on the bike and headed north on the M1. Just past Peats Ridge, she turned off the motorway. She passed by an array of roadside farms, the scent of freshly cut grass filling her helmet. Being so in touch with your surroundings was one of the joys of being out on the bike.

She pulled into Jerry's Cafe. The large carpark was full of all shapes, sizes and ages, and that was just the bikes. She guided hers into a space between a fresh-off-the-lot Harley and an adventure bike with knobbly tyre treads caked in mud. She dismounted and scouted the packed wooden tables and benches for her friends Debra and David, long-time weekend bikers who lunched at Jerry's almost every Saturday.

At the table opposite the community library box a familiar crop of frizzy shoulder-length blonde hair stood out, the only woman in the group of six. Gen set off across the grass in Debra's direction.

'My blood pressure and cholesterol have gone right up,' Benny, a tall man decked out in jeans, a black leather vest and a white tee complained.

'Five point nine's a disaster.' Red, dressed similarly but sporting full sleeve tattoos, clapped him on the back.

Gen suppressed a laugh. Most people would cross the road if they saw these men walking towards them, but she knew better. They were so like her dad. Rough looking on the outside, but soft and squishy within. She buried the familiar flare of longing. Her dad would have hated that description.

'I take my meds every third day,' Tommy interjected in his broad English accent. 'Best advice I ever received.'

Gen had almost reached the crew when a man carrying a small dog stepped into her path. He shoved his Jack Russell into her arms. 'Say 'ello to Patch.'

She had no choice but to accept the dog. 'Umm ... hello Patch.' Dogs and quirky people were not unusual to bike pitstops. 'Is he yours?'

'Going on three years. Dogs are life, you know?'

'He's lovely.' She patted Patch a few times then offered him back. The man held the dog to his chest and headed towards a shiny bike with a sidecar.

'Making friends as always?' Debra wrapped her arm around Gen's shoulders. 'David, look what the cat dragged in!'

'Geneva!'

David, six-foot-four with an ever-increasing waistband, pulled her into a hug. It was rare for Gen to feel small, but in his hold, she felt tiny.

'Good to see you, David.' She gave him a squeeze then let go.

'You look tired.' Debra held Gen's chin and examined her face.

'It was Amber's funeral yesterday.'

'Oh love, I wish we could have come.'

'Hugh wanted it small, family only. Rough on the kids.'

'The papers said they know the mongrel who did it,' David said.

'Love, leave her be,' Debra said. 'She didn't come here to talk about that.'

'It's okay,' Gen said. 'The police think the guy whose land she was found on murdered her, but I'm not so sure.'

'Why?'

Gen shrugged and made a face. 'My gut?'

They both gave her a sympathetic look.

David patted his stomach. 'Well, my gut says it's time for a pie and chips.'

'Honey, weren't you all just discussing cholesterol?' Debra said. 'The doctor warned you that —'

'I'm almost seventy, love. I'm not being dictated to by some snooty doctor who's barely out from under his mother's skirt.'

Debra pursued her lips at Gen. 'See what I have to live with?'

Gen smiled fondly at the pair. They were always like this, but underneath all the back and forth they loved each other deeply.

A tall, slim man, the only one at the table she hadn't met before, untangled himself from the bench seat and stood. 'You can have this seat. It's my turn to take orders.'

'Thanks ... Sorry, I missed your name.'

'Joe.' He asked everyone what they wanted, writing nothing down. Either he had an amazing memory, or lunch would be a mess.

Gen faced Debra and David. 'I wanted to show you something.'

Deb nodded curiously.

'A man watched Amber's burial from behind a tree yesterday, and I think he returned to her gravesite later.'

'You didn't recognise him?' David asked.

'Never seen him before in my life.' She pulled the folded sketch from the inside pocket of her jacket.

'Could he have been a parent of one of the kids from school?' Deb asked.

'He rode an Indian Chief, looked more a part of my scene.'

David placed his elbows on the bench and rested his chin on laced fingers. 'How old was he?'

'Late fifties or so? I didn't get a great look. But he had on a black leather vest, like MCs wear. This is what the patch looked like.' She handed over her sketch of the bird-like logo.

'What about the rockers printed at the top and bottom of the logo? They should have displayed the club's name or location,' Benny interjected, and the whole table turned their attention to Gen.

'Couldn't read them. The design in the middle was what stood out.'

Debra placed her hand over Gen's. 'Sorry love, I haven't seen that one.'

Dave's palms slapped the table. 'We have!' He pointed at Deb. 'Remember when we ran into that guy, I think his name was K2, at the rally last year?'

'No, I don't, and neither do you.' Debra widened her eyes pointedly at her husband.

'Come on, the eyes of the bird were really creepy, looked like they were following you around. Except I don't think it was a bird, it was some kind of creature on fire.'

'David!'

'What?'

'Gen doesn't need to be getting involved with Phoenix.'

'Shhhh,' Red hissed loudly.

Gen sat forward. 'Who are Phoenix?'

'They broke away from the Rebels a few years back.' Red spoke quietly, and they all leaned in. 'Claimed they hated the criminal element taking hold, but it probably had more to do with the pressure from Strike Force Raptor.'

But Raptor only dealt with the criminal elements of bikie culture. The New South Wales state police formed the strike force to dismantle outlaw MCs after an ongoing street war between the Comancheros and the Hells Angels resulted in a deadly brawl at Sydney airport.

'So, Phoenix are one percenters?' Gen asked.

'Officially? No, they reformed into a social club, and strictly controlled membership. They've stayed under the radar ever since, but it's hard to believe they all just walked away from the life.'

'How do you know all this?' Benny asked.

Red shrugged. 'People talk.'

Gen's brows drew together. 'But what would Amber have to do with members of a hardcore bike club?'

'Not sure,' Deb said. 'But you should stay away from them.'

'Do you know who their president is? Maybe I can talk to him and —'

'Now do you get why you needed to shut up, David?' Debra crossed her arms.

His face crumpled as realisation dawned. 'Deb's right, love. You don't want to mess with those types.'

Gen looked past Debra. 'Do any of you know them?'

'K2 is the pres, or at least he was when they set up,' Red answered. 'But like David said, a bird like you shouldn't go messing around with them.'

'Bird?'

'Phoenix are old school – eye for an eye and brothers above all else. Their clubhouse has military-style fortifications and if you do them wrong they always make you pay. They also treat women who enter their world, who aren't family or claimed as "old ladies", as useful for one thing only.'

'I don't want to spend time with them, I —'

Joe came back with the food and conversation ceased. Gen got the distinct impression no one wanted him to know what they'd been talking about. Everyone busied themselves with their food, and before long, Red and Benny said their goodbyes. Soon after, Deb and Dave stood to leave. Gen gave them both a hug.

'Sorry it's been a while, and thanks for the tip.'

'Don't thank us.' Debra elbowed her husband in his stomach. 'Bugalugs here should have kept his mouth shut.'

They waved one last goodbye and walked away to their BMW tourer.

Back at her bike, Gen geared up as fast as she could. There was no need for her friends to be so over-protective. She'd grown up on the fringes of bikie culture, understood how the clubs worked. At least now she had a club and a name to work with – if you could count K2 as a name. Now she just had to track him down.

11

Gen flew through the first twisty section of the Old Pacific Highway, starting each corner wide, counter-steering to initiate the lean in and then gently twisting the throttle, feeding in power to exit the turn. She kept her chin pointed to the furthest bit of clear road she could see; if she let herself get distracted by anything on the outside of the turn she'd end up where she was looking.

Not unlike the current police investigation. They might have followed every lead at the farm, but had they looked further afield? Or had they concluded that Stubenitsky was Amber's abductor because that's all they'd focused on? Gen had to be careful not to do the same. She needed to consider the remote possibility Amber had decided to leave Hugh, and even look into her dad's biker circles and any potential connection to one percenters. The answer could also lie in the foster child, Roger, or be related to Hugh's unusual behaviour the night she disappeared.

She guided the bike around a wider turn. A rock face rushed past on her right, and through the bush on her left she glimpsed the gleaming waters of the Hawkesbury River.

But what if she discovered something she couldn't step back

from? Something that could have serious consequences for the kids? She'd already failed Amber once. Was she being selfish, trying to relieve her guilt by proving it hadn't been a random attack?

The road curved sharply. She glanced up and a red four-wheel drive filled her vision. *Shit!* She'd taken the bend too late. Jerking the handlebars to the left, she managed to pull the bike out of the turn just in time. One second later she would have hit them, gone flying over her handlebars and slammed into the rock wall. She wouldn't have survived.

Sucking in breaths, she reduced her speed. Her hands shook. She needed to get her head straight. As she reached Peats Ferry Bridge she pulled into the wide viewing area overlooking the water.

Her dad would be horrified. She'd broken the first rule he'd ever taught her. *Never ride while distracted, wild one, it'll get you killed.*

She removed her helmet, placed it on the seat and climbed over the steel Armco safety barrier. She sat on the railing and stared out at the Hawkesbury River, a wide expanse of tidal water spotted with oyster farms. A light wind swirled, carrying a hint of salty tang. The roar of the trucks and cars flew past on the adjacent Brooklyn Bridge, echoing her still-racing heart and thoughts. She had to address them if she was going to get home safely. She plucked her phone from her pocket and searched 'Phoenix MC Australia', then added the name 'K2'. No useful results. How else could she source the info? Who knew about MCs?

She tapped her phone against her chin. A guy at her favourite bike shop had invited her along to a clubhouse party once. She'd declined, but they'd always got along well; maybe he could help with this. Better still, there were three bike gear shops along that stretch in Auburn where she could ask. She checked the time. There was no way she'd make it to Parramatta Road before close today. She would have to wait until morning. Her phone buzzed with a message from Jesse.

What time? I'll bring pizza.

Would he know anything about Phoenix or K2?

He might, but he would warn her away like her friends had today. She stood and put her phone away.

Parramatta Road it was.

She climbed back over the barrier, geared up and kept her focus on the road the whole way home.

A familiar knock rapped on the front door. Gen raced downstairs and caught her reflection in Hugh's grandfather clock as she passed – tracksuit pants, fitted black metal tee and hair shoved into a pile on her head. Maybe she should have changed before Jesse arrived? She tucked a stray hair behind her ear.

You sure you don't like him a little bit? A voice that sounded uncannily like Amber's filled her head.

Shut up, I just want him to take me seriously.

She opened the door and Jesse held out a white pizza box, the scents of garlic, cheese and pepperoni teasing her tastebuds.

She smiled and gestured to the end of the hallway. 'Go on through.'

He placed the box on the dining table. 'Supreme still your fave?'

How on earth did he remember? She nodded. 'It's a treat not to have to decide what's for dinner. I'll grab plates.' She reached into the cupboard. Behind her a chair dragged across the floor. Gen whirled around. He'd pulled out the chair closest to the kitchen.

'No!'

Jesse stilled. His gaze searched hers, then softened. 'Amber's?'

Her face heated as she came around the bench. 'I know it's stupid.' She slid the chair back into position and ran her hands along the top of it. 'We've kept it free all these years.' Her eyes lowered. She released her hold and drifted back to the cupboard. 'I guess it doesn't matter now.'

She pulled out two plates and paused, getting the burn at the back of her throat under control.

'It's okay to miss her.' Jesse's hand came to her shoulder. She closed her eyes. She could lean back. Absorb his strength like she once had. Before he'd ditched them.

Her eyes shot open and she stepped around him. 'Beers are in the fridge.' She pointed, hoping her clipped tone would put an end to further discussion about feelings. He grabbed the beers and sat on the chair next to Amber's.

Gen carried the plates to the table, and he tracked her every move with an intensity that sent awareness skittering across her skin. She needed to steer them back to solid ground.

She sat at the table. 'I spoke to Dennis Stubenitsky's son last night.'

'How did you find him?'

Her lips twitched. 'Toni.'

'Of course.' He opened the box and offered it to her. 'I'm surprised he talked to you.'

'He was still rattled by everything, the police, the press, but as soon as I said I didn't think his dad was guilty —'

'Geneva!'

'What?'

'The last thing he needs is false hope.'

'It's not false. I don't believe a seventy-two-year-old farmer with no criminal history whatsoever suddenly decided to abduct a woman he'd never met. It's preposterous.'

'Trust me, I've seen stranger things in my time.'

'Erwin never saw his father behave violently, or wear a baseball cap.'

'What does —'

'Amber said her abductor wore a baseball cap, but Erwin swore his father hated them, thought they were stupid.'

'Maybe he bought a cap for that exact reason.'

'Oh come on.' Gen tore off a piece of pizza and munched on it aggressively. 'Okay, how do you explain the two men I heard at the property on Monday night, the ones on motorbikes?'

'Local dealers who knew the house was empty and used it as a place to store drugs. Sometimes the easiest, most obvious solution is the truth.'

'Nothing about this has ever been easy or obvious.'

'Agreed.' He chewed absently. 'I *am* surprised the sniffer dogs didn't pick up on whatever the men retrieved.'

'They would have if it were drugs, wouldn't they?'

'They were cadaver dogs, so maybe not. Each canine team is trained to track specific scents.'

'What if one of the guys at the farm was the man watching Amber's funeral?' She grabbed another slice of pizza. 'What did he say when you spoke with him?'

'The moment he saw me he ran to a motorbike and took off.'

'What kind of motorbike?'

'An older-looking touring bike.'

Like an Indian Chief. She knew it. It had to be the same man she'd seen later, at the cemetery. She paused, debating the pros and cons of telling Jesse about Phoenix.

DYING TO KNOW • 139

'Did you notice anything about him?'

'Other than the beard looking out of place against the suit? Not really.' He took a swig of his beer.

'It all seems too much of a coincidence. The strange bike rider at the funeral. The bikes at the farm.' She wiped the grease from her mouth with some paper towel, then scrunched it into a ball and tossed it onto her plate. 'I feel like I'm missing something.'

'Or you're seeing things that aren't there.'

'If that's what you really think, why are you here?'

Jesse leant back in his chair, completely unruffled by her accusatory tone. 'Anything else?'

She folded her arms across her chest. She certainly wasn't telling him about Phoenix now. 'I asked Erwin about his foster siblings. He remembered a boy called Roger, who was a bit older than him, really into motorbikes.'

Jesse raised an eyebrow.

'Roger was removed from the Stubenitskys because he was being bullied at school. Apparently Dennis was upset because wherever Roger moved to, he ended up getting involved in a gang. Considering his love of bikes, it could have been an MC. Is there any way we could find out who he was?'

'How?'

'You must work with Family and Community Services in your job. Couldn't you ask one of the case workers to check the Stubenitskys' foster care records?'

Before Jesse could answer, Gen's phone rang.

'Sorry, I have to get this.' She accepted the call. 'Charlie!'

Crying and sniffling filled the line.

'Charlie?' Gen cupped the phone closer to her ear. 'Are you okay?'

There was no response, just more sobbing. Gen met Jesse's concerned gaze and shook her head in confusion. 'Honey, talk to me. What's wrong?'

'I want ... to come ... home.'

'Take a deep breath, sweetheart.' Two slow exhales and inhales came down the line. 'Good. Now tell me what's going on?'

'Lily had a huge fight with Grandpa and ran out the front door.' His breath hiccupped. 'It's my fault she got in trouble.'

'Lily's run away?'

His crying increased.

'It's going to be okay, Charlie. I'll sort it out.' Gen put her free hand out to Jesse. *I need to borrow your phone*, she mouthed. He unlocked it and handed it over. Gen dialled Lily's number, but it rang out. She sent a text.

> Lily, this is Gen on Jesse's phone. Are you okay? Call me please, I'll come and get you, wherever you are.

'Charlie, is Grandpa or Grandma there? Let me talk to them.'

'No. They say mean things about you,' he whispered.

'Sweetheart, it's okay. I'm sure —'

'Charles Forsythe, hand me your phone.' Hugh's mother's shrill voice got louder with each word. 'Is that you, Geneva?'

'Hi Helen, is everything okay?'

'Lily went for a walk, but she's back now.'

'But Charlie —'

'Overreacted.'

'Leave me alone.' Gen heard Lily shouting in the background.

'Go to your room now!' William roared.

Gen reached for her handbag, searching for her car keys. 'Perhaps I should come and try to calm things down?'

'That won't be necessary. Charles, tell your aunt everything is okay.'

'Sorry for ringing, Gen. I love you.'

'Charlie, you can call —'

'We have it from here, Geneva,' Helen interrupted. 'It might be best if you give the children some space to settle. Please don't call them. You'll see them Monday night, when Hugh gets back.'

The line went dead, and Gen stared at the phone. A roar of anger exploded from her lips. She picked up the plates and dumped them in the sink, then slumped back into her chair.

Fuck!

'Gen?' Jesse leant forward.

'What?' she half-yelled, half-spat at him.

'Are the kids okay?'

'Did it sound like they're okay? They fucking hate that mausoleum! The funeral was one of the worst days of their lives and then they were forced to go and stay with their grandparents, and I did nothing to stop it.'

'There wasn't much you could do.'

'I should have tried.' Her voice broke. 'There's no point talking about the case anymore. Thank you for the pizza.' She stood up.

'Where are you going?'

'To sit on the sand and listen to the waves until I can trust myself not to go over there.'

'I'll come to the beach with you.'

'I'm not interested in talking.'

'Don't expect you to.'

'Stop being nice to me.'

'I'll stay quiet and just walk next to you.'

'Whatever.'

She locked the house up and hiked down the hill to the beach, Jesse's silent strength a fixture by her side.

She charged along the promenade, energy shooting through her like a bullet ricocheting in a steel box. Jesse kept his promise, not uttering a word the whole way, which was more irritating than she could have predicted. She reached the edge of the beach, toed off her sneakers, strode to the high tide mark on the sand and plonked her butt down. Staring at the luminous foam, she stubbornly ignored the man beside her. Whole conversations hovered between them, unspoken.

'What are you doing here?' she snapped.

'You need someone at your back.'

'I don't mean now. I mean, why are you in our lives again?'

'I owe you.'

'It's not like we were serious, Jesse. I've had more action from Bentley welcoming me home.'

'Are you saying I kiss like a slobbering dog?'

Gen's mouth twitched and she looked to the star-littered sky. 'I can't believe you're fishing for compliments.'

'There was more than just a kiss between us, Gen.' His tone softened.

Gen pulled her knees to her chest. 'Then why did you leave?'

He was silent. Waves rolled into the shore then drew back out to sea. Their ebb and flow were inevitable, but the rhythm was varied, unpredictable, like the people in her life. She released a breath.

'Forget it. That's all in the past. What I don't understand —'

'Gen, wait. I think you need to know what happened back then.'

'I do. You got offered your dream job in the Tactical Operations Unit and jumped at it.'

'Upstairs took me off the case.'

'What? But you worked so hard.'

'That was the problem. I refused to let the investigation into Hugh drop.'

'Why?'

'When nothing of note came from his personal financials, I applied to expand the search to include Forsythe Commercial Real Estate – in particular, any accounts involving Hugh.'

'And?'

He shook his head. 'That's when the police minister requested I be removed from the case.'

'What? Why would he —'

'His golf partner at the time was William Forsythe.'

Gen sucked in a breath. How could William be allowed to step in like that? He had a clear conflict of interest. He might have resigned from the board of Forsythe Commercial Real Estate when he got into state politics, but everyone knew it was still his company. Was he just anxious to keep up appearances, or was there something to hide? A chill washed through her. Whatever it was, it was important enough to him to derail Jesse's career. She swallowed against the congealed lump of pizza rising from her gut.

'I'm so sorry, Jesse.'

'Hugh filed an official complaint about my relationship with you, which he said was inappropriately close. It was a condition of my transfer that I stay away from the family. My brother and father advised me to back right off, or my career would be finished.'

'So why have you risked it now?'

'Because I made the wrong decision. The clean break seemed easier at the time, especially after what I'd let happen between us.'

'There were two of us there, Jesse. And it was just a kiss.'

'I crossed a line. There's a reason police aren't supposed to date victims of crime.'

'I wasn't the victim.'

'No?'

Gen leant her chin on her knees and stared at the patchwork of lights on the opposite shore. Jesse's career had been as important to him back then as being a journalist had been to her.

'Do you think Hugh had something to do with Amber's death?'

'I thought he was hiding something. But between the casino camera footage and Tobias's statement, Hugh's alibi was solid, and he had no apparent motive. According to everyone, the marriage was strong.'

Gen dug her heels into the cold sand. 'What if it wasn't?'

'Explain.'

'The other day Tobias hinted that Hugh thought Amber might be about to leave him.'

'Do you believe that?'

'They were fighting a lot that last week. But she was doing everything she could to fix things, was still fully engaged. I'd have been more worried if she'd gone quiet.'

'So why did Hugh think she was leaving?'

'Something about money going missing from the joint accounts, but there has to be another explanation for that. Amber knew the turmoil of an acrimonious divorce. She wouldn't have wanted that for the kids.' Gen shivered.

Jesse slipped off his battered leather jacket, but she shook her head. 'I'm fine.'

He folded the jacket and placed it in his lap. The cedar scent of his cologne battled the salty waft of the ocean. Gen lay her cheek on her knees, facing away from him. Waves crashed gently against the shore, the foam shining white under the light of the full moon. She picked up a handful of sand and let it run through her fingers.

'How did you get into the Tactical Operations Unit then?'

'Dad called in a favour. Got me on the next trial course. I passed all the tests and —'

'Lily cried and cried when you didn't come back.'

He rubbed the back of his neck, looking anguished.

Gen ran her hands down her shins. 'You still haven't answered my question.'

'What question?'

'Why are you here now?'

'Because I want to see things through this time. With the case. With us.'

'Jesse there is not, nor will there ever be, an us.'

A pause ballooned between them. She could almost feel it getting buffeted by the wind.

'Is that why you tried to get out of seeing me today?' he asked.

She grimaced internally. 'I had to work.'

'I went by the restaurant.'

Shit. 'I needed to get out on my bike.'

'Why weren't you honest with me?'

'I don't know. I'm drowning in leads so tenuous I wonder if they're real. I'm not even sure if I'm doing the right thing pushing for further investigation. What if I'm opening up Pandora's box? I can't bear to hurt the kids more.'

'Maybe you should let it go. Live your own life. I could take another look at the case but leave you out of it?'

She pulled her knees in closer. 'Please don't tell me to walk away. Amber never would have given up on me.'

A howl of wind filled the air, and she ignored Jesse's stare.

He shifted. 'Can you promise one thing?'

She half-turned her head in acknowledgement but didn't meet his eyes.

'Don't lie to me again. And I promise I won't walk away. I've got you, Gen – even if you fall, okay?'

Silence roared louder than the crashing waves. She wasn't lying by not mentioning Phoenix, just delaying the discussion until she knew more.

He bumped her shoulder with his. 'Geneva?'

She brushed the sand from her calves and stood. 'Now we know where Amber ended up, I want to retrace her steps from that night.'

'You know the police did that already.'

'I know, I do, but I need to find some way to process what happened on her last day.'

Jesse stood. 'I'd like to come. I could answer any questions that arise about police procedure.'

Gen deliberated. It would be great to tap into his knowledge of how things ran back then. 'I'm working every day until Friday. You free straight after school starts?'

He nodded and followed her off the beach.

'I want to take my bike, it'll give us more flexibility. You happy to ride pillion?'

'If you tell me how.'

They sat on the steps and cleaned the sand from their feet before putting their shoes back on. Jesse stood and offered his hand to help her up.

The warmth of his smile hit her in the centre of her chest. She placed her palm in his, got to her feet and dropped his hand straight away. He'd been so open with her, admitted his mistakes. She took a breath. She could forgive what had happened last time, but she wouldn't forget.

12

Geneva weaved through the stalled traffic along Parramatta Road. After a nod of permission from the driver of a ute, she pulled through the gap in front of his vehicle and entered the Redline Motorcycle Accessories parking lot. She parked behind a white van, hoping to conceal her bike. If she could get information on Phoenix from one of the shops up the road, she might be able to leave Auburn without being identified.

She'd debated posing as a reporter, but authenticity was king in the world of bikes, so she'd thrown on blue frayed jeans, her bike boots and a black fitted 'born to ride' classic tee. She tied her hair into a low ponytail, wore no make-up and generally tried not to stand out. Not always easy as an almost six-foot female bike rider.

She dismounted, locked her gear away and crossed the small bridge over the creek. The weeds and grasses growing on the bank were the only hint of greenery among the concrete jungle of car yards and bike shops that made up this industrial stretch of Sydney.

Opening the door into the yellow-themed warehouse, Gen's ears filled with the loud riffs of an electric guitar. She unzipped her leather jacket and glanced around the shop as if searching for the right section. The clientele was mixed. A surfer type dude, in board shorts and a Rip Curl tee, exited past her with a small bag. In the far aisle two younger men tried on gloves, and at the checkout an older guy in expensive bike gear was paying for an armful of clothes. No doubt he owned the perfectly detailed Harley parked closest to the door; image more important than the bike itself. Her dad would have had a quick chuckle over that.

A short girl in staff uniform with blue streaks in her hair and a nose ring approached with a warm smile. She didn't exactly scream biker scene expert.

'Hi, I'm Stacey, do you need help?'

'I'm looking for casual shoes, like reinforced sneakers?'

'I'll show you what we have.' She led Gen to the shoe section. 'Have a seat.' She pointed to a tattered black vinyl bench.

A few minutes later Gen pulled on a pair of brown basketball style boots which would provide zero protection in a bike accident. She wandered back and forth in front of the mirror. She needed to find an in with Stacey. 'Do you ride?'

'A Kawasaki Ninja 250r. My parents hate it.' Stacey giggled. 'It's bright green and matches my boyfriend's.'

'Nice.' Gen smiled and toed off the boots. 'They're a no.'

'What about you?'

Bingo. 'Boyfriend or bike?'

'Both.'

'A Ducati Streetfighter.' She pulled on tan sneakers she wouldn't be caught dead in.

'And boyfriend?'

Gen leant in conspiratorially. 'Actually, maybe you can help me with that.' She glanced around. 'I met a guy at a rally a little while ago but lost his number. He was in a breakaway MC. Phoenix. Do you know them?'

Stacey scrunched up her nose. 'MCs aren't really my thing, but one of the other guys here plays on the fringes. Hey Chop,' she called out before Gen could protest. 'Have you heard of Phoenix?'

Could the girl scream it a bit louder? Gen bent to undo the laces, keeping her head down.

A man around six foot and built like a brick outhouse swaggered over.

'Heard of them. They're a closed shop. Why?'

'My friend here —'

Gen flashed her palms and shrank behind them. 'It's okay.'

'But —'

She widened her eyes at Stacey and whispered, 'Girl stuff, yeah?'

Chop looked between them and smirked. 'Now I'm interested.'

'Sorry, Chop.' Stacey shrugged. 'The sisterhood has spoken.'

His expression dropped to a sulk. 'Don't need no gossip shit anyway.'

'Naw, don't be like that.'

He started back to the counter, then called over his shoulder, 'If you change your mind, I reckon Pat at Redline could help.'

'Ahh okay, thank you.' Gen's face burned with heat. She picked up the cheap lace-ups and handed them to Stacey. 'Sorry, they're not quite right either.'

'All good.'

'Thanks so much for your help though.'

'Good luck finding your bloke.'

Gen ducked her head and exited the shop, crossing back to the Redline carpark. Asking questions at her regular bike shop could get tricky, but she needed to find the guy who'd been at Amber's funeral.

She entered the two-storey warehouse. Metal shelving was scattered higgledy-piggledy around the main floor, making the huge space like a maze. One entire wall displayed bike helmets, organised from lower-end basic colours to the high-end graphic designs. Two faded red dilapidated change rooms stood off to the left, surrounded by racks of clothing. Gen spotted Freddie at the counter, a long-term employee who had a sandy-blond ponytail, a beard to his chest and attitude galore. He waved Gen over.

'Hey gorgeous,' his voice boomed through the space. 'Watcha need today?'

'Hi Freddie. Got any aftermarket helmet headsets?' Gen knew they didn't stock them, but it gave her a reason to be in the shop.

Freddie tapped at the keyboard, his silver skull ring shifting to cover the 'O' of the word 'LOVE' tattooed across his knuckles.

Gen glanced around to make sure no one would overhear, then leant in. 'Any chance you've heard of Phoenix MC?'

He stopped typing and looked up. 'What do you want with them?'

'It's kinda private.'

'So are they.' He folded his arms across his chest. 'Tell me the reason you're looking, and I might be able to help.'

'I want to write an article —'

He shook his head. 'You definitely don't want to be sniffing around them.'

'Are they one percenters?'

His expression hardened. 'We don't stock the headsets.'

'Please Freddie, I want to write about how Raptor unjustly targeted certain people, like tattoo artists, and the impact on their livelihoods.'

He shrugged. 'Suppose it's your face to risk. Pat in the demo section can help – but, babe?' His expression turned serious. 'Tread carefully. It's such a pretty face.'

'Freddie, you're a gem.'

'So, when are you coming on a ride with me?'

Gen laughed. 'One day, I promise.'

He led her to the front of the store where they found a slender guy with sleeve tattoos that spoke of an Irish Catholic upbringing, including a claddagh, a shamrock and a Celtic cross.

'Hey Pat, this is Gen. She rides a Ducati, also has a Bonneville, and she's looking for some info.'

Pat looked her up and down. 'A little learning is a dangerous thing.'

'Ah, but knowledge is power.' Gen put her hands on her hips and looked him up and down just as he'd done.

He barked out a laugh. 'I like you already.' He waggled his eyebrows suggestively. 'How can I learn you?'

She pointed at his wedding ring.

He chuckled. 'Cheryl's been on the back of me bike for thirty years. Knows it's all in good fun.'

'I'm sure she does.' Gen glanced around the showroom, which was full of Indian brand bikes. 'They're beautiful.'

'Used to have a Harley, but with those Nike Bikies posing on 'em now, we've started calling 'em Leb sleds. I'd rather ride one of these.'

MC culture was full of blatant racism. Us and them. It was part of the gang mentality, totally out of step with the rest of society. It was why Gen had never dated anyone from an MC. That, and the sexist bullshit. Paternalism dressed up as flirtation. She had no desire to fit in with the cult-like 'do as you're told' culture. With the exception of the weekend social groups, men ruled the world of motorcycle clubs. They claimed that 'old ladies' held power, but ultimately the women and girls were expected to be subservient to the men, and women certainly weren't included in Friday night 'church', the weekly chapter meetings where decisions were made by the senior ranks. At least not in any club she'd come across.

'Freddie said you could help me with an article I'm writing on the impact of Strike Force Raptor on MCs.'

He scanned the display floor and frowned. 'Not here, but I can take lunch in thirty. Meet me at the Broken Spoke on Granville Street.'

Gen found the pub and parked on a side street around the corner. The faded paint of the curved facade and cracked ceramic tiles hinted at better times for the art deco-style building. Gen scrolled her socials while she waited, her heel jackhammering against the road.

Twenty minutes later Pat rode into the space next to hers. They entered a brightly lit public bar, the stench of yeast strong in the air. The dings and blings of the poker machine escaped as a man dressed in a fluoro vest, shorts and work boots exited the casino room. The cheering crowd of a televised boxing match roared from above the metal bar. Pat pointed to a silver table in the corner. 'Take a load off. I'll grab drinks.'

'I'll get them.'

'Never look a gift horse in the mouth, I always say. Tooheys New, thanks.'

'Food?'

'Burger, no chips.' He patted his belly like a buddha and laughed. 'Watching me weight.' He sauntered to the table.

Gen ordered and carried two schooners back to the table, hers non-alcoholic.

He took a sip then leant back in his seat. 'What do you need to know?'

It was tempting to delve straight into questions about Phoenix, but that might make him doubt her cover story. The last thing she needed was him getting suspicious.

'I'm writing an article about the impact of Raptor on individuals.'

Pat's face darkened. 'Those pigs took away me livelihood. Banned anyone associated with an outlaw MC from working in security, tow trucks, car repairs or tattoo parlours.' He pointed to his tattoos. 'Used to own my own joint. Now I have to work at that warehouse to support me family, and I don't do well with a boss.'

'That's tough.'

'The fuckers picked on us because we're easy targets. Great political punching bag. I don't wanna cause no harm to no one, but I'm not living under rules made by a society I've got no respect for and that has no respect for me. You know what I mean?'

Gen nodded.

'We're just a bunch of mates who liked to get together, tinker with our bikes and party. No different from any club. Our clubhouse was in an industrial area; we didn't bother no one. We even ran toy drives for the children's hospital.'

'So what happened?'

'After the bullshit between the Comancheros and Hells Angels at Sydney airport it all went to shit. Look at our pres. The cops caught him with a bit of dope. He had no police record and they went after him anyway. He had to leave the country.'

Now she was getting somewhere. 'So your club still exists?'

'We broke away.' He chuckled. 'Now we're a drinking club with a bike problem.' His chuckles turned into guffaws. 'The cops might have taken away our clubhouse, but we've found a way around. I have a farm out in the boonies, with a stage for bands, a fire pit and kegs. You should visit sometime.'

'Oh wow, thanks.' *Wow?* Christ, she sounded like a groupie.

'You'd have to come on a ride first though. Only way I know I can trust you.'

'Fair enough.'

The waitress slid two plates in front of them and snatched up the number from the table. 'Anything else?'

Gen shook her head. Pat nicked a chip from her plate. She pushed the plate into the middle of the table, and he laughed and helped himself. She ate a few bites of her burger, then put it down. Time to dive in.

'So a few groups broke away from the big MCs? I heard of one called Phoenix. Do you know of them?'

He grunted. 'Surprised you do.' He licked the last of his burger from his fingers.

'A friend met them on a ride.'

'God I miss those.' He wiped the napkin across his face. 'You should have seen us in 2010. We did a run to Gosford. Four thousand bikes. Colours and banners flying everywhere. Nothing the pigs could do because we outnumbered them. The road was full of Harleys and bikers. Real bikers, not the thugs you find these days. They've fucked it up for everyone. Especially the Mongrels. Mongrels is right, they're just crooks.'

She had to get him back on track. 'Are Phoenix part of that crowd?'

'They can be mean motherfuckers. You don't want to land in their sights and neither do I. I'm not saying any more about them.'

Damn. She sipped at her drink. His expression had soured. She had to put him back at ease.

'What about Ulysses?'

'Now there's a true social club. Weekend warriors.'

'My friend David rode with them after the Vietnam War.'

'Lots of the old timers joined up after 'Nam. It's hard to find the kind of mateship you develop in war when you return home, people who respect the bond, and that's rule number one in an MC. In the real clubs, I mean. That new lot don't care about loyalty, they just want to flash their cash around wearing stupid diamond earrings and arse-showing jeans. Most of them don't even own a bike. How the fuck the cops see them as the same as us real bikers is anyone's guess. Total bullshit.'

Gen wasn't going to get any more information about Phoenix out of Pat.

'Sorry, I think we've been longer than thirty minutes. Do you need to get back?'

He skolled the last of his beer. 'Let me know if you need to chat again. Nice to have lunch with a pretty lady.'

'I wouldn't say it like that to your wife.'

He chuckled as they walked out to their bikes. She waved him off. What a total waste of time. She'd have been better off asking Jesse. Now she'd have to wait until their trip on Friday.

13

Gen kicked off her shoes at the front door. Her feet throbbed after a twelve-hour shift, but doing a double was the only way she could get Friday off and still be around for the kids. She unpacked the taco ingredients she'd bought on the way home. A zing of excitement charged through her. Lily and Charlie would be home any minute.

She poured a dash of olive oil into a saucepan, seared the skirt steak then added taco spice mix and water, and turned up the heat.

Would Lily still be angry with her? She'd been furious at Gen for not standing up to Hugh, for not stopping him from taking them to his parents'. And what about Charlie? He'd been beside himself on the phone. Gen wiggled her jaw to release the tension. God, she wished she'd managed to secure some kind of legal say in their lives. The blunt tone of the lawyer she'd visited years ago skidded into her head.

'*You have no legal recourse, and even if you did, could you afford to fight the money and influence their father has behind him?*'

'*Surely with his alcohol issues …*'

'He has addressed that by attending rehab. Your best bet, if you want to remain in the children's lives, is to play nice. Make yourself needed.'

The smell of burnt meat tugged her back to the present. 'Oh shit!'

She snatched the saucepan from the stove and inspected the damage. She could salvage the top layer, but the meat on the bottom was inedible. She scooped the unaffected meat into a fresh pan.

What Charlie and Lily really needed was Amber, so maybe it was only right that Gen was on the outer, toeing a line she detested.

She scraped the burnt meat into the bin, put the pan in the sink to soak, and returned to the mixture she'd saved.

Tonight, she would make sure they enjoyed a peaceful family meal. Friday's funeral had put a strain on them all. She also had to find some way to stop Hugh questioning her suitability as the children's primary carer.

Tasting a small mouthful of the meat, her shoulders sank. She added water, powdered chilli and some paprika, crossing her fingers the extra spice would mask the burnt tang. She returned the mixture to a low simmer, grated a large bowl of cheese, chopped up lettuce, tomato and onion, and turned on the oven, ready for the tacos.

A moment later the front door swished open.

'Gen?' Charlie called eagerly. It might only have been three days, but it was the longest they'd been apart since she'd moved in.

She raced to the front hall. Charlie dropped his overnight bag and wrapped his arms around her, and she squeezed him tight, burying her face in his hair.

She looked up at Lily. 'I've missed you both so much.' Her gaze dropped momentarily to her niece's outfit. A white knee-length baggy broderie anglaise dress and beige ballet flats. Where the hell had that ugly ensemble come from?

'For goodness sake, it's only been three days.' Hugh pushed past them all. Heat flared inside Gen, but she'd promised herself she'd make tonight work.

'Do you want me to say I missed you too?' she teased.

'I wouldn't believe you.' He glared over his shoulder, but the corners of his mouth lifted. Sometimes it felt like Hugh was an annoying little brother she had to manage.

She unwound herself from Charlie and faced Lily, arms outstretched. Lily stepped into her embrace and Gen breathed her first full breath since Friday. She rubbed her niece's shoulder blades and Lily's body relaxed. Then Lily's pocket buzzed. She disengaged from Gen and followed her father down the hall, focus buried in her phone.

At least she'd hugged her back.

Gen picked up the kids' discarded overnight bags and dropped them near the stairs to the laundry, then joined the rest of the family in the kitchen.

'How was Melbourne?' She turned to Hugh who sat at the dining table, tapping on his phone. He swiped up and his mouth thinned.

'Hugh?'

He looked up with a scowl.

'You okay?'

'Fine. What stinks in here?'

Great. Back to cranky pants. She took a breath.

What would Amber do?

Gen stepped up to the stove and stirred the meat. 'That enticing scent is tonight's dinner.'

'Smells like crap.'

Gen swallowed the swear word wobbling precariously on the tip of her tongue. She picked out a small amount of the mixture and tasted it. 'It's fine.'

'We ate at my parents' house.' Hugh poured himself a whiskey and headed for his office. 'I've a tonne of work. I'll be here early in the week but have to go to Melbourne on Thursday. You'll be around to attend Lily's scholarship interview on Friday? She needs a guardian with her.'

'Wouldn't miss it for anything.'

Hugh's office door clicked shut.

'I want tacos. Five.' Charlie's voice lowered to a whisper. 'The chicken cockle, whatever, had mushrooms. Dis-gusting.'

'Coq au vin,' Lily corrected.

Gen stepped between them before war erupted. 'Five tacos coming up. Charlie, would you please take the bags to the laundry for me?' He carried them downstairs while Gen filled a tray with taco shells. 'How many do you want, Lil?'

'None. I've got homework to do.' She moved towards the stairwell.

Gen gritted her teeth. The Forsythes would have insisted Lily's homework was finished yesterday. Gen couldn't let her hide in her room again.

'I was hoping you'd tell me about your weekend,' she said in the least demanding tone she could manage. She placed the tray in the oven and turned back to find Lily slumped onto a chair.

'It was exactly what I knew would happen. Dad dumped us there Friday. The only time we spent with Grandma and Grandpa was on Saturday at a photoshoot, and tonight at dinner.'

'A photoshoot?' Gen's gaze narrowed.

'Some stupid magazine article.'

So *that's* what the weekend visit was about. A publicity stunt for William's political campaign. Forget what the kids needed. She took a steadying breath. 'What did you do the rest of the time?'

With a flourish, Lily gestured to her outfit. 'Mrs Wood, the *nanny*, took us shopping for more "appropriate clothing".' She made air quotes with her fingers. 'I worked with a flute tutor both days. Mrs Wood took Charlie to his basketball game and training, and the rest of the time we were told to stay quiet in our rooms while Grandpa entertained important visitors.' She glared at Gen.

'I'm sorry, sweetheart, but they're your grandparents. I couldn't stop your dad taking you there.'

'Grandpa only wanted us there for his stupid political shit.'

'That's a dollar to the swear jar,' Charlie teased gleefully, ambling back into the room.

'Let's send that one to the keeper, okay mate?'

'Can I get a glass of milk?' he asked.

Gen nodded, then sat opposite Lily. 'You going to tell me what happened Saturday night?'

'Grandpa was laying into Charlie about not behaving like a proper Forsythe man and I told him to back off. He said I'd better learn how to behave, or he'd teach me some manners, or let a boarding school do it for him. I couldn't take being there anymore, so I ran. I was just in the park up the street. I needed to get away from them.'

Charlie sat heavily beside Lily. 'It was my fault.' His upper body caved in on itself. 'I was crying. Lil just tried to protect me.'

'It's okay to cry, Charlie. Don't ever let anyone tell you otherwise.' Gen glanced between them. 'I'm so sorry, guys. I'll ask your dad not to send you there again.'

Tears pooled in Lily's eyes. 'What if Dad sends me away, like Grandpa threatened?'

Gen reached across the table and took their hands. She made sure Lily met her gaze before she spoke. 'I'll never let anyone send you away.' Lily grasped tighter onto Gen's hand.

At least the kids were back safe under her care. She'd have to find a way to get through to Hugh. He'd always told Amber how much he hated growing up in that house. Surely he'd understand how the kids felt.

Lily wiped her eyes. 'I have to get out of these clothes. I feel like some kind of Amish mail-order bride. Then I do have to do some prep for Friday's scholarship stuff.'

'How about I bring you in a hot chocolate to drink while you study?'

'Yes please.'

Gen gave Charlie a hug on her way back to the kitchen. He moved to a stool at the bench and Gen set an empty plate in front of him. She placed all the components for tacos between them and they ate. He didn't complain once about the slightly burnt taste of the meat.

Half an hour later, Gen walked upstairs with a hot chocolate and knocked on Lily's door. No response. She cracked the door open a little. 'Lil, I have your drink.'

Still no answer. She poked her head around the corner and Lily jumped and stuffed something under the covers.

'You're not supposed to come in without knocking.'

'I did knock. You didn't answer.' Gen's gaze flicked to the lump under Lily's hand. She placed the mug on the bedside table. 'You know you can talk to me about anything?'

'There's nothing to talk about.' She grabbed her closed computer and opened it. 'I have work to do.'

It was a clear dismissal.

'Fine, but not too late to sleep, okay?'

Lily nodded and began typing. Gen pulled the door closed behind her and wrapped her arms around her waist, resisting the urge to burst back into the room and gather Lily in her arms. If only she would open up about what was going on.

Between working and helping the kids settle down, it had been an exhausting week. Lily, constantly distracted by her phone, withdrew more and more each day, slipping up to her room every chance she got.

On Friday morning, for the first time ever, Lily missed the school bus. Gen threw on jeans and a Harley tee she grabbed from her dirty clothes pile and herded the kids to the car.

She weaved in and out of the bumper-to-bumper traffic, determined to deliver both children to school on time. She dropped Charlie with five minutes to spare, then cut through back streets and pulled up at the ornate wrought-iron gates of Shellwood Ladies College just as the old-fashioned school bell tolled.

'I'll meet you here at two-thirty and we can walk to the exam together then head over to the interview.'

Her niece didn't move.

'Lil? Sweetheart, the bell's rung.'

Lily looked at her, tired smudges beneath her eyes.

Gen engaged the park brake and faced her niece. 'Talk to me.'

'What if I don't want to go to this school anymore?'

'You're not happy here?'

Lily shrugged and looked out the passenger window. Gen hated losing the chance to read her face.

'What if I don't get the scholarship?' She spoke almost under her breath.

Gen wanted to grab a hold of her and never let go. Instead, she tucked her hands between her thighs and kept her tone light. 'We'll deal with it.'

'Right.' Exasperation flooded Lily's tone.

'Sweetheart, what's all this about?'

'Never mind.'

'Whatever happens, we'll face it together.'

Lily sighed. 'I'd better go.' She collected her bag and climbed from the car.

Gen opened the passenger window and leaned over, trying to catch Lily's eye. 'Love you.'

'You too,' Lily mumbled, then turned and walked through the gates, eyes to the ground.

Something was really wrong. Gen switched off the engine and grabbed her handbag from the backseat.

A knock rapped on the driver's side window. One of the school security guards circled his hand in the air, gesturing for her to wind the window down.

'Ma'am, is everything okay?'

'Yes, I …' Gen turned to look for Lily, but she'd disappeared.

'I'm going to have to ask you to move on.'

Gen checked the gates again.

'Now please, ma'am.'

She restarted the engine and drove off, the ache in her chest growing more painful the further she got from her niece. Maybe she should cancel the ride with Jesse today? Make an appointment with Lily's mentor at school instead?

But Lily had her scholarship exam this afternoon. She took a deep breath. *What would Amber do?*

She'd tell Gen to stop overreacting. Of course Lily felt overwhelmed today – the exam was a big deal, she was bound to be struggling, especially after everything that had happened the week before.

She entered her street, and Jesse's ute was parked just before the turning circle. She drove into the carport and switched off the engine.

Jesse sat on the front steps, wearing blue jeans and an unzipped black leather jacket with a white tee underneath. He turned his phone over and over in his hands, his gaze on her. Her stomach flipped. Their conversation on the beach seemed to have pierced the armour she'd built against him. And that wasn't safe.

Nor was the impending proximity of their bodies on her bike.

She opened the car door and half-stood. 'Sorry I'm late, I had to drop Lily at school.' She gestured to the passenger seat as he walked towards her. 'We might take this instead, it'll make for a more comfortable day.'

His warm smile lost its shine for a moment, then grew wider. 'No way. You promised me a ride on the back of your dad's bike.'

'You may regret it after a few hours.'

'No pain, no gain, right?'

His smile had to be the most infectious one she'd ever encountered, other than Charlie's.

She locked the car. 'Don't complain when your butt gets sore.' She entered her workshop, pulled on her jacket and boots, and waved him over to her dad's old bike.

'Before we head off, some safety tips. We won't be able to hear each other, so if there's a problem, tap my leg three times and I'll pull over. Okay?'

He nodded.

'It'll feel counterintuitive, but you need to let your weight lean into corners. The easiest way to do that is if you look over my shoulder in the direction we're turning. Left turn, left shoulder.'

'Got it.' He rested against her work bench, legs crossed at the ankles, as calm as could be.

'Don't make any sudden moves, and if we have to go over a speed bump or rough patch, it helps to lift your bum like you would on a horse. There are handles near your hips here, to help you feel more secure, particularly at speed.' She pointed them out, avoiding eye contact. 'Or you can hold my waist if that feels safer.'

He didn't move or say a word. She met his gaze.

'You okay with this?' he asked.

'Yes. Just don't make it weird.' She walked to the shelf, snagged a spare helmet and held it out to him. 'Try this, see how it fits.'

She picked up her helmet. 'Hold it by the straps, like this, and pull them apart. Forehead in first, then slide the helmet on.' He followed her instructions like a pro. She stepped closer, did up the straps and wiggled the helmet about on his head. Her gaze slid to his. Every time they were face to face he watched her too closely, like he was peeling back her layers. The bike might be the better option after all.

She stepped back. 'Fits well.' She put her helmet on, swung her leg over the seat, kicked the foot stand up and turned the ignition key on. 'Keep your weight to the centre of the bike, like you would if you were mounting a horse. Hold on to my shoulders and swing your leg —'

He'd settled in behind her before she'd finished her sentence. Right behind. Every inch of his thighs was pressed against hers. She pushed the starter button and the engine rumbled to life. She forced herself to focus on that sensation instead.

'Ready?' she shouted.

He gave her a thumbs up and she closed her visor.

Driving up the street, she concentrated completely on the bike, getting a feel for its manoeuvrability with the extra weight on the back.

Jesse leant into the first corner as if he'd done it a thousand times before. His hands stayed loose yet very present at her hips.

Five minutes later they entered the laneway behind the supermarket where Amber had gone missing. Gen parked the bike in the only free spot in the car park, one away from where Amber's car had been found. Cold rippled through her. She switched off the engine and removed her helmet.

'I'm going to wander around. See if I can get any idea of why she might've been targeted.'

'Case detectives sometimes re-enact what they think happened. Do you want to try that? You play Amber and I'll be her abductor?'

She nodded. 'I'll start over there.'

Striding past the spot where Amber had parked, she crossed the lane and climbed the narrow set of stairs leading to the main street of Mosman. At the top, she turned left and entered the supermarket, spotting fisheye lens security cameras that were far more sophisticated than the ones that had been in place twelve years ago.

She found the baby goods aisle and her mouth dried. If she had gone to the shops that night, would the abductor have targeted her instead? She bent her knees, trying to see the world the way Amber would have. At half a foot shorter, her sister would have struggled to reach the top shelf. Maybe it was as simple as that. Maybe she asked someone for help. The wrong someone.

Gen expelled a loud huff. Now she was doing it. Blaming Amber like the reporters had as the weeks drew out after her abduction.

Abductee Amber Forsythe: living a secret life.

Amber Forsythe, was she having an affair?

Mothers who run from responsibility: a deep dive into the mind of Amber Forsythe.

The only person to blame for Amber's abduction and death was the person who took her.

Gen marched through the checkout and hurried back to the car park.

Back down in the laneway, Jesse, who she'd forgotten was supposed to be following her, stood two car spaces before the ute taking up the spot where Amber's car had been found.

Just like Amber had described her attacker doing.

Gen's body felt like live wire.

She retrieved an imaginary key and pretended to bleep open the car doors. Tucking her chin down, she walked with speed, taking a wide berth around Jesse. His stare followed her. Her breath shallowed. She charged towards the driver's door of the ute.

Large hands grabbed her by the shoulders. Gen whirled around, fists raised.

'Whoa, it's me. You're okay.'

A tremor rippled through her and Jesse pulled her against his chest. Had Amber's body felt primed to flee like Gen's just had? Had she dismissed the instincts screaming at her?

Gen slid from Jesse's hold and returned to her bike. She flexed and closed her fingers a few times, then grabbed her helmet and climbed on.

'Did you follow me into the supermarket?'

'Yes.'

Gen put on her helmet. How had she missed him? Unlike Amber, she'd known she was being followed. 'How did you get back to the car park before I did?'

'I slipped out before you got to the register.'

'I want to see the supermarket videos from that night. And the casino footage. Can you get them for me?'

'Gen, you're not a police officer. A team of detectives went over it frame by frame.' He tilted his head. 'I thought today was about closure.'

'It is, but what if I can pick up a detail about Amber they wouldn't know to look for.'

'I can't justify accessing the evidence now I'm at Youth Command. All downloads are recorded against our login details.'

'But —'

He put up a palm. 'If it will help you finally move on, I'll see if my brother can get you access.'

She'd follow up with Toni too, see what her police contact could get.

'Let's keep going.' She shut her visor and waited for Jesse to gear up.

Ten minutes later they entered the feeder lane for the Harbour Bridge. They passed the second set of concrete pylons and turned onto the Cahill Expressway. To their left, a panorama of deep blue water connected the Opera House, Circular Quay and Milsons Point. This was why she rode a bike. Did the people in the SUV behind even notice the sun's rays bouncing off the wake of the ferry, or the shimmering sparkle of the water through the dark tinted windows of their vehicle?

Following the M5 out of the city, they eventually reached Campbelltown. Trucks and cars jostled between the lanes. Gen's focus narrowed to the cars immediately around her, prepared for sudden lane changes.

Forty minutes later, just after the bridge over Gibbergunyan

Creek, she decelerated, easing the bike onto a verge. The black SUV that had been behind them since the city flew past.

Turning onto the access road, she slowed further. Her mouth dried. This was the place where Amber's phone had been found, where the signal had dropped out that night. She guided the bike deeper into the bush, lifting her backside to accommodate the rocky terrain. Jesse followed her lead. A hundred metres along, there was an easement to the left. She pulled in and switched off the engine.

Eucalypts surrounded the area, their bark covered in tiny scribbles made by moth larvae. A thick undergrowth of wild grass covered the ground surrounding the tall cream trunks. Such an average Australian bush location. No landmarks, no hiking trails, no reason to even pull in. An ache rose in her throat. Was this where Amber spent the last moments of her life?

Her body swayed as Jesse got off the bike. She kicked the bike stand down and dismounted. Small rocks crunched beneath her boots. Gen stared out over the bush. Amber's phone had been found in the undergrowth, about fifty metres into the scrub, the screen completely shattered. Police photos showed no discernible tyre or foot impressions on the easement – it was as if the entire area had been swept. Search dogs had located a fist-sized rock buried in the undergrowth in the opposite direction from the phone. The sandstone had been covered in Amber's blood. Gen squeezed her eyes shut.

'No. No! Please, no!'

Slaps of fists and palms against flesh. A loud thud, a crack.

'You okay?' Jesse asked.

She blinked and stared into his eyes until the ghost screams faded and the bird sounds and traffic noise returned.

'What do you think happened?'

He searched her face, then shoved his hands in his pockets. 'I agree with the coroner's conclusions. Amber was killed here and then her body was taken to Windsor to be buried.'

She walked along the edge of the bush. 'But why not bury her here?'

'No time. Her phone had been smashed intentionally, so we concluded her attacker found it, saw she'd been on a call and got the hell out of here before the cops arrived.'

'Okay but why not leave her here?'

'They could have been worried about evidence on the body.'

'But they left the rock behind.' She crossed her arms across her stomach. 'What if she wasn't dead when they left here?'

'Gen,' he touched his palm to her upper arm. 'Chances are we'll never know what happened that night but allowing your imagination to run wild will only lead to more pain.'

She shrugged him off. 'Coming to this place has just made me angry, made me want to search harder for answers.' She checked her watch. 11:08 am.

'Let's go.' She tilted her head towards the bike. 'I need to be back at Lily's school at two-thirty.'

They geared up and Gen steered the bike back onto the motorway, watching for a spot where she could legally turn around and join the northbound lanes. As the gap to cross appeared up ahead, a roar of engines filled her helmet. Four Harley-Davidsons flew past, pulled into the two lanes in front of her and hit the brakes. Gen reacted instantly, working to keep the bike under control. *Idiots!*

Two sports bikes pulled up either side of her, keeping pace. Her gaze darted to her rear-view mirror. A black SUV, flanked by two more Harleys, closed in from behind. What the fuck were they playing at?

Jesse twisted to look back and the bike shifted. Gen pulled his leg closer to hers, hoping he got the message to lean into her. She didn't need him destabilising the bike.

She scanned the riders. All men, dressed identically in black, from their boots, jeans and leather jackets to their full-face helmets and gloves. There was nothing to identify them, and smears of mud masked every number plate.

Gen squinted into the mirror, trying to identify the car's driver, but the tinted windows hid the interior. She couldn't even make out how many people were in the vehicle.

She gripped the handlebars tighter. This was no impromptu stunt.

The pack slowed, forcing her to decelerate with them. She gauged the gap between the bikes in front. If she were on her own and on her sports bike, she might have had a chance of breaking away, but with two of them on the Bonneville there was nothing she could do.

A chill slithered up her spine. Jesse was a policeman. Is that why they were being targeted? What did these men plan to do?

The bikes turned right, and Gen had no choice but to comply. They cut across the northbound lanes onto Belanglo Road and followed it until they traversed a bridge. The surface transitioned to gravel, and a sign welcomed them to Belanglo State Forest. Gen swallowed. *It's okay. We're going to be okay. It's just a misunderstanding. We'll be on our way again soon.*

They forced her into a turnout area about a kilometre from the motorway. The SUV pulled in front, and the rumbling bikes surrounded her. She checked the road behind and in front for a passer-by, but the area was deserted. She killed the engine and twisted to Jesse.

He shoved his visor up.

'No! Keep your visor down. If they recognise you as a cop, this could escalate rapidly.'

'I'll handle this.' He lifted his body in preparation to dismount.

Gen pushed him back down. 'At least stay on the bike with me.'

The men switched off their engines. Quiet flooded the air.

The back door of the SUV opened, and a pair of black boots with silver hardware stepped into view.

Jesse stiffened behind her, and she squeezed his leg. He had to stay calm.

A huge man, six foot five and wider than a rugby prop, folded himself from the back seat of the car and turned to Gen. He was dressed in black leathers, wore wraparound sunglasses and a black kerchief covering his nose, mouth and neck. He strode towards them, an open-faced helmet in his right hand.

'Geneva Leighton.'

Her pulse tripped. The man had said her name like a flirty caress, as if they were old friends. She drew herself up tall. 'And you are?'

Ignoring her question, the man spread his legs, folded his muscular arms across his huge chest. 'Off the bike, pig.'

Oh shit. 'Please leave him alone.'

Jesse removed his sunglasses and crossed his arms. 'Walk away now, before things get out of hand.'

'Think you're in charge here, Johns?' the large man sneered.

Double shit.

'You going to hurt a cop?' Jesse taunted him.

Her heart raced, pounding like it was going to explode. *Shut up, Jesse!*

'Nah, gonna let you stew in the SUV while Geneva here comes for a little ride.'

'She's not going anywhere with you.'

'Eleven against two.' The man's tone was filled with ridicule. 'Whatcha going to do?'

Two more men climbed from the SUV, their faces masked by kerchiefs and sunglasses. They stood tall, arms folded across their barrel chests, unmoving.

She blinked rapidly. Someone needed to defuse the situation.

Gen faced the large man, infusing her voice with more bravado than she felt. 'Where do you want to take me?'

'If you do as you're told neither of you will be hurt.'

Her mouth dried. He hadn't answered her question. These men weren't like any bikers she knew. The men of the clubs could be impulsive, but kidnapping was extreme. Were these men even bikers or just criminals?

She exhaled a shaky breath.

'You promise we'll *both* be safe if I come with you?'

He nodded. 'We'll even let you ride your own bike. We just want a chat.'

She stared at the man.

Jesse angled himself closer. 'You can't go with them.'

'Do you know who they are?'

'No.'

'I'm losing patience,' the stranger growled.

Jesse shifted, looking about again, as if assessing his chances.

Gen squeezed his leg. 'There's no other way.' She lifted her chin at the man, her heart in her throat. 'I'll go with you.'

Jesse dismounted, tore off his helmet and leant in, his lips touching hers. He whispered against them, 'If you get a chance to escape, take it.'

'N—'

He smothered her refusal with an open-mouthed kiss. The bikers hollered. After a moment of shocked stillness, she relented and played her part. He eased back until his lips just brushed hers again. 'Better for them to think we're a couple. Remember what I said.'

'No.'

'Promise me.'

'Put your dick back in your pants, Johns. You'll see her soon enough.'

Gen grabbed his cheeks. 'Don't do anything stupid.'

'I'll be fine. You focus on staying safe.'

Two men stepped up next to Jesse, grabbed him by the arms and led him to the SUV. He twisted, struggling against their hold.

'Not one hand on her,' he shouted back. One of the men shoved Jesse's head down and forced him into the back seat. They climbed in either side of him.

Gen swallowed down her terror. *Please stay safe.*

The group's leader stepped in, blocking her line of sight. Her breath shallowed. What now?

'Phone.' He put out his hand and she reluctantly pulled her phone from her jacket. He switched it off and zipped it away in his pocket.

'Follow me. And don't try anything funny,' he said, and jerked his chin towards the SUV, 'or he'll pay.'

Without another word, he put on his helmet, mounted the long-handled Harley in front of her and started it up. She engaged the ignition on her own bike, blood rushing in her ears. What choice did she have? These men would enjoy hurting Jesse, that much was clear.

The other bikes started up, their deafening roar thundering through her chest. Gen's breath burst in and out sharply. The riders peeled off, dust rolling behind them, leaving just her and the man in charge. He did a U-turn and led her back to the motorway. They headed north.

14

Windsor turnoff, three kilometres. Gen read the sign and her mouth turned to sandpaper. Was she being taken to the farm where Amber had been found?

They reached the turnoff a few minutes later but drove straight on through the roundabout towards Richmond instead. They'd been riding going on ninety minutes.

She forced herself to take deep, controlled breaths. Adrenaline would serve her well, but only if she didn't let it overload her.

Bushland flashed past and a eucalypt scent filled her helmet. A sign welcomed them to Londonderry. The scent dissipated and they rode on.

Gen struggled to control her racing thoughts. Is this how Amber had felt in the boot of the car? Scared. Second-guessing everything. A wave of shame washed through Gen. Their situations weren't even close to being the same. Amber had been hit without warning, then woken in the dark, alone and terrified. Gen had spoken with her abductor, had even been assured of her safety.

If the man's word could be trusted, that was. A bead of sweat ran down her neck.

After what felt like forever, they pulled alongside a wire security fence. A row of fir trees blocked any view of the land beyond. The man slowed, turned right and pulled up at a gate. He removed his kerchief and sunglasses, eyeballed a camera on a pole and the gate opened.

Gen glanced back to the road. Following him in there would be stupid. She'd be trapped.

An image of Jesse being bundled into the SUV flashed in her mind.

She rolled her shoulders and followed the man through to a second perimeter fence and another gate with a camera. They drove through, and a huge property opened out before them, completely ringed by the fence and fir trees. A large dam lay at the centre. Spaced evenly around it stood six structures, the largest a two-storey corrugated-iron building.

They parked beside the building, and the side door swung open. No one appeared.

The man dismounted and removed his helmet. Gen followed suit, then froze. He'd shown his face. Her gaze dropped to her feet. *Shit.*

'Nice ride.' His voice came from beside her.

'Thanks.' Her stare remained fixed on the ground.

He chuckled. 'You're going to have to look up sometime.'

Sweat covered her palms. She looked up into the most intense ice-blue eyes she'd ever seen. Long black eyelashes and matching shoulder-length hair would have made him almost pretty, if it weren't for the thick black whiskers covering his chin. Above the neckline of his black tee, tattooed wing tips escaped, finishing at his collar bone.

He grinned, aware of the impact he made. It dimmed his attractiveness.

'This way.'

He led Gen to the open barn door. Male voices and laughter echoed from within, and her guts surged. As soon as she walked in there, she'd be outnumbered again. She slowed, looked back at her bike. Maybe it would be safer to make a run for it. But they had Jesse. *Fuck!*

Stillness in her peripheral vision drew her attention. The man had stopped walking.

'I gave you my word: no one will touch you.'

'How do I know your word means anything?'

'You don't, but what are you going to do? Run?' He swept his open palm in invitation towards the door. 'Ladies before arseholes.'

She lengthened her spine and stepped through the door. Wolf whistles and catcalls greeted her from the men spread around the bar-like space. There was a smaller room extending from the far wall, and to the right, a doorway led down a corridor.

She surveyed the main area. A long metal bar stretched the length of three full-sized glass-fronted fridges, filled to the brim with drinks. Above them, the club motto, Family Reborn, was emblazoned on the wall. It sat alongside a framed vest displaying the club logo: a mythical bird, wings outstretched, surrounded by fire. Her pulse skittered. This was Phoenix headquarters.

Gen moved into the room, scanning the men. Most were muscular, covered in tattoos and wearing their biker cuts – leather vests displaying their logo and rockers. She stopped and the man behind ran into her.

She instinctively jumped away from the contact.

'Should nickname her Rabbit,' one of the men sitting at a long table drawled. He threw his head back with a bellow of laughter, revealing a tattoo of a skull covering his entire neck. Beside him, in a high-backed chair, sat a man made of pure muscle, with an undeniable presence and energy. The ringmaster of this circus.

'You're okay, babe,' her escort whispered in her ear. She tensed.

The men hollered louder, making lewd gestures. 'Mac's found himself some pussy,' a bear of a man yelled out. Gen's head whipped in his direction.

'Fuck off.' The comment slipped from her mouth before she could think better of it. Her gaze snapped to the man in charge. His eyes, the same striking blue as the man they'd just referred to as Mac, drilled into her, stern and unmoving, then a deep baritone laugh burst from his mouth.

'You're no rabbit are you, gypsy girl?' said Mac.

'My name is Geneva.'

'Gypsy suits you better.' Phoenix's leader stood, and, *holy moly*, he was tall. Gen was an inch off six feet, but this man towered over her. He ambled behind the bar and opened a fridge. 'Beer? Water? Soft drink?'

This had to be the most bizarre situation Gen had ever been in. She took a deep breath. 'Why am I here?'

'The name's Viking. I'm the president of Phoenix.'

'And the rest of the ... crew?'

The shutters came down on Viking's face. He slammed a bottle of water on the bar, dragged a metal stool out to the middle of the space and pointed at it. 'Sit.'

Shit. She sat, tucking her shaking hands between her thighs.

Viking returned to his throne, legs sprawled, and took a swig of his Coke.

'Talk.'

'What about?'

'Don't play innocent. You've been asking around about our club.'

She ran a palm over her hair. 'I'm doing a story on the impact of Strike Force Raptor and —'

'Bullshit.'

'Excuse me?'

'My bullshit radar never fails, and you are spewing your brand all over us. Respect is the most important tenet of this club. Respect, loyalty, brotherhood and secrecy. You've managed to trash three of the four already, so I suggest you change lanes.'

Mac leant in. 'Or that cop of yours might not remain so comfortable.'

'What the fuck?' Viking nailed Mac with a glare.

'Later.' Mac cocked his head at Gen.

She scanned the faces around her: angry, tense and suspicious. She swallowed. These were dangerous men. And if she didn't tread more carefully, Jesse would pay. She nodded to the water bottle.

'May I?'

Mac handed her the bottle, and she unscrewed the lid.

Viking's radar was solid: she had no choice but to tell the truth. She took a swig of water.

'I apologise for any offence I've caused.'

'Noted.'

'My sister is Amber Forsythe.'

'We know. What's that got to do with us?'

He wasn't going to make this easy for her. 'I was asking about Phoenix because I think someone from your club came to my sister's funeral.'

His gaze slid from hers and took in each man in the room, one by one. Each shook his head.

'No one wears colours outside of the clubhouse without permission. That's how we stay off the police radar.' He glowered at Mac, who shrugged.

'The man wore a suit to the funeral, but later that day I saw the same man leaving the cemetery, wearing a cut with a phoenix on the back. Exactly the same design as yours.'

'What did he look like?'

'He had a long silver beard and drove an old-style Indian.'

'Fuck.' Viking stood and whirled on Mac. 'What the hell's Dad been doing?'

Mac put up his palms. 'I've no idea.'

'Fucking pain in our arse.' Viking paced. 'I'm starting to think he needs someone on him twenty-four seven.'

'He'd hate that.'

'Yeah, well, he'll hate it more if Raptor declare us outlaws. Everything we've worked towards will be screwed.' He snapped his gaze back to Gen. 'What about your cop?'

Her heart slammed against her ribs.

'He's not my cop. We're friends. He's helping me find out what happened to Amber. Unofficially.'

Mac stepped in. 'Didn't look like friends when he had his tongue down your throat.'

Her face warmed.

'Enough of this BS.' Viking dismissed Mac with a sweep of his hand. 'What does the cop know about us?'

'Nothing. Jesse approached the man at the funeral to find out who he was, but he rode off.' Her gaze darted between Mac and Viking. 'And I didn't mention seeing him or the Phoenix cut at the gravesite later.'

Idiot that she was. If she had and something went wrong here, at least Jesse would have some idea where to start looking for her.

'So what *did* you tell him?'

His gaze bore into her. She had to give him something else, and this could be her one chance to find out if Phoenix were involved with the farm. 'I mentioned the two guys who collected something from the house in Windsor.'

Once again, he scrutinised the surrounding men and each shook their head.

He crossed his arms. 'You talking about the farm where your sister was found?'

She nodded.

'Were the guys wearing our colours?'

'I didn't see them. I was hidden behind a door.'

Mac chuckled. 'Of course you were, gypsy girl.'

A man wearing an apron emblazoned with the image of a naked woman emerged from the corridor. 'Grub's up.'

Viking didn't take his gaze off Gen. 'You lot head out back.'

Her pulse surged. He was done with her, but what did that mean? She slid her feet to the floor, ready to run.

'What now?' Mac asked.

'Get Dad in here.'

Mac stared at Viking, a silent debate taking place between the two. Then Mac bowed with a flourish. 'As you wish, big brother.' He left the room, and Viking sat like he had the weight of the world on his shoulders.

After several minutes of excruciating silence, footsteps approached from outside.

'Where's the fucking respect?' a voice carrying the scars of at least a pack a day for forty years roared from outside.

The man Gen had seen at the funeral barged into the room, followed by Mac. The man marched up to Viking, fists clenched, gaze furious, and jabbed him in the chest. 'You don't get to summon me like some fucking nom, kid. You might be pres now, but I'm still your father —'

'Dad!' Viking tilted his head in Gen's direction. 'We got company.'

His gaze swung to her, and he flinched. 'Geneva? What the fuck are you doing here?'

Geneva balked. She'd never met this man.

'What the hell were you doing at her sister's funeral?' Viking retaliated.

Ignoring the question, the grizzled man stalked to the fridge, pulled out a beer and took a long swig.

Viking's shrewd gaze narrowed. 'Thought you didn't know him?'

Gen shook her head and whispered, 'I don't.'

The man pulled up a stool next to her and sat. 'Sorry about that, darlin'. The boys caught me off guard.' He offered a tattooed hand, and she shook it tentatively. 'I'm K2.' He gestured to her water. 'You might want something stronger than that for this.'

'Fuck's sake. Between you and Mac ...' Viking snatched two beers from the fridge and offered her one. She took it, reminded of her eighteenth birthday and the first time her dad had handed her a beer. Shame washed over her. These men weren't at all like her dad. He would be horrified by them, and what they'd done. She discarded the bottle and turned to Mac.

'Where's Jesse?'

'The cop's fine.'

'I want to talk to him.'

Viking shook his head. 'Can't have anyone tracking your phone here.'

'Is he okay?'

'He's in one piece.' Mac's tone shut down any further questions.

What did that mean, *one piece*? Had they hurt him?

Viking crossed his arms. 'Okay Dad, spill.'

'You're not too old for me to take you out back and teach you a lesson, you know.'

'Like to see you try,' Viking muttered under his breath.

K2 faced Gen, his expression softening. 'How much do you know about your dad's past?'

Her dad? She stared at his jagged nails, narrowing in on the black bruised bed of his thumbnail. Her dad had taken part in social rides back in the day, but he'd died four years before Amber disappeared, on a trip overseas with mates. Druggie mates, her mum had called them.

Oh shit.

'Was my dad involved in drugs?'

K2 shook his head. 'He smoked pot like the rest of us, but he had honour. Wouldn't stoop to dealing.'

This whole thing was like a maze of secret tunnels without an exit. 'Then what's Dad's past got to do with you?'

'Stretch – that was your dad's nickname – he and I knew each other as kids. Grew up together. Best mates.'

'I never met you.'

'By the time you came along, your mum had banned me from his life. Bad influence and all.'

Lucy did hate everything to do with her dad's bikes. An ache spread through Gen's chest. 'How did you meet Dad?'

'Stretch's dad, Joker, and my dad, King, fought together in Vietnam. When they returned, things were rough. Society turned its back on 'em. The only place they fit was with the Rebels. A couple of years later your dad and I were born. Stretch and I became nominees when we were old enough and rode together with the club.'

The Rebels? No way. Her dad had written off one percenters as dangerous thugs and drug dealers.

She narrowed her eyes. 'I never saw any Rebel cuts at my dad's gatherings.'

'Stretch patched out when your sister was born. We only reconnected after your parents' divorce, but he still wanted nothing to do with the old club, not with you girls around. Took me a while longer to come to my senses.'

'So Phoenix isn't a chapter of the Rebels?'

'Nah, when the cops formed Raptor, a few of us could see the writing on the wall and the club was being infiltrated by arseholes anyway – loose cannons who were all about personal gain and had no loyalty – so we formed our own club. No one with a criminal record allowed.'

She raised her eyebrows doubtfully.

'Doesn't mean we're choirboys, but there's a code. If you're found guilty of a crime, you're out.'

Gen stared at the concrete floor. Had her dad's past somehow caused Amber's death? Is that why K2 was at the funeral? 'What does all this have to do with my dad?'

'You know he died on a trip to Vietnam?'

'He said he was going there for a memorial service.' She pushed the heel of her hand down her thigh. 'Mum said he was probably killed because he was hanging out with drug dealers.'

'Fuck, that bitch is a piece of work.' K2 shook his head, took a sip of his drink, then looked back at her apologetically. 'Sorry.' He took another gulp of beer. 'Stretch and I went to Vietnam to stand in for our dads at a memorial service at Núi Lé. We celebrated with a few after. Stretch left early and was hit by a car. He was in and out of consciousness in hospital, but he asked me to keep an eye on you if he didn't make it. When he died, I looked for you and Amber, but Lucy had moved. I had no idea how to find you.'

Gen scratched at the edge of the label on her beer. Her racing thoughts tangled in her mind. It was so much to process. But at least she knew for sure that her dad had told her the truth before he left. And he'd been thinking of them right before he died.

'It wasn't until Amber was all over the news that I found you. I tried to reach out, but your mum threatened to make trouble for the club.'

Gen tore at the label, peeling it from the glass. From the moment their dad died, Lucielle had tried to remove all memory of him from their world.

'When I heard Amber's remains had been found, I took the flowers to her grave. Stretch would have wanted that.'

'You left the yellow posy?'

'Didn't manage to keep my word to him before, so it was the least I could do.'

K2 skolled the rest of his beer and slammed the bottle on the table. He glared at Mac, then Viking. 'Your turn. Why the fuck have you dickheads dragged Gen here to this shithole?'

'She's been asking about Phoenix,' Mac said. 'Managed to get a cop involved.'

'Well, shit.'

15

All three men turned to her with fierce expressions.

'He was riding pillion with me when he' – she pointed at Mac – 'pulled us over. I never said a thing about Phoenix to Jesse.'

K2 and Viking glared at Mac.

'What? Last time I checked I'm still the Sergeant at Arms. It's my job to protect the club however I see necessary.'

'And you thought you'd do that by kidnapping a cop?' Viking spat out.

'We needed leverage to be sure she'd tell the truth. She's been going around asking questions about Phoenix. And we had to find out if the cop thought we were somehow connected to her sister's death.'

'And what's your plan for the cop now?' The tone in Viking's voice sent a chill up Gen's spine.

'You can still leave Jesse out of it. I swear I haven't said a word about your club to him.' Her gaze darted between the three men. 'I'll tell him I have no idea who took us today. That you were all masked, demanded to know why I was at the house in Windsor, and that was it.'

'That'll only work if he doesn't report today,' said Viking.

'I'll make sure he doesn't.' God knows how, but she had to make sure they didn't hurt him.

K2 leant forward. 'What happened in Windsor?'

Gen ran through the events again.

K2 turned to Viking. 'Can you ask Feral to look into the two bikers?'

Viking gave an exasperated huff.

'Feral?' Gen asked.

'He's our ...' Mac paused, then smirked. 'Our computer expert, the one who found where you live.'

'How?'

'Not hard through the Redline store loyalty program,' said a skinny man leaning on the doorjamb of the adjoining room. He had long brown hair that hadn't seen shampoo for a while.

'Shut it, Feral,' Viking snapped.

She hadn't even noticed Feral enter the room. He might be her only chance to find anything on the men at the farm. '*Can you find out who the bikers were?*'

Feral grinned but said nothing.

She turned to Viking imploringly. 'Please, those men might be involved in Amber's murder.'

'Think about what happened today thanks to your poking around,' Mac said. 'Other clubs won't be nearly as hospitable.'

Viking stood. 'Best leave it be.' He moved towards the bar and Gen stepped in his way.

'I'm not going to stop until I find out what happened to my sister.'

Viking stared down at her.

She expelled a breath, couldn't manage another, pinned by his gaze.

His focus moved over her shoulder, in Feral's direction.

'There are two MCs with competing territory around Windsor,' Feral said. 'Want me to look into it?'

K2 put a hand on her shoulder blade. 'Come on, son, I owe her.'

Viking pointed in her face. 'That cop better not tie us to anything.'

'He won't.' Gen met his glare. 'I promise.'

Viking nodded to Feral. 'See what you can find.'

K2 squeezed her shoulder then joined Feral and chatted quietly with him.

Viking looked back down at her. 'You best be on your way.'

'What about Jesse?'

'Raz is with him,' Mac said.

'Tell him to get to the hardware store at the Crossroads and keep the cop in the SUV till Gen pulls in to the car park. You escort her there. And Mac?'

'What?'

'You and I will have words later.'

At her bike, Mac handed over her phone. 'Don't turn it on until the Crossroads.'

She put it in her jacket pocket. 'How will I know if Feral found anything?'

'I'll be in touch.' He jumped on his bike, and she followed him back up the drive.

Gen's stomach churned as Mac waved her off down the Crossroads ramp and continued along the motorway. How could she make Jesse keep quiet about today? It was an impossible task.

She pulled to a stop at the hardware store, her head on a swivel. Jesse was nowhere to be seen. Was he okay? She checked the time on her watch. Oh shit! Lily's exam and interview. If she didn't leave in the next minute or two, she'd never make it.

Gen plucked her phone from her pocket and turned it on. *Come on.* The signal connected, and as she dialled Lily, an SUV skidded to a stop beside her. Jesse jumped out and had barely closed the door when the black vehicle roared away.

'Thank God!' He ran to her, pulled her into a fierce hug, then leant away and scanned her top to bottom.

Gen put up her finger to silence him as she reached Lily's message bank.

'I'm running late, Lil. If I'm not at the gate by two-thirty head to the auditorium for the exam. I'll meet you there after, for the interview. You've got this. Love you!'

She hung up and pointed to the helmet dangling from his fingers. 'Put that on. We need to leave.'

'What?'

'I've got to get to Lily's school for the interview.'

'I'm not going anywhere until we talk.'

'I don't have time for this. Get on.'

'Geneva, you have been missing for three hours. I was held *hostage.* You don't get to just go on with your day!'

'Lily needs me. Let's go!'

'No. We can ring the school. Get them to reschedule.'

'I can't do that to her.'

'You've got to be fucking kidding me.'

'Jesse, *now*!'

'I think she'll understand if you're a little late, all things considered.'

'Oh yeah, and what am I going to say? "Sorry, Lil, I got strong-armed by a bunch of bikies. But hey, better late than never, right?"'

He folded his arms across his chest. 'Are you more involved in the biker scene than I know?'

'No! But I am leaving now, Jesse, with or without you.'

Jesse shoved his helmet on. 'Afterwards, we're going straight to the station.' She'd never heard that tone from him before.

He swung himself onto the saddle behind her, but his body didn't press against hers and his hands didn't come to her waist. Hot anger emanated from him the whole drive. She had no idea how to convince him not to report today's events, but at least she'd bought herself time to work it out. Right now, she had to get to her niece.

16

She pulled up to the school and leapt from the bike the moment Jesse dismounted. She ran for the gate, undoing her helmet as she went.

No sign of Lily. She raced to the auditorium and entered the foyer, breath coming in loud gasps. She scanned the space, then approached the teacher sitting at the sign-in desk. 'Could you please tell me where Lily Forsythe's interview is being held?'

'Forsythe?'

'Yes, Lily, Liliana. She's in Year 10.'

'And you are?'

'Geneva Leighton, her aunt. I'm an official guardian.'

The woman typed into her laptop. 'I'm afraid Lily didn't check in for her exam.'

'What do you mean?'

'She was a no-show.'

'That doesn't make any sense.'

The woman glanced at her as if to say, *What do you want me to say?*

'Is she still in class? I could go and get her.'

'I'm sorry, it's too late. She missed her slot.'

'But surely if I can find her …'

'The schedule is full.'

Gen wasn't going to get anywhere with this woman. Better to take Lily to the headmistress's office and ask for help there.

'Can you tell me what class she's in?'

'English, but she's been marked absent.'

Absent? Was she sick? Gen checked her phone. No message. She tried calling Lily again, and then the home phone, but both rang out.

She sprinted back to her bike.

Jesse checked behind her. 'Where is she?'

'She didn't turn up to her exam and she's not in class. I'm going home to see if she's there.'

Five minutes later Gen pulled into the driveway and ran for the front door. It swung open when she turned the handle.

'Lily? Are you here?'

She headed upstairs, two at a time, burst into Lily's room, and sucked in a breath.

Lily sat in front of her wardrobe mirror, scissors in hand. Piles of long blonde hair lay all around her. Her tear-filled gaze met Gen's. 'Dad's going to kill me.'

Crouching behind Lily, Gen ran her hand over the choppy, messy bob. 'I like it.' Their eyes met in the mirror. 'Wanna tell me what's going on?'

'I looked too much like Mum.'

Her words hit like a punch to Gen's gut. Lily was struggling way more than she'd realised.

Gen held out her hand for the scissors and began straightening the back of the bob. 'And the exam and interview?'

Lily groaned.

Gen focused on Lily's hair and stayed quiet, even though it

went against all her instincts, which were screaming at her to do something, *anything*.

Lily palmed the shorn hair into a pile. 'If I don't have a scholarship, I won't have to go to that school.'

Gen blinked, careful to keep her tone calm. 'I thought you liked it there.'

Knuckles rapped on the door and Jesse stuck his head around. 'Sorry to interrupt. I have to —'

Lily scrambled to her feet and glared at Gen. 'What's *he* doing here?'

'I took him for a ride on the bike this morning —'

'But he ... I told you ...' Lily shook her head and folded her arms across her chest. 'Forget it. No one listens to me anyway.'

'Lilybelle ...'

'Stop calling me that!' She whirled on Jesse. 'Get out of my room!'

He withdrew and Lily pivoted to Gen. 'You too! You're just the same as everyone else.'

'Lily, I'm sorry. I —'

'I said *get out*!' She pointed to the door.

Gen hesitated, and Lily turned her back on her. Reluctantly, Gen left the room. She had to find out what was happening at school, and a way to fix it. But first, she had to deal with Jesse.

She entered the kitchen. Jesse pushed a cup of peppermint tea across the bench to her. 'Sorry, I should have left you both alone.'

'She's been struggling since Amber was found, but I didn't realise how much.' Gen ran a hand over her hair. 'She won't talk to me.'

'Speaking of ...'

She put her hand up to stop him. 'I know we need to debrief. But honestly, there's not much to tell.'

'Are you kidding? You were gone three hours. Who were they? Where did they take you? What did they want? I almost went crazy in that car. I had no idea if you were okay.'

'I don't know who they were. They kept their masks on.' Her gaze slid to her tea. Lying to him was going to be even harder than she thought. 'Can we meet later and talk properly?' She glanced at the stairwell. 'I'm so worried about Lily I can't think straight, and I need to pick up Charlie.' Gen sank onto a stool, head in her hands.

Jesse squeezed her shoulder and sat next to her. 'She's going to be okay.'

'Is she? I've never seen her like this. And Hugh is going to lose it about her missing the exam, not to mention cutting off her hair.' She pressed the heels of her hands into her eyes. 'Sorry. This isn't your problem.' She stood. 'I'll meet you at the beach when the kids are in bed. The rotunda, around ten?'

He shook his head. 'We need to go to the station, make a statement.'

'Jesse.' He met her gaze. 'I really need you to ... Could you please just hold off on reporting it until later? I know what I'm asking is huge —'

'Gen, I could lose my job.'

'I know. I will explain tonight, I promise.'

God knows how.

Jesse took a breath, gathering himself, then stood, arms outstretched. She sank into his chest, and he stroked her hair. 'It scared the shit out of me when they took you.'

'I know. I'm sorry.'

'Wasn't your fault.'

'You won't report it yet?'

He sighed. 'I'll wait, but please don't make me regret it.'

He kissed the top of her head, and she pulled back. Seeing the open vulnerability in his eyes, she slipped from his hold.

His gaze searched her face, then he shoved his hands in his pockets and nodded to her handbag. 'Don't you have to go?'

She checked her watch. 4 pm. 'Shit!'

She retrieved her car keys and gestured to the front door. 'Come on. I won't be held responsible for what Lily might do if I leave you here.'

Gen threw the car into reverse and accelerated away. Jesse's question from earlier arrowed into her thoughts like a javelin. *Are you more involved in the biker scene than I know?*

She wasn't, but could her dad's involvement with the Rebels be at the root of all this? She'd always treasured how bikes had kept her connected to him. But the Rebels had never been an MC to mess with. If her dad had been involved in the outlaw scene, had that somehow got Amber killed?

Today had been like an echo from her teen years. The joking around, the brotherhood, the belonging. But was she putting the kids in danger by agreeing to keep Phoenix a secret from Jesse and the police?

Newspaper headlines from last year flickered through her mind. The exposé on the infiltration of the police and military by one percenter MCs and white supremacists. No. She couldn't risk it. She and the kids could be vulnerable to retaliation.

Somehow, she had to keep Phoenix a secret from Jesse but still convince him not to report today's events.

She pulled into the deserted school car park. Charlie sat in the gutter bouncing a tennis ball between his hands. She flexed and unflexed her fingers on the steering wheel. She'd put Jesse in danger today and let both the kids down. Maybe, in pursuing a resolution to Amber's case, she was doing more harm than good.

He jumped in the passenger seat with a huge grin. 'How was your day?'

This kid, he was all sunshine. 'Good. How was yours?'

He ran through every event, from cricket training to what his friends did at lunch to his teacher using basketball statistics to explain how graphs work.

This here, this was what truly mattered. The kids' happiness and joy. She'd help Lily through this rough patch, and they'd all find their equilibrium again.

Gen added jam to the scones she'd bought on the way home and took a plate out to the driveway where Charlie was practising lay-ups. She took a second plate upstairs and knocked on Lily's door.

No answer.

She could hear murmurs, as if Lily were talking to someone, but Gen couldn't make out the words.

She knocked again. 'Lil, I've got scones.'

'Not hungry.'

'Come on, honey, you need to eat.'

The door swung open and Lily snatched a scone, took one bite, then dropped it back on the plate. 'There, I ate. Happy?'

Gen's mouth fell open and the door clicked closed. The murmuring resumed.

Gen returned to the kitchen, set aside the rejected scones, and opened her laptop. She emailed the school requesting an urgent meeting with Lily's mentor. She couldn't leave things any longer.

As she packed the excess scones into a container, her phone buzzed. 'Hello?'

'Ms Leighton? It's Alisa Smith, I'm Lily's new mentor. I hope you don't mind me calling so late on a Friday, but I've been trying to talk to someone about Lily all week. Mr Forsythe hasn't returned my calls or emails.'

'Why didn't you call me? I'm Lily's primary school contact.'

'Oh dear, I'm so sorry. I came on board halfway through this term and the file only lists you as an emergency contact. Must be a clerical error. I'll have it corrected.'

'Thank you.'

'In your email you mentioned being worried that something is happening to make Lily unhappy at school?'

'I am. She's always been happy there, but in the last few weeks it's become clear that something's wrong.'

'We've noticed changes in her behaviour too. That's why I've been reaching out to her father. She's late to class, isn't handing in homework or assignments, and, to be honest, a number of teachers have said she's become quite rude.'

Gen stared up at the ceiling, towards Lily's room. What was going on? 'That's incredibly out of character. I'm sure you're aware her mother's remains were found two weeks ago?'

'I am, and the school is so very sorry for your family's loss. We understand that this is a difficult time, and we've tried to reach out to Lily to offer support. But I need to warn you, her scholarship is in jeopardy. She missed her exam today, didn't show for her one-on-one music lesson yesterday and failed her science exam last week.'

'Failed?'

'The only questions she answered were her name and student number. It's a condition of her current scholarship that she maintains an A-grade average.'

'Surely you can take into consideration the family situation.'

'Of course. That's why I wanted to talk.'

'When exactly did you first try to contact her father?'

'Ten days ago. The school sent an email when she missed an assessment. I've sent two emails and left four voicemails since.'

Gen slid open the back door and stepped onto the deck. She let the rhythm of Charlie dribbling the basketball settle over her as she took a deep breath. 'So where do things stand?'

'I'm trying to organise special consideration for her scholarship exam, but the truth is it's very competitive and we have to be seen as being beyond reproach.'

'I understand.' Something about this whole mess wasn't sitting right. 'Has anything changed at school? Have the teachers noticed anything socially?'

'Not that I'm aware of, but let me check and get back to you.'

Surely the school could have thought of that themselves.

'I think it would be helpful if we could meet as soon as possible, with Lily, you, Mr Forsythe, and myself. I'm free after school Monday or Wednesday next week?'

'I'll make any time that suits.'

'Perhaps you could check with Mr Forsythe?'

'I'll ask, but I doubt he'll come. He's away for work a lot, and I don't think we should leave it any longer.'

'In that case, let's meet in my office at three-thirty on Monday.'

'Okay. And thank you, I know your day should have ended by now.'

'I'm just so relieved to have finally made contact.'

Gen hung up and leant on the balcony. She wasn't sure she had the skills to get Lily through this. Not when Hugh was going to go absolutely apeshit about the missed exam, let alone her hair. Then again, if he'd answered his emails or phone, they could have tackled the problem ten days ago.

A text sounded on her phone. She checked the screen and opened Hugh's message.

Home 7 pm. Make sure kids there.

That sounded ominous. He'd better not be sending the kids to his parents' again. Not after the disaster last weekend.

She had to talk with him before he saw the kids. She grabbed a beer to drink while she made dinner. She was going to need a little liquid courage tonight.

Gen left the goulash simmering on the stove and went out to the garage. Charlie had finished his homework and was settled in front of the TV. Lily hadn't emerged from her room, but that was the best place for her to be right now.

Gen checked her watch, then the driveway. Hugh should be home any minute. She massaged her jaw. If she could get him to burn his anger out on her, it might protect Lily from his unfiltered venom.

A silver limousine pulled into the drive.

Gen focused on slowing her breath, calming her pulse down.

Hugh exited the vehicle and spotted her in the garage. He rolled his suitcase along the drive towards her.

'What now?' His voice rang with contempt.

She blinked slowly. 'Can we have a chat before you go inside?'

'What have you done?'

She pulled out a chair for him, thankful they were doing this on her territory. 'We need to talk about Lily.'

'How did her interview go?'

'Please sit.'

'Geneva, I'm exhausted. I just want to grab a scotch, eat some dinner, and go to bed.'

'Well, Hugh, sometimes the world doesn't revolve around you.' *Shit. Rein it in, Gen.* She put up her palms in surrender. 'Sorry.'

Hugh wiped off the seat and sat. 'You have five minutes.'

'I'm asking you to hear me out before you react.'

Hugh uncrossed his legs and moved to stand again. 'I've already had enough —'

'Lily didn't go to the exam or interview today.'

He looked to the house. 'Is she sick?'

'No, she's ... her mentor rang this afternoon. Said she'd left messages for you.'

'I don't have time for all the junk that comes in from the school. You agreed to handle it. That's part of our arrangement.'

'And I do, but the mentor is new. She didn't realise I'm the primary contact.'

'For God's sake, Geneva, you're supposed to be on top of all this. If you weren't so obsessed with playing detective ...'

Heat flared up Gen's neck. She closed her eyes and swallowed. If she followed Hugh down that well-worn path, they'd never get to what was important. She softened her tone.

'Lily is very unhappy at the moment.'

'What does she have to be unhappy about? I provide everything she needs. An elite education, top of the line clothing, a beautiful home.'

'Those things don't matter. I'm trying to tell you Lily is struggling.'

'Well, fix it.'

'I can't – at least, not alone. She needs you, her father, and you're never here.'

'I'm working so she can have everything she needs.'

Gen stood and paced the garage, had to, or she would explode. 'She just found out her mother is never coming back.'

'Whose fault is that? You filled her head with nonsense, made her believe there was hope Amber could still be alive.'

'I never said that to either of the kids.'

'No, but they watched you obsess over that website.' Hugh pointed at her. 'You did this. Confused her. My dad's right, you're a bad influence. You need to clean up your act.'

'*Me* clean up my act?' Gen pushed the heels of her hands into her temples. 'You're the one who's barely home, and mainlining scotch when you are. The school has been trying to contact you for ten days, Hugh. Where the fuck have you been?'

'Don't you swear at me!'

'Your daughter needs you but you're never here! It's me who's shown up for them every day of the last twelve years!'

'And look how that turned out.'

'How *dare* you!' Gen's hands curled into fists, poised to attack. But this wasn't about her. The kids needed her to be their advocate, their protector.

'Okay Hugh, I'll give it to you straight. Lily has been rude to teachers, failed a science exam and may very well lose her scholarship. That poor girl is spiralling and what she needs, more than anything, is some of your time.' She folded her arms across her chest. 'Oh and she cut her hair.'

'She can't lose her scholarship. Forsythes don't fail.'

'That's all you care about?'

He shook his head. 'You live here because you look after my children, but I'm beginning to wonder if that's what's best. It might be time to reconsider, send them to boarding school like Dad suggested. At least I could rely on the care they'd get there.'

She let out a frustrated scream. 'Kids need love and affection from their parents and role models.'

'Exactly.' His lip curled. 'If you want to stay living under my roof, with my children, you will change your ways.'

'What the hell is that supposed to mean?'

'No more investigations into Amber's death. And if you don't sort things out with Lily, she can board next term.'

'But —'

'No, Geneva. I'm drawing a line.'

Gen glared at him.

'And I know you've been seeing Johns behind my back. That ends now too.'

'Behind your back? You're not my father, Hugh. You get no say in who I see.'

'I do if you want to be around my children.'

'The kids need me.'

'They'd be fine without you. Might even toughen them up.'

She turned to the bench, taking slow breaths to quell the fight response zipping through her veins. He hadn't always been like this.

Gen stood outside the birthing suite, holding the biggest bunch of freesias she could afford. Her belly knotted in anticipation. What if there was no room for her in Amber's life anymore?

She pushed the door open. Amber lay in bed while Hugh sat in a chair next to her, staring down at the bundle in his arms. His face was filled with awe. He looked up, eyes wet, and gave Amber a smile of a pure amazement. 'I will never let anything or anyone hurt her.'

Amber turned to meet Gen's gaze and joy lit up her face. She held out her hand. 'Come and meet Liliana – Lily for short.'

Gen walked over.

'Lily,' Hugh said, 'this is your Aunty Gen.' The name sent a wave of warmth through Gen's chest.

She stared down at the cherubic face. Lily's eyes opened and Gen swore they met hers. A tiny hand escaped the swaddling, and Gen stroked her niece's soft skin. Her heart swelled. 'Welcome to the family, Lilybelle.'

Hugh cuddled the baby and beamed with pride.

It was hard to believe the same man sat before her now.

'Amber would be horrified at you.'

'Don't you dare bring her into this. If you had gone to the shops that night she would still be here, taking *good* care of our children. And I can guarantee Lily wouldn't be in trouble at school. Amber understood what's important.'

'You mean what's important to you.'

'I'm not discussing this any further. The ball is in your court.'

As much as she wanted to tear him in two, he was right. She had no power, no recourse. If she wanted to be part of Lily's and Charlie's lives, she would have to do as he said.

He stood. 'Now, what's for dinner?'

17

After a tense dinner that Lily missed, Hugh finally disappeared into his office. He hadn't once checked in on his daughter.

Gen rapped lightly on Lily's door.

'Come in.' Lily was curled up on her bed, facing the wall. Gen waded through the floordrobe and sat on the edge of the bed.

'You okay?'

'Fine.' The tremor in Lily's voice betrayed her, as if she were battling tears.

'How can I help?' She rested her palm on Lily's shoulder, but her niece curled further into herself.

'I'm just tired.'

Hand sliding to the purple and pink floral bedspread, Gen let the pause stretch for a few beats. Then she sighed and moved to the door.

'Gen?'

She froze, afraid to spook her niece out of talking.

'How angry was Dad?'

'He was … disappointed, but I promised we'd do everything we could to fix things at school.'

'He didn't come in to say goodnight.'

'He has a lot on at work.'

'He always does.'

'He loves you, sweetheart, he just —'

'It doesn't matter. I'm going to sleep.'

Gen's heart pinched. 'Love you, Lil. We'll sort everything out, okay?'

Lily put in earbuds, pressed a button on her phone and the faint beats of a rap song echoed throughout the room.

Gen pulled the door shut behind her and leant her forehead on the wall. It was like all light had been drained from Lily's world. The meeting at school on Monday couldn't come soon enough.

She moved to Charlie's door. She tapped quietly, having promised years ago she would always go in and give him a goodnight kiss, even if he was asleep.

She sat on the edge of the bed, and he wrapped his arms around her neck. She rested her cheek on his head gently, inhaling the pine scent of his freshly shampooed hair. Her breathing slowed into the even rhythm of his as he fell back to sleep.

Hugh's threats slid into her thoughts. In her pursuit for truth she was jeopardising moments like this, risking being carved from the kids' lives completely. But could she accept that justice for Amber might never be found? She stroked Charlie's hair.

Toni would tell her to trust her gut, but at the moment she had no idea what was instinct, what was fear, and what was just indigestion.

She checked her watch: 9:45 pm. She eased her body off Charlie's bed and tiptoed out of the room.

Down one floor, Hugh's bedroom light shone from under the door. She knocked.

'Yes?'

She cracked the door so he could hear her. 'Are you staying in the rest of the night?'

'I'm in bed, aren't I?'

Gen flipped him the bird from behind the door. 'I'm going to visit Toni.'

'Make sure you're back to take Charlie to cricket in the morning.'

'I'll be home to sleep.' No response. 'Hugh?'

'What?' he slurred.

'You won't leave?'

'Of course not.'

She pulled the door to, wishing she could slam it.

She texted Jesse.

Hugh's threatened to bar me from the kids if I see you. Anywhere more private we can meet?

2/48 Winston Rd, Neutral Bay.

??

My place.

See you in 10

She slipped her leather jacket over her tee and jumped on her bike, the hollow in her chest threatening to swallow her whole.

During the drive over, fears and mistakes rushed through her mind, vying for pole position. By the time she climbed the stairs of Jesse's 1940s apartment block, exhaustion weighed down every limb. Faint guitar chords escaped from under the door of Jesse's apartment, accompanied by his smooth baritone voice, tender and warm, singing 'Fields of Gold'. Gen lifted her hand to knock, then paused. She still hadn't figured out how to explain today's events in a way he would accept. In a way he deserved.

Emotions simmered in her belly. Sadness. Guilt. Regret. And something she'd buried years ago. A yearning. An urge to free fall into the connection that still burned between them. She touched her fingers to her lips ... Who was she kidding? She dropped her hand away.

Armour on, Leighton. She rapped on the dark wood door. The strumming inside stopped, then the door swung inwards. Jesse was dressed in light-blue jeans and a black fitted tee displaying every muscle. Her face warmed.

Jesse cocked his head in question when she didn't enter. 'You're welcome to come in.'

'Thanks. Sorry we had to meet here.'

'All good.'

Taking note of his bare feet, she removed her heavy riding boots then stepped inside, their arms brushing ever so slightly, awareness prickling across the surface of her skin. If she couldn't lock these reactions down, she'd have to leave.

He took her jacket and hung it by the door. 'I was about to have a glass of wine?'

'No thanks.' That was the last thing she needed.

'How about a hot chocolate?'

'That sounds good.' She followed him into the studio apartment. A well-used dark-brown leather lounge sat to the left of the front door, facing a wall-hung television. To the right, a breakfast bar flanked the kitchen, with Danish-style wooden stools tucked underneath. Past a closed door, against the far wall of exposed brick, lay a queen-sized bed dressed in a midnight-blue quilt and topped with patterned scatter cushions. An acoustic guitar lay sideways across it.

She pointed to the instrument. 'You play beautifully.'

A red tinge rose in Jesse's cheeks. 'It relaxes me.' He put the guitar in its stand, then circled past her to the kitchen.

'Your home is lovely,' she said.

'My mum and sister helped decorate.'

A milk frother hissed and she stepped up to the guitar, running her hand over the neck. There had been an almost haunting quality to the song he'd been playing, so different from the assured, in-control Jesse she knew.

He handed her a mug, and the earthy scent of chocolate filled her nose. He slid a glass door open, just to the left of the bed. 'Thought we'd sit outside. It's a warm night.'

She followed him onto a balcony furnished with an old rattan lounge and two matching side tables. The balcony wall was glass, revealing a blanket of lights spreading down the hill to a partial view of Sydney Harbour.

Jesse sat on the left side of the lounge, and Gen sank into the soft cushion on the opposite end. She took her first sip of the frothy cocoa. Time to face the music. She turned to Jesse. His gaze darted from her lips.

'What's going on with Hugh?' he asked. 'Is everything okay?'

'Not really.' She took another sip of cocoa, but she struggled to swallow past the new lump in her throat. 'He threatened to kick me out.'

'He can't expect you to look after the kids —'

'Out of the house and out of the kids' lives.' She focused on the lights of a plane as it tracked its way out to sea.

'Surely —'

'I have no legal right to the kids, only a verbal agreement that he can rescind at any time.' Her voice wobbled. 'I don't care about finding a new place to live, but the kids … He threatened to send them to boarding school if I don't fall into line.'

'What does he want you to do?'

'Besides not seeing you? Stop investigating Amber's murder.' She glanced sideways at him. 'But I can't.'

'Why not?'

'She needs justice. I owe her that. I owe her so much. She pretty much raised me once Mum and Dad split.'

'But your mum was around, right? I remember meeting her when Amber went missing. She was a wreck.'

'We lived with her, but she was always super focused on whichever man was in her life at the time. She loved us in her own way – at least, that's what Amber used to say – but we were expected to slot in around her partner.'

'And your dad?'

'He wanted to stay involved, but my mother made it difficult, and her second husband had cash to splash, so she had a good lawyer. The courts only gave Dad access two weekends a month.'

'You must have missed him.'

'Heaps. Which offended my mother, of course. And my new stepdad, who hated everything about me. But Amber was always there, telling me how much she loved me. She was my shelter.'

'Why didn't you tell me all this when she first went missing?'

'Are you kidding? Amber was taken because I was too selfish to go to the shops when she asked. I was absolutely mortified. If I'd told you what a rock she'd been for me I'd never have been able to face you again.'

'I would have understood.'

'How? I still don't.' Gen ran a hand through her hair. 'And now I'm failing her all over again.' She trembled with the frustration. 'That man is sucking me dry. He's not my partner, my husband, or my boss, but he has so much control over me. And there's not a damn thing I can do, because I have no legal right to those kids.' She discarded the mug, sat forward, and put her head in her hands.

Her eyes filled. 'I'm ...' Her voice cracked. This wasn't how she dealt with things. She stood and gripped the edge of the glass.

Jesse moved in behind her and rested his palms on her upper arms, as if holding her together. He breathed, slow and steady, and her chest convulsed with the effort to keep everything in. The yearning returned. To lean into him. Just for a moment. She softened back into his chest, and he wrapped his arms around her. She blinked against the welling in her eyes.

His chin brushed against her temple. 'It's okay.'

The dam burst. The fear, the pain, the exhaustion, it all came flooding out. He gently stroked her arms as her body expelled the lot.

Gradually, the tears ran dry. He pulled her in tighter, kissed the top of her head, and instead of pulling away she matched her breathing to his. She grew aware of every point of connection between them. He shifted. Warm breath caressed her ear, sending a tug of longing through her.

She turned in his arms and met his gaze. He didn't blink. This was what she needed. To forget. To lose herself in him. She lifted onto her toes.

He pulled back slightly. 'You sure?'

'I'm sure.'

His hands cupped her cheeks. He searched her face and a shadow fell from his.

He brushed his mouth across hers, tugged gently at her bottom lip. Tingles radiated through her and her mouth parted on a silent sigh. He pulled at her lip again, slower this time, with more intent, and her body trembled. His tongue touched hers and his hands slid down her sides, exploring the dip of her waist, his fingertips brushing the edge of her breasts. He deepened the kiss, and she could take it no more. She pushed him onto the sofa and straddled him, revelling in the feel of him. She pulled off his tee, running her fingers through the sprinkling of hair across his chest. He threaded his fingers through the hair at her nape and took back control, his arousal pressing between her legs. She groaned and ground down on him, needing to feel him completely.

He eased back from the kiss. 'Gen ...'

'No talk. I want this. I need it. Please.' She climbed off him and walked backwards into the apartment, eyes never straying from his. She threw off her shirt and bra, then wriggled out of her jeans and underwear. He followed her into the room, and she stepped into him and brushed his mouth like he first had hers. Then she drew him onto the bed. He braced above her, his gaze raking her bare skin, searing every inch.

The pulse point at his throat beat fast. She saw the moment he made up his mind. She gave him a slow smile as he stood and shucked his jeans, then reached into a drawer and put on a condom. His fiery stare met hers and her breath shallowed. He was so beautiful.

He knelt at the end of the bed, kissed her ankles. Cherishing. Worshipping. A balloon of tenderness swelled in her chest. His parted lips brushed up the inside of her calf and then her thigh, never losing connection to her skin. She eased her legs apart, willing him on. His breath caressed the mound of her sex as his lips followed the dip of her hip. She trembled, desperate to pull him to her but also hungry to feel where his mouth would touch next. He kissed her abdomen, her belly, the underside of her breasts and continued up. Her body vibrated with sensation and need. He lingered over her nipple, his tongue circling the rigid peak. Every nerve ending lit up. His tongue traced up her neck and, finally, his mouth reached hers. She'd never felt so wanted in all her life. She slid her hands along his chest, and he threaded his fingers through hers, one hand then the other, and held one each side of her head. He pulled back slightly, his heavy-lidded stare meeting hers, making sure. She arched up and took his mouth, wrapped her legs around his thighs and pulled him closer. He slid into her and she moaned, losing herself in him completely.

A buzzing sound woke Gen. Jesse's arm lay heavy across her waist, his chest rising and falling against her back. She blinked the wall into focus.

Her mobile, which must have fallen from her pocket during her hasty strip, buzzed again from the floor. She slid a little from Jesse's hold and reached down to pick up the phone. An unknown number appeared on the screen with a message.

Have news. Wollombi pub Monday. Noon. Alone. M.

M. Mac. That was fast.

I'll be there.

She dropped her phone back on the floor.

Jesse pulled her back against his chest. Tension built in her muscles. What the hell had she been thinking last night? She stared at the wall, itching to slip out of bed, to disappear and avoid the inevitable scene that awaited her. She needed to get back to the kids, get ready for whatever news Mac had.

Maybe if she just gently slid out from under his arm ...

'I can hear you thinking.' Jesse's breath caressed her cheek. She tried to sit up, but he nuzzled her neck.

'I need to go.' She patted his arm, swung her legs to the side of the bed and grabbed her bra from the floor.

He traced the base of her spine with a finger. 'Who was the text from?'

'Lily.' She stood and yanked on her underwear and jeans, ignoring the hot imprint he'd left on her skin.

He switched on the bedside light and sat up. 'We need to discuss yesterday and file a report.'

She slipped her top over her head and pulled on her socks, searching for the right words.

'Gen, the longer we leave it, the harder it'll be to explain the delay.'

'I know.' She retied her hair at the base of her neck, took a deep breath and met his stare. 'We can't report it.'

'What?'

'I didn't see anyone's faces. There's nothing to tell.'

'Doesn't mean we can't report it. I noted down details, heights, mannerisms and such, while I was waiting for you outside Lily's school.'

She opened and closed her mouth without speaking.

His eyebrows drew together. 'You're lying.'

Dammit. She was going to have to put him off a different way.

'The men who took us were old friends of my father.' She picked up her mobile and tucked it in her back pocket. 'They wanted to show me the dangers of nosing around outlaw MCs, wanted to scare me a little.'

Jesse stood, pulling on a pair of tracksuit pants. 'You can't be okay with that.'

'I don't like the way they went about it, but I understand. They're not bad guys, they just want to keep me out of trouble.'

He scoffed. 'That's bullshit. What about me? They kept me in that car for three hours.'

'I'm so sorry they involved you.'

'Who are *they*?'

'I promised I wouldn't tell.'

'What the hell?' He began to pace, then threw his arms in the air. 'You can't have it both ways, Geneva. We're either a team or we're not.'

'Jesse, please calm down.'

'Don't treat me like an idiot.'

'I'm not. Please Jesse, you have to understand, once I told them about what happened at Windsor, they promised to tap into their resources to help me.'

'Men like that can't be trusted. They won't have your back, Gen.'

'They had my dad's back. Besides, we all want the same thing.'

'Do we? Cause I want a genuine relationship with you, Gen. I thought tonight was the start.'

She flinched. 'I never promised you that.'

'You implied it.'

'I told you on the beach last Saturday that there would never be an us.'

He pulled a shirt on roughly. 'It sure didn't feel that way when you had your hands all over me.'

'Don't be an arse, that was just sex.'

'That was way more than sex and you know it. You're scared.'

'I don't have the time or energy for this.'

'Right,' he spat out.

Silence stretched heavy between them. He sat on the edge of the bed, elbows on his knees. Hurt filled his face and his hands dragged through his hair.

Gen shoved her hands in her pockets so she wouldn't reach for him. 'There's so much going on right now, with the kids and Hugh. I can't be pulled in another direction.' She knelt in front of him. 'If Hugh finds out about what happened today, he'll definitely remove me from the kids' lives.'

'Could you blame him?'

'Fine.' She stood and folded her arms. 'If you report it, you'll do it on your own. I won't back you up.'

'You'd do that to me?'

What sort of person was she becoming?

'I'm sorry, but I can't lose the kids. Please, Jesse.'

His lips pinched tight and he closed his eyes. Then he sighed deeply. 'I won't report today if you promise to keep me informed of everything that's happening.'

'I can't tell you who —'

'No, but you can tell me if you see them again. I need to know you're safe.'

She stared at the ground.

'Geneva, look at me.' She forced her eyes to meet his. 'I know if you give me your word, you'll keep it. Now stop avoiding and promise me.'

'I promise to keep you in the loop.'

'I'm trying to have your back here.'

'Jesse, last night —'

'Won't happen again. I don't do friends with benefits.' He strode to the front door and took her coat from the hook. The hollow in her chest returned. She pulled on her boots and jacket, then reached for the door handle.

'And Gen?'

She turned.

'I want to know exactly what M tells you at the meeting on Monday. We will plan a course of action together.' His eyes blazed.

He'd seen the text, and had wanted her to share. She'd let him down again.

She nodded and slipped out the door. She used the ride home to box away how good his touch had felt. She was doing the right thing, walking away. It was best for everyone.

18

Gen rode past Jerry's Cafe and travelled on towards Wollombi. Being a Monday morning, she had the single lane road to herself. Bushland whizzed past in her peripheral vision. The weekend had gone smoothly. Well, as smooth as it could with a moody teen and an even moodier father, who was resolutely ignoring said teen.

On Saturday a resistant Lily had eventually agreed to getting her hair tidied up by a hairdresser. Gen had tried everything she could to connect with her niece on the way there and back, but her efforts were countered by the brick wall of Lily's phone.

Hugh had been absent from family dinner again on Sunday night.

Gen had no idea what to do about Lily or Hugh. They were both pulling away from the family.

Hopefully the meeting at school this afternoon would help Lily.

She hit the throttle, accelerating past fields of green spotted with country cottages and cows. Her thoughts turned to Jesse. They hadn't spoken since Friday night; she'd needed the space and imagined he did too. She really shouldn't have let things go that far. A flash of his intense gaze as his lips met the hollow of her hip tugged at her. But not in her centre, no, it pulled firmly at her heart.

She forced her focus to the world around her, the slight dip in temperature as she went through a valley then back up the hill, the scent of newly laid manure filling her helmet.

What she needed to do right now was fortify herself for the meeting with Mac. The fingers of her left hand drummed against the hand brake. What was his news? If Feral had found the identity of the riders at Windsor would it help solve Amber's murder? Or just create more questions? Could she even trust what Mac said?

Approaching the tiny town of Wollombi, she eased up on her speed. The one-pub town had a few shops, a tiny bespoke winery and a police station. The police station had always struck her as odd. The town's population was only 188 people so unless they were the rowdiest group of non-conformist outlaws ... Then again, it was a popular biker rest stop.

She parked outside the Wollombi Tavern, which had stood by the Great North Road since the 1840s. A covered balcony jutted out to one side, its tables made of old wine barrels topped with horizontal slabs of tree trunks. The balcony overlooked fields sparsely littered with campervans. In a sunken outdoor area on the north side of the pub lay a grass courtyard covered with wooden benches and tables. A couple with a Bull Terrier nursed beers at the first one. Three tables behind, in the far corner, sat Mac, dressed in blue jeans and a plain white tee. No colours today. He slid his Ray-Bans up on top of his head, looking like he'd stepped off the set of a bad-boy modelling shoot. Yet there was no catch of breath, no rush of heat to Gen's face – not like when Jesse had opened his door on Friday night.

She plonked her gear on the table and sat.

Mac leant across and grazed her cheek with his lips, a practised move she was sure usually brought women to their knees. 'Gypsy.'

'You know that term is offensive these days?'

'And you know I don't care for society's rules.'

'Why do you call me that, anyway?'

'You have a gypsy's heart. You want to roam free, explore the world, live on the fringes, like me.'

'I think you've read me wrong. I live a very predictable life in the suburbs raising my niece and nephew.'

'That's not who you really are though, is it?'

Gen shifted in her seat. He had called it too close to the mark. Or at least, too close to who she used to be. Who she'd thought she would become.

Most people would assume Mac was dangerous because of the lifestyle he led, but the true threat lay in his ability to read people. No one outside of Gen's family had seen her so clearly before. Other than Jesse. She clasped her hands together in her lap.

'What did you find out?'

'I got us beers.' He gestured to the two steins on the table gathering condensation. This was his meeting, he was making sure she understood that.

'I don't drink alcohol when I'm riding.'

The corners of his mouth twitched. 'Yours is non-alcoholic.'

He'd read her right again. Her skin itched with discomfort. She checked her watch. 'I have to leave at —'

'In one hour, I know.'

'How?'

'Feral.'

His hacker clearly hadn't kept his investigations to the bikers of Windsor. She shifted in her seat again. What exactly was she getting into here? Maybe she should have told Jesse who she was meeting.

'You called me here, Mac. What do you want?'

He swigged his beer again, his gaze steady on hers, as if he were reading her soul. 'I assume you managed to keep the cop on a leash.'

She nodded.

'Then no questions till I'm done.'

She tucked her hands under her legs.

'Feral looked into the two one percenters near Windsor. The Black Crows are connected to a European club and specialise in trafficking small-time drugs. The Warriors run drugs too, but they also head up a money-laundering operation for an international crime syndicate.'

'How's an MC involved with money laundering?'

'They recruit and coordinate teams targeting casinos and one-arm bandits. They also provide muscle.'

She frowned. What did that have to do with Amber?

'The Warriors used the house in Windsor as a money drop.'

She sat tall. 'So the Stubenitskys were involved with them?'

'No. The whole point is to use abandoned houses to store drugs and cash until they can move them. But they got caught out this time. The wreckers came a week earlier than expected – something to do with asbestos in another house. When the police were called in, the Warriors wouldn't have been able to get to their money.'

'Someone gave them a key to the security fence.'

He shrugged. 'Not hard to bribe a worker.'

'But —'

He placed his hand on the table. 'One of the Warriors used to be a foster kid at the farm. Roger Bronson, otherwise known as Brick.'

She sat back. *Rog the Podge.* 'Your guy is good.'

'Used to be with the police.'

'Really?'

'Clubs aren't just made up of school washouts like me. We have lawyers, police, doctors and ex-military.'

'So just like any social club?'

Mac's lips twitched. 'Sounds about right.'

Gen crossed her arms. 'Just because the Warriors used the house doesn't mean they had anything to do with Amber's death.'

'You haven't let me finish.'

She tucked her hands under her thighs again.

'Feral uncovered another connection to the overseas syndicate.' He leant in. 'Sure you want to know?'

She bit her cheek against her impatience and nodded.

'The real estate company owned by the Minister for Liquor and Gaming, William Forsythe, has sold a number of properties to the extended families of high-level syndicate members.'

Cold slid between her shoulder blades. 'Are you saying William's corrupt?'

'There's no evidence other than the suspect sales. But given the syndicate's connection to the Warriors, their connection to the farm where Amber was found and her connection to Forsythe Commercial ... that's a few too many coincidences.'

'Why haven't the police looked into any of this?'

'Lots of deals are done under the table in property, particularly in Sydney – it's a lucrative market. It would take years of forensic accounting to pick it up.'

'Then how did Feral uncover it in one night?'

'He knew which dots to connect.'

'So wait ...' Gen sucked a breath down to her diaphragm in an attempt to slow her racing pulse. 'You're saying Forsythe

Commercial Real Estate might be involved in organised crime. Do you think Amber was a part of it? That she knew?'

'That I don't know. We're not sure who's involved, but it is a huge red flag that the property where she was found was also being used by the Warriors.'

'It seems stupid to use the place again if they knew Amber was there.'

He shrugged. 'They'd gotten away with it for twelve years. If Stubenitsky's son hadn't decided to have the place demo'd, her remains never would have been found.'

Gen leant her elbows on the table and buried her face in her hands. This was so much bigger than she had suspected. Had Amber somehow uncovered the link? Was that what had got her killed? How involved was Hugh?

She reared away from the table and strode down the embankment to the river. She stared at the trickling water and focused on her breath. If Hugh was involved, Lily and Charlie were in grave danger. And if William was at the centre of everything, she couldn't ever let the kids go to their grandparents' again.

Could she go to the police with any of this? She had no actual proof.

Footsteps approached and a hand squeezed her shoulder. 'You alright?'

'Trying to figure out what to do with all this information.'

'Nothing.'

'I can't do nothing!'

'You have no choice. Trust me, you don't want to put yourself in the sights of the syndicate or the club any more than you already have.'

'But if I tell Jesse he can —'

'I said no cops.'

'But —'

'No. The cops would demand to know where you got your information. Mention Phoenix and you'd be throwing Feral under the bus. Besides, the other clubs have connections in the police force too. Trusting anyone is dangerous.'

'You trusted me.'

He eyed her, his gaze inscrutable. 'Dad insisted we do what we can to protect you, and you forget, I can read you like a book.'

'Mac, I can't leave it. I couldn't live with myself.'

'You have to.'

'What if I investigated Forsythe Commercial Real Estate on my own? As a cadet I was given stories to research and fact-check all the time. What if I can put the connections in place?'

'It's too dangerous. I would have thought it was more important to be around for Lily and Charlie. Isn't that what Amber would have wanted?'

'That's low.'

'It's the truth.'

Gen headed back to the table to collect her gear.

He fell into step beside her. 'You going to be okay?'

'I need to figure out what to do. I can't expose the kids to danger, but I don't think I can just leave this alone. If Hugh had anything to do with Amber's death that means the kids aren't safe with him.'

He reached out and took her arm gently. 'There's one more thing.'

'Not sure I can take any more.'

'You need to know this. That cop, Johns. A member of his team was dismissed from the Tactical Operations Unit for police brutality. The kid he hurt was a drug runner for the Warriors but had turned informant to get out of charges.

Before he could testify, Johns and the other cop pulled the kid over for a search. He ran, there was a fight and the kid ended up with brain damage. Unexplained transfers were found in the other cop's bank account. He was dismissed from the force and sent to prison, but Johns was present at the attack too. Two months later he transferred from the TOU to Youth Command. Quite a step down for a career policeman.'

'Are you saying Jesse is corrupt?'

'The PCYC would be the perfect recruitment tool for organised crime.'

'Jesse would never do that.'

'How can you be sure?'

'I know him.'

'Did he tell you why he left the TOU?'

'No, but —'

'Think about it. Do you trust him enough to put Charlie and Lily's lives in his hands?'

And there was the rub. She had trusted Jesse once and he'd cut and run without a word, because it was best for his career. For all his talk, she had to face facts: Jesse's priority was Jesse.

Gen checked her watch. 'I need to go.'

'You won't tell Johns?'

'Not about Brick or the syndicate.'

He grabbed her arm again, and this time his grip was firm. 'None of it.'

She looked to his hand and when he removed it, she nodded.

'Please thank Feral. And thank you for meeting me.'

'This freebie is for Dad. Next time, you'll owe me.'

19

They rode back next to each other on the M1. Every time her mind strayed, she narrowed her focus to the heat and rumbling of the bike, the sound of the wind rushing through her helmet.

Gen broke away at the Pacific Highway and managed to avoid heavy traffic until she reached Chatswood, where she got caught at her first red light.

She put her feet to the ground and waited. Could she trust the information Mac had given her? His motivations? What if Phoenix was somehow involved, or there was some old grievance with her dad she was unaware of? The men weren't exactly angels; they'd had no problem holding a policeman hostage. Still, her gut told her Mac was telling the truth. And Forsythe Commercial being at the root of all this made sense.

But if that were true, she and the kids were in much bigger trouble than she'd realised. Her breathing shallowed. She had no resources to go up against organised crime gangs and corrupt officials. Too much was stacked against her. And she had no idea who to trust.

A horn beeped from behind, jerking her focus from the fears tumbling in her head. She raised her hand in apology and set off around the corner. Her priority had to be to shield the kids. But how? And is that what Amber had been trying to do all those years ago? Had Hugh tried to stop her?

The police had dropped all investigation of him because of Tobias's alibi, and pressure from the police minister. She needed to see the casino footage, and the supermarket videos. To put her mind to rest all had been above board in the investigation, there at least. Especially after the corruption Mac intimated. Hopefully Toni could access the videos for her. Otherwise, she'd have to ask Jesse again.

Could she even trust him? Jesse said he wanted a relationship with her, said he would always be there for her, but he was still lying to her, hadn't shared a thing about his jailed team member or why he himself had left the TOU. Was he a dirty cop too? A bitter taste coated her tongue.

She merged into the queue of traffic entering the M2. And what if she did somehow confirm everything Mac had shared? What if Hugh really was involved with a crime syndicate? Could she betray him, tell the police? It would allow her to apply for custody of Lily and Charlie, but it would also take away the one parent they had left.

How the hell could she navigate them safely through this?

The meeting with the mentor was a bust. They'd tried to tease out what had caused such a huge change in Lily's behaviour, talked about counselling to deal with the news about her mum, but in the end they all left none the wiser about what was going on. Any more infractions and Lily would face detention.

The second they left the room Lily took off to band practice. Gen checked her watch. *Dammit.* She was late for Charlie. Again.

At 4:35 pm she pulled into the driveway a little too fast, jumped out and knocked on the door. Timmy's mother answered, dressed in a linen dress, hair neat, nails perfect.

'Hi Sonya, I'm sorry I'm late.'

'No problem. I knew to build in a little extra time before we had to leave for swim training.'

Ouch.

'Charlie, your mum's here.' The woman blanched and then mouthed, *Sorry.* 'I mean aunt.'

Gen shrugged. 'Happens all the time.'

'By the way, I did canteen with Erica today and she asked if I could get Hugh's phone number from you.'

'What on earth does she want with him?'

'Something about selling her house.'

'She's barking up the wrong tree. He works in commercial.'

'Apparently he helped her during her divorce, got more money from the sale of the home and holiday house than she could have anywhere else.'

'Wouldn't she have his number then?'

'She said something about the one she had being out of service now.'

Gen found it hard to imagine Hugh going anywhere near Erica Sykes. She was a short stocky American who loved the sound of her own voice and had no important connections for Hugh to mine.

'I'll check if he's okay for me to pass on his details and text you.'

Charlie bounded down the hallway like an excited Border Collie, pulling up short when he reached Sonya. 'Thank you for having me, Mrs Carrough.'

'A pleasure, Charlie. See you at basketball on Saturday.'

'Where's Lily?' Charlie asked as he and Gen climbed in the car.

'Band practice.'

He went unusually quiet. She flicked a glance his way. He was frowning.

'She's been weird lately.'

'What do you mean?'

'She's always on her phone.'

'That's pretty normal for a sixteen-year-old girl.'

He wasn't wrong, though. Gen was sorely tempted to search it but couldn't bring herself to invade Lily's privacy like that. Her niece would never trust her again.

Gen inhaled, trying to calm the stress bubbling through her. She was being pulled in so many directions, it felt like at any moment she'd snap.

As Gen prepped dinner, her thoughts drifted back to what Mac had told her. The investigation was getting too unwieldy to make sense of on her own. She needed help wading through everything.

She set the soup simmering on the stove and rang Toni. No answer. She sighed and sent a text.

Are you free to talk today?

At airport. Off to WA. Man trapped at Big Bell mine.

Damn. Gen sent a reply.

Hope all goes well.

Everything OK?

Not even close, but there was no point worrying her friend when she'd be too far away to do anything.

Just need to hash out a few things. All good.

Her phone rang.

'Hey lovely, I haven't got long. What do you need?' A bleep sounded. 'Welcome to the flight, Ms Tsui,' said a nasal female voice.

'Sorry Gen, I'm walking down the airbridge.'

'It's okay. How long will you be in WA?'

'Until they rescue the guy.'

'You're in seat 3D, on your left. Enjoy the flight,' a young man's voice interrupted.

'Thank you.' Toni's voice returned to the line. 'Okay, I'm in my seat. What's going on?'

Gen let herself out onto the deck, closing the door behind her. 'Did you manage to get the videos from the car park and the casino?'

'Sorry, my source is on long service. I tried another guy, but he hasn't gotten back to me yet. What are you hoping to find?'

'Not sure, but my gut says there's something.'

'You always had great instincts.'

'Hmmmm.'

'I wish I could pack you in my bag for WA. Imagine, you could help with the background research, maybe even try your hand at a freelance article.'

'As if you need me.'

'You have a special ability to draw people out.'

'Sure doesn't feel that way right now. Lily's shut up tighter than a clam.'

'What's going on?'

'Excuse me?' the same male voice interrupted. Toni covered her phone, then came back a second later.

'Sorry Gen, I have to hang up, they're getting ready for take-off. I'll try to call when I land. Love you!'

Gen hung up and squeezed her eyes shut. Dammit, she was going to have to ask Jesse. The memory of Jesse's lips brushing her shoulder slid into her consciousness. She shook the image away. *That rubbish ends now.* He couldn't be trusted. He might even be corrupt. She needed to keep their interactions confined to the safe lane going forward.

She took a deep breath and typed.

Just wondering if you've managed to track down those videos for me?

Her phone buzzed with Jesse's reply almost immediately.

How did the meeting with M go?

She had no idea what to say. She couldn't share anything Mac had told her, but she had no idea how to divert him. Was she making a mistake trusting him with this?

Went fine.

Meet tomorrow morning to discuss?

I have a shift.

Early, before kids are up.

What choice did she have? She typed a reponse.

6 am. Won't have long though.

See you at mine.

Rotunda better tomorrow.

Why couldn't Toni have tracked down the videos?

She went back inside, stirred the minestrone she'd prepared for dinner. One thing at a time. Gen headed upstairs to Lily, who'd stomped straight to her room when she got home. Crinkling and thumping noises came from behind the door.

Gen knocked, but there was no answer. She tried again, rapping harder this time.

'What?' Lily shouted.

'Can I come in?'

The door swung open. Lily had her hand on her hip, music blaring from her headphones. Gen surveyed the room. A pile of colourful clothing spilt from a plastic garbage bag. The bookcase, still filled with books, had lost all colour – Lily had turned the spines in. Looking around the room, Gen realised she had removed everything that gave the space personality. It was devoid of colour and trinkets. The mirrored wardrobe doors were stacked to the side, revealing an almost barren railing and shelves. Only a selection of black and dark-blue clothing remained alongside the dark-green school uniforms. On the desk lay a box of black hair dye.

'Thinking of changing your hair colour?'

No response.

Gen needed to find a way to connect. The books on the top shelf hadn't been turned around yet – Lily probably couldn't reach them. Gen lifted out the first in a series of dystopian fiction and turned the spine inwards.

Lily paused in tying up the bag. A crack in her demeanour. Gen turned all the books until the top shelf resembled the others.

She pivoted and found Lily on the floor in front of the mirror, a stick of eyeliner in her hand. Gen had no idea she was even interested in make-up, let alone owned any.

She sat cross-legged next to Lily, who ignored her. Gen reached for the dark eyeshadow palette she spied on the floor and began applying it in the style of her teenage years. Lily's eyes widened.

Gen's mouth twitched, but she kept going. She picked up the deep purple lipstick and applied it to her lips.

Lily removed her headphones. 'Can you teach me how to get the eyeliner closer to my lashes?'

Gen gently lifted the outside corner of Lily's right eyelid, placed a dot, then followed an invisible line inwards and placed two more dots.

'Join them, with light strokes.' She handed back the black pencil and waited for Lily to complete the line. 'Now colour the area in stronger.'

'Can you do the dots on my other eye?'

'How about you tell me what's been going on first? Seems there are a lot of changes in your life. And I haven't seen any of your friends around lately.'

'That's because they're not my friends anymore.'

Gen's hand hovered in the air. She was desperate to ask why but needed to give Lily the space to share. She placed the dots on Lily's left eyelid then handed the pencil to her. Lily's gaze lowered, and she twirled the stick in her fingers.

'One of them told everyone in my year that I copied her answers on a test, that I cheated.' She glanced up, tears in her eyes. 'I promise I didn't.'

'Oh honey, of course you didn't.' What was wrong with those kids? Gen put her arm around Lily's shoulders. 'Did she tell the teachers the same thing?'

'No, but she lied and told the kids she did, and that the school refused to punish me out of pity, because my mum was missing. It was horrible. Everyone believed her. People avoided sitting next to me during tests. I know it doesn't sound bad but —'

'It sounds awful.' Why the hell hadn't the teachers picked up on this? 'Who told these lies, Lil? I can go to the school and —'

'No!' Lily's eyes widened in panic. 'If you tell the school what happened she'll make my life worse. She already started a new rumour when Mum was found. Told everyone she died

because of —' Her breath caught on a sob. 'Because you —'
She hiccupped another sob.

'It's okay, sweetheart.'

'It's not!' Lily wailed. 'She said you were in a bikie gang, that
you got Mum killed. I haven't talked to anyone at school since.'

Lily fell into Gen's arms and the tears poured out.

Gen rubbed Lily's back. Every molecule of her body wanted
to hunt the bully down, expose her for the callous coward she
was. She wiggled her jaw back and forth to relax it. Anger
wouldn't help Lily now. When Lily's breathing slowed Gen
pulled back slightly and met her niece's eyes.

'We need to fix this, but I won't do anything at school
without talking it over with you, okay?'

'Promise?'

Gen nodded, grabbed a tissue, and dabbed at the eyeliner
tracking down Lily's cheek.

'So who have you been talking to on the phone?'

'New friends.'

'From where?'

'Around.' Lily pushed to her feet. 'I better wash this off
properly before Dad gets home.'

She strode away and closed the bathroom door before Gen
could think of a response. *Around?* What did that mean? Who
were these new friends? She scanned the room but there was
no sign of Lily's phone.

God, she wished Toni were here to talk things through.
Should Gen go to the school and insist they get to the bottom
of the bullying? Lily may never forgive her, especially if it did
make the situation even worse. Gen ran her hands through her
hair. What would Amber do?

Silence rang in her head.

20

Gen woke with a start to the blare of her alarm. She stretched out her achy limbs and forced herself out of bed. Hugh's loud arrival home at 1 am last night had woken her. Afterwards, she'd struggled to get back to sleep. Each time she'd been close to drifting off, her worries filed through her mind like flashcards.

She sighed. She had better get moving if she was going to make it to the beach by six. She pulled on jeans and a black tee from the floor, scraped her hair back into a ponytail and headed downstairs. A voice from the kitchen stopped her in her tracks.

'What are you doing up so early?'

What the hell was Hugh doing awake? He'd come in so late last night she'd been sure he'd sleep in.

She found him at the kitchen bench, newspaper in hand. 'Shouldn't I be the one asking you that?'

'It is a workday, Geneva.' He looked her up and down. 'Well, for some of us it is.'

Gen sidestepped the dig. She needed to get out of the house without arousing suspicion.

'I need you to drop these at the dry cleaners today.' He held up a crumpled suit and shirt.

'I'm not your housekeeper, Hugh.'

'For Christ's sake, can't you cut me some slack? I'm running myself ragged.' He went to the cupboard and shook a few ibuprofen into his palm, swallowing them dry.

Gen eyed the pile of clothes. The reek of stale smoke and sweet perfume oozed from the fabric. 'Amber might have fallen for your BS, but I'm not her.'

He looked her up and down again, like he was searching for something. 'Clearly.'

'Partying hardly qualifies for sympathy.'

'Forget I asked.'

Gen paused. If she wanted to know what Hugh was up to, it would be a lot easier to have him on side. She put out her hand. 'I'll drop them in on the way home from work, but you'll have to pick them up.'

Hugh threw her a smile laced in practised charm. 'You're a life saver.' He started up the coffee machine. 'Want one?'

She shook her head. 'I'm heading out for a ride.'

He pointed his coffee cup at her. 'Make sure you're back to get the kids up. I need to be able to rely on you. Especially with the way things are at work.'

'What's going on?'

His face went blank. *Dammit.*

'I'm going to shower. Be back by the time I need to leave.'

She grabbed her keys and headed for her bike.

Five minutes later, she parked in a side street where her bike would be less visible, then crossed to the white rotunda at the centre of Balmoral Reserve. Her stomach was a writhing ball of nerves and doubt. Half of her wanted to challenge Jesse head-on with what Mac had told her, but the other half wasn't even sure she could trust his response. On Friday night he'd seemed so open. Real. Even when she refused to back him with a report to the police, he hadn't deserted her. But maybe it was all an act to gain her trust.

Dark clouds loomed above. Jesse sat on the stairs, dressed in black running shorts, a navy fitted tee and a white baseball cap. As she approached, he stood and handed her a piccolo with a dash of milk. He still remembered. More manipulation or an act of kindness? Mac had severely messed with her head.

'Thanks.' She took it and pointed towards the island. 'Do you mind if we find a place out of sight?'

'Embarrassed to be seen with me?'

Gen flushed. 'Don't want to tempt fate where Hugh is concerned.'

He swept his open palm forward. 'Lead the way.' They crossed the bridge to the island and sat on a wooden bench, leaving a substantial gap between them. The growls and barks of two dogs asserting their dominance carried across on the light morning breeze. The promenade was already heaving with joggers and dog walkers, swimmers making their way to the baths, and the occasional parent pushing a pram.

Jesse reached into his pocket and removed a memory stick. 'Ethan and I have stuck our necks out for this. If it comes out I've shared this information with you, the breach will be investigated.'

'I won't share it with anyone without checking with you first.' She put her hand out, but his fist closed around the stick and dropped back to his lap.

'What happened yesterday?'

She knew he wouldn't give up. 'Jesse, I promised him I wouldn't share anything he told me. Surely you understand – after all, I just made you the same promise.'

'It's a bit different.'

'How?'

'Policeman versus outlaw biker.'

'How do you know he's an outlaw?'

'Who else would have the balls to kidnap a policeman?'

That question niggled like a pebble in a shoe. She levelled a gaze at him. 'Why *did* they think that would be okay?'

'What?'

'They knew you were a policeman when they pulled us over. Why would they think you wouldn't report the incident?'

'I would have except you begged me not to! And threatened not to back me up if I did. Remember?' He ran a hand through his hair. 'I only gave in when you promised to keep me in the loop. Are you going to keep your word?'

She hated this, had no idea who to trust. 'I'm caught between a rock and a hard place, Jesse. I need M's help. He has resources and access you're not allowed to use.'

'So, you're happy breaking the law?'

'Well I've trusted the system for twelve years and it got me nowhere. I have to pursue whatever avenues open up to me, no matter what.'

'Is that what I am, an avenue for information?'

'Yes.'

Hurt flickered across his face.

'I mean, initially, but that's not what the other night was.'

He raised an eyebrow.

'I was confused and I needed to burn off the tension between us.'

'You think that explanation makes things any better?'

'Look, can we put Friday behind us? I'm sorry, I shouldn't have let things go that far. But if we're going to keep working together —'

He looked crushed. 'Working together? I thought we were friends.'

'If we're going to be *friends* who work together, I can't keep revisiting Friday. If you need to, then I'm sorry but we might need to take more space.'

Jesse sighed, held out his hand and dropped the memory stick into her palm.

She stood and tucked it into her pocket.

'Got what you came for and now you just leave?'

'Don't be like that.'

'Like what, Gen? You're running around, using people, letting the kids down, and now you're getting mixed up with a dangerous group of criminals and you just want me to stand by meekly and let it happen? Clearly you don't know me very well.'

'I will never let those kids down.'

'Seems to me Lily's in one hell of a mess and yet you're too busy keeping secrets to help her.'

'You want to talk about secrets? You've hardly been open, have you?'

'What do you mean?'

'You never explained why you left the TOU. It was your dream job, worth abandoning us for, apparently.'

'I had no choice, Gen. I already explained what happened.'

'Oh yeah? Mac told me your team member was dirty, was charged with police brutality and that's why you moved to Youth Command. How do I know you're any different?'

'Mac, huh?'

She mentally kicked herself. 'You haven't answered my question.'

'Ralph, the team member you mentioned, betrayed every oath he ever uttered. In the end he bashed a seventeen-year-old kid who'd got mixed up in the wrong crowd but was trying to make things right.'

'And where were you?'

'Trying to pull Ralph off him. Not a day goes by that I don't wish I'd reported him sooner. His behaviour had become unpredictable, he was pushing the boundaries of procedure more and more, but when I challenged him, he begged me to let him get help privately. His wife did too. My gut told me to back off, that letting him deal with his issues quietly would be best for my career too.' Jesse's shoulders hunched and he stared at the ground. 'But that night, after the ambulance took that boy away, I couldn't look at myself in the mirror. The right thing to do all along was report Ralph's suspect behaviour to Professional Standards but I took the easy route. I swore I'd never do that again.'

That sounded like the Jesse she thought he was. Could she trust him after all?

'I have two regrets in my life, Gen. Walking away from Amber's case and not reigning Ralph in before that boy got hurt. I made my amends about Ralph by testifying for the prosecution. But I still need to make things right with you and the kids.'

Gen felt a pang of sympathy at how awful that must have been for him, but the analytical part of her, the one she'd committed to listening to, noted he'd left out any mention of his partner taking bribes, and the suspicion that had been cast Jesse's way.

She still didn't know if she could trust him.

Gen checked the time. 'I need to get back before the kids wake up.'

She threw her coffee cup in the recycling bin and gave him an awkward half-wave. 'Thank you for the videos.'

'Gen.' He stepped closer. 'I do have your back. Please trust that.'

'Right. Thanks.' She gave another awkward wave and practically bolted back to her bike. She was desperate to look at the videos but would have to wait until after work. She couldn't afford to miss another shift.

As she turned down her street, Hugh's Porsche was reversing out of the driveway. She checked the time. He'd left early.

It was a gloomy morning, and the restaurant was quiet. Gen was relieved when the boss sent her home early; he was probably glad to see her go. All shift she'd been distracted; the memory stick she couldn't bear to leave at home burning a hole in the pocket of her work pants.

She had to find something in the videos to keep the case open, to buy her time to investigate the connection between Forsythe Commercial Real Estate and the crime syndicate. If there even was one. She let herself into the house and called out. No answer. She knocked on Hugh's locked office door just in case, to confirm she was alone. He couldn't catch her watching the videos. Not after yesterday's threat.

She locked her bedroom door, opened her computer, and inserted the stick. She'd never seen these videos before; she'd been picking the kids up from school when they were played at the inquest.

Six files came up as thumbnails, all dated the night of Amber's abduction. Gen's throat tightened. She was about to watch Amber's last free moments on earth.

She clicked on the first, a grainy screenshot from above the supermarket's automatic doors, facing into the store. Two checkout operators, both teenage girls, served a customer each. A businessman entered and bought cigarettes.

Two minutes in, Amber rushed through the doors, head down. She bypassed the trolleys and turned right, towards the baby goods aisle. A minute later she reappeared on screen carrying a packet of nappies under one arm and texting as she went. Amber's phone records had shown that she'd sent numerous texts to Hugh that night. All unanswered. Amber placed the nappies on the conveyer belt and looked up to greet the young woman serving her. Gen's hand pressed at her chest. It had been so long since she'd seen her sister's face. Her beautiful warm smile.

Amber glanced again at her phone and her expression fell. She paid and walked quickly from the store. As a pensioner wheeling a trolley took Amber's place at the checkout, the video finished. Gen sat back. That was it? She should have been more specific, requested the complete tapes of the night. What if the man in the baseball cap had appeared earlier?

She settled a pillow behind her back and opened the second file. This one showed the angle from outside the store, covering the entrance. A minute in, her sister appeared up the stairwell from the back lane. She strode along the footpath, handbag hooked over her shoulder, and turned left into the supermarket.

Five minutes later, Amber appeared back on camera, a packet of nappies tucked under her arm. She set off briskly to the stairs, disappearing off camera again. No one followed her and not one motorbike had passed by in shot.

Gen rewound the tape, paused on the image where Amber exited the supermarket. She touched her fingers to the grainy image, a lump forming in her throat. This was the last image of Amber alive. She traced her sister's heart-shaped face. Even doing a last-minute dash to the shops, she'd managed to look elegant. Her gorgeous blonde hair curled down her back, as if she'd just left the hairdressers, not run around all day after a busy four-year-old and a baby. Gen's vision blurred. She wished she could dive into the video, defend her sister from what was about to happen.

She allowed the tears to fall. Amber was so petite, an easy target. She hadn't stood a chance.

After a minute, Gen grabbed a tissue, wiped her eyes and blew her nose. This was getting her nowhere. She threw the tissue in the bin and her emotions along with it.

The detectives had cleared every staff member and customer who'd been present, as well as the woman who had raised the alert. Unfortunately, she hadn't even seen Amber, just the abandoned car in the back laneway.

The police were right, there was nothing.

The third video was from the Imperial Casino and was of much higher quality. Gen watched Hugh and Tobias, both looking almost boy-like, swagger through the entrance, laughing and jostling one another. A group of young women tottered past and both men pivoted slowly, their leering gazes tracking the girls. Hugh grinned wide, slapped Tobias on the back. A rush of heat raged through Gen. Hugh looked as if he didn't have a care in the world, while Amber had been fretting all day, texting him constantly.

The men walked off camera and the video ended.

The next angle was from above a roulette table. Hugh paid the croupier for ten large stacks of red chips and pushed a pile onto one square. The croupier spun the wheel, threw the ball the opposite direction on the track. As the wheel slowed, the ball fell into place and Hugh punched his hands in the air. The croupier pushed his winnings over. The process repeated and Hugh won again. A crowd started to gather behind him.

Gen checked Tobias. He was watching on from Hugh's left, forever the sidekick.

A waitress came into view, delivered three drinks. Hugh drank a whole one down then grabbed another. Tobias nursed his.

Thirty minutes later Hugh's winning streak had well and truly ended. The crowd dispersed and he stood, swaying on the spot. Hugh had drunk three whiskeys in his time at the table. Was that enough to cause the stumbling, bumbling idiot walking off screen?

She clicked on the third video from the casino, which focused on the bank of hotel lifts. Tobias appeared, supporting an unfocused, meandering Hugh around the waist, guiding him towards a lift. They entered alone and the doors closed.

The final video showed the lift's interior. Hugh leant into the side wall, and Tobias propped him up. They got off on floor nineteen and turned left down the corridor. The footage returned to the beginning still. There were no more videos to watch. The coroner had noted at the inquest that the hotel didn't have surveillance cameras in their corridors and neither Tobias nor Hugh had appeared on any other footage until morning.

Gen groaned in frustration. The videos had given her absolutely nothing. What did she do now?

She climbed from the bed and plodded down to the laundry to the pile of dirty clothes she'd ignored this morning. She separated the colours and turned out the pockets of each item, making sure there were no erroneous tissues. The action tilted her thoughts to the film she'd found in Amber's dress. She pulled her phone from her back pocket and checked. The order status was still listed as pending.

She set the laundry cycle to wash and headed back upstairs. Her thoughts scrolled through every tangent and possible lead and kept coming back to what Mac had said about Forsythe Commercial Real Estate. William sold himself as an upstanding moral crusader. Would he really risk his reputation and political career by associating with organised crime or outlaw bikie gangs? She tried to picture him sitting on the stool at

Mac's clubhouse, shooting the breeze with Feral and Viking. The image refused to form.

What if William Forsythe's political career was connected to Amber's murder? The police had investigated the possibility and ruled it out, but they hadn't been looking for connections to an organised crime syndicate. And how could she uncover any links anyway?

Gen groaned and set the laptop aside. She needed caffeine. Heading for the kitchen, she passed by Hugh's office and stilled.

Could she?

She checked the time. One hour before the cleaner was due to come. She called Hugh's mobile. No answer. She dialled his executive assistant.

'Hugh Forsythe's office, Kelly speaking.'

'Hi, it's Gen. Is he there?'

'He's in a board meeting, won't be out until five. You want to leave a message?'

'I'll wait until he gets home.' She hung up.

She stared at the door. She wasn't going to get a chance like this again in a hurry.

She wriggled the handle. As expected, it was locked. She searched the kitchen drawer for a spare key but found none. She walked to his bedroom, hesitated on the threshold.

In for a penny, in for a pound.

She checked the bedside table, nudging around the neat piles of books and the vintage twin bell clock, but there was no key. Bentley sat in the doorway, watching. She rifled through the drawers but still no key.

She returned to his office door and knelt. The lock looked the same as the one on her door, which had a simple latch button at the back.

She mentally sifted through the lock-picking research she'd done before going to the farm. Maybe the credit card trick would work here.

She collected her card from her handbag.

Approaching the door, she shook out her hands. She slid the plastic in the tiny gap between the door and its frame, shuffling it up and down. The latch gave way and the door opened inward. She pocketed the card and scanned the room. The floor was carpeted in cream. A Scandi desk sat in front of two glass doors. A brown and khaki striped rug defined a sitting area featuring a brown leather lounge and designer coffee table. On the walls hung a series of metal-framed pictures of city buildings. In the corner, a fireplace sat empty; above it hung a huge mirror bracketed by light fittings. The room looked like the set of an American movie about a wealthy businessman at the top of his game, not a middle-aged man working for his father.

Gen licked her lips. Once she crossed the threshold there'd be no turning back. Her gaze landed on two photos resting on the mantel. The first was a portrait of the kids that Helen had commissioned last Christmas. The perfect grandchildren of the perfect politician's son. The second was of the Forsythe clan with William and Helen sitting at the centre, their children and grandchildren arranged stiffly around them. Amber was nowhere in sight.

Gen strode into the room and stopped in the middle of the space. Everything was perfectly placed and squared, right down to the open picture book on the coffee table. Every molecule in her body wanted to tilt the book out of position, but she resisted.

A wet nose pushed against her palm and Bentley leant against her leg. She patted his head, then bent down and scratched under his chin, searching his eyes.

'I've got to do this, right?'

Bentley nuzzled her hand.

'You'd better wait outside. You know how he is about this room.' She pointed to the indent Bentley had created over the years, sleeping outside the door. 'Keep an eye out.'

She circled the desk. On it sat an antique wooden Victorian desk clock, and a freestanding screen but no computer. He'd have his laptop at work, and she didn't know his password anyway. She tried the top desk drawer and it slid open. Everything inside was neatly packed: pens, notepad and stapler all lined up. The notepad was unused. She lifted it up. There was nothing underneath.

She massaged her temples. There had to be something here. She couldn't face another dead end. She slid out the second drawer. It was filled with files. She walked her fingers across the labels. *Banking. Car insurance. Car maintenance. Miscellaneous. Tax.* She pulled out the thick banking file.

The first page was a typical bank statement. National Bank of Australia. Account name: Hugh Richard Forsythe. There were deposits and withdrawals listed, but nothing stood out. She flicked through the file, losing interest fast. Then a new account appeared. Westpac Bank. Account name: Liliana Forsythe. The balance increased by large amounts of interest each month, but no other transactions were recorded. Gen continued shuffling through the statements, finding an account for Charles Forsythe. The interest payments were the same.

These were the accounts he'd set up with the money from Amber's insurance payout. She swallowed. At least he'd done as he'd promised there. Her thoughts slid to Amber's inquest, five years ago, where Hugh had pushed to have her declared legally dead. They had such a fight about it. He'd said he was doing it for the kids, so that the insurance payment could go into investment accounts for them, saying the longer it was there the more it would build up. She'd screamed that the kids needed hope that their mother was alive more than they needed to accrue interest. She'd thought she'd been doing the right thing, but it seemed Hugh had been right all along. Had he already known Amber was dead?

She fanned through the rest of the pages. At the back of the pile her eye caught on an orange triangular bank logo she didn't recognise: TNC Bank. Account name: Forsythe Commercial Real Estate. *Weird.* What was Hugh doing with work bank-account statements in his personal files? She took a photo of the first page and turned the paper over to capture page two.

Keys jangled in the front door, then a lock turned. *Oh shit.* Gen jostled the statements into a pile and closed the folder.

'Hello?' a northern English accent called out. Nancy, the cleaner. If she saw Gen in here, she might mention it to Hugh.

Bentley scrambled to his feet and set off at a lope towards the front door.

Gen stuffed the banking file back in place, shoved the drawer closed, straightened the chair up to the desk and darted for the door, bashing her leg against the table in her haste. She bit her lip to keep from cursing and realigned the table with the indentations in the rug. She dashed the last few steps, depressed the lock button, and eased the door closed as quietly as possible.

Heading to the front door, she sucked air deep into her lungs to slow her breathing, praying desperately that she'd left no sign of being in Hugh's office.

21

A loud crash woke Gen. Heavy footsteps approached her room. She reared out of bed, glancing around for something she could use to protect herself. Her door slammed open, bouncing against the wall, and the light blazed on.

'What the fuck were you doing in my office?' Hugh filled the doorway, chest heaving, face flushed.

'What ...?' Gen blinked against the bright light, adrenaline rampaging through her body. 'I haven't ... I wasn't ...'

'Don't lie to me.'

Gen grabbed a hoodie from the floor and slipped it over her T-shirt and tracksuit pants. 'Keep your voice down, you'll wake the kids.'

'Don't tell me what to do!' Hugh marched forward and jammed his finger in her face. 'You broke into my office.'

She coughed against the alcohol-infused breath that invaded her airways.

'Hugh, the cleaner was here today —'

'Don't you dare. She knows she'd be dismissed immediately if she went in there.'

'Maybe you're being paranoid.'

'Then how do you explain the strands of Bentley's hair on the rug? I've never, not once, allowed that dog into my office.'

'Oh come on. You could have carried them in on your clothes.'

'You're lying.' Hugh grabbed her arm and dragged her out of the room and down the stairs. 'Tell me what you were looking for.'

'Let me go!'

'Not until you tell the truth.'

'You're hurting me, Hugh. Amber wouldn't want you to behave like this.'

'Fuck Amber!' He stormed into the kitchen and picked up Amber's chair. 'I'm so sick of all this shit!' He carried it out onto the deck and threw the chair over the balcony.

'No!' The chair landed with a sickening crunch next to the pool.

Gen stared at the crumpled heap below. How was she going to explain that to the kids? 'What is wrong with you?'

'There will be no more talk of Amber, you hear me?'

Gen's fists clenched at her sides, primed with every bit of contempt that had built up over the years. 'What are you so worried I'd find in your office?' She turned and marched towards it. 'Maybe I should take a good look.'

He seized her by the upper arm, and she whirled on him. 'If you touch me one more time, I will have you charged with assault.'

'Fine. Get out.'

'You can't throw me out.'

'This is my house —'

'Hugh —'

'You have ten minutes to pack up your things and leave.'

'Or what?' She crossed her arms.

'Or I call the police and have them remove you.'

Her eyes widened. 'You don't mean that. What about the kids?'

'They're better off without you.'

'You can't send me away, not after what happened with Amber.'

'I can do whatever I want.'

'It's not all about you, you self-absorbed arse!'

'You have nine minutes.'

'I promised them I'd never leave.'

'You shouldn't make promises you can't keep.'

'What promises have you kept, ever?' she hissed.

'How dare you!'

'No, Hugh, how dare you? I stepped in for those kids when you were barely functioning.' Her breath heaved in and out.

'That was years ago.'

'Was it? Seems to me you've fallen off the wagon again.'

'Things are stressful at work, how many times do I have to tell you?'

'Those kids love me. They need me.'

'You're a bad influence.'

'Fuck you, Hugh! At least I'm here for them.'

'Not anymore.' He tapped his Tag Heuer. 'Eight minutes.'

He was really going to do this. *Fuck*. She needed to defuse the situation. 'Please calm down, Hugh. Sleep on it.'

'I can't trust you to be in this house.'

'Look, I'm sorry. I did go into your office and it was wrong. I'll never do it again. I've just been so worried about what's going on with you. I wanted to help.'

'I am none of your business.'

'Hugh, please.'

He folded his arms across his chest. 'Seven minutes.'

'Aunty Gen, what's going on?'

She turned. A sleepy-eyed Charlie wrapped his arms around her waist. She pulled him in close, her eyes pleading with Hugh.

'Your aunt has decided to move out.'

'No! I won't let you lie to them.' She knelt and bracketed Charlie's cheeks with her palms, her heart wrenching at the distraught expression in his eyes. 'Honey, your dad and I have had a disagreement. We just need a little time to sort it out.'

'Who's the liar now?' Hugh yanked Charlie from her arms. 'Gen *is* leaving.'

'No!' Charlie's anguished cry almost destroyed her. He pulled against his dad's hold. 'Please Gen, we need you!'

'I need you too, mate. I'll fix things.' She stepped forward and Hugh held Charlie tighter. 'Hugh, think about what you're doing!'

'I am. For the first time in ages. This is what's best for all of us.'

'All of us? You mean you, you selfish ...' Her gaze fell to Charlie. 'I will not disappear from their lives.'

'You will if I have anything to say about it.'

Tears ran down Charlie's cheeks. He pulled and squirmed against his dad's hold, reaching for Gen.

She pulled her phone from her pocket and started filming her drunk brother-in-law as he clutched and wrangled his crying son. It was the only thing she could think to do.

He set Charlie aside and lurched forward. He gripped her wrist, trying to prise the phone from her hand.

Lily ran from the hallway. 'Dad!' she screamed. 'Let Aunty Gen go.'

'Hugh, stop! You're scaring the kids. Please!'

Hugh twisted Gen's arm up and behind her back.

Lily waved her phone in the air. 'If you don't step away, Dad, I'm calling the police.'

He dropped Gen's arm and began to pace. Gen ran to Charlie, who was huddled against the wall, shaking, his eyes wide.

'It's okay, sweetheart. You're okay.' She guided him to Lily, keeping Hugh in her peripheral vision the whole time.

'Are you okay?' Lily's eyes were like pools of despair.

'I'm fine.' She pulled both kids in for a hug. 'Go back to your rooms. I'll be up in a minute, I promise.'

She waited for Lily's door to bang shut, then whirled on Hugh. 'You son of a bitch. How many times did you lay your hands on Amber? Did the police know?'

'I never hurt her.'

'I don't believe you.'

His fists balled. 'I swear to God, Geneva, if you don't leave this house now —'

'I'll leave, once I've said goodnight to the kids, but I will be back tomorrow morning to drive them both to school.'

'I'll drive them.'

'You'll still be over the limit.'

'I don't want you in my house.'

'I'll take the car and pick them up from the driveway tomorrow. But Hugh, I'm going to tell them to call me if they are the slightest bit scared. Your behaviour tonight was unhinged. I will send the recording to your father if I feel I have to.'

'Are you blackmailing me?'

'No, I'm keeping Lily and Charlie safe.'

'I would never harm them. I protect them with everything I have.'

'Like you did with Amber, huh?' Gen's lip wobbled and before she could show any more weakness, she turned on her heel and marched up the stairs.

Her entire body shook, her thoughts tumbling and tripping over one another. She didn't want to leave the kids alone with him. Maybe she should take them with her? But if she did, he'd definitely call the police on her. She entered Lily's room and found Charlie curled up in his sister's arms. She knelt at the side of the bed.

'I'm so, so sorry.'

'Why was Daddy angry?' Charlie's eyes were red from crying.

'I made a mistake.'

'Say you're sorry.'

'It's not that simple, sweetheart, but I promise we'll sort it out. Both of us love you guys very much.'

'So, you're not leaving?' he asked.

'Just for tonight. Go to sleep now and I'll be here in the morning to take you to school.'

'He was scary.'

Gen ran her hand over his head. 'Your dad is struggling much more than I realised.'

Hugh's footsteps thumped up the stairs. 'It's time.'

Gen's gaze darted to Lily, who had yet to say a word.

She tilted her head towards her brother. 'I have him.'

Gen squeezed Charlie. 'Love you.'

'Love you too.' He clung to her neck, and she gently untwined his arms.

She turned to Lily, hugged her tight.

'Are you really okay?' Lily whispered in her ear.

'I'll have my phone on all night. Call if you need me.' She pulled back and checked Lily's eyes. 'Are you going to be all right?'

Lily blinked. Gen touched her forehead to her niece's and whispered, 'I'm not leaving. I'll be in the car in the driveway.'

The relief she saw in Lily's expression almost broke her in two. 'Just don't tell Charlie because he might try and sneak out to me.'

'*Now*, Geneva.'

She kissed each child once more, then slid from the bed. Hugh followed her to her room and watched from the doorway as she filled an overnight bag. She moved downstairs, ignoring him, and went to the kitchen to grab the car keys. Her stomach turned at the empty space where Amber's chair had been.

Hugh was right about one thing: they couldn't go on like this. She had to find a way to retain access to the kids. He was getting more unbalanced by the day, and if the Forsythes were in bed with a crime syndicate, the kids weren't safe with any of them. She just had to find the evidence.

She strode down the hall and out the front door, her eyes burning, her body trembling, terrified at leaving the kids alone with Hugh. But she had no choice. He'd call the police if she didn't leave.

The door locked behind her.

22

Gen sat in the front seat of the four-wheel drive, gaze fixed on the light escaping around the edges of Lily's blind. It was 1 am. The kids really needed to go to sleep.

An owl hooted. Six counts later, it hooted again. It had kept up a steady rhythm since she came out to the car half an hour ago. There must be a predator nearby.

Gen reached for the door handle. It was too much, expecting Lily to look after Charlie after all they just witnessed. She opened the door and began to climb from the seat.

The light went off. She continued to watch the window, one foot in the car, one foot out. Should she check on them anyway? But what if Hugh caught her? She sighed, slumped into the driver's seat, and pulled the door closed. The last thing the kids needed was Hugh going off again.

She dropped her head back to the headrest. The situation was getting out of control. Maybe she should move out? Keep looking after the kids but have her own space at night. But that would leave the kids without a buffer. What if Hugh turned his anger on them?

Had he ever aimed it at Amber? Gen hadn't suspected anything at the time. Then again, she'd been so caught up in her own life, so obsessed with her cadetship, could she honestly say she would have noticed the signs?

Gen eased her seat back as far as it would go and stared at the roof. She'd known something wasn't right. Especially that final week. Hugh had barely been home, and when he was, he and Amber fought constantly.

On her way downstairs for breakfast Gen heard raised voices from the kitchen and paused in the stairwell.

'Please, Hugh,' Amber said. 'Please, just walk away.'

'You don't understand!'

'Our family should come first.'

'Why won't you fucking trust me?' Hugh snapped.

'Because you shut me out!'

A minute later the front door slammed. Gen entered the kitchen and Amber turned to the stove, swiping at her eyes as she stirred porridge.

Before Gen could ask what was going on, Charlie's cry blasted through the monitor. Ten minutes later, when Amber returned with both kids in tow, she pretended nothing had happened.

With Hugh's behaviour tonight and what she'd learned from Mac, that argument took on a new light. His current stress levels seemed the same as they had back then. Could he have played a part in Amber's disappearance? Was he capable of murder? She reared up and checked Lily's window again, then exhaled. The light was still off.

Even if Hugh was innocent in Amber's death, his behaviour now was out of control, and that meant the children were at risk. She needed to find out, collate whatever evidence she could.

Gen peered at his bedroom window. No light spilt from around his curtains. She crept down the driveway and pushed open the back gate. It creaked loudly. Her gaze flew to Hugh's window, but his room remained dark. She snapped photos of the wreckage of Amber's chair from numerous angles, then returned to the car. She wasn't going down without a fight.

She placed her phone in the cradle by the seat and lay back down, beginning to shiver. No point blasting the heat; running the engine would attract attention. Mrs Rosen next door would call the police and Hugh would probably have Gen charged with trespass.

She tucked her tee into her tracksuit pants and pulled her sweatshirt hood over her head and ears. She found a beach towel behind her seat and covered herself with it, then placed her leather jacket over the top.

She was going to need to step up and fight. No more keeping the peace. Tomorrow, after work, she would contact a family lawyer, show them the video of Hugh, drunk and out of control, and the photos of the chair he'd destroyed. She'd also check her arms for bruising and record any she could find.

He would not remove her from the kids' lives. She'd die before she let that happen.

The morning cackles of a kookaburra woke Gen. She opened her eyelids and groaned. It was barely first light.

The kookaburra's low hiccupping chuckle started again, building into a raucous laugh. Gen rubbed her eyes and set the seat back to upright. She checked Lily's bedroom window. The blind was still down. Hopefully the kids had slept better than she had.

Climbing from the car, she stretched her arms above her head then bent forward, reaching for toes she hadn't come close to touching in years. She unfolded stiffly and pressed the remote for the garage. Rubbing her hands together, she blew mists of hot air between them as she waited for the door to rise.

She put her phone on charge and then splashed her face with water at the tiny sink. Her fingers hurt with the heat, but at least she could feel them again. She glanced at herself in the rusted mirror and for the first time in years, wished she wore make-up. She looked exactly how she felt – exhausted and unkempt. Luckily, she could do her job in her sleep, which is pretty much what she would be doing today.

She patted her hair down with water, finger-combed out the matted knots, applied deodorant and changed into her work clothes. Then she returned to the car and sent Toni a message telling her about last night and, just in case, asking if she could stay.

At 6:30 am her phone bleeped with a text from Charlie.

Dad said he's leaving in an hour. Are u going to be here?

I'm in the driveway.

The front curtain moved aside, and a grinning Charlie waved. Then he jumped, his smile fell, and the curtain dropped back into place. *Fucking Hugh.*

She scrolled through the photos and video she'd taken the night before and checked they had saved to the cloud.

At 7:30 am on the dot, a limousine pulled up at the end of the drive. Hugh exited the house, not a hair out of place, no sign of the irrational man from last night. The kids followed him out and he locked the door. He strode past Gen without a glance, climbed into the limo and it drove off.

Gen leapt from the car and Charlie ran into her arms. She wrapped him up tight, inhaling his scent. Lily lagged behind; her focus absorbed in her phone.

'Morning Lily.'

'Morning,' she mumbled as she typed.

'Shotgun!' Charlie broke from Gen's hold and ran to the passenger side.

Lily climbed into the back seat without complaint, still typing. In the past month her phone had transformed from a communication tool to an extension of her arm.

Gen got in the driver's seat and twisted around to face the back seat.

'Lil, could you put your phone down for a moment?'

Her niece jabbed at the buttons on her phone, then looked up and crossed her arms. 'Why?'

Gen inhaled slowly. 'I want to know how you are this morning. Are you okay?'

'We're fine, everything's fine. Is that all?'

'Noooo.' Gen dragged out the word. 'I need to hear from Charlie.'

'I'm okay. Over breakfast Dad explained it was time for you to live your own life, get your own family.' Charlie's voice wobbled on the word *family*.

'*You* are my family, Charlie, you and Lily. Your Dad' – *the absolute bastard* – 'and I have a few things to sort out, but I promise everything will be back to normal soon.'

Lily made a disparaging noise. 'Like we've ever been normal.' She pulled headphones over her ears and faced the window.

Gen's head pounded, the lack of sleep fogging her brain. She should pull Lily up on her behaviour, but she was probably acting out because she was scared. Gen stared at the back of her niece's head. 'Lily, honey —'

The music from Lily's headphones blasted louder. Gen sighed and turned to Charlie. He stared at his lap, twirling a loose thread from his shorts around his finger.

She reached across and squeezed his hand. 'It's going to be okay, honey.'

'Please don't leave us, Gen.' He looked up at her, his eyes like saucers.

'Never.'

She held his hand the whole drive to school.

She dropped off Lily first, her niece barely managing a thank you as she leapt from the car. A suburb later, Charlie leant across the console and gave her a hug before he ran off to join his friends on the cricket field.

All the way to work, a boulder weighed on her chest. She had to do better. So did Hugh. The kids were paying the price for their mess.

Breakfast service stayed constant all morning. At 11 am, her manager pulled her aside.

'There's a Tobias at the back door to see you. Said it's important. Take your break now, but don't be longer than fifteen, okay? And in the future, tell your "friend" to deal with whatever's going on outside of work hours.'

'Sorry, I'll make sure he knows.'

Gen grabbed a bottle of water and headed out the back to the staff car park. What was Tobias doing here? Had something happened to Hugh?

She opened the flyscreen and walked over to the far row of the car park, where Tobias stood next to her car.

'Tobias?'

He wouldn't meet her eye. 'Sorry, Hugh asked me to come by. I don't know what's happened, but he is really pissed with you.'

'No more than I am with him.'

'I need your house and car keys.' He put out his hand.

'What? No.'

'He said he'll report you for theft if you don't hand them over.'

She looked to the sky with a deep sigh, scrubbed her hands over her face.

Tobias leant back against the four-wheel drive and folded his arms. 'What happened last night?'

'I stuffed up.'

'He said he couldn't trust you.'

'He's been acting weird lately, so ... I had a little look around his office to see if I could figure out what's going on.'

'Why didn't you just ask?'

'I did. He said, "Nothing". But he's distracted, quick to anger, and drinking way too much. I know you've noticed.'

Tobias shrugged. 'Maybe the two of you do need a little space.'

'I'm not leaving those kids alone with a man who drinks nightly and comes and goes on a whim. Please, there must be something you can do to help.'

'I can try to get him to change his mind. But you know how he is.' He rubbed the back of his neck, then met her gaze for the first time. 'I have a spare room if you need it.'

'Thanks, but I can stay at Toni's if need be.' Not that she actually planned on moving out. She still had the damning video and photos. 'I'm worried about the kids. He's like he was in the week leading up to Amber's death.'

'Gen —'

'What if he's got himself into trouble?'

'What do you mean?'

'Something at work.'

'Then I'd know about it.'

'You sure? Even if it involved his dad?'

'What exactly did you find in his office?'

Did she risk it? His loyalty might be to Hugh, but Tobias had always helped Gen when her brother-in-law went off the rails. Besides, Hugh already knew she'd been in his office.

'Forsythe Commercial bank statements.'

His stare drilled into her then his eyebrow quirked up. 'That's it?'

'Is there any good reason for him to have company bank account statements in his personal files? He's not the CFO. He manages building management contracts and new commercial acquisitions.'

'Yes, but he's a Forsythe, and on the board.'

Tobias was right. The statements were no smoking gun.

She toed a discarded bottle cap along the asphalt and sighed. 'I'll stop by his office on the way home from work. Apologise again. Can you please talk some sense into him before then?'

'I'll try.' Tobias put out his palm. 'But I still need the keys.'

'How am I supposed to get home?'

'Geneva, I don't want to be in the middle of this. He will call the police if you don't give them to me.'

'Fine, I guess I'll walk. But I'm not moving out.'

'We'll get it sorted. Give me a chance to talk with him.'

'Geneva, we need you back out on the floor!' her boss called from the back door.

'Coming!' she called over her shoulder. She pulled the keys from her pocket and handed them to Tobias. 'Promise you'll try to get through to him?'

'The kids need you. I know that.'

'Then why's he doing this?'

'He's stubborn. You have to find a way to make him think he's won. Giving over the keys is a good start.'

'I hope you're right.'

'You know he can't stand to lose. No Forsythe can.'

He unlocked the car and got in. She grabbed the door before he closed it. 'Thanks for your help, Tobias.'

'Geneva!' Irritation filled her boss's voice.

She jogged to the back door of the restaurant. She was lucky to have Tobias on side. Right now, she needed every bit of help she could get.

After the waitressing shift from hell, when a bunch of businessmen had leered and jeered through their extra-long lunch, Gen race-walked home. By the time she lumbered into the driveway sweat was pooling under her armpits. A pile of mail stuck out of the letterbox. She grabbed it, removed the two envelopes addressed to her, and stuffed the rest back in. She tucked the letters and her overnight bag in the top box of her bike, changed into her boots and rode to Macquarie Street as fast as was safe, relieved to find a park close by.

She spilled out of the spinning glass door into the foyer of Forsythe Commercial Real Estate, turned left and approached the long aubergine reception desk. She had to get past the gatekeeper of the week, a young blonde with long styled waves and a toothy smile. Her gaze dropped to Gen's bike jacket, and her expression seemed to light with recognition.

Gen's brows knit together. She didn't remember meeting this girl. Then again, the reception staff turned over at such a pace it was barely worth introductions.

'I'd like to see Hugh, please.'

'You're Geneva, his sister-in-law, yes?' A whiff of floral perfume sent Gen's internal alerts pinging, straight back to Hugh's dry cleaning last Wednesday. She took in the vivacious, petite twenty-something before her and her eyes rolled before she could catch them. Could Hugh be any more of a cliché?

The girl's face lost its sparkle then rallied into an expression of aloof professionalism.

'Take a seat, please.' She pointed to a row of sleek black leather lounge chairs by a window that looked out onto Sydney's Botanic Gardens. 'I'll let Mr Forsythe know you're here.'

Gen crossed the marble floor, the thuds of her boots echoing through the cavernous space. She slouched on the lounge.

Dammit. Who Hugh slept with was not her problem, and now she'd lost her chance at sweet-talking her way upstairs. What if Hugh told the receptionist not to let her come up?

She had to get through to him before things went any further. She would apologise again, profusely if need be, but if he still wouldn't budge, she'd use the video. She would do whatever it took to be back under the same roof as the kids.

Her attention slid to the receptionist, who held a mobile phone to her ear. A moment later the girl's face softened. Gen couldn't make out what was being said, but the giggles tittering across the space screamed of intimacy. The girl discarded her phone and looked at Gen. 'I'm sorry, Mr Forsythe is in meetings for the rest of the day. He said to —'

'Geneva?' The low, cultured tone of Hugh's brother, Bill, echoed from near the lifts. 'It's okay, Ms Sinclair, I'll attend to Ms Leighton.'

'But Hugh ... I mean, Mr ...'

Bill's expression hardened and the girl broke eye contact. 'Of course, Mr Forsythe.' She angled her body away and reached for something on her desk. Gen stood and walked over to Bill, who waited with a smile plastered on his face.

'I understand you and Hugh are facing a few challenges?'

'More than a few, I'd say.'

'He said you've moved out.'

'That's not —'

'No need to explain to me. My baby brother is a royal pain in everyone's life at the moment. I was hoping you might know what's wrong.'

This family. No wonder Hugh had issues. 'You mean other than his wife's remains being found and the police confirming her murder?'

'No need to be snippy. Is he drinking again?'

'Why don't you ask him?'

'I'm asking you.'

'I need to talk to him.' She stepped towards the lifts, but Bill didn't budge. 'He is drinking.' She'd pay for that later. She tucked her hands in her pockets.

'Perhaps we could help each other?' Bill indicated the lift and scanned his security pass. The doors opened immediately. He swept his hand through the air, inviting her to enter, then followed her in and pushed the button for the top floor.

'We'll go to my office first.' Bill typed into his phone as he talked. 'Make sure we're on the same page.'

Gen checked the time. 'Okay, but I really need to talk to Hugh before he leaves for the day.'

'We won't be long.'

She followed him down a wide corridor to his corner office. Gen entered the room and then froze on the spot. William Forsythe sat at the desk, arms crossed, impatience filling the lines on his face. Hugh stood facing the floor-to-ceiling windows overlooking the gardens. She could imagine the smirk on his face.

She pivoted to leave but Bill closed the door and moved in front of it.

'You prick.'

'Charming as always, Geneva.' William's haughty tone grated like chalk on a board. She tried to dart past Bill, but he gestured to his father.

'You'll listen if you want to see Lily and Charlie again.'

She whirled around and marched over to the desk.

'No one,' she pointed at William and then directed her voice to Hugh's back, 'I repeat, no one will keep me away from my niece and nephew.'

'I think the police might beg to differ.' Hugh turned around.

Gen sucked in a breath. His right eye was swollen and bruised. 'Oh my God, Hugh, what happened? Are you —?'

'Stop the act, Geneva, Dad and Bill know what you did. They wanted to have you arrested for assault.'

Gen blinked. 'But —'

'Enough!' William slapped his palm on the desk.

What the hell was going on?

'You are here as a courtesy, Geneva. I can't afford any adverse attention right now, not with the state election so close. You will back off from any further pointless investigations into your sister's death.'

That's what this was about? The election? But how had Hugh ended up with a black eye? She scanned the cold faces in the room. Fine. Game on.

'I'll back off if I can live with the kids again.'

'Not happening.' William dismissed her with a wave of his hand. 'The children are going to boarding school next month.'

'No! They need stability —'

'Exactly what boarding school is for.'

'After all they've been through —'

'Those kids need a stern spine and a firm hand.'

She stepped towards Hugh. 'I will not let this happen.'

He crossed his arms and smirked. 'Our lawyer has advised getting a restraining order after your attack last night. He's currently outside court, awaiting my call.'

'You bastard, that is not what happened.'

Hugh put out his hand. 'Hand over your mobile.'

'No.'

Bill spoke into the intercom to his EA. 'Get our lawyer on the line.'

'Wait. Stop.' Gen paced. 'Let me think.'

Hugh stood in her path. 'Delete the video.'

She could delete it from her phone then retrieve it again from the cloud. She brought up the gallery in her photos folder.

'What are those?' Hugh peered over her shoulder. 'You took photos of my files? Delete those now, or I *will* have you charged with breaking and entering as well as assault.'

'It's your word against mine.'

'I distinctly remember seeing you swing for him after you threw a dining chair over the balcony,' Bill cut in.

'You weren't even there!'

'That's not what I'll tell the police.'

'The kids would back me up.'

'Coercion from an aggrieved carer,' William interjected. 'No judge in his right mind would grant access of two vulnerable children to an aunt with anger issues.'

'Don't forget her connection to bikers,' Bill interjected.

'What?'

William raised his eyebrows again. If he did that one more time, she just might slug him.

'I don't know what it is you think —'

'Geneva, Hugh has asked nicely, and I'm losing patience. Delete every photo and video you took.'

What choice did she have? She pressed delete with Hugh watching on.

'Now clear your cloud service too.'

Her gut churning, she did as William commanded.

'Your job was to take care of Lily and Charlie.' Hugh's mouth twisted. 'Your services are no longer required.'

'I'm not hired staff you can just terminate, Hugh, I'm family. Amber wouldn't want this.'

'Your sister is dead,' William bit out. 'She doesn't get a say.'

'You callous bastard.'

'You're a negative influence on the children.' William looked her up and down. 'That's become even more apparent lately, especially with the trouble at Lily's school and that horrendous haircut of hers.'

The pressure inside Gen's head felt like it could shoot her into space. All her evidence was gone. She had nothing left to fight with.

'I can't just abandon Lily and Charlie.'

'You could be put on the boarding school visitor lists. Perhaps even have them for a weekend every now and then – *if* you learn to behave.'

How could she live each day not seeing the kids? They were her world.

'Can I at least take them out for dinner tonight, to explain?' she asked Hugh.

'How do I know you won't run with them?'

'I would never …' She needed to tell the kids she'd never stop working to sort this out. To ask them to trust her. 'What if I bring takeaway to the house? We can eat near the pool. You'll be able to see us the whole time.'

'I won't be there.'

'Who's looking after them then?'

'Carol, our nanny.'

Her stomach knotted. How would Lily and Charlie survive this? She stood taller, lifted her chin. 'She could watch over us.'

'You can have an hour. Between six and seven. But the nanny will be under strict instructions to end things if you step out of line.'

Gen nodded, the retort she wished she could use blistering her tongue.

'I'll have Carol pack up the rest of your room. You can pick up your things while you're there, and clear the garage out next month, after the kids have moved to their new schools.'

William stood. 'If you stir up trouble with the children or continue to investigate Amber's death, you're done. No second chances. Hugh will get his restraining order and you will be erased from the children's lives forever.'

Geneva locked glares with William for one full breath, then turned her back and stalked from the room. The entitled bastards might think they'd won, but she'd find a way to beat them at their own game. She'd get the kids back, and somehow, she'd expose everything the Forsythe family was working so hard to keep hidden.

23

By the time she climbed back on her bike all the wind had evaporated from her sails. Who was she kidding? She had no money, no connections and no influence. She had no hope against the political and financial might of the Forsythe family. Her best bet was to talk Hugh around.

Her phone buzzed in her pocket. She pulled it out and opened Toni's text.

> You know where the key is! I've taken leave and fly back on the red eye Thursday. Hang on two days and we'll sort things together.

Gen's vision blurred. She needed Toni more than ever and she hadn't even had to ask. She looked at the sky, blinking rapidly to clear her tears. A bank of clouds moved in from the east.

A restraining order. She groaned. She had no legal claim to Lily and Charlie as it was. A criminal charge would sink her. She needed to find out how Hugh had really got that black eye. What had happened between the time he got in the limo this morning and this afternoon?

A double-length bus stopped behind a queue of cars, blocking her view of the gardens. Traffic built up further, broken traffic lights causing gridlock. A car horn blasted, then another. Everyone remained stuck in place.

Why hadn't Tobias told her about Hugh's black eye? Had he known about the situation she was walking into?

Her jaw tightened and she dialled his phone.

He answered after two rings.

'Why did you send me into an ambush? You said you understood that the kids need me.'

'Geneva? What are you talking about?'

'The restraining order.'

'What? When I delivered the keys, Hugh calmed right down.'

'And why didn't you give me a heads up about his black eye? It wasn't there when he left the house this morning.'

'I don't understand.'

'Yeah, right.'

'Gen, I'm worried about Hugh. Tell me what happened.'

Perhaps she'd been unfair in assuming Tobias had set her up. He was the only person who had a chance of getting through to Hugh now. She ran him through the meeting.

'So what are you going to do?'

'I'm not giving up.'

'Look Gen, we don't come from their world, but I work in it every day. Deference to pedigree matters to them, right? You need to play up to that. It's the only way people like us stand a chance of belonging.'

'Why are you even friends with him if he makes you feel that way?'

'He wasn't always such a snob. Amber was good for him.'

'God, I wish she was here.'

He hummed his agreement. 'She understood how to play the Forsythe game.'

'The game?'

'People born into privilege need to feel like they're in control. The easiest way to get what you want is to make them believe they came up with the idea in the first place.'

'But I want to stay in the kids' lives, live with the kids again. How can I make the Forsythes feel like that was their idea? It's not possible.'

'Then make it happen a different way.'

'It's not as simple as that.'

'It is if you want it enough. If you make it your only priority.' He cleared his throat. 'I have a meeting to get to. You going to be okay?'

'Yeah. Sorry for being stroppy.'

'Believe it or not, I'm on your side. If you need anything, call.'

Gen hung up. How had she not seen how alike Amber and Tobias were? They both appeared to follow Hugh around, but they were actually propping him up. She ran through the conversation again. What had Tobias said? Make it happen. Deference would see the kids in boarding school. She needed to find a way to keep them in Sydney.

But how? She had no resources or assets, except her bikes. Her gaze fell to her Ducati. It would fetch a good price, and her dad's bike was a collector's item. Their sale should give her enough money for a decent lawyer.

Her palms stroked the handles. The bikes were all she had left of herself and her dad. Could she bring herself to part with them?

Her hand dropped away.

For Charlie and Lily? In a heartbeat. And her dad would agree.

She'd list the bikes later tonight. In the meantime, she needed to buy a phone for the kids, one only they knew about, and sneak it to them over dinner. Her hands tented over her mouth and she blew out a breath. How was she going to explain why she was moving out?

She shoved her helmet on. She wouldn't think about that now. She'd buy the phone, go to Toni's, and then, once she was set up there, she'd figure out how to talk to Lily and Charlie.

Gen placed a takeaway order at the kids' favourite Italian restaurant, took a quick shower, and headed for Balmoral. Toni's Milsons Point home was a good thirty minutes away in peak hour, and she didn't want to miss a second of the time she had with the kids. She picked up dinner on the way and pulled into the driveway at 5:58 pm. Close enough. She bounded up the stairs to the front door, clutching the takeaway bag in her hand and balancing the pizza box against her hip. She rapped on the door three times, excitement surging through her. She couldn't wait to get both kids in her arms.

A petite woman in her late fifties, dark hair scraped into a low tight bun, answered the door.

'Hi, I'm Geneva, the kids' aunt.' She stepped forward to enter the house, but the woman blocked her way.

'Carol Wood, the children's nanny. Mr Forsythe asked me to give you a message.'

Gen's body tensed. He'd better not have cancelled the visit.

'I've packed up everything from your room. The boxes are in the garage out front. He said you have until the end of the month to remove your things from the property. Anything left after then will be donated to charity.'

He really did think he could treat her like hired help. She took a deep breath. She would not let his fuckheadery distract her from her limited time with Lily and Charlie.

'Mr Forsythe also insisted I don't let you enter the house.'

'But I'm supposed to have dinner with Lily and Charlie.'

'The children will meet you on the pool deck after they've finished their homework. You can use the driveway entrance.'

'I only have one hour.' Gen unclenched her teeth. 'The children can finish their bloody homework once I've gone.'

Carol took a step back. 'I'll send them down soon.' She closed the door.

Gen traipsed down the driveway and let herself in through the pool gate, struggling to undo the latch without dropping the pizza. In the end she had to place it on the ground then let herself through. She unpacked the plastic cutlery and box of pasta on the glass-topped table and checked the time: 6:04 pm. Whining drew her attention to the sliding door. Bentley stood with his nose to the glass. She slid the door open and bent to scratch the scuff at his neck. He nuzzled her hand.

'Hey boy, I missed you too. What are you doing downstairs?'

Fast thuds descended in the stairwell and Charlie came flying at her. 'Gen!' His arms wrapped around her waist.

Gen's throat thickened. He was so happy to see her. Lily appeared around the corner behind him. She seemed hesitant, as if unsure what to do. Gen reached for her and pulled her into the hug.

Lily softened in her arms. 'Please tell me you're taking over from Mrs Wood.'

The clamp around Gen's ribcage tightened another half-twist. She faked a smile. 'I brought Gino's.'

Charlie's face lit up. 'Supreme?'

She nodded at Charlie, then turned to Lily. 'And spaghetti carbonara for you.'

Lily beamed. 'Thank you!' For a moment she looked like the old Lily, relaxed, happy and warm. Then her phone buzzed, and she pulled it from her pocket and stepped away. Her thumbs flew over the keypad.

Charlie charged to the table and opened the pizza box.

Gen moved next to Lily. 'Who are you chatting with?'

Lily mumbled something inaudible and shifted her shoulders, blocking Gen's view.

Gen paused, willing Lily's focus to return. She checked her watch, then touched her palm to Lily's shoulder. 'Please put your phone away.'

Lily kept typing for a moment, then placed her phone face-down on the table and sat. Gen passed her a plastic fork, and they all began eating.

Lily's phone buzzed again, and she reached for it. Gen covered her hand.

'Honey, I only have an hour with you.'

'An hour, why?' Charlie asked mid-chew.

Gen's gaze flicked between them. Lily's eyes narrowed.

Time to rip off the Band-Aid.

'It's taking a bit longer to sort things out with your dad than I thought.'

'Right.' Lily pushed her pasta away.

'But —' Charlie said at the same time.

Gen held up her hands. 'Let me finish. He needs time to calm down. I'll stay at Toni's for a few days, but that doesn't mean I've moved out for good, or that I'm no longer here for you.'

'What if he gets scary like last night?' The fear on Charlie's face almost brought her unstuck. She'd never forgive Hugh for putting them through this.

She checked the balcony. Carol had stepped away. This was her chance. She slipped the mobile she'd bought out of her pocket. 'That's why I got you this. So, no matter what, you can contact me. If you need me, I promise I will come straight away. Best put it away before Mrs Wood sees it though.'

Charlie slipped it into his jeans pocket.

Lily's lips thinned. 'What's going on?'

'I'm making sure there can't be a repeat of last weekend, where you couldn't call me.'

Lily shook her head. 'You're not telling us the whole truth.'

Gen blinked slowly. 'I can't, Lil. It's adult stuff.'

'Adult stuff. Right.' Sarcasm dripped from every syllable.

Charlie placed his half-eaten slice of pizza back in the box. 'Who will look after us when dad's away?'

Gen's gaze shifted to the balcony and Charlie groaned.

She reached out and squeezed both kids' hands. 'It's only for a little while.'

'You said that yesterday,' Lily snapped.

'I promise I will still be here for you. No matter what.'

Lily's eyes filled.

'Honey, it's going to be okay.'

Lily shoved her chair back. 'I wish they'd never found Mum's stupid body. It's her fault everything changed.'

'Lily —'

'I have homework to finish.'

'Please don't go. It might be a few days before I can see you again.'

'Whose fault is that?' Lily glared.

'Please.'

'Go and live your life. That's what you want to do, right? Dad says you're dating Jesse.'

'Lily, it's not like that. I'm not dating Jesse, and I'd never abandon you.'

'You already have.' Lily stormed off, each footfall up the stairs causing a wrench in Gen's chest.

Charlie pulled his chair closer to Gen's. 'I believe you.'

She blinked hard, willing the tears away.

'You'll fix things, Aunty Gen. You always do.'

She swallowed.

'And you owe another dollar to the swear jar.'

'What?'

'I heard you at the front door. You said the b-word to Mrs Wood.'

Gen smiled, but inside her guts churned. Could she really fix things this time?

24

Gen opened her eyes and Toni's spare room blinked into focus. Like the rest of the ground floor apartment, it was classically decorated in muted tones of khaki, cream and soft pink. She dragged herself from bed and drifted into the open-plan living area. Toni had lovingly restored every room. The peacock feathers, candles and throw rugs gave the place a warm, homey vibe.

Gen opened the glass front door. Outside, a small courtyard led into a walled-off garden area. She inhaled a breath, the scent of the flowering frangipani next to the entrance filling her nostrils. If she was going to turn things around today, she had to clear her mind.

Last night had been one of the hardest of her life. Walking away from Charlie. Being unable to get inside to fix things with Lily. The kids had been front and centre in her every waking thought for the past twelve years. How could Hugh expect her to just move on? How did he think the kids would cope?

Everything was such a mess.

She returned to the kitchen island, her limbs like limp noodles, her head like someone had filled it with wet sand. She prepared a pot of tea, forcing herself to focus on the task.

She felt like she was being pushed downhill in a go-kart with no brake. She'd never thought Hugh would go this far. They didn't always get along, had never been friends, but they were family. Or at least, she'd thought they were. Perhaps blood really was all that mattered to him?

Had he discarded Amber just as easily? What if she had rebelled against the Forsythes' plans?

Gen exhaled and shook out her hands. Time to take back some power. She retrieved her computer, sat at the bench and looked up advertisements for Bonneville motorbikes. Most fetched between $11,000 and $12,000.

Next, she researched the cost of family lawyers. Her shoulders sank. If Hugh dug in, which he most certainly would, the whole legal process could end up costing her over $100,000. Selling her dad's bike would barely make a dent.

She sighed, made an appointment with a firm for the next day.

Researching the value of her Streetfighter didn't yield much more hope: $15,000. And she'd need some of that to buy a small second-hand car to transport the kids around.

But it was a start. She opened her email to activate the seller account she'd registered. Three emails downloaded into her inbox: her Bikesell account activation, the Shellwood parents' newsletter and an update from Rewind Images Lab, the photo restoration company where she'd sent Amber's film. She clicked it open. *Confirmation of delivery.* She bit at her thumbnail. She hadn't received anything from them. Then she remembered the envelopes she'd grabbed from the letterbox yesterday. The ones she'd shoved in her top box. She jogged straight out to her bike.

The first letter was the registration renewal for the Streetfighter, not exactly what she needed right now, but the other was from Rewind Images Lab. Excitement raced through her. She headed back inside, discarding the unwanted renewal papers on the bench. Turning the lab envelope over, an ache mushroomed in her chest. Inside were the last photos her sister had ever taken. An opportunity to see the world through her eyes again. She cleared the tea to the sink – the last thing she wanted was to damage the photos – then sat on the stool and slid her finger under the flap.

Here goes, Amber.

She skimmed a letter apologising for the poor quality of the prints and set it aside. She pulled the stack of photos out of the envelope, goosebumps fanning across her arms. The right half of the first photo was washed out and the rest had squiggles of magenta across it, but she could still make out four-year-old Lily cradling baby Charlie in bed, a look of deep concentration across her sweet face. Gen stared at the photo for a moment, then placed it on the bench. In the next shot Lily was kissing Charlie's head. The following photo was a complete blur. The fourth was of a workbook page. Handwritten columns of numbers, and three-letter abbreviations or initials or something. She squinted closer; the writing looked like Hugh's. The fifth image was of a different page, but in the same format. The next nine photos were similar. Something about them had been important to Amber. The final photo showed the front page of a real estate contract. The image had thick magenta stripes masking the buyer's name, but the seller was listed as Sykes. Erica Sykes. So it was true, Hugh had helped her sell her house. But why did Amber have photos of the contract?

Gen held it closer to the pendant light, tilting and twisting. It didn't reveal anything more. She activated the torch on her phone and ran the light over the image. Her heart sped up. There was another name at the bottom of the page. She squinted, then sighed. It was unreadable.

Could the contract have something to do with the sales Feral had uncovered between Forsythe Commercial Real Estate and the families of organised crime figures? Was *this* why Amber had been killed?

What about the other photos? She glanced over at the workbook images. She needed help. She needed someone with the resources to decipher what those figures meant.

She dialled Jesse, holding her breath as the line rang. They hadn't spoken for days, but the information contained in these photos might be exactly what she needed to fight Hugh. She couldn't afford to let anything get in the way.

Jesse's voice message kicked in. She groaned and hung up. Maybe he was on the early shift. She dialled the PCYC main switch. A woman answered.

'Hi, could you please put me through to Sergeant Jesse Johns?'

'Sorry, Sergeant Johns is on leave. Can someone else help?'

'Leave? When does he get back?'

'He's not rostered on for the rest of the month. I'll put you through to Constable Brady.' The line began ringing again. Gen hung up, dialled Jesse's mobile again. Message bank.

'Jesse, what's going on? The PCYC said you're on leave. Please call me.'

She spread the photos across the bench. After five minutes of pointless staring, she packed everything up and headed to Jesse's apartment. Maybe he hadn't heard his phone.

She ran up to his door and knocked. No answer. She knocked again. Still no answer. *Dammit.* She typed a text.

Where are you? Just called past your place. Please ring asap.

She paced the street, debating her options. She could wait for Toni to get back, but that was two whole days away. If she wanted to stop the kids going into boarding next month, she needed to get things sorted fast. And she needed to know if those photos had any bearing on things before she met with the lawyer.

Mac might help. She stilled, his final comments echoing in her mind. *This freebie is for Dad. Next time you'll owe me.*

She bit her lip. It was actually Feral's skills she needed. All Mac had to do was put them in touch. Surely that didn't count as a favour? She sighed. She'd owe him, but any chance to get the kids back was worth it.

She dialled.

'Knew you couldn't stay away for long.'

'Mac, I —'

'Couldn't stop thinking about me, could you?'

'Umm ...'

A laugh boomed down the line. 'Just fuckin' around, Gypsy. What's up?'

'I found some photos Amber took.'

'Of?'

'A ledger or something. I'd like to show them to Feral.'

'You injure me.'

'Please, Mac. This is serious. Hugh has kicked me out. He's keeping me from the kids.'

'Want us to pay him a visit?'

'No!' She rubbed her forehead. 'What I need is to figure out what these photos mean and why Amber took them.'

'Feral's with his missus, but he should be back soon. We can meet at yours in a few hours.'

'Can I come to you? It'll take an hour to get there anyway. I want to get onto it as soon as I can.'

'Give me a sec.'

He muted the phone. The space between her shoulder blades itched. She scanned the street, but nothing was out of place. It was just nerves.

A few seconds later he came back on. 'Viking's okay'd it. Text when you get to the first gate, and I'll escort you in.'

'Thank so much, you've no idea what this means.'

'I'm sure I can find a way for you to make it up to me.'

'Seriously?'

'When am I ever serious?'

'See you in an hour.'

Gen pulled up at the security gate and texted Mac. Two minutes later the gate slid open. Butterflies backflipped in her stomach. She checked the empty road behind her, looked to the fortified compound ahead. Maybe this wasn't the smartest idea. Could she really trust a bunch of bikers, possibly outlaw ones, just because her dad used to be friends with their ex-leader? She should have waited for Jesse.

Mac ambled through the second gate and gave her a roguish smile as he waved her through the first. She stopped, and he swung himself up on the back of her bike. The second security perimeter gate closed behind them as they drove down the road. She pulled in beside the clubhouse and they dismounted. Gen removed her helmet and retrieved the envelope from the top box, holding it tight to her chest.

'Better gulp as much fresh air out here as you can,' he said. 'Feral's office ain't pretty.'

She followed him through the empty building. 'Where is everyone?'

Mac tilted his head. 'Working on their bikes out back.'

He opened the door of Feral's office. Gen coughed against

the mixed stench of day-old pizza, smoke and sweat that flooded out. Mac hadn't been kidding about the fresh air.

'Welcome to my lair.' A chuckle came from a gamer chair facing a bank of seven computer screens, some dark, one with a video security feed and another with an open search engine. 'Mac said you have something to show me.' Feral put out his hand.

The room's only light was the blue haze emanating from the computer screens. Nests of cables and cords covered the desk and lay in all directions on the floor, as if multiplying on their own. She handed over the photos.

'Pull up a chaise lounge.' He pointed to a milk crate. She sat and felt immediately like a preschooler.

Mac remained standing, one leg bent back, foot to the wall. He pulled out a pack of cigarettes. 'Fuck man, you really are feral.' Mac lit up, inhaled, and blew out a stream of smoke. 'It's disgusting in here.'

'You know where the door is.'

'Yeah, it's the only reason we're all still breathing.'

'Piss off. Thought you wanted my help.'

The low hum of a computer fan filled the room.

Gen flicked a glare at Mac, then placed her hand on the arm of Feral's chair. 'I really appreciate you helping me.' Feral switched on a lamp and spread the images out on the desk. He leant in closer, then tapped on his keyboard. A dark screen lit up with a search engine and he typed in TOR, then clicked on the link. A purple browser popped up.

'What's that?'

'Protects my privacy.'

'Is it legal?'

'It was developed by the US Navy to protect sensitive info.'

'You didn't answer my question.'

'Using it is legal, but what I'm about to do fits more in the don't-ask, can't-tell category. Now, quiet.'

Gen watched every stroke he typed, every number entered and search result produced, but it quickly became clear she wasn't going to be able to make sense of what he was doing. He activated a new screen. This time numbers scrolled with speed. The typing continued in a blur, then a third screen lit up with real estate sales results, and a fourth with the homepage of TNC Bank. Its orange triangle logo seemed somehow familiar.

Feral typed feverishly, oblivious to Gen and Mac's presence.

Mac tapped her on the shoulder. 'Want a coffee?'

'No, I'll stay.'

'Go.' Feral flicked his hand in the air. 'Your hovering's distracting. I'll be at least another fifteen.'

'Do you want a drink, Feral?' Gen asked.

'Latte. Two sugars.'

She followed Mac to the door, then glanced back at Amber's photos.

'He'll look after them or he'll have me to deal with.' Mac stepped forward and lightly punched Feral's arm. 'Right?'

'Yeah, now fuck off.'

The furious drumming of the keyboard returned, accompanied by the low-level hum of the fans cooling the computers.

Mac tilted his head, indicating for her to follow, and led her down the corridor to an industrial-sized kitchen with immaculate stainless-steel benches.

'Wow.'

'Bear runs a tight ship.'

He led her to an espresso machine in the far corner. 'Grab the milk?' He pointed to the fridge.

Gen pulled out a three-litre container and placed it on the bench next to him.

'Piccolo?' he asked.

'Get f—' She coughed to cover the rest of her statement.

'You can say it. We don't have a swear jar here.'

'Wait, how do you know about that?' She folded her arms.

He shrugged. 'Just a guess you'd have a jar.'

'Why?'

'Because you've got to find some way to rein in your natural instincts.'

'You know what, you *can* fuck off.'

He laughed. 'That's more like it.' The coffee grinder stopped any further conversation.

They drank their coffees, then took Feral's back into his office. He paused in his typing and put a finger in the air.

'One minute.'

Gen took up her assigned position on the crate, while Mac leant back against the wall. A few taps later, Feral slapped the desk. 'I fuckin' knew it!'

'What? You knew what?'

Feral sipped his latte and turned his chair to face her.

'Those photos your sister took. I couldn't read all the columns, but they gave me enough trails to follow. See the first column?' He pointed and she nodded. 'The three letters are an abbreviation for a suburb. MOS equals Mosman. DOV is Dover Heights. And so on. When I matched the seven digits of the second column with sales recorded in these suburbs and entered the third column of six numbers, it became clear that the six numbers are a date of sale. I think the last three columns are the seller, the buyer and the amount paid in cash.'

'In cash?'

'It's a way to launder money. The real estate broker finds a seller, a cleanskin, prepared to sign a contract saying they were paid an amount which is usually on the lowest end of believability for the property. The buyer, someone looking to clean money, then pays the rest of the property's value to the seller in cash.'

'Wait. What do you mean by clean money?'

'Convert illegally gained cash into a legitimate form.'

'But why would a seller agree to do that?'

'They are guaranteed top dollar for their property and are often paid a cash bonus by the buyer. Meanwhile, the buyer legitimises his illegal proceeds. It's a win-win.' He shrugged. 'For everyone except the government.'

'So,' Gen said, 'the seller on that real estate contract, Erica Sykes, agreed to take part in money laundering?'

'Not necessarily. If the seller isn't financially literate the broker often presents the deal as a way to minimise tax, and tax avoidance is an area of law many people are happy to push the boundaries of. It probably never entered Sykes's head that the buyer could be using the process to launder funds.'

'Okay.' Gen processed what he'd told her for a moment. 'But the buyer essentially gives money away.'

'Sometime later, the property is re-listed and sold for its full value and the buyer gets most of his money back, all cleaned.'

'Surely that's not legal?'

'No, but it's hard to track. Especially if the buyers aren't people flagged by the police or ASIO.'

'People like relatives.'

'You're catching on.'

'But how does the broker get paid?'

'Commission, sometimes paid in kind, like gifts of rare art, or by deposits into an offshore account.' He pointed to the screen with the orange bank logo. 'Hugh is listed as a signatory on a TNC bank account. Their headquarters is in the country of Georgia, so non-CRS.'

'I'm not following.'

'Common Reporting Standard. It's a global agreement requiring financial institutions to collect and report information on foreign tax residents. Georgia didn't sign the agreement, meaning records there can't be subpoenaed by overseas law enforcement. It's the perfect way for individuals and companies to avoid tax and hide dubious profits.'

'And Hugh has an account in Georgia?'

'The account is for Forsythe Commercial Real Estate, but like I said, he's a signatory.'

'So why did Amber photograph the logs?'

'My guess? She discovered her husband was keeping a private record of dodgy transactions, probably to protect himself in case things went south, and she took the photos to figure out what he was up to.'

Gen took a minute to let that sink in.

'Or,' Feral continued, 'she was a knowing participant and wanted to keep her own bargaining chip.'

'No way she was involved!'

'Woah!' Feral's hands flew up in defence. 'Don't shoot the messenger.'

Mac leant in. 'Let's get back on track. If this is a record of illegal real estate transactions, can you identify who was involved?'

'Not all the numbers and letters are visible, because of the poor photo quality. But if I had the contracts, like that last photo, then yeah, I reckon I could.'

Amber must have figured out what Hugh was up to. Is that why she was murdered?

But he'd been in the hotel all night. Could a different Forsythe be the killer?

'Who would have had to be involved for the laundering to work?'

'Not clear, but they'd need a —'

Feral's phone rang.

'What?' His eyes zeroed in on Gen. 'How long?'

He hung up, collected the photos into a pile, and held them out. 'Get her out now. Pigs just passed by Franco's house. Looks like we're about to be raided.'

'Fuck!' Mac snatched the photos from Feral. 'Come on.'

'Wait!' Gen said. 'We haven't finished.'

He grabbed her arm. 'There's a shitstorm headed our way. Trust me, you don't want to get caught up in it. Get moving.'

'Thanks Feral!' she called out as Mac dragged her through the doorway and down the hall. He handed her the photos and she tucked them in the inside pocket of her jacket.

'Helmet on. I'll send you out the back gate. Turn right at the end of the track and loop back to the freeway three roads along. Do not come back here.'

'Thank —'

'Get the fuck out of here.'

Mac pressed a remote, and a gate just big enough for a bike to fit through opened behind the barn. She drove through and the gate closed behind her. She glanced in her rear-vision mirror. Mac was already turning away, raising his phone to his ear.

She rode along a dirt track for a minute, her body jolting with every rock and uneven bump, then turned onto a sealed road and finally sat her bum on the seat. Her thighs quivered. Before the freeway she turned into a petrol station and dismounted. She filled the bike with fuel and took the chance to stretch out her leg muscles. Before remounting the bike, she transferred the photos to the top box so they wouldn't get crushed.

An hour later, she exited onto the Falcon Street off-ramp and pulled to a stop at the traffic light at the top. Another bike, a Harley ridden by a guy dressed in black jeans, a black canvas style jacket and a full black helmet, pulled up next to her. The hair on the back of her neck rose. He'd been in her side mirrors on the M2, over half an hour ago. Was he following her? She gripped her handlebars and when the light turned green she hit the throttle and shot out into a small gap in the traffic, the front tyre lifting from the road with her speed. She manoeuvred her bike into the empty second lane, then accelerated away as fast as she could.

Heart hurtling, she checked her mirrors. It was only when she passed through Neutral Bay that she remembered she wasn't going home to Balmoral, but to Toni's in Milsons Point. She re-routed, head on a swivel, alert to everything around her, but spotted no sign of the bike. Was she just being paranoid?

She parked on Toni's street and dismounted as fast as she could. No one else entered the dead-end road, but her instincts screamed. She checked all around then ran through the gate, locked the front door behind her and shut herself in the bathroom. The glass front door meant anyone could see inside the flat.

She dialled Mac.

'What the fuck do you want?' Viking answered, his brisk clipped twang undeniable.

'Viking? Is everything okay? I need Mac.'

'The police took him in after executing a search warrant on his room. If I find out you set him up, you will pay.'

'I would never do that.'

'Yeah, well, I don't believe in coincidences, and trouble seems to follow you around.'

'I'm sorry.'

'You will be if you call him again. Now fuck the fuck off and stay there.'

25

Gen closed her eyes and tried to make sense of things. Mac had been arrested? What had the police found? She could see why Viking might think it had something to do with her, but Phoenix were bikers. Run-ins with the police couldn't be a surprise.

But something didn't sit right. Like Viking said, it was too much of a coincidence. Especially after everything Feral had figured out. She scrubbed her hands across her face. She needed answers, but she had no idea where to turn. She tried Jesse again and groaned when it went to voicemail.

'What the hell, Jesse? You said you'd be there for me this time. Answer your damn phone!'

She hung up and reared to her feet. She'd go over to his house and camp on his doorstep until he returned home.

Her phone rang in her hand. She sighed heavily when she saw who it was.

'Gen, it's Tobias. I ... Where are you? I need to talk to you.'

'I can't right now. There's a lot going on and I need to find —'

'Something's really not right with Hugh.'

'What?'

'I'd rather not say over the phone. Can we meet?'

'I'm at Toni's.'

She gave him the address and kept herself busy while she waited, boiling the kettle and tidying up, resisting the urge to call Hugh herself to find out what was going on.

Ten minutes later the garden gate squeaked open and Gen let Tobias in. 'What's he done?'

'He's in a panic. Won't let anyone in his office. His secretary isn't putting through any calls. He's insisting no one interrupts him.'

'He probably has his latest girlfriend on the desk.' She grabbed her boots from the front door and sat on a dining chair to put them on. 'I don't have time for this crap.'

'Something *is* wrong.'

'Even if there was, what could I possibly know, Tobias? He kicked me out, remember?' She did up the zips and Velcro pads and stood.

He wandered to the kitchen bench, glanced over the papers there. 'Have the police found out something more about Amber's death?'

'Why would you think that?'

'Yesterday, you said you'd found something weird.'

Gen turned her back to him and made a pot of tea. Not that she'd be able to swallow it, but she needed time to recall exactly what she'd said yesterday. She'd only told him about the bank statements she'd found in Hugh's files.

She whirled around. 'Did you tell him about the statements? Is that why he ambushed me with William and Bill?'

'I swear I didn't! But last night he was agitated, rambling about how you could wreck everything.'

If Hugh knew about the existence of the workbook photos, or even a hint of what she'd uncovered this morning, he'd be going ballistic. But how could he know? The only people she'd shown were Mac and Feral.

She crossed her arms and stared Tobias down. 'Why are you really here?'

His focus slid to the pile of bills on the bench, as if he were trying to collect his thoughts. He sighed and his voice deepened. 'I'm worried about the kids. Hugh's losing it. He's paranoid and acting erratically.' He finally met her eyes. 'I know what it's like to feel unsafe at home. I don't want that for Charlie and Lily.'

She pulled out her phone and checked it for messages. Neither of the kids had contacted her. Charlie would have rung if he was scared. Unless Hugh had found the phone she'd given them.

Tobias pushed his glasses up to the bridge of his nose. 'I didn't grow up in the best of environments. I got good at identifying the warning signs: mood swings and volatile behaviour. Had to, to survive. Hugh is panicking, in fight-or-flight mode. Usually I can talk him round, but not today.' He held his palms out, beseeching. 'I need to know what's going on so I can help.'

Gen bit her cheek. Tobias had been there for her many times since Amber had disappeared, especially when Hugh spiralled. If he was going to help this time he needed to understand how serious things were. 'I think Hugh is involved in something that got Amber killed.'

'What?'

'I'm not saying yet.'

'Illegal?'

She nodded. God, she hoped she was doing the right thing telling him.

'Dammit. What are you going to do?'

'I think I have to take it to the police.'

'But what about the kids? He's the only parent they have left.'

Her eyes met his. 'Maybe they're better off without him.'

'Tell me ...' His voice faded and he put up his hands. 'Actually, don't. I don't want to know. If he's broken the law, I'm required to report him.'

He paced, then looked up at her. 'Is there any other way, for the sake of the kids?'

'I don't think so. Tell me again about the night Amber went missing. It still feels like he hasn't come clean.'

'What are you talking about?'

'It never sat right with me. Unless he was interstate, Hugh always came home, even if it was really late. Then the night his wife is abducted he stays overnight in a hotel. He'd never done that before.'

'He was pretty drunk.'

'I think what I've uncovered might show motive for Amber's murder.'

Tobias stared into her eyes, and she held his gaze, determined not to waver from his challenge. He sank to the lounge with a deep breath, leant forward, elbows on knees, and pushed his hands through his hair.

'I'll deny it if anyone asks, but I wasn't with Hugh the whole time that night.'

'I knew it!'

'I left him for a few hours with a woman he'd chatted up downstairs.'

'The hotel video never showed you leaving the floor.'

'Because I didn't. I went into the woman's room down the corridor, watched television for a few hours, to give them privacy.'

'Why didn't you tell the police this?'

'Because I never saw her again and Hugh couldn't remember a thing about her. If I told the police he had no alibi ...'

'What the hell did you two do? They could have identified her from the hotel video.'

'Listen! When I went back to the room, I found Hugh passed out naked on the covers. There was a photo left on the bed showing the woman astride him in the throes of sex. It only showed her from the neck down. On the back of the photo were the words: *Time is running out.*'

'What the fuck, Tobias?'

'When the police found us the next morning and told us about Amber's disappearance, Hugh begged me to give him an alibi for those missing hours. I knew he couldn't have had anything to do with what happened to Amber, so I agreed.'

'But what about justice for Amber? What if the people behind that note had something to do with her murder?'

His face filled with regret and shame.

'How often did Hugh cheat?'

'Occasionally.'

Gen lifted her chin. 'And you'd play wingman.'

'He still loved Amber.'

'That's what all cheaters say. Next you'll blame Amber for him straying.'

'Hugh's ego is —'

Gen threw her hands in the air. 'I don't give a flying fuck about Hugh's ego.' She needed to calm down. She inhaled and exhaled slowly before speaking again. 'What happened next?'

'After the police left, Hugh came clean with me. He'd started gambling. Owed some dangerous people serious money.'

'Gambling? He's never had a problem with that before.'

'Once an addict ... The creditors wanted him to do something for them. He never told me what, but they weren't taking no for an answer.'

The laundering. It must be. Hugh got Amber killed. She'd never been surer of it.

'I don't know what you've found, but if the people he owed money to had anything to do with Amber's death we need to make sure the kids are safe before you go to the police.'

'The safest place for the kids is as far away from Hugh as possible.'

'That might be so, but we can't do anything about that right now.'

'You conceited arse! There is no *we*.'

'But I can help!'

'What did you expect me to say, Tobias? Because of your lies we might never be safe. Amber thought you were a friend. So did I! You need to leave.'

'You can't tell anyone what I've told you.'

'That's not up to you.'

'I'll deny it.'

Gen folded her arms and glared. 'You coward.'

'What are you going to do?'

'I don't know, but I'm not figuring it out with you.'

'I'm sorry, Gen —'

'A little late for that, don't you think?'

He collected his suit jacket and opened the door to leave, then looked over his shoulder. 'Be careful. If I were you I wouldn't do anything you can't undo.'

'And if I were you, I'd fuck off before I throttle you.'

She needed to get to Jesse now. He could take her to whatever police department was best suited to deal with this mess.

She grabbed her jacket from the bathroom floor and slipped her arms into the sleeves. The doorbell rang. She poked her head around the corner to check it wasn't Tobias again, and spotted two uniformed police at the door, a young woman who looked fresh out of the academy and guy in his thirties, both with serious expressions. What now?

She threw the door open.

'Geneva Leighton?'

She nodded as they held up their IDs.

'Is Lily Forsythe here?'

'No, she's at school.'

The man handed her a letter with an official judicial crest.

'We have a warrant to search the premises.'

'What?'

'Lily Forsythe is a missing minor and her father believes you might be hiding her here.'

'What the hell? Lily's missing? Why didn't anyone call me?'

'Please step aside.'

'She's not here.'

'Ma'am, we need to check.'

'Fine, but you're wasting time.'

The officers tore around the small apartment, checking wardrobes, the bathroom, under the beds, any place a person could hide. Gen checked her phone but there was nothing. No message from Hugh, Lily, Charlie or the school.

'Please tell me what's happened.'

'Lily wasn't in roll call this morning,' the female officer said. 'And she didn't attend any of her classes. When the nanny arrived to take care of the children this afternoon, she noticed the family car missing and reported it to her employer.'

'But Lily can't drive.' Had someone taken both her and the car? 'Where's Charlie?'

'In his dad's care.'

'Fat lot of good that will be. I want you to take me to him.'

'That's not a great idea right now. Mr Forsythe is adamant you are behind the abduction.'

'I would never abduct my niece. My God, where the hell is his brain?'

The male cop exited the main bedroom and walked to the door. 'Is there a garage attached to this property?'

'A carport out back.'

'I'll check, but otherwise the place is clear.'

'Can I leave now?'

'Where are you headed?'

'Someone needs to be out there looking for Lily.'

'Leave that up to us.'

'I did that once, never again. Besides, I have a much better idea of where to look than you lot.'

'Ms Leighton —'

'Unless you are going to arrest me, please get out of my way.'

He pulled a business card from his pocket and handed it to her. 'Here's my number if you get news of her.'

She tore a scrap from the shopping list and scribbled down her number. 'Can you please call me if you hear anything?'

The female officer nodded reluctantly, took the paper and they left.

Gen shoved the officer's card in her jacket pocket, locked up and dialled Lily's number as she ran to her bike. It went straight to voicemail. She dialled Charlie. It did the same. She called the phone she'd given the kids. It rang out.

She shoved her helmet on and rode as fast as she could to Balmoral, scanning the streets for the family car as she went.

Lily couldn't drive, hadn't even got her learner's permit yet. So where could she and the car be? Had someone taken her?

She pulled up alongside Balmoral promenade and jumped off her bike, barely pausing to kick down the stand. She ran to Rocky Point Island, tugging off her helmet as she went.

'Lily! Lily?'

She searched the area top to bottom, her heart sinking as she cleared each spot. Her niece wasn't there. She jumped back on her bike and headed for the cemetery. She sprinted from her bike to Amber's grave, but there was no sign of Lily there either. She dialled the kids' numbers again. Voicemail. She dialled Hugh. The phone rang twice then cut out. Stupid fucking wanker!

Tears welled in Gen's eyes. She couldn't lose Lily too. She'd never survive it.

She called Jesse and screamed when she got his voicemail again. 'Fucking answer your fucking phone! Lily is missing!' Her voice broke. 'I need you.'

She sank to the ground and cradled her head in her hands. Why hadn't she put a tracker on Lily's phone like other parents did? She should have at least figured out who Lily was always talking to these days. Maybe that was it. She shot to her feet. Her phone rang. It was the phone she'd given the kids.

'Lily?'

'Aunty Gen?'

'Charlie! Are you okay?'

'I'm scared. No one will tell me what's going on.'

'Do you know where Lily is?'

'No, and everyone is panicking.'

'Where are you?'

'In my room.'

'Charlie, why didn't you call me sooner?'

'I forgot about this phone and Dad has my other one. I'm sorry.'

'It's okay, sweetheart.'

'It's not. This is my fault.'

'Charlie.'

'It is. I caught her packing clothes. I knew she was skipping school today, and I didn't say anything.'

'Slow down, sweetheart. Tell me where she was going.'

'She said she was going to meet her boyfriend. Made me promise not to tell.'

'She has a boyfriend?'

'A guy she's been talking to online.'

She was meeting a stranger? *Oh fuck.* 'Honey, I have to go, but I'll call back in a minute.'

'This is bad, isn't it?'

'Stay where you are, and I'll call you back as soon as I can.'

'Please don't get her in trouble. I said I wouldn't tell.'

'You did the right thing, honey, I promise.'

Gen hung up, snatched out the business card the officer had given her. He answered immediately.

'Lily was meeting with someone she met online today. Someone none of us knew. A boyfriend. What if he was catfishing her? What if she's been taken?'

'Ms Leighton, slow down. I was about to call you. We've found your niece. She was in a motor vehicle collision near Avalon. She's been flown to Westmead Children's Hospital.'

'Oh my God. Is she okay?'

'I don't know any more details for now but I'm sure if you —'

Gen hung up and ran.

26

Gen skidded into a spot on the verge of the drop-off zone, leapt off the bike and ran through the hospital's main entrance to the front desk.

'Lily Forsythe. She was brought in by helicopter after a car accident.'

A man in his sixties looked up with a wan smile. 'Slow your horses, love. How do you spell her surname?' Gen enunciated each letter between puffed breaths, tapping her hand on the counter impatiently as he typed.

'She's in the Intensive Care Unit. ICU. Level three. Lifts are over there.'

'Thank you.'

Gen charged for the lifts and frantically pressed the call button. The doors opened straight away, and she rushed in and jabbed at floor three. The doors moved to close, but a wrinkly hand reached through, and the doors slid back open. An elderly man dressed immaculately in a suit and fedora stood aside, holding the lift open for his wife who, using a cane for support, hobbled aboard.

Gen's fingers drummed on her leg. 'What floor would you like?'

'That's very kind, dear.' The woman turned to her husband, who still hadn't released the door. 'I think it was floor four, or was it five?'

Gen pressed both. She didn't care as long as the elevator got moving. The man tipped his hat at her and finally stepped into the lift. Gen stared at the numbers above the doors. *Come on. Come on.* Finally, the lift groaned to a jerky stop and the doors parted at level three. She squeezed through the still-opening gap, dodged around a large family and followed the signs to the nurses' station.

'Lily Forsythe? She was brought in after a car accident.' Gen's heart thrashed in her chest.

'Are you family?'

'Her aunt, Geneva.'

The nurse's demeanour changed completely. She smiled and came from round the desk. 'Follow me. Lily asked for you continually before they put her under.'

Gen's eyes filled with tears. Lily had needed her, and she'd been nowhere nearby.

The nurse stopped outside a glass-walled room. Gen craned her neck, but the bed inside was empty. 'She's in the next room along. I wanted to warn you first, she's on a high dose of morphine after her operation so is slipping in and out of awareness. And she's pretty banged up.'

Gen let out a shaky breath.

'She has a long recovery ahead. The surgeon had to remove her spleen, she has two broken ribs, there's a hairline fracture to her left orbital bone and her nose had to be reset. There's also a lot of bruising as a result of the car rolling.'

How close had Lily come to dying?

The nurse's palm came to Gen's shoulder. 'Are you okay?'

Gen wrapped her arms around herself. 'I need to see her.'

'Of course.' The nurse led her to the next room and Gen pulled in a breath. Lily's face was swollen and blue, her hair lay in a matted halo around her head. An oxygen mask covered her nose and mouth and a tube led from her arm to a drip.

Gen watched for the rise and fall of her chest. Only then could she exhale.

She slid a chair to the edge of the bed and took Lily's cold hand in hers. She sandwiched her niece's fingers between both palms and blew hot air on them. 'I'm here, honey. You're safe now. You're going to be okay.' Gen's eyes welled and she kissed the back of Lily's hand. 'I'm here.'

The monitor beeped steadily. The nurse checked Lily's chart then fiddled with the IV. 'My name is Aisha, I'm the nursing unit manager tonight. Lily's nurse, Nate, will be along in a minute. He's just wrapping up a phone call with the police.'

'The police?'

'It was a hit and run accident. The police want to talk with Lily and the driver as soon as they wake.'

'Who was the driver?'

'Nate might know more after the call.' Aisha wrote a note in the chart, walked to the doorway, and turned. 'Can we expect Lily's parents to come in? It's just, there's only two visitors allowed in an ICU room at a time.'

Gen sat taller. 'Her mum died twelve years ago, but I assume her father is on his way.'

'If it's just him, it'll be fine,' Aisha said and left the room.

A minute later a male nurse with short dark hair entered. 'Hi, I'm Nate. I'll be with Lily until seven tomorrow.'

Gen's shoulders eased at his warm smile. 'I'm Gen, Lily's aunt. Aisha said you were talking to the police? Do you have any idea what happened? Why it took so long to notify us she was here?'

'Lily had no identification at the scene. The police tried to contact the owner of the car, but he didn't answer their calls. It took a while to track him down, as he was out of the office in meetings.'

Fucking Hugh! Gen took a deep breath. Lily needed her full attention right now.

She stroked her niece's head, closed her eyes to prevent the tears that threatened. 'Nate, do you have any idea what happened?'

'They were clipped by a car who ran a red light near Avalon Beach. The other driver fled the scene.'

'Aisha said the car rolled?'

'Witnesses said it spun, hit the kerb and turned end to end a few times. The firies used the jaws of life to get Lily out. The driver's neck was injured, but Lily took the brunt of the impact on her side.'

'Who was the driver?' She looked to the corridor. 'Is he on this floor too?'

'All I know is he's an eighteen-year-old, so he couldn't come to the children's hospital.'

Gen squeezed Lily's hand. 'What were you doing at Avalon, sweetheart? Why didn't you come to me?'

'What the hell are you doing in here?' Hugh marched into the room, his voice bouncing off the walls. He pivoted to Nate. 'Get her out. She is —'

'Sir, you need to calm down.'

'Remove that woman from my daughter's room. Now!'

'Hugh! Stop it.'

He pulled out his phone. 'I'm calling the police. It's her fault my daughter is in that bed.'

'My fault? You've got to be fucking kidding!'

'That is enough!' Nate stepped between them. 'Gen, please come with me while we sort this out.'

'But Lily asked for me. I need to be here when she wakes up.'

'You're never getting near her again.' The venom in Hugh's voice made Gen take a step back.

Aisha ran into the room. 'What's going on in here?'

Hugh whirled on the unit manager. 'If anyone in this hospital lets her' – he pointed at Gen – 'near my daughter again, I will sue.'

The monitor on Lily's machine beeped quicker.

'Gen,' Nate placed a gentle hand on her forearm, 'this is not good for Lily.'

Gen's fingernails bit into her palms as she glared at Hugh, a man she'd had no idea she could hate so much.

She bent across the bed to touch her lips to Lily's cheek. 'I love you, honey. I'll be just outside.'

She brushed past Hugh, ignoring him completely, and followed Nate down the corridor.

'Thank you. I don't think we were going to get through to Mr Forsythe.'

'No one ever can.'

'We do have a problem, though. As next of kin he has every right to dictate who has access to his daughter. I'm afraid I'm not going to be able to let you back into Lily's room.'

'But you don't understand. I've raised Lily since she was four, after my sister was murdered.'

Understanding filled his expression. 'I thought I recognised you. You held those vigils for your sister every year. I'm so sorry.'

'Thank you.' Gen shoved her hands in her pockets. Her gaze sank, unfocused. She had to get Nate to help her, whatever it took. Her eyes rose to meet his. 'Amber was my older sister. When she disappeared, Hugh fell apart and I stepped in to raise Lily and her younger brother, Charlie. I've lived with them all ever since – until Hugh kicked me out this week.'

'I wish I could help, I really do, but we have to follow hospital policy.'

'So you're going to throw me out?'

'You can't return to Lily's room.' He lowered his voice. 'But there's a parent waiting room barely anyone uses. If you want to stay in there, I could give you updates. It might give Mr Forsythe time to calm down. Emotions are always high when people first deal with an emergency.'

Hugh would never back down. But at least she would be close by.

'That sounds good. Thank you.'

He led her to the end of the corridor and pushed open the door to a small room with tea-making facilities, a couple of chairs and a bright-purple lounge.

'You can set up over there.'

'Thanks. Is Lily ... will she be safe?'

'As long as she remains stable through the night, the prognosis is good.'

'I mean from the driver that hit them.'

'The police think it was an accident, that the driver drove off in a panic. You'd be surprised how often it happens.' He squeezed her arm. 'Lily is my only patient. I won't let anyone get to her.'

'You'll keep me updated?'

'As long as Mr Forsythe doesn't say I can't.'

'Thank you. And I'm sorry for the disturbance before.'

Nate closed the door behind him. Gen boiled the kettle and made herself a strong cup of tea. There was no milk in the fridge, so she added a little cold water, then settled herself onto the lounge and sipped at the bitter liquid.

A tear slipped down her cheek. Lily needed her and she wasn't even allowed to be by her side. Gen leant her head back. Was the driver the online boyfriend Charlie had told her about? She sat up. Charlie! She discarded the mug and dialled the phone she'd given him.

'Gen? How's Lily? Is she okay? Can I talk to her?'

Gen's shoulders relaxed at the sound of Charlie's voice. 'She's sleeping right now but she's good.'

'Dad said she was in a car accident.'

'She was, but the hospital staff are amazing, and they expect her to make a full recovery.'

'Can I see her?'

'Not now. They want her to rest.' She sat forward. 'Who's staying with you?'

'Ugh, the stupid nanny. She won't let me call Dad or tell me anything. Can you come home, please?'

Gen pinched the bridge of her nose. 'Sorry, honey, I need to stay here with Lily, but you can call anytime, and I promise I'll answer.'

'They're making me go to school tomorrow.'

'It's pretty boring here, and don't you have a basketball game in the afternoon?'

'Yes, but ... is Lily really going to be okay?'

'Yes, sweetheart. She'll be back to bossing you around before you know it.'

'Can you tell her I love her?'

Gen swallowed. 'Of course.' One little white lie couldn't hurt. Charlie must feel so alone right now. 'How about I come to your game tomorrow afternoon?'

'But what about Lily?'

'Your dad will be here. Besides, you need me too. One o'clock, right?'

'Yes.'

'Are you going to be able to sleep now?'

'I think so.'

'Okay sweetheart. Sleep tight.'

'Gen?'

'Yes?'

'I love you.'

'Love you too, monkey.'

Gen cuddled the phone to her breast.

Hugh was trying to blame her, but he was at the root of all this. His illegal dealings, his gambling debts, his obsession with his father's approval. If he hadn't removed her from the house, she might have realised what Lily was up to this morning. And her niece certainly wouldn't have lain alone in that hospital bed for so long if Gen hadn't been erased from the school's notification list.

She was done taking the blame for everything. She'd let her mother put her in that role for too many years: the too-difficult child who caused problems in her mother's marriages. She'd taken the blame again when her sister went missing.

She stared at Amber's face on the lock screen of her phone and a small breath slid from her mouth as realisation pinballed through her. It would have made no difference if she'd gone to the supermarket that night. Amber was taken because of what she'd discovered. If she hadn't gone to buy nappies, they'd have got to her some other way.

Gen allowed her heavy eyes to close.

A gentle knock at the door roused her. Nate stuck his head around the corner. 'Everything okay?'

'You tell me.'

He slipped into the room. 'Lily's vitals are good. As long as the surgeon okays it during morning rounds, she'll be moved to a ward.'

'Can I see her?'

'That's what I came to talk to you about. Mr Forsythe had it put in Lily's notes that you are not allowed access to her room or her records.'

'Can he do that?'

'Unfortunately, yes. The thing is, while he was out of the room on a phone call, Lily woke and asked for you. I didn't know what to say. In the end I told her the truth, that her dad made you leave but you were waiting down the hall. That you refused to leave the hospital until you knew she was okay.'

'Thank you.'

'She asked me to give you a message. She said to tell you she's sorry.'

A hot, tight feeling spread at the back of Gen's throat. Lily was a victim in all this. It was the adults in her life who should be apologising. 'How is she now?'

'She's asleep, we gave her another dose of morphine.'

'Thank you so much for your kindness. Could I ask one more favour?' Gen undid the necklace from around her neck. 'Would you please give her this and tell her that no matter what, I love her, that I am fighting to see her, and I will never give up.'

'I ...'

'Please, I don't want to get you in trouble, but she needs to know I haven't abandoned her, not after what happened with her mother.' She held out the necklace. 'She knows what this means to me.'

'I'll get it to her.' His nose scrunched up in apology. 'I hate to say this, but you'll need to leave this room before change of shift. Parents aren't supposed to be in here overnight.'

'Can I stay until Lily is okayed to move?'

'The surgeon does rounds at six. I'll come past then and let you know.'

'I can't thank you enough.'

'She's lucky to have you in her corner.'

'I wish someone would tell her father that.'

'I tried. He's ...'

'A rude, pompous arse?'

'I wouldn't have put it quite like that.' He grinned. 'But I can't disagree.'

Geneva woke again to echoing footsteps approaching the door. She sat up, rubbed her eyes, and ran her hands over her hair. A gentle knock sounded, and Nate entered. His face looked a little drawn, but he still had a smile for her.

'The surgeon has cleared Lily to be transferred to the gastroenterology ward. She'll stay there a few days because of her spleen.'

'But she's awake and okay?'

'Still a bit groggy, but good.'

Gen held a palm to her chest. 'Thank you. Is there any way I can get updates on her?'

'Not officially. But I'm back on shift at 7 pm. You could call me?'

'You'd let me do that?'

'When she's alert, the only person she asks for is you. The only time her eyes lit up was when I gave her your necklace. Honestly? I'm doing it for her.'

Gen passed him her mobile and he entered his number into her contacts.

'I'd better go,' he said. 'I've got handover then I'm off to bed.'

Gen packed up and, as much as it hurt to leave the hospital, she headed for Toni's. She'd have a shower and then go through all the evidence she'd collected. She was meeting with the lawyer at ten. She had to be ready.

27

Lack of sleep pulled on Gen's muscles as she parked the bike outside Toni's apartment. Barely able to lift her head, she trudged through the gate into the garden, retrieved her key from her bag, lifted it to the lock and stilled. The door was wide open. Was Toni home early?

Her gaze caught on the glass-covered kitchen floor, then scanned the room. She hissed in a breath. The island bench had been swept of every ornament and vase. The dining chairs were overturned. The lounge had slashes all over its back. No pictures or paintings remained on the walls. The apartment had been completely ransacked. She stood transfixed in the doorway.

'Toni?'

There was no answer, no sign anyone was present. She pulled out her phone.

'If you're still in there, you need to leave. I'm calling the police.' She stepped away from the door, just in case, and dialled.

'Police. Fire. Ambulance. What's your emergency?'

'Someone broke into my friend's apartment. She's not here.'

'Is the intruder still inside?'

'I don't think so.'

'Are you alone?'

'Yes.'

'I'm sending out a patrol car. I want you to remain outside the premises. Is there someone you can call to wait with you? It could be up to two hours before the officers can get there.'

'Two hours?' She checked her watch and her shoulders slumped. 'Okay.'

She left a message at the lawyers asking to reschedule for the afternoon, then dialled Toni's number, but couldn't bear to leave a message. Her focus snagged on the shattered remains of the delicate blue porcelain egg Toni's grandmother had sent her from Shanghai.

The absolute destruction felt pointed, personal. Why would someone do this to Toni? Gen's life was the one in a mess, it would make more sense if she had been targeted.

No!

She bolted for her room. Gen's clothing and underwear lay shredded across slashed bed sheets. She threw everything aside, searching for her laptop and the folders on Amber. She rifled through the piles of ruined things, panic building. It was all gone. Everything she'd recorded was gone.

The break-in wasn't a robbery. It was a warning, a targeted attack. She checked Toni's room. Jewellery was scattered around as if someone had thrown the storage box through the air; a few clothes had been pulled out of drawers, but here, the destruction was half-hearted.

As far as Gen could tell, the only things missing were her files and her computer.

Viking was right. Trouble followed her everywhere, and now she had brought it right to her best friend's door.

She returned to the front entrance, sank to the steps and rested her head in her hands. How had everything gotten so out of control so quickly?

The operator had told her to call someone to sit with her, but the only person she wanted was in Western Australia. If she'd had her own home, Toni's wouldn't have been touched, and Hugh mightn't have so much control. She'd built no life for herself, just lived on the sidelines, waiting in reserve, every decision driven by guilt. It was time to change. She would make sure the kids were okay, but she had to stop trying to be Amber. To stop protecting Hugh.

She needed to tell the police everything she'd uncovered. And for that she needed Jesse. He'd know who to trust, who she should report this to.

She dialled his number again. It rang twice.

'Geneva?'

'Oh thank God, where have you been?'

'I just heard. Is Lily okay?'

'She's good, considering.' Gen ran her fingers through her hair. 'Are you ... Can you please come to Toni's? There's been a break-in.'

'Are you okay? Have you called the station?'

'They're sending someone, but it could be a few hours. And I need to talk over some things with you first. So much has happened in the last twenty-four hours.'

'Text me the address. Are you safe?'

'I'm out in the garden.'

'Wait there until I arrive.'

'I will. And Jesse?'

'What?'

'Thank you.'

The line disconnected. It would be a relief to hand over the investigation to people who knew what they were doing. She was so out of her depth.

She groaned out loud. What investigation? She had no proof left. The intruder had taken her files, notes, and computer.

The photos! She'd thrown them in the top box on the way home from Phoenix headquarters and in her desperation to get to Lily, she'd forgotten all about them.

She ran to her bike, unlocked the top box, and let out a shaky laugh. She wasn't beaten yet.

Holding the envelope to her chest, she walked back through the gate. She heard rustling behind her and twisted to check, but an arm snaked around her throat. She tried to duck away, but the pressure on her windpipe increased. She pulled at the man's forearm with one hand, clutching the envelope with the other.

'Help!'

His hand flew to her mouth.

She stomped on her attacker's feet and bit at the flesh of his palm. His fist slammed into her stomach and she doubled over in pain. She gasped for breath. Coughed.

He yanked her upright and his arm dug into her neck again. If he didn't stop, she'd choke.

'Shut your trap,' he sneered. 'And hand them over.' He held out an open palm.

Nausea and pain clouded her brain. What did he want? Then it hit her. He wanted the photos. That's what the break-in was about. But how did he know she had them?

His arm squeezed tighter. Spots appeared before her eyes. If she passed out, he'd take the envelope anyway. She held it out in front.

'They're only old family photos.'

The pressure on her neck eased a little.

Was this the guy who'd killed Amber? She twisted, trying to catch a glimpse of his face. He tightened his hold again and snatched the envelope from her hand. With only one arm free, he'd lost his hold on her. She fought hard, stomping and kicking and hitting him. He grunted. She reached her hand behind her and scratched his face as hard as she could.

'Bitch!'

For a split second she was airborne, then her shoulder slammed into the brick wall, followed by her cheekbone. She crumpled into a heap on the ground. Footsteps retreated.

A car screeched to a stop outside on the street. The gate slammed open.

'Gen!' Jesse ran to her. 'Are you okay?'

'That way,' she stammered, pointing to the harbour. 'He's getting away.'

Jesse glanced towards the path, then back to her.

'Go!' she screamed hoarsely.

He took off. Gen rolled to her hands and knees. Her head pounded and her face stung. She climbed to her feet and breathed against the rolling nausea, scanning her body. Her throat hurt, her temple throbbed, and there'd be bruises everywhere, but she wasn't seriously hurt. She hobbled to the edge of the path, holding her stomach. Footsteps approached and an out-of-breath Jesse ran up to her.

'I lost him, sorry.'

'No!' She bent in two, hands on knees. 'He took them.' Her voice came out in a raspy sob.

He crouched in front of her. 'Took what? Are you okay?'

'The photos. He took the photos.' She swayed.

'Woah. Let's get you inside. Then you can tell me what's going on.'

He hooked an arm around her waist and guided her to the door. He scanned the apartment and frowned, then settled her on the lounge. He filled a plastic cup with water, then pulled two tablets from his wallet and handed them to her.

She shook her head.

'By the look of that lump on your temple, you're going to have quite a headache.' He pushed the tablets into her hand. 'It's paracetamol. Now, let's check the rest of you over.'

'A few grazes and bruises. Honestly, I'm fine.'

'Christ, you're a tough one,' he mumbled under his breath, then ran his hands over her head, pausing at her neck. His thumb traced her skin and his lips thinned. 'What happened?'

'He had his arm around my neck, but I'm —'

Jesse's eyes flared. 'When I get my hands on that fucker ...'

Tears welled in Gen's eyes. His hands came to her cheeks. 'Are you hurt anywhere else?' His tone had gentled.

'Just a sore head and belly.'

'Belly?'

'He punched me when I screamed.'

His eyes darkened further, searched her face, and then the anger dissolved. He'd reined it right in. How could she ever have doubted his character?

He put his hand in the air. 'How many fingers?'

'Three.'

'Blurriness or nausea?

'Not really.'

He took her hand in both of his. 'Can you tell me what happened? What he looked like?'

Gen closed her eyes.

'He grabbed me from behind, so I didn't see him. But he's tall. Wore a black tracksuit, with three white stripes down the sleeve.'

'On the phone you said officers were on their way.'

'The operator said it could be a few hours.'

'I'm going to call. Upgrade this to an assault.'

'Could you hold off? Just for a minute?'

'Geneva —'

'Please, I need to tell you everything that's happened first. I think we're going to need to report to someone much more specialised than a beat cop.'

He rubbed his chin, then he stood, went to the freezer, and returned with a bag of peas. He held it to her temple until she took over. 'Toni have any antiseptic cream?'

Gen blinked, thrown by the shift in topic. 'First-aid drawer. Third down in the bathroom.' He reappeared a minute later with a white tube of cream, a hand towel and a damp face cloth.

'I'll attend to your face while you talk.' He dabbed the wet cloth at her cheek, easing the pressure when she winced.

She ran through everything – how Hugh had kicked her out, finding the photos, meeting with Mac and Feral, the Forsythes' connections to a crime syndicate and a money laundering scheme, Tobias admitting he'd lied when he'd given Hugh an alibi, Hugh's cheating and gambling debt, Mac's arrest and, finally, Lily's accident.

Jesse set aside the cloth and gently dried her face with the hand towel. He dabbed cream onto the graze.

She reached up and held his forearm. 'Jesse, do you know anything about this? Do you know why Mac was arrested?'

'I want you to promise to stay calm.'

'Has there ever been a time in the history of the world when telling someone to stay calm has worked?'

'Point taken.'

'Just tell me.'

'He was arrested on suspicion of Amber's murder.'

'What?'

'The objects they found in his room? It was the jewellery she was wearing the night of the abduction.'

'No!' She leapt to her feet, then clutched at her skull. It was as if the sudden movement had set off a bomb in her head. She sank back to the sofa. The back of her throat burned – with tears or pain or God only knew what. She covered her face with her hands.

'Why would Mac help me if he was behind everything? It doesn't make sense.'

'Maybe he was trying to keep tabs on what you knew?'

Oh God. She'd been so stupid. How could she have never suspected him?

'Are you sure?'

'He'd kept the personal items of other murder victims too. We believe he was a hit man.'

'But how does that connect to Hugh and the laundering? To what Amber uncovered? It doesn't fit.'

'I need to explain what I've been doing the past few days.'

'The PCYC said you were on leave.'

'I was called into head office. Strike Force Chameleon.'

She blinked at him blankly.

'They're part of a worldwide investigation looking to break apart a cartel targeting Australia's real estate market and casinos. They called me in to warn me off further interaction with the Forsythes.'

'You mean —'

He nodded. 'The Forsythes are suspected of being the Australian brokers for the cartel, a group made up of five crime families from around the globe.'

'Fuck.' Her bottom lip wobbled. 'Fuck!' she screamed, then winced. 'Those bastards had Amber killed, didn't they? How long have the police known?'

'It's a little more complex than that, but yes, they think a hit was put out on Amber because she discovered what was going on.'

Gen stared at the broken pieces of a dainty pink and white teacup. Toni's favourite.

'How could he? She loved him so much. I'm going to fucking tear Hugh limb from limb when I see him.' She swatted at the stupid tears that spilled from her eyes.

'We're not sure if he was cognisant of what happened to Amber.'

'Oh come on, if he wasn't directly involved, he had to have at least suspected.'

'I agree.'

'I don't understand how Mac connects to all this.'

'He was hired to kill her.'

'Who by? Hugh? His family?'

'The strike force is still investigating that.'

'Why would Mac mention the Forsythes' dodgy sales to me then? It makes no sense.'

'Maybe he thought he could scare you off looking into things, by mentioning a possible organised crime connection. He did forbid you from sharing the info, especially with me.'

The explanation still didn't sit right, but it wasn't like she could ask Mac himself. She rubbed her temples. 'I can't believe K2 —'

He shook his head. 'Not Phoenix. Just Mac and two of his mates. They worked with the Warrior MC, planned to bring Viking down.'

'But Viking's his brother!'

'Mac was fiercely against leaving the Rebels. He planned to stage a revolt and take over.'

'No,' she shook her head. 'Mac gave me the information to help identify the Warriors.'

'He was going to have you destroy his competitors for him. His plan was to merge the two clubs. He would become president and they could take over the whole territory.'

'How do you know all this?'

'I can't tell you that, but let's just say there is someone in his world who didn't want him to succeed.'

'There's an informant in Phoenix?'

'I really can't say anymore.'

'My God. All these years I thought my family was messed up, but they have nothing on this lot.' A tear slipped down her cheek. 'I trusted Mac. How stupid am I?' She turned to Jesse. 'He even convinced me to doubt you.'

Her chest felt like it was about to collapse in on itself. She couldn't have made more of a mess of this if she'd tried. 'If I hadn't gone to Phoenix with the photos, you'd have the proof Amber uncovered.'

She rubbed at the stabbing pain across her breastbone, wincing when her fingers brushed her shoulder. She frowned. 'All that doesn't explain about my attacker. Who was he? How did he know I had the photos?'

'Mac placed a call to a burner phone two minutes before the raid. I think he must have sent someone to retrieve the photos.'

'It's like the Forsythes and Mac were always one step ahead.'

Jesse's tone sharpened. 'Who pays for your phone?'

'Me.'

'Any issues lately? Overheating? Excess data usage?'

'No.'

'What about your bike?'

'What about it?'

He raced from the apartment and she followed. He sat on his haunches and ran his hands over the frame.

'Shit.'

'What?'

He pulled a round tag, about the size of a twenty-cent piece, from behind the number plate.

'Is that what I think it is?'

He nodded.

Her hands curled into fists. 'How long's it been there?'

'No way to tell. And with this type of tracking device, we can't trace the signal to the owner.'

He pushed the tracker back in place.

'What are you doing?'

'They don't know we've found it.' He stood. 'We'll leave it, until Strike Force Chameleon has a chance to decide what steps to take next.'

They returned inside and she sat.

'Will the officers even believe me? I don't have any evidence left.'

She closed her eyes and felt a wave of exhaustion almost take her under.

The lounge sank next to her. 'You might not have the photos anymore, but you can tell the forensic accountants what and who to look for. Can you remember any dates? Names?'

'Erica Sykes. A month before Amber was killed. A house in Clifton Gardens.'

'Anything else?'

'Not exact numbers, but there was another sale when Hugh returned from his stint in rehab.'

'I want you to write down how the columns were set out, and what Feral thought each was for. We can also ask the restoration lab if they kept copies of the photos.'

'What about the raid? Wouldn't there be something on Feral's computer?'

'He wiped it clean.'

Jesse passed her a notepad and pen he'd found by the smashed printer. 'Are you up to it?'

She nodded and jotted down all she could remember.

'I'll stay until the officers get here, give them an account of what happened when I arrived, but then I'd like to drive to headquarters. That's if you think you'll be okay. I want to talk with the Strike Force team. They're good people and I trust them. I'll also pay a visit to my contact in Internal Affairs. If we're going up against the Forsythes and the cartel, I want to confirm everyone on our end is clean. We can't risk any tip-offs.'

Twenty minutes later, the beat officers arrived, and things ran just as Jesse described. Once he'd finished his statement, she walked him to the door. His gaze slid to her grazed cheek and he shook his head slightly, then hooked his hand around the back of her neck and pulled her to his chest. Gen wrapped her arms around his waist and allowed her breath to fall into rhythm with his. After a minute he eased away, and she stuffed her hands in her pockets.

'You will come back?'

'Try and stop me.'

28

The officers took Gen's statement, some photos, dusted for prints and took samples from under her nails, where she'd scratched her attacker. Then they filled her in on Lily and the crash investigation.

Lily's condition was improving hour by hour. Her boyfriend, an eighteen-year-old in his final year at Hoxton Park High, held a provisional driver's licence and had agreed to skip school to take Lily to visit her mum's grave. They'd met in an online support group for children who'd lost a parent.

He'd caught the bus to Balmoral and met Lily at the house, where she gave him the keys to the car, and they drove to Macquarie Park Cemetery. They spent the morning at Amber's graveside, then drove to Palm Beach for lunch, and were headed back to Balmoral when they were hit by an unidentified ute. Police had a partial number plate for the runaway driver and were confident of tracking them down.

Not long after completing their report, the officers received another call-out. Gen assured them she would be fine until Jesse returned. If the attacker had wanted to harm her further, he'd surely have done so at the time.

Still, she made them confirm the deadlock worked before

they left. Gen looked around. She couldn't let Toni come home to this.

She grabbed a dustpan, brush and garbage bag and started the clean-up. She tipped pan after pan of swept-up mess into the bag until it was full, put it near the inside of the front door and started filling a new bag. Her headache flared and she went to the bathroom to find more paracetamol.

Her mobile rang from the lounge room, and she rushed to get it.

The caller ID flashed: *Hugh Forsythe*. Her stomach crept up her throat, but if she didn't answer, he might get suspicious.

'Yes?'

'Geneva, I need you to meet me at Balmoral as soon as you can.'

No fucking chance, arsehole. 'I can't right now.'

'We have things to discuss.'

'We can talk on the phone.'

'It needs to be in person.'

'No.'

'What do you mean, no? Are you that uninterested in your niece's condition —'

'I know she's improving and doing well.' Silence filled the line. 'What did you need to talk about, Hugh?'

'You need to come here. It's urgent. It's about the kids.'

'If it's so urgent, tell me now.'

This was ridiculous. They were going round in circles, but there was no way she would risk meeting Hugh without back-up. The last time she'd done that he'd ambushed her, and that was before she knew what she did now.

'I'll come in an hour when Jesse can come with me.'

'Of course.' The sneer in his voice caused a rush of heat to flash up her neck.

'Fuck you, Hugh.'

She jabbed the phone violently, ending the call. *Dammit.* When it came to the kids, she'd always come running, and he knew it.

She exhaled. Lily was doing well in hospital and Charlie was safe at school. So, what was Hugh up to now?

Shit. Charlie. She checked her watch. His basketball game started in half an hour. She texted Jesse.

> Promised Charlie I'd go to his basketball match at 1. You okay if I go?

> Please stay at apartment. Things more precarious than we knew. Back in 45.

Gen's chest sank. She'd be letting Charlie down again, but if Jesse didn't think leaving was a good idea, she had to trust him. She typed a text to Charlie.

> Sorry matey, I won't make basketball today. I owe you the biggest pizza and ice-cream night, and any movie of your choice.

She sent it off. Almost immediately, it shifted from delivered to read. She watched for the typing bubbles to appear, but there was nothing.

She tried again.

> I know you're disappointed. I really am sorry.

Delivered, read, but again, no dots. Which was really unlike him. Charlie always answered. She tried again.

> Charlie?

She tried ringing, but it went straight to voicemail. Something wasn't right. She called his school.

'Sorry, Charlie was pulled out of school this morning to visit his sister in hospital. His uncle picked him up.'

'His uncle?' Bill had never stepped foot in Charlie's school before. 'Bill Forsythe?'

'No, Tobias Church.'

Gen paced. Why would Tobias take Charlie to the hospital while Hugh stayed at home?

She dialled the hospital switchboard and asked to be put through to Lily's ward.

'Hello, I'm from Shorewood Boys Grammar, I'm trying to get in touch with a student of ours, Charlie Forsythe. He's visiting his sister, Lily, who is on your ward.'

'One minute please.' Hold music came on the line, then clicked back to the woman who'd answered.

'I spoke to her nurse. Lily's only visitor this morning has been the family nanny. She's still there now. Do you want me to pass on a message?'

'No! No, thank you. I'll try his father again.'

Adrenaline raced through her veins. If Charlie wasn't visiting Lily, then why had Hugh asked Tobias to pull him out of school?

Her phone buzzed with a text from the burner phone. *Of course!* Hugh had confiscated Charlie's phone yesterday but Charlie still had the one she'd given him.

Can u pls come?

She rang his number immediately, but it went to voicemail again. Another text came through.

Can't talk.

Why?

He'll hear.

Who?

Dad.

Where are you?

Home.

Walk out the back, I'll meet you in the park.

Can't.

Why?

Dad won't let me leave. He's drinking.

Are you ok?

Scared. Pls come.

Oh my God. What the fuck was going on?

She dialled Jesse but it clicked straight through to voicemail. 'Jesse, I have to go to the house in Balmoral. Something is going on with Hugh. Charlie's really scared. I won't go inside the house, I promise, but I have to make sure he's okay. Can you meet me there when you get this?'

She tried Jesse's number again, just in case it went through this time, but it didn't. She could try calling headquarters, but she had no idea who exactly Jesse was meeting with. Tracking them down would take time, and Charlie needed her now. She quickly texted back.

Charlie, run out front when I pull into the drive.

She grabbed her jacket and bolted for her bike. *Hold on honey. I'm on my way.*

29

Gen screeched into the driveway and flicked down the stand. As soon as Charlie came out, they'd walk up the road and take a taxi to Jesse's house. It was the only place she was sure they'd be safe.

She dismounted, locked her helmet in the top box then stared at the front door. *Come on, Charlie. You must have heard me pull up.* She checked her phone. Nothing.

She typed a quick message to Jesse.

I'm at the house but Charlie hasn't come out. Are you on your way?

She waited a minute, but the message remained unread. She opened her chat with Charlie and typed.

I'm in the driveway.

No typing bubbles appeared.

She hesitated. Maybe she should wait for Jesse. She stared at Charlie's last message. *Scared. Pls come.* She couldn't leave him in there alone any longer.

She climbed the front stairs, raised her hand to knock, then withdrew it and twisted the door handle instead. It eased open.

If Hugh was drunk at this time of day, there was every chance he was passed out on the lounge. She could slip upstairs to Charlie's room, and they could leave without a confrontation. She snuck down the hall to the stairwell.

'In here, Geneva.' Hugh. *Fuck.* She pulled out her phone, ready to dial 000.

'Charlie,' she called up the stairs, 'I'm here. You can come down now.'

Hugh emerged from the back room. 'Geneva, please come and take a seat.'

She froze, unable to reconcile the man she'd thought she knew with the man she now knew he'd become.

He snatched her phone and moved to stand between her and the front door.

'What the hell, Hugh? Give me back my phone.'

'When we've had a chat.'

'I didn't come here to talk, I came for Charlie.'

He gestured, indicating that she should go through to the back room. She rocked on her feet. Was Charlie in there? Better to do as Hugh said until she could figure out where her nephew was.

She entered the kitchen. Tobias sat at the dining table, Charlie's phone in front of him and, next to it, the phone she'd bought for the kids. 'Tobias?' She whirled on Hugh. 'What are you up to?'

He shrugged. 'Had to get you here somehow.'

She tried to march past him to go upstairs, but he blocked her path.

'Charlie! Are you up there?' she yelled, then turned to Tobias. 'Is he even here?'

Footsteps thundered above, and Charlie came bounding down the stairs. 'Gen Gen!'

330 • Rae Cairns

Charlie buried his head in her middle. He seemed okay.

'Are you coming with us to see Lily?' The relief in his tone, the joy at having her there, momentarily filled her with warmth.

'Okay Charlie, you've said hello.' Hugh stepped in. 'Back upstairs.'

'But —'

'Now!'

Tobias stood. 'I think you should listen to your father, Charlie.' There was an edge to his tone. Charlie flinched, and Hugh shot Tobias a warning glance.

Gen's gaze darted between them. 'What's going on here?'

'Go play your Xbox, Charlie.' Hugh's tone gentled a little. 'I just need a few words with your aunt before we leave.'

Gen knelt in front of Charlie and held her palms to his cheeks. 'Are you okay? We can walk out the front door right now if you want.'

His gaze flicked to his dad, then he leaned in close. 'I'm okay, but please don't leave without me. They've been fighting ever since Uncle Tobias brought me here.'

A warning buzz fanned out in the pit of her stomach.

'I'm not going anywhere without you, I promise.' She kissed his forehead and stood.

She waited until Charlie's bedroom door banged shut, then faced Hugh. 'What the fuck is going on?'

'Have a seat.'

She glanced at the stairs. She could run up to Charlie's room, barricade them in until Jesse arrived. But that would put Charlie right in the middle of whatever this was.

'You've got me here. Talk.'

Hugh looked briefly to Tobias, then he lifted his chin. 'I've bought you a plane ticket to Europe. You leave tomorrow morning. When you land in London, enough money will be deposited into your bank account to cover you for six months.'

She made a *what the fuck?* face at Tobias, then turned back to Hugh. 'Have you lost your mind?'

'In return for your cooperation, Forsythe Commercial Real Estate will buy you a three-bedroom apartment, anywhere you want, up to the value of two million dollars. And upon your return next year you'll get official visitation rights to the children.'

'You're using Lily and Charlie as bargaining chips?'

'I'm doing this to protect them.'

She scoffed. 'Right, like you protected Amber.'

'You know what? I'm sick of your holier than thou bullshit. Amber liked the things I provided her with. If it weren't for me —'

'If it weren't for you, I'd be travelling the world and Amber would be very much alive.'

Tobias's chair scraped back, and he stood. 'This isn't getting us anywhere.'

'Us? What exactly is your role here, Tobias?'

'Legal representative for Forsythe Commercial Real Estate.'

'Well then, don't let the door hit you on the arse as you leave. Nothing about this is legal.' She paced the room, highly aware both exits were blocked. Her muscles tensed, and rage boiled in her gut. She nailed Hugh with a glare. 'Admit you got my sister killed.'

'I don't know what happened.'

'Yes you do!'

'If she'd backed off like I'd asked, I would have been home that night.'

'Don't you dare blame her. Not with what you're involved in!'

'It's only white-collar stuff, nobody gets hurt.'

'Are you fucking kidding me?'

'Hugh.' Tobias's tone carried a note of warning.

She pointed upstairs. 'Your twelve-year-old son is scared and locked away in his room, your sixteen-year-old daughter is in hospital because you were too busy to be there for her, and your wife, your *wife*, was murdered by your employers because she was trying to make you do the right thing.'

'That's not true!'

Gen threw her hands in the air. 'Stop bullshitting yourself. Who do you think owns the money you're laundering?'

'Enough!' Tobias yelled.

Gen whirled at the steely tone she'd never heard from him before, then froze. He held a gun at his side, a black pistol, and was wearing black leather gloves.

'What are you doing?' Hugh's voice rose an octave. 'Put that away!'

'You said you'd get her under control.'

Hugh stepped in front of Gen. 'I will. Just give me another minute.'

'She knows too much.' He lifted the gun and pointed it at Hugh's chest.

'What the fuck?' Hugh's palms flew into the air in surrender.

Tobias? *He* was behind everything? The events of the past few weeks tripped over one another in Gen's scrambling brain.

My God. She'd shared her suspicions with him, told him her plans to go to the police.

The corners of Tobias's mouth lifted. 'Naive little Gen. Thought you were so clever cosying up to Mac, didn't you? Have you figured it out, yet? How he was the one who bashed your sister's skull in?'

The burn of bile hit the back of Gen's throat. She clenched her fists and her weight shifted, ready to step forward, but Tobias's gun hand twitched. What was she thinking? Charlie was in the house. She had to get him out.

'I've had Mac tracking you ever since the funeral. And drip-feeding you information while I set the final pieces of my plan in place. He wasn't, however, supposed to get caught.'

'You?' Hugh's head drew back. 'You hired the man who killed Amber?'

Tobias placed the weapon on the flat of his palm and offered it to Hugh.

'Take it.'

'What?' Hugh shook his head and jammed his hands under his armpits. 'I'm not touching that thing.'

'This ends now.'

Gen locked her knees against her shaky legs. 'Jesse is on his way. He's right behind me.'

'No he's not. You said you'd be an hour because you had to wait for him. By my calculations, we have at least another thirty minutes before he gets here.' He shoved his outstretched hand closer to Hugh. 'Take the gun.'

'No.' Hugh shook his head. 'I organise vendors, contracts. That's all.'

'Time to get your hands dirty.'

Gen slid her right foot back, then her left, slowly transferring her weight. She had to get to the stairwell, get to Charlie.

'She's my sister-in-law. This is not what I do.'

Tobias grabbed Hugh's hand. 'In that case, I'll adjust the parameters.' He curled Hugh's fingers around the gun. Held them in place. 'When Jesse arrives, he'll discover the scene of a murder-suicide.'

'What?' Hugh whimpered.

'You're going to kill Geneva and then turn the gun on yourself.'

Gen inched further back, heart pounding, barely able to breathe.

'What makes you think I won't turn it on you?' Hugh's voice quavered.

'I have an employee on standby at the hospital. If they don't hear from me, they'll be at Lily's bedside in a heartbeat.'

Tobias's gaze shifted to Gen.

She froze, mind whirring. She had to buy some time. Surely Jesse had her message by now.

'No one will believe that story,' she said. 'Where would a man like Hugh get a gun?'

Tobias scoffed. 'He's working with a crime cartel and a bunch of one percenters. All the evidence was kindly supplied by you and Amber.'

'He won't spare Charlie,' she appealed to Hugh's back. 'Charlie knows Tobias was here.'

Hugh spun and pointed the gun at Tobias, hands shaking. 'I'll shoot you right now.'

Tobias scoffed and stepped closer. 'You don't have the balls.'

'Why are you doing this?' Hugh's voice filled with gravel. 'We're best friends.'

'We were never friends.' He plucked the gun from Hugh, made a show of clicking the manual safety off. 'You used me to prop up your ego. But being an errand boy suited me, gave me the chance to bring down the great Forsythe empire. You'll be gone, and William and Bill will go to prison. Every thread of evidence leads back to the three of you. I'll be free to step in and take over the business.'

Hugh jammed his hands under his armpits, rocked on his

feet. 'Why? We gave you a great job, a great life. Why would you do this?'

'William was as industrious in his affairs as he was in business. He knocked up his secretary, my mother, at the same time as your mother fell pregnant with you. Only, while your arrival was hailed as a triumph, we were sent interstate, paid to disappear into the night. Couldn't risk any illegitimate kiddies destroying the image of the perfect Forsythe family. Not when William planned to go into politics one day.' Tobias paced; the air thick with threat.

Hugh and Tobias were half-brothers?

Gen gave herself a mental shake. None of this shit mattered. She had to get to Charlie now. Each time Tobias changed direction she edged closer to the stairs.

'We did just fine without him – until Mum died in a car accident when I was ten. I was sent to my maternal grandmother in Sydney. She believed she had to beat the sinner out of me.'

'Why didn't anyone contact Dad when your mum died?'

'The Department of Community Services tried, but William wasn't listed on the birth certificate. He threatened to sue if they pursued him further.'

Another step. She'd almost made it. The next time he turned his back, she'd run.

'I worked hard, got a scholarship to the college every Forsythe has attended since day dot. It was no accident we were placed in neighbouring rooms.'

'Why didn't you tell me? You know I never felt like I belonged in the family.'

'Oh yes, poor second son Hugh. You pathetic piece of shit.'

Gen's heel hit the bottom step. She bent her knees, ready to spring, when a creak came from above. Her gaze shot to Tobias. He hadn't heard it.

Go back to your room, Charlie, she willed him. *Please, go back to your room.*

'You had every advantage in the world and you squandered it.'

She glanced up the stairs. Charlie's feet came into view. Her heart beat so fast her head began to spin. It was now or never. She ran. She made it two steps up before she was jerked back, yanked by the ponytail, and thrown aside. Tobias raised the gun and aimed it up the stairwell.

This can't be happening. 'Run, Charlie!'

Hugh lurched for Tobias's arm. A shot fired, but no cry rang out.

Tobias backhanded Hugh and he fell to the ground.

Gen dived for Tobias's ankle, held it tight. He kicked her in the stomach and pain radiated through her. She gasped for breath but kept hold. She was going to die here, she knew, but she would buy Charlie enough time to escape.

Tobias's foot came down on her arm with a sickening crunch and she screamed. The barrel of the gun bore down on her. She rolled away, her vision blurring with pain.

Get out, Charlie. You can do it. Please get away.

A loud bang echoed, sending a searing heat through her head. Then everything turned black.

30

A low-pitched keening brought Gen back into consciousness. The floor felt sticky beneath her cheek. She squinted her eyes open, just a little. The noise was coming from Hugh, cowering beneath the barrel of Tobias's gun.

'On your knees.'

'Please,' Hugh begged. 'Please, spare Charlie. He has nothing to do with any of this.'

'He's seen too much. But I'll make it quick if you kneel now.'

Behind Tobias, on the stairs off the kitchen leading down to the driveway, a shape shifted into view. A step creaked. Tobias caught Hugh around the neck with his upper arm, then pivoted them both to face the kitchen. He pressed the gun to Hugh's head.

'Back off!' Tobias bellowed towards the intruders. 'Or I'll kill him.'

Gen rolled onto her other side, used her good arm to climb to her knees. The room spun. She blinked against the pain and focused on the stairs. She put one foot flat to the floor.

Get to Charlie. Get to Charlie.

'The house is surrounded,' a deep male voice came from the stairwell. 'Put your weapons down and lie on the ground.'

A thwack sounded behind her. She checked over her shoulder. Hugh was lying unconscious on the ground and Tobias was running at her.

Gen lurched towards the first stair, her vision spotting.

An arm came around her throat. Tobias pinned her against his chest.

'No!' Tears poured down Gen's face. 'Get out, Charlie!' she rasped. 'Please get out!'

'That you on the stairs, Johns?' Tobias yanked Gen's broken arm and she screamed.

'Hear that? Come any closer and she's dead.'

She swayed.

Tobias shook her. 'Pull yourself together. If I go down, so do you.'

Two men dressed head to toe in black tactical suits stepped from the back stairs into the room, guns trained on Tobias's head. At least, Gen hoped that's where they were trained, because with her blurry vision it looked like the sights were on her. Her entire body shook.

'I've got you,' the man on the left spoke in a warm baritone.

Jesse? She blinked the man into focus, but couldn't see his face through his mask, only his eyes. Her bottom lip trembled.

'I won't walk away. I've got you. Remember the beach?'

The beach? What was he getting at? She forced her mind past the fear, past the pain.

I won't walk away. I've got you, Gen – even if you fall.

She met his green-eyed gaze, and he nodded.

'Now!'

She sagged her knees, putting her entire weight onto Tobias's arm.

The front door burst open behind them and a loud bang echoed through the house. Gen fell backwards. Her eyes stung, her ears rang. The weight leaning across her neck didn't move. Neither did the body beneath her.

'Geneva! God, are you okay?' Tobias's arm was pulled off her neck and she rolled off his body onto her haunches, her crushed arm hanging useless beneath her. She coughed and dry retched, the smoke dissipating from around her. Tobias had a bullet hole through the centre of his forehead. Two metres away, Hugh lay still, a pool of blood around his head.

An officer removed the gun from Tobias's hand. Another held out a plastic bag to Jesse and he dropped his gun in.

She retched again as she lurched to her feet. Jesse tried to support her around the waist, but she shrugged him off and stumbled towards the stairs. Her knees gave way after two steps.

'Charlie.' She gave a hiccupping cry. 'Charlie!'

'He's outside.' Jesse crouched down next to her. 'He's safe, outside. Used what he'd learnt at parkour to get across the roof to your neighbour's.'

Two paramedics rushed in, put an oxygen mask over Hugh's face, lifted him onto a gurney and rolled him away.

Gen turned wide eyes back to Jesse. 'Lily!'

'Lily is safe under police guard at the hospital.'

'I want to see her.' She tried to stand again, but her muscles wouldn't cooperate. 'I need to hold Charlie.'

Outside, the ambulance's siren blared, growing faint as it sped away.

'How about I help you outside?'

'Is Hugh going to be okay?'

'He was cold cocked but he's alive. Let's get you checked out.'

She took the stairs down slowly, with Jesse's help.

'Gen!' She turned at Charlie's cry. He broke from the police officer who was with him, bolted towards her then pulled up short, eyes widening as he took in her head and arm.

She sank to her knees, the need to hold him overwhelming. 'I'm okay, honey, I promise, but I could really do with a hug.'

He stared, his eyes following the blood trail running down her head. 'You got hurt.'

'It looks worse than it is, I promise. You're so clever getting yourself out of there.'

'What about Dad? They wouldn't let me see him.'

A hit to the head could kill someone. She looked into Charlie's eyes. 'The doctors will look after him.'

Hugh had better pull through.

Another ambulance screeched to a stop and the doors swung open.

Charlie threaded his arms gently around her waist. She lay her cheek on the crown of his head, wrapped her good arm around his back and mouthed, *Thank you,* to Jesse.

Two paramedics approached, wheeling a stretcher. 'Ma'am, we really need to check your injuries.'

They helped her onto the lowered gurney. Every muscle and limb screamed in protest as she lay down.

One paramedic knelt at Charlie's side and spoke quietly, while the other inspected Gen's wounds, moving her right arm carefully. Gen hissed out a breath.

'Lucky for you the bullet just grazed your head. It'll need wound debridement and antibiotics, but it looks like the bullet missed everything vital. The arm will need setting.'

Gen turned to Jesse. 'I'm not leaving without Charlie.'

'He can ride to the hospital with you.'

'I can't go anywhere but Westmead. I have to get to Lily. I need to see for myself that she's safe.'

Jesse and the ambulance officers stepped away and had a whispered conversation, then Jesse returned to Gen's side.

'They've agreed, for safety reasons, to take you to Westmead emergency. I have to finish up here and debrief but I'll meet you on the ward.' He ran the back of his hand gently down her cheek. 'In the meantime, try and stay out of trouble.'

The other officer came over. 'Let's get you on the rig.' They rolled Gen into the ambulance. Charlie scrambled in and sat in the chair at her side. The female paramedic climbed in and helped Charlie with his seatbelt. Charlie grabbed Gen's good hand and squeezed. 'You're going to be okay, Gen Gen, I promise.'

The doors closed, someone tapped twice on the side of the ambulance and the vehicle began to move.

A tear slid down Gen's cheek. They were alive, thank God, but would they ever be okay again?

31

Gen lay her forehead on the sheets of Lily's bed and closed her eyes. It had been four hours since she'd been released from emergency with her head bandaged and her arm set in a cast. Lily had been moved to a private room at the end of the corridor, and Gen had been escorted here under police guard. A constable was stationed outside the room, assigned to protect them until the police could assess the threat posed by Hugh's criminal connections.

Gen's eyelids shot open. Her niece's chest rose and fell. She checked the recliner in the corner where Charlie lay, soft snores escaping his mouth. Her spiking pulse eased. The kids were safe.

Lily had roused as soon as Gen entered the room but had exhausted quickly, and after a long hug and a few tears she had drifted back to sleep. Charlie would have a lot to process, but she'd be at his side every step of the way.

No one was ever taking her from her kids again.

Her stomach twisted. What had happened to Hugh? She'd had no update since being brought in.

She settled her breath in time with the puffs coming from Lily's mouth and smiled at a particularly loud snort from Charlie.

A soft knock sounded, and Toni stuck her head around the door. 'Up for a visitor?'

Gen leapt to her feet and fell into her best friend's embrace.

'Hey,' Toni rubbed her back and Gen let the silent tears fall. 'If I'd known I'd get such a dramatic welcome I'd have come earlier.'

'God it's good to see you.'

'Let me take a look at you.' She leant back and scrutinised Gen from head to toe, pausing at the gauze where the bullet had grazed her head.

'I'm okay.'

'Oh yeah, you look pristine. Just another day in suburbia.'

Gen grinned.

'Toni? Aunty Toni?' Charlie blinked a few times, then jumped up and threw his arms around her.

She hugged him tightly. 'I hear you were quite the hero today.'

His face fell, and Gen squeezed his shoulder. 'Mate, it's okay, say whatever you need.'

'How is Dad?'

Gen hesitated; her gaze lifted to Toni's. 'I haven't heard yet.'

'Jesse's in the corridor. I can stay with them if you like.'

Gen looked back to Charlie. 'Are you okay if Toni stays with you while I find out about your dad?'

'You'll come back?'

'Oh honey, I'll always come back. You're going to start begging me for space.' She ruffled his hair, took a step away, then pulled him in close and touched her forehead to his. 'I love you. You and Lily will always be my family. There is nowhere else I want to be, okay?'

'Okay.' He turned to Toni. 'Bet you can't beat me at Thunderwars.'

'You're on, you little monkey. You owe me a win.'

Gen took one last look at the three people she loved more than anything in the world, and quietly left the room.

Outside, she found Jesse talking with the guard, quietly but seriously.

'Everything okay?'

'It's all under control for now, just a lot of departments involved and things to sort. I was just telling the constable here that the only person to stand him down from duty will be me. Right, Craig?'

'Absolutely sir. I'll still be here when you get back.'

Gen narrowed her eyes. 'What's going on?'

'Hugh needs to see you.'

'If he thinks he can separate me from Lily and Charlie ever again, he's wrong.' Her voice dropped in pitch. 'I will never back down.'

'Do you trust me?'

Gen searched his face and, surprising herself, nodded.

'It's important you see him.'

Gen looked back at the closed door to Lily's room.

'We've put another guard at the nurses' station. They're watching the elevator and the stairs.'

'What about the guy who attacked me this morning?'

'He's been arrested, thanks to the scratch you left on his cheek. Rounded up by Strike Force Raptor in a raid on the Warriors.'

'Who is he?'

'Matthew "Trip" Miller.'

'Trip? The guy from the Stubenitsky farm?'

'One and the same.' Jesse checked his watch. 'Toni can stay with the kids, but I need you to come with me now.'

She sighed and stuck her head into Lily's room. 'I'm just going to get us some dinner. Toni will stay with you, okay?'

Toni's eyebrows drew together in question, but she nodded.

'What about Dad?' Charlie asked.

'I'll have news when I get back.'

She closed the door and stared into Jesse's eyes. He would never leave the kids here if he thought they were in danger. She knew that in her soul. She followed him down the hall, and he led her out to the car park.

'We're taking the car? Surely it'd be quicker to walk to the main hospital?'

'He's been moved to North Shore Private. That's all I can tell you for now.'

'Is he okay?'

'He's stable.'

'What about everything else?'

'It's one hell of a mess. Forsythe Commercial Real Estate was also under investigation by AUSTRAC.'

Gen screwed up her face in confusion.

'They're responsible for investigations into suspected money laundering. So, as well as New South Wales Police, the Federal Police are involved, as are a hundred other acronyms, departments, and task forces, including Raptor. It's going to take a while to sort out.'

'What's happened so far?'

'All Forsythe assets have been frozen, and William Senior issued a very public resignation from his ministerial position. He, Helen and Bill are all at headquarters under questioning. They lawyered up, but the evidence is damning. All the money in the world won't get them out of this.'

'I wish I could have seen his face when he was asked to resign.'

'All this brings me to you and the kids. The assets frozen include the house and any funds Hugh had. That leaves you in a very difficult position. Police liaison can help with temporary accommodation.'

Gen shook her head. 'Toni will have us, until I can sort something, although she's not allowed dogs. I'll have to find somewhere for Bentley.'

'If you like, I'll see if my brother can take him. He loves dogs. I'm sure he'd be happy to care for Bentley for as long you need.'

'In that case, we'll be fine. I was already planning to sell my bikes anyway.'

'You were?'

'I needed money for a lawyer to fight Hugh. Those kids are everything to me. As long as they're safe and happy, I'm fine. I'll get another bike in the future.'

Jesse pulled into a spot outside North Shore Private and led her to a floor of specialist offices.

'This doesn't look like a ward.'

'The police have taken extra precautions, so no one can find him.'

'Of course. Special consideration all the way.' Anger burned her gut. Even when it looked like Hugh would get his comeuppance, he was still getting preferential treatment. Well, she wouldn't be cowed by him. He wasn't keeping her away from the kids. Never again.

'Do you want me to come in with you?'

'I've got this.'

'I'll be outside.'

'Always at my back, right?

He smiled warmly. 'Always.'

She pushed open the door.

32

Gen's gaze bounced around the space. A Federal Police officer sat in one corner, static hissing occasionally from his radio. The room was mostly bare except for a bed and a bleeping monitor showing Hugh's heart rate and oxygenation. Everything reeked of bleach.

Hugh looked like a little boy. He was dressed in a blue hospital gown, his head bandaged, hair sticking up in spikes and his face sunken and pale. They locked gazes, taking one another's measure.

'What do you want, Hugh? I need to get back to the kids.'

'That's what —'

'Before you start, let me make myself clearer than I ever have. You will *not* – not now, nor ever in the future – remove me from those children. I'm the closest person to a mother they've known in the last twelve years. They need me, they love me, and they *will* have me in their lives. I will fight you with everything I have, and I will win, so if you have called me here to demand I drop them to some nanny hired by your parents you can fuck right off. Nothing and no one will ever part me from Lily and Charlie again.'

He stared at her silently, then closed his eyes and gave an almost imperceptible nod.

Or had she imagined it?

'Don't you dare —'

'Give me a moment, Geneva.'

She fixed him with a glare.

'Please?' His tone softened.

She dragged a chair into the middle of the room and sat. 'You have two minutes.'

'You always were the strong one.' His voice had turned raspy. 'Amber and I used to talk about how there was no one else on earth we could entrust our kids to if anything happened to us. You were in the will as our next of kin.'

'What?'

'There are some papers on the side table over there. Please, take a look.'

'If this is another game ...'

Gen snatched up the papers and read. The letterhead said Brown Family Law.

The document stated that Geneva Leighton was to take over legal guardianship for Liliana and Charles Forsythe. Behind it was a court order.

'You need to file those on Monday.'

'I don't understand.'

'I have agreed to testify against the syndicate.'

'What about your parents and brother?'

'They dragged me into it in the first place. Well, them and Tobias. Apparently, he lured Dad into the scheme not long after he joined the firm. I was brought in once Dad went into politics and had to resign from the company board.'

His gaze dropped to his lap. 'I honestly had no idea about

Tobias.' He shook his head. 'And Dad's still denying he's his father.'

Gen closed the file and pointedly checked her watch.

'You're right, that doesn't matter right now.' He clasped his hands in his lap. 'It's a condition of my plea deal that I leave Australia. It's a worldwide investigation, and the Federal Police believe they can only keep me safe if I'm out of the country.'

'But what about the kids? Hugh, you can't take them away. They need —'

'Stop, please?'

Gen exhaled and nodded.

'I'm signing guardianship over to you. I know you'll keep them safe. The official story will be that I ran. Disappeared. I can't see them again.' Tears filled his eyes and his voice quavered.

Oh Hugh.

'It's my own fault. You were right, it was my need for approval that got us into this. Got Amber killed.'

'Then why did you always treat *me* like shit?'

'I hated that the kids preferred you.'

Gen rolled her eyes and moved to stand.

'Wait.' He rubbed his forehead. 'The truth is it was easier to blame you for Amber's death, to tell myself she was taken in a random abduction that wouldn't have happened if you'd gone to the shops.'

'But she knew about the laundering, or at least suspected.'

He nodded. 'She asked about the Erica Sykes property sales, and I told her to leave it alone. For the next month she tried everything she could to get me to talk. But what could I tell her?'

'The truth.'

'She would have left me.'

Her nostrils flared. 'I know you slept with a woman that night at the casino. And all about the photo left to force you to pay your gambling debts.'

'What woman? I've never been in debt.'

'Tobias was lying about that too?'

'He's always been good at misdirection. He came up with the restraining order idea. I even let him give me the black eye.' His gaze clouded. 'The night Amber disappeared is like a blank slate in my mind. I wouldn't be surprised if Tobias drugged me.'

That would fit with Hugh's behaviour on the casino footage.

Hugh rubbed his eyes. 'I still can't believe he had Amber killed.'

Silence filled the room, and Gen took a deep breath. She didn't want to think about that man ever again. She tapped the file on her lap. 'I just want to make sure the kids are okay. They have so much to deal with.'

He sighed. 'You always were the best person for them, once Amber was gone. Will you take them?'

'You don't need to ask. Can they write to you?'

'No contact. Not until the court case is over, and probably not even then. I will never expose them to risk again.'

'How do you know no one will come after us, to draw you out?'

'Hence the story that I ran. Someone's going to leak it to the media that I've run off with my girlfriend, that I never cared about the children anyway.'

'It will kill the kids to hear that. You need to explain things to them.'

'I can't! I'd rather they hate me and stay safe. You'll have to help them through it.'

She shook her head. It might break them.

'Geneva, this is important. They have to believe the story. I can't have them slipping up. It could cost them their lives.'

'Where will you go?'

'They haven't said, and I wouldn't tell you.'

A knock sounded and Jesse stuck his head around the door. 'We need to go. We've already been here too long.'

'Okay.' She looked back at the broken man in the bed.

'For what it's worth, I am sorry, Gen.'

She stayed quiet, torn between consoling and condemning him.

'I did do one thing right. The money from Amber's insurance is in trust for the kids. It's not a heap, but it should help you put a new roof over their heads. There are details in the folder about how to access it and the law firm to talk to.' He raised his gaze to meet hers. 'Forgive me?'

'It doesn't matter what I forgive.' Gen's emotions felt like they were in a blender. 'But for what it's worth, this is the first time in a long while that I've truly liked the man I see before me.'

His lip quivered and he looked away. 'Keep them safe.'

'Always.' Gen walked from the room. Jesse went to hug her, but she pulled the files tighter between her cast and chest and stepped back. If he touched her, she'd break.

She had to fix things with him, but there was something else she had to do first.

'Can we make a quick stop on the way back to the kids?'

33

They walked in silence to Amber's grave. In the distance, the sky was a palette of pinks and oranges. On the grave sat a small posy of flowers, identical to the ones K2 had left only a week before. This time, there was a card.

Sorry, little lady. May your sister find her peace, too.

Hopefully K2 was doing okay after the fallout from Mac. She knew he'd be devastated. But that wasn't her burden to bear. She sat cross-legged at the head of Amber's plot.

'Soooo, it's been a week.' She imagined Amber rolling her eyes at the understatement.

She told her sister everything that had happened. At the end, she sighed a deep breath.

'You always seemed to have everything together, like you didn't need me, but I would have been there for you, Amber. If you'd talked to me, I could have helped.' Gen swallowed. 'I need to build my own life now.' She patted the ground, then stood. 'Love you, Ambs.'

Jesse walked alongside her to the car. He opened the passenger door, and she climbed inside.

He crouched down beside her. 'You okay?'

'I'm ... It's going to sound strange, but I really am.'

He shook his head.

'What?'

'Toughest person I ever met. Those kids are lucky to have you.'

'They are, aren't they?'

He closed the door, then walked around to the driver's side and climbed in. As he reached to put the car into gear, she covered his hand with hers. 'Can you give me a minute?'

He turned off the engine. She twisted to face him, but his eyes remained fixed ahead. What did he think she was going to say?

'The kids and I, we have a lot of challenges ahead. Housing, schools, not to mention the bucketloads of therapy we're all going to need. But if you're prepared to wait – I know it's not fair to ask, but if you are, I would really like to try ... us.'

He continued to stare forward, remained completely still.

'You're like a rock.'

He gave her an incredulous look.

'That's a good thing! I mean, you're solid and calm, and I've never felt as safe and at peace as I do around you. I'd like to be the same for you.'

His lips twitched. 'Calm and peaceful?'

She laughed. 'Maybe I can offer complementary traits instead.'

He pinned her with a look. 'I'll wait.'

34

One year later

Gen reached into the cardboard box and pulled out the last Christmas bauble: the photo-covered ball that Amber had made when Charlie was born. It had pictures of everyone important to the kids: Amber, Hugh, Gen, their paternal and maternal grandparents.

Lucielle had been reaching out more lately, especially to the kids. It would never be easy, but the events of the previous year had shifted something, and she seemed to realise that they all needed her.

Gen turned the bauble around and stared at the photo of her dad, then Amber. She let the familiar yearning for them wash over her, no longer a crashing wave of questions and guilt but gentler, like the ebb and flow of the tide. *Miss you guys.*

She handed the ornament to Lily, whose blonde hair, grown out again, swished as she hung the bauble on the tree.

'It's my turn to do the star!' Charlie yelled.

'Inside voice, mate,' Gen said.

He grinned and dragged a chair across the carpet to the pine tree in the corner. The excitement on his face when he and Jesse had brought the tree home had been priceless – rivalled only by Jesse's expression. You'd have thought they'd raised the tree from a sapling. They'd placed it in the corner of the lounge in their Marrickville semi, and there was barely enough room at the top for the glass star Charlie held.

He scrambled up on the chair and stood on his tippy toes. Jesse stepped forward and held the chair to keep Charlie from toppling forward.

The star safely in place, Charlie climbed down and grinned. 'It's huge!'

Gen packed up the empty boxes and set them aside. 'So guys, I have some news. I'm going to be a student again.'

'You are?' Jesse tilted his head.

Charlie groaned. 'Why would you want to study?'

'Because, mate, I've been accepted into a Master of Political Science program. They liked my proposal to research the role of lobbyists in gambling reformation.'

'That's amazing, Gen.' Lily gave her a hug.

'It sounds boring!'

'Bloody hell, Charlie, don't hold back.' Gen gave him a wan smile.

'That's a dollar to the swear jar!'

'That damn thing will haunt me for all my days.'

Jesse laughed and stood. 'We need to celebrate.'

'Yeah, school holidays!' Charlie danced in a circle.

Gen went into the kitchen and checked on the roast. Toni and her new boyfriend were arriving soon for their regular Sunday dinner.

Family was who you made it.

'Gen! Can you come back into the lounge room?' Lily called out.

'Come on, Gen, hurry up!'

The impatience in Charlie's tone made her chuckle. It had been a hell of a year with numerous ups and downs, and Gen was incredibly grateful to the team of school counsellors and psychologists that had guided them through it. The kids had been devastated when their dad disappeared from their lives, but they were slowly adjusting to the story that Hugh had left. The challenges would continue – none of them had emerged unscathed – but the moments of fear and abandonment were becoming less frequent.

After the media circus had finally calmed down, Gen had heard nothing more about Hugh. She caught herself sometimes wondering where he was. Did he feel any sense of redemption, given the sacrifice he'd made?

She walked into the lounge. Lily grabbed her hand, guided her to the couch and made her sit. Charlie did the same to Jesse. Butterflies danced in her belly.

What if he said no? She scanned his features, alight with love and joy for the kids he'd taken on as his own.

Charlie carried a box over to the mantel and hung up his stocking, just as they'd practised. Lily did the same. Then Charlie handed a stocking to Jesse. He was doing things a bit out of order, but they were probably too excited to wait any longer. Jesse turned the stocking over and read his name that had been cross-stitched on by Lily.

'Jesse,' Gen said, and turned to face him, 'we were hoping, as an early Christmas present for us all, that you would move in with us.'

He stared at the stocking, silent.

Charlie's face fell, his gaze darting to Gen in panic. Bentley walked over to press himself into Charlie's leg. Gen lay her palm on Jesse's forearm. 'It's okay if it's too soon. It's just, you feel like such a part of this family —'

'Don't you say another word.' He strode to the mantel, hung up his stocking and then faced them with an enormous grin. 'Best present ever.'

He held out his arms and the kids rushed in for a hug. He crooked his finger at Gen, and she joined them, giving him a soft kiss on the lips.

'Ewwww, get a room.'

'Yuck.'

Jesse's laughter echoed through the house.

The kids drifted back to the couch and Gen looked into his eyes. 'Scared me for a minute there.'

'Told you, I'm not going anywhere.'

Charlie cleared his throat and held out the box. 'There's one more.'

Gen pulled out a red stocking. She turned it over and read the bright-green stitching. *Mum.*

Her eyes welled.

Lily stepped forward and guided her to the mantel. 'Hang it in the middle space. It's where you belong.'

But what would Amber say?

She looked at both kids and blinked away the tears. Her sister would ask Gen what the hell she was waiting for.

She attached the stocking to the mantel, and Lily stepped closer. 'Is it okay if we call you Mum from now on?'

'Come here.' Gen spread her arms wide. 'I wouldn't have it any other way.'

ACKNOWLEDGEMENTS

The one constant between this book and my first has been the amazing support I've received from family, friends, readers, industry professionals and other writers. Thank you to everyone who has been in my corner this year!

To my wonderful literary agent, Jeanne Ryckmans, from Cameron's Management, thank you for your guidance and encouragement. I'm so grateful to be under your wing.

To Roberta Ivers, my brilliant publisher at HarperCollins, I am tremendously thankful for the expertise, commitment, insight and enthusiasm you bring to my stories.

To everyone at HarperCollins Australia, thank you for your invaluable contributions to this book. Special mentions to Andy Harper and the HarperCollins design team for the sensational cover; to Shannon Kelly, my in-house editor, for your astute guidance; to Caitlin Toohey and Sara Zarriello for expertly managing my marketing campaign; to Hannah Lynch and the rest of the fabulous and hard-working publicity team; and to the entire HarperCollins sales team and account managers for getting my book into bookshops and the hands of readers. Thank you also to Vanessa Lanaway for the detailed structural and copyedit, and to Lauren Finger for her eagle-eyed proofread.

Research is one of my favourite things and, while internet

searches are great, it was the generosity of people with experience, knowledge and stories that gave me the magic touches for this book. Thank you to the incredible officers at Cabramatta PCYC who allowed me to spend a day among them, asking questions about their work and its impact on their lives. Huge thanks also to Darren Bennett, Executive Director of Criminal Investigations for the NSW Crime Commission, and Angella Whitton, who patiently answered my questions about policing.

Thank you, Melissa Doyle, for the fabulous brainstorming session about media cadetships.

To my husband, Peter, thanks for answering my endless motorcycle-related questions.

To the people in the motorcycle community who shared their stories, insights and perspectives with me, I can't thank you enough for your generosity and candour.

Sincere thanks to Penelope Janu for her advice on legal procedures. Thank you also to Peter Janu for helping me streamline my explanations on money laundering.

Any mistakes in aspects of the law, policing, motorbikes and journalism are mine alone. *Dying to Know* is a work of fiction; no characters are based on real people and, while many of the suburbs exist, I have created elements including streets, businesses, houses and locations to suit my story.

I am dearly grateful for the support, advice and guidance extended to me this year by other writers. Special thanks to Sulari Gentill, Michael Robotham (and Viv), Anna Downes, Hayley Scrivenor, Ali Lowe, Vanessa McCausland, Nina Campbell, Petronella McGovern, Ber Carroll, Sara Foster, Nicola Moriarty, Sarah Bailey, Anna Snoekstra, Rob McDonald, Sarah Barrie, Tim Ayliffe and Chris Hammer, your words and support came at the most helpful of times.

Huge thanks also to the booksellers, podcasters, bloggers, reviewers, journalists, festival organisers and writing organisations who welcomed me so warmly into the industry.

To my awesome and talented writers' group, The Ink Wells – Pamela Cook, Terri Green, Laura Boon, Joanna Nell, Penelope Janu, Michelle Barraclough and Angella Whitton – thanks for always being there! Special thanks to Pamela and Laura for reading early drafts of *Dying to Know*, and for your invaluable feedback and faith in the manuscript.

To my mum, thank you for guiding me through second-book wobbles and believing in me. Thank you also to all the family and friends who've cheered me on!

To Pete, Amy and Ben, thanks for listening to me talk incessantly about my imaginary friends and for keeping me laughing through all the ups and downs. I love you dearly. You too, Alfie; thanks for keeping me company every day.

And to you, the reader, thank you for picking up my book. I hope you enjoyed it and would love to hear your thoughts. You can find me at raecairns.com, on Facebook @raecairnsauthor and Instagram @raecairnswrites. And if you'd like to know what I'm writing or reading next, please join my newsletter via my website.

THE GOOD MOTHER

RAE CAIRNS

Want to read more?
Turn the page for a taste of Rae Cairns's thrilling debut,
The Good Mother
Shortlisted for the 2021 Ned Kelly Award for Best Debut Crime Fiction

She's protected them from the truth. Can she save them from her past?

Sarah Calhoun is a regular Sydney soccer mum, but she's keeping terrifying secrets from everyone she loves … and her past is about to catch up with her.

When two men from Northern Ireland hunt her down, she's forced to return to Belfast to testify at a murder trial. Caught in the crossfire of an obsessive policeman driven by a disturbing past, and a brutal IRA executioner, Sarah faces an impossible choice: lie and allow a killer to walk free, or tell the truth and place her children in the line of fire.

With her family and innocent people at risk, Sarah must find the courage to fight for the truth. But righting the wrongs of the past just might cost her everything …

This fast-paced, explosive thriller will keep you on the edge of your seat to its gripping finale.

'This story wouldn't let me go' Michael Robotham

'Fierce, action-packed … A wild, original ride from start to finish'
Sarah Bailey

'Taut, propulsive … Brilliant' Anna Downes

'Past and present collide on and off the page in this explosive debut'
Sunday Telegraph

'The kind of book the phrase "nail-biting" was made for …
Genuinely terrifying' *Books and Publishing*

Prologue

Northern Ireland, 2014

Never before, not even during the darkest moments of her life, had Sarah Calhoun believed she could become a killer. But staring down at her mother's ring, she finally understood. There was no action she wouldn't take.

No lie. No betrayal. No sin.

No matter who you were, there was always something, or someone, who could push you to the point of no return.

She reached for the band of gold and twisted it round and round. She had to do this, or even more would die.

He'd given her no choice.

One life to save many.

1

Sydney, Australia
Three months earlier

Sarah bounded up the sandstone stairs of her rundown Federation cottage, her breath sending puffs of white into the cool morning air. She checked her watch. Two minutes shaved off her time. She'd never run competitively again but she was definitely getting closer to form. Stretching out her quads, she savoured the salty scent wafting up the hill from Bronte Beach. A buoyancy moved through her, and Sarah surfed the endorphins that years of running had hardwired her body to crave. But it was more than that. For the first time since the divorce two years ago, she'd found a space her family loved and, with Evan's generosity in the settlement, had finally given her kids back a home.

She deactivated the front door alarm, stepped into the hallway, then shrugged out of her running jacket and hung it on a hook by the door, catching a glance of her newly lean body in tights and a crop top in the hallway mirror. At thirty-nine, she was the strongest and fittest she'd been in years.

Now if only she could bring her thick unruly hair into line. She retied the wayward chestnut strands into her ponytail. Tinkling giggles drew her to the family room, where she found Sophie, her eight-year-old, sitting on the floor and squealing with delight as their Labrador puppy licked black paste off her fingers.

'Honey, Vegemite isn't very good for Fudge. And what did we say about eating on the floor?'

Sophie dropped her half-eaten piece of toast to a plate and jumped up for a hug, her toffee-coloured bob brushing Sarah's bare stomach.

'But Fudge hasn't had a picnic before, and I wanted to show him how.'

Before Sarah's arms had a chance to fully enclose her, Sophie ran off and entered into a tug of war with Fudge over a blanket the puppy had dragged halfway out the dog door. Sarah couldn't help but laugh. Buying her kids a puppy was one of the best ideas she'd had. The divorce, however amicable, had seriously upended her kids' lives but Fudge's unpredictable antics had reintroduced some much needed joy into their world. She walked to the fridge and removed the lunches she'd packed before her run. The familiar grind and gurgle of the coffee machine joined the hullabaloo.

'Mum, can you sign off my homework?' Ally emerged from the study, waving a bunch of papers. Sarah did a double take. From the length of her skirt, her older daughter had edged yet more centimetres taller this week, but it was her twelve-year-old's face, left exposed by the knotting back of her curly blonde hair, that caused the tug in Sarah's chest. No longer cute like Sophie, Ally was maturing into the alarming beauty of a teenager. Too soon her girl would move out into the world. How would Sarah protect her then?

'Earth to Mum.' Ally waved a pen in the air. 'Signature? And don't forget I finish dance rehearsal late today.'

'Ally, that hem is too short. Go change into the new uniform I bought you.'

'This one's already longer than every single one of my friends'.'

'I'm not their mother. Go change.'

Her daughter glared, her sapphire eyes sparking.

'Now.'

Ally smacked her homework on the bench and stomped upstairs to her room. Sarah caught the rolling pen before it fell to the floor. Ally didn't understand yet. It was better not to stand out, not to be noticed. She corrected a wrong answer on the homework, then signed. Maybe she should enrol Ally in more of the dance classes she loved. That would keep her busy, and it had worked with Riley. Even at sixteen, sport took up every spare minute of his life. His single-minded goal to play professional soccer made it easy to discourage him from the traditional distractions of teenage life, in particular the nightmare of girlfriends and all the risks they posed. Sarah glanced towards the dining table. Where *was* Riley? Normally he'd be inhaling a pile of Weet-Bix by now. She checked her watch.

'Riley, get a wriggle on,' she called up the stairs. They'd all better get moving if she was going to make the client presentation this morning. She'd need her wits about her for this one; the stakeholder was going to be unhappy with the results of the focus groups Sarah had coordinated. While her coffee finished brewing, she gathered the papers and bills scattered across the bench into an orderly pile. Her gaze caught on a sticky note stuck to an orange folder she'd never seen before: *Mum.* She flipped the folder open and scanned the handwritten letter attached to the front of a document. Her face began to burn. She strode to the stairwell.

'Riley.' Silence. 'Riley, get down here now!'

No feet came pounding. Nothing. She checked the space outside the kitchen door where his school bag should have been. What had he done? She dashed back to Sophie. 'Was Riley awake when you came down?'

'I haven't seen him since last night.'

Sarah grabbed the folder and ran for the stairs. With each stride up, her knuckles whitened around the file. How could he go behind her back? This wasn't part of their plan.

She rushed into her son's bedroom. 'Riley James Barker!'

The dark room was quiet. The jagged shadows of his soccer trophies loomed from the shelves. He'd left early for school, sneaked out before she was awake. She sucked in a breath laced with the outdoorsy scent of his deodorant, then sank onto the unmade bed, staring at the letter in her hand.

Dear Mum,
I know you won't like this, but please, please, please
try to understand. I need to go on this FIFA Youth
Development camp. Only two players were selected
from Australia, and there will be scouts from all over
the world there. Dad has filled out all the forms and
paid for everything. It's being held in Dublin, Ireland.
All you need to do is sign the travel permission form.
I know I should have told you earlier, but I thought
you'd freak out. Please say yes.
Love Riley

Sarah closed her eyes. The stink of burning gasoline overwhelmed her senses. Screams. A crack. A flash. A spray of blood across the floor. Surging to her feet, she parted the curtains and threw open the window. Riley could not go to Dublin. Everything she'd done to protect her family could come unstuck.

A herd of schoolboys passed on the footpath below, chattering and hollering. Her boy should have been amongst them, heading for the bus. *God damn Evan.* He knew she'd never let her sixteen-year-old travel alone. Especially not to Ireland. What was he thinking? She plumped up a pillow that had been discarded on the floor and returned it to the bed.

This couldn't wait; she needed to visit Evan and put an end to this trip now. She tugged the quilt into place, had a quick shower, dressed in a navy blue pant suit and headed downstairs to her phone. She'd have to ask the other researchers to cover her section of the presentation.

The elevator doors opened onto Evan's fifteenth floor law office. Every chair in the waiting room sat perfectly spaced, each picture frame squared and matching in tones of red and grey. Everything uniform, predictable and masculine. Everything that is, except for the pastel floral arrangement adorning the reception desk, and the diminutive Mrs Farley sitting behind it. Now in her late sixties, Evan's personal assistant was five foot if she were lucky and used her glacial grey eyes to preside over all who entered Evan's domain.

Sarah smoothed down her suit jacket and moved towards the desk. 'Good morning, Mrs Farley.' Never Gladys. Not even in her fourteen years of marriage to Evan was Sarah allowed that familiarity.

'I'm sorry, Ms Calhoun, Mr Barker is in meetings all day. Can I make you an appointment for tomorrow?'

Sarah swallowed the urge to deliver a snappy retort. 'This can't wait. I need to see him now.'

'Mr Barker said you would say that.' Mrs Farley reached to the shelf behind. 'You'll need these.' She passed over a pile of magazines. 'Please take a seat.'

Sarah tossed the magazines onto a side table and perched herself on the chair facing the long corridor. Every cell in her body wanted to burst into Evan's office and demand he see her straight away, but it would be a mistake. His biggest issue during their marriage had been her 'irrationality'. Her overzealous protectiveness.

A familiar feeling of outrage flared. He knew what she'd been through in her twenties, what her work in Belfast and Crossmaglen had involved. The vulnerable youth, caught in the crossfire of the brutal paramilitaries in the last gasp of The Troubles. Kids shot, kids torn in two by bombs, kids drawn into and then enslaved in a sectarian conflict, the genesis of which had nothing to do with them. She hadn't cared which side they'd come from; all she knew was they needed her help, her support – her reassurance that there was a future away from the violence. It had been nothing like she'd expected when she took on the job. Never knowing who to trust, who to turn to, never sure of people's loyalties and connections.

But the terror she felt was about more than her work, something Evan didn't know anything about. She'd been drawn in deep and she'd gotten too close to dangerous people. She'd been shocked to the core by the street value of human life and how far some people would go to retain power. When she'd left – when she *had* to leave – she knew she'd never be able to go back. Evan didn't know that she'd seen too much, knew too much, nor how far the people there would go to make sure she kept it all to herself.

Riley couldn't go to Dublin. It was less than two hours from Belfast – only 170 kilometres – and even closer to Crossmaglen. But Evan would only listen if she were calm.

She crossed her legs and concentrated on mapping out what she was going to say. Music interrupted, piped from speakers spread around the ceiling, the familiar melody of 'Clair de lune' grating across her skin. Evan had played it over and over while each of their children had grown in her womb. Her right foot tapped in the air. Back then he'd been everything she believed she wanted – safe and honest, a family man. But he'd always needed more than she could give. Uncrossing her legs, she shifted upright in her seat. That was unimportant now. Being a good father had always been his priority. It was the reason she hadn't fought shared custody. So, what was going on now?

She fixated on his office door. Riley was scheduled to leave in four weeks. What could be more important than their son's safety? She stretched her head side to side. When 'Moonlight Sonata' started over the speakers, she pushed to her feet. 'I'm going to the bathroom. If Evan comes out, please ask him to wait.'

Mrs Farley gave a dismissive nod.

Before Sarah reached the ladies room, Evan's office door swung open. His eyes, the same almond shape and colour as those of their daughters, studied her from behind on-trend square black glasses.

'Sarah.'

'Evan.'

His mouth pulled into a thin line. 'Please don't start until you've heard me out.'

He waved her into his office – a huge corner room, with a wall of windows overlooking Sydney Harbour. Sunlight caught on his new platinum wedding ring. Why hadn't she thought to get Evan's wife on side first? Felicity oozed calm, and she understood how to keep Evan happy, better than Sarah ever had. The door clicked shut. It was too late now. Sarah sat while Evan moved to his chair on the other side of the desk. He rubbed at the manicured stubble on his chin for a moment before he spoke.

'Look, I understand you might feel uncomfortable.'

'Uncomfortable? Allowing Riley to go on this trip is irresponsible.'

Evan looked down at the desk, a faint sigh slipping out of his mouth. He removed and folded his glasses. Sarah's foot jackhammered against the floor while he took care to place the glasses in their case. His gaze returned to hers. 'This trip is the chance of a lifetime. And Riley's earned it, through his dedication and hard work. I'm struggling to think of one good reason why he shouldn't go.'

'For starters he'd be on his own on the other side of the world for four whole months.' Sarah forced her rising voice to lower. 'He's not an adult yet.'

'He's not a baby either. Riley is talented and smart.'

'Exactly! He goes into Year Eleven next year. Now is too important a stage of school to miss.'

'The camp has study periods built into the timetable and his teachers have already agreed to send work over with him.'

'There's no way he'll work hard enough. He's too young.'

'He's worked hard for this. You can't stop him following his dream. He'll never forgive you.'

At least he'll be alive! Her fingers dug into her thighs to stop her shouting the words. Evan had no idea how precarious life could be. 'Our job is to parent, not be his friend. It's too much of a risk.'

'It's Ireland, for Christ's sake, not Afghanistan.' Evan ran his fingers through his hair. 'Look, I understand it felt unsafe when you worked in Belfast, but Northern Ireland has been at peace for years. And even if it wasn't, Dublin is in the Republic, a whole different country.'

'Please, Evan, you don't understand.'

'I've looked into the program. Have you? Or did you merely react with your need to wrap the people you love in cotton wool? You give me one logical reason why Riley will be "at risk" in Ireland, and I'll back you.'

Sarah stared into her lap. Gerry's terrified expression flashed like a still shot in her mind. She'd never shared with Evan about that night, about Gerry, about Michael, about Daniel. No way she could confess it now. Not after all these years.

'I shouldn't have to explain it. If you thought like an adult —'

He stood and threw both hands in the air. 'That is not a reason.' He turned away to face the windows. Words tumbled in Sarah's head, but not one false argument she concocted made sense.

When Evan turned back, his expression had hardened. 'Riley needs to follow his dreams, not worry there's a bogeyman around every corner. I will not let your fears control his life. I've promised Riley I will back him, no matter what. Even if we have to take you to Family Court.'

Sarah flinched as if she'd been struck. He wouldn't, would he? She took in the tight set of his mouth. Her pulse sped up. 'Surely you don't mean for custody?'

'No, of course not. All we need is a Court Order of Consent. Because Riley is sixteen, they'll take his wishes into consideration. Unless you can give serious and well-evidenced welfare concerns, the court will rule in my favour.'

376 • Rae Cairns

Evan meant it. This couldn't be happening. Riley couldn't go to Ireland. What if they found him? She launched to her feet.

'This is wrong. He's too young. He's not ready to be on his own so far away. They're the facts.'

'Only your version, Sarah.'

She hitched her handbag onto her shoulder. 'If anything happens to Riley in Dublin, anything at all, I will never forgive you.' She turned away and marched from the room.

There had to be another way to stop this. She had to protect her son.